The
SERPENT
and the
EAGLE

a novel

Daniel Spicehandler

caislan press

Box 28371, San Jose, California 95159

Printed in the United States of America

Library of Congress Catalogue Card Number: 83-70293

ISBN 0-937444-05-7 Hardcover
ISBN 0-937444-06-5 Paperbound

caislan press

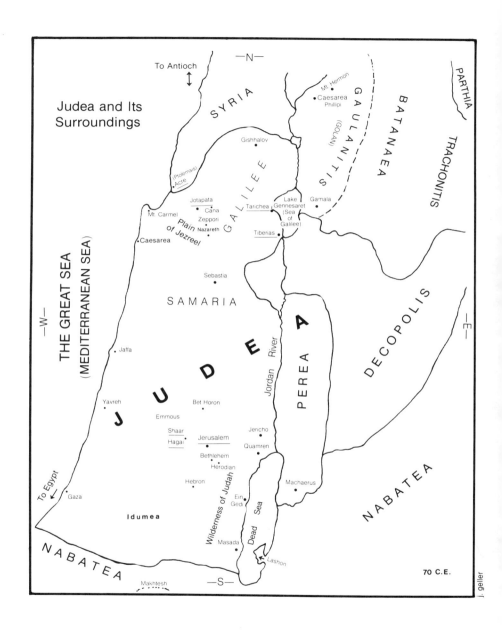

Judea and Its
Surroundings

—N—

To Antioch

PARTHIA

SYRIA

Mt. Hermon

Caesarea
Phillipi

GAULANITIS (GOLAN)

BATANAEA

TRACHONITIS

Gishhalov

GALILEE

(Ptolemais)
Acre

Jotapata
Cana
Zeppori
Nazareth

Mt. Carmel

Plain of Jezreel

Caesarea

Tarichea

Lake
Gennesaret
(Sea
of
Galilee)

Gamala

Tiberias

Sebastia

SAMARIA

THE GREAT SEA
(MEDITERRANEAN SEA)

—W—

DECOPOLIS

—E—

Jaffa

J U D E A

Jordan River

PEREA

Yavreh

Bet Horon

Emmous

Shaar
Hagai

Jerusalem

Jericho

Quamren

Bethlehem

Herodian

Hebron

To Egypt

Gaza

Wilderness of Judah

Ein
Gedi

Idumea

Dead Sea

Machaerus

NABATEA

NABATEA

Masada

Lashon

70 C.E.

j. geller

Makhtesh

—S—

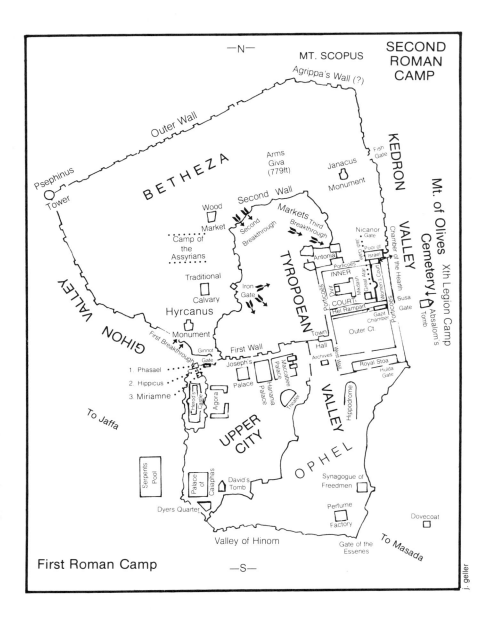

—N—

MT. SCOPUS

SECOND ROMAN CAMP

Agrippa's Wall (?)

Outer Wall

KEDRON VALLEY

Psephinus Tower

BETHEZA

Arms Giva (779ft)

Janacus Monument

Fish Gate

Mt. of Olives Cemetery

Xth Legion Camp

Second Wall

Wood Market

Markets

Third Breakthrough

Nicanor Gate

Chamber of the Hearth

Absalom's Tomb

Camp of the Assyrians

Second Breakthrough

Antonia

Porticoes

Pool of Israel

Traditional Calvary

TYROPOEAN

INNER

Porticoes

Great Altar

Gazit Chamber

Susa Gate

Hyrcanus Monument

Iron Gate

COURT

Hel Rampart

Outer Ct.

First Breakthrough

First Wall

Town Hall

Ginnol Gate

Archives

West Wall

1. Phasael
2. Hippicus
3. Miriamne

Joseph's Palace

Maccabee Palace

Royal Stoa

Hulda Gate

To Jaffa

Herod's Castle

Agora

Hanana Palace

Theater

Hippodrome

GIHON VALLEY

VALLEY

UPPER CITY

OPHEL

Serpents Pool

Palace of Caiaphas

David's Tomb

Dyers Quarter

Synagogue of Freedmen

Perfume Factory

Dovecoat

Valley of Hinom

Gate of the Essenes

To Masada

First Roman Camp

—S—

j. geller

I willingly surrender to the Romans and consent to live; but I take Thee to witness that I go, not as a traitor, but as Thy minister.

Bellum Judaicum
Josephus

to the city of jerusalem

PREFACE

Why Josephus?

Because he lived in a cataclysmic age, not unlike our own, partook in its major events and later recorded them. Rome was floundering between the need for further conquests and a desire for order and consolidation. The world at large was seeking a more viable philosophy to add vitality to the pagan way of life. A new faith was rising upon the ashes of less satisfying ones. Together these phenomena seemed to be balanced precariously upon the fulcrum of one land cursed with catastrophe as it was blessed with creativity — the ancient land of Judea.

And its people?

Caught as they are today between two giants, they fought to survive. Some took up arms; others fell back upon the holy law of their forefathers. Was it then the act or the word? the sword or the pen? In more philosophical terms, was it *time*, meaning national memory, or *space* defined as land which that same law had once promised them, that allowed them to defy history and choose life. Was it the serpent or the eagle?

Sitting in the valley below King David's Tomb and watching goats tinkle and munch their way up toward the walls made of the stones Josephus touched, I feel myself an intruder upon this city and its tombed history. This book was conceived in the days of glory after the Six Day War and completed in the frightening days of the more recent *Yom Kippur* War. Here was a city I had fought for when I was a boy in 1948, a city perhaps about to be rent again by its many lovers. How strange it is to be huddled in its shadows, among the grasses that fed its people during many sieges: to be overwhelmed now by daisies and poppies watered by the last spring rains that gush down the wadis as far south as the Fortress of Masada, and finish the story of my people's destruction which has almost occurred twice in my lifetime.

I gaze across the village of Silwan and down the biblical Gehenna knowing that jackals cringe in the surrounding caves awaiting a new catastrophe, the same beasts who scavenged among the dead legions of Titus and the bands of the Sicaris. Lizards blink at me from between the slits of boulders that Simon bar Giora and Eleazar ben Yair's men died upon, and know I am an intruder upon their secrets. I must stop. The *sharav* has ceased to blow and a cool breeze raises the sun which now intrudes upon my own secrets as it casts a shadow across my history.

Jerusalem 1982

Part I
JERUSALEM

*Passing on to your present
passion for liberty, I say
that it comes too late.*

Bellum Judaicum

CHAPTER I — THE COASTS OF THE EARTH

The sea is always violent off Jaffa and the boulders guarding the harbor hiss against alien intrusion. Incoming ships cast anchor beyond the breakwater and lower small boats for passage through the treacherous waters churning around the black portals that open onto the coasts of Judea.

From the open hold of *The Palmyra*, Joseph ben Matthias, followed by Lucia Paulina, stepped into the last of a dozen lighters that bobbed against the ship like puppies at their mother's breast. The lighter was already packed with legionnaires who had been picked up earlier from the military vessels in the convoy that arrived that morning from Rome. One centurion offered Lucia a cushion which she refused as she sat on a crossplank beside Joseph. A sailor unleashed the line and the helmsman steered clear of the ship and through the convoy.

Just as they came by the last ship and turned toward the shore, an officer, fully armed, leaped off the deck and on to the gunwale of the lighter. He agilely balanced his stocky body until some soldiers cleared a space for him to step into the boat.

"You never go ashore with all that weight," said Joseph. "It's trouble enough getting through as you are."

The officer seated himself amidship, glittering in the noonday sun. "Josephus," he called back in surprise. "I had no idea that you were in the convoy."

"Nor I you, Titus. Or that you had been released from jail."

"I see you have won the beautiful Lucia Paulina."

Lucia was looking beyond the officer and at the line of boats ahead that were passing through the straights between the boulders. She grabbed Joseph's hand. "What an exciting way to enter," she exclaimed.

"She accompanies the Queen of Golan as her lady-in-waiting," said Joseph to Titus.

"Then our destinies all carry us to Judea."

"Golan," said Lucia, "is not part of Judea. At least not yet."

"Josephus here seems to have accomplished his mission."

"If failure is an accomplishment, then I return with success."

"And is Titus Flavius satisfied with his own achievements?" asked Lucia coldly.

"Well," said the legate Titus, "satisfied enough to have been given back the XVth. I rejoin my legion at Gaza."

"Neither one of you should be so quick with his accomplishments or failures," said Lucia, withdrawing her hand from Joseph and wiping it on her cape. "Your so-called achievement which you seem so

2

pleased over can still be undone, and your failure, as you name it, Josephus, may yet be the greater accomplishment.''

"Joseph. In my own country, call me Joseph.'' He turned to the legate. "The Apollonaris hasn't been stationed in Judea since Pompey surpressed the first Jewish rebellion more than a hundred years ago.''

"From what I gather, we have the same mission again.''

"I already warned you not to be too sure what your mission here is,'' said Lucia. Perhaps the Queen and Josephu— Joseph here will save you your burden.''

"I'm a soldier of the *Pax Romana*,'' said the legate, addressing Joseph rather than Lucia. "Perhaps my effort may crown Queen Berenice with the whole of her late father's old domain.''

"If it is peace I carry,'' said Joseph, "it is an imposed one.''

The shore rose and fell, cutting the land from the sky. A wave carried the lighter high enough for Joseph to see beyond the coastal plain, where the contours of the Judean hills herded across the horizon. Nestled among them lay Jerusalem, his destination. Beneath his tunic, sprayed by the sea, he sweated. He doubted that his people would accept the terms Rome had offered him as representative of the *Sanhedrin*, the Supreme Council of the Jews, and quell the tide of rebellion; doubted too whether his countrymen wanted Berenice, a known Romanizer and mistress of the very legate who now sat opposite them.

The lighter came crashing down making the wine Lucia had urged upon him before they landed burn in Joseph's stomach. Throughout the journey back from Rome, he had been seasick, hardly the voyage he had planned with Lucia. The extravagant last few days in Rome had been tempered by the return to the burden of his inheritance. Not even in their stop at Alexandria did he feel well enough to make love, and he had refused Lucia the luxury of his body. He once asked his father why all pleasure made Jews feel guilty. Without looking up from the holy scroll that he had been studying, the old man had answered: "The Lord God of Abraham is our highest pleasure, the crown of all our joys.'' Joseph ben Matthias, priest on his father's side going back to Evyatar, King David's High Priest, and inheritor on his maternal side of Maccabee royal blood, did not look forward to the intractible task that awaited him. At one point during his six months in Rome he had almost accepted a position offered him by the senior counsellor to Emperor Nero, and oddly enough it was Epaphroditus' daughter, Lucia Paulina, who insisted that he return to Judea and take up his true responsibilities.

"Incredible, aren't they?'' cried Lucia, standing as the waves washed over the lighter, while the legionnaires huddled beneath their capes. The lighter rose again, this time shuddering in midair before splashing down hard against the panels of the sea. "Makes my palate itch," she laughed sticking out her tongue and scratching off the salt with her small teeth. It was the same gesture she had made when she first met Joseph standing in her father's atrium beside a statue of Janus, the two-faced god of Rome. She had taken his hand and without introduction led him off to one of the changing rooms along the colonnaded walk. Lucia always laughed before she made love.

"Do you think your brother will be on shore to greet us?" asked Lucia above the screech of sea gulls. The lines across her forehead and her marble eyes made her look older than her twenty years.

As they approached the boulders, the shoreline threatened. Joseph wiped the sea from his face. How different were the candescent beaches of Ostia, Rome's port, from these iron waters of Judea whose only light was the gray froth that chewed the edges of the waves. Rome was as different from Jerusalem as that clean shaven general, with his exposed thighs, was from the curly headed helmsman in his black burnoose.

"Yes. Mati will be there," lied Joseph, who also knew that his father would be absent since at that moment Matthias was walking up the Great Altar of the Temple for the ceremony of *Sukkot*, the last pilgrimage of the year to Jerusalem.

But Lucia was already distracted by the flirtations of two centurions who offered her a drink from their wineskins. Joseph never ceased to wonder at the capacity of Romans for drink; how they could rule the world as soberly as they did. Though his stomach churned, he was offended that they had not offered him any. In order to keep from becoming sick, he concentrated on the helmsman whose knuckles reddened as he fought the current drawing them through the straits and toward the harbor. One of the centurions leaned over and whispered something in Lucia's ear. She looked at Joseph and laughed as the officer tucked the goatskin rug tighter around her lap. The act reminded Joseph how she had led him to the hold of the ship yesterday and after yanking off a piss smelling sheepskin protecting one of the catapults stored there with other heavy weapons, had spread it beside a quickfirer and pulled him down in broad daylight beside her, showing him that making love to one's wife could be promiscuous.

Without warning the lighter veered to the starboard, heading for a sabre tooth rock jutting out the far end of the straights. The helmsman rose at the same time withdrawing a short dagger from beneath his burnoose and flung it in Joseph's direction. Then he leaped overboard.

4

The lighter crashed against the rock, casting Joseph into the sea. When he tried to lift himself back into the boat, he saw that the legate's seat was empty and that Lucia had been thrown to the floor on top of one of the centurions. The helmsman had disappeared. Joseph's grip slipped as his body was sucked down into the socket of a whirlpool, the current churning in his nostrils. He began to swallow the sea.

The words of the wiseman, Bannus, his old teacher, droned in his ears: *Anticipate the moment before it is conceived. Perceive catastrophe and reconcile it.*

He surfaced and saw that the lighter had passed safely through the straights. Lucia was at the helm. Swimming toward the shore, Joseph was again dragged down by the current. He was fighting the tide when he realized that he was being pulled down by a cape whose clasp in the shape of a golden eagle was stuck in the mouth of the Roman legate. Titus lay near the bottom, his eyes barely open. Out of the shell of his armor, his arms flexed like claws as he tried to undo the clips of his iron vest. Joseph came up for air.

"He's down there. Just below you," shouted Lucia, still at the helm. "His cape has just surfaced. Save him!" The legionnaires stood watching.

The sun blazed in Joseph's eyes. He knew the dangers of rescuing a drowning man, especially one heavier than himself. Taking a deep breath, he plunged down again.

He found the legate lying calmly on his back, all but one clip of his armor undone. His eyes were lidded like the alabaster statues in the Roman Forum. It was the way Joseph remembered him at their first meeting in the baths when he too had urged Joseph to return to Judea. Titus rolled over, his short legs clamping around Joseph's neck. Like buoys in a turbulent sea, they shot up to the surface.

One of the centurions heaved the legate out of the green bay with one hand and Joseph with the other. Lucia was on the floor again, this time with her knee between Titus' legs as she pumped at his hips. The legate's eyes rolled with the color of the sea.

Joseph sat unnoticed in the seat from which he had been thrown a few moments ago. As his breath came back, he convinced himself that he had dived after Titus Flavius. He was about to toss the goatskin rug around his shoulders, when Lucia reached up and pulled it away, wrapping it instead around Titus.

"Turn him over," said Joseph. "Then stick a finger down his throat. If he's still alive."

"This isn't a drinking bout," said the centurion.

"He just had one," said Joseph. "With the sea."

A moment later Lucia rose. "He'll be all right," she said, wiping the vomit onto her lavender cloak.

The lighter was approaching the shore and already vendors were leaning over the quay, their arms hung with trinkets for sale. On his own strength, the legate lifted himself on to a crossplank opposite Joseph and Lucia. "You've saved my life," said Titus. "Let's hope that I don't ever have to do the same for you."

In order to bypass the Jewish rebels who had blocked the coastal road to Gaza, Titus Flavius decided to move eastward to Emmaus from where he could turn southward to his destination. Joseph was concerned that this contingent of the XVth Legion was accompanying him in the direction of Jerusalem.

At Emmaus, where the Sharon plain began to rise into the hills of Judea, the column halted. Joseph noted that the town was empty, the inhabitants, as he well knew, already in the Holy City for the festival. They camped by a stream across which a caravan of Nabateans smoked and watered their camels. The beasts sucked hard in the mud of the nearly dried stream.

Joseph slept listlessly, without dreams. Each time he awoke, his eyes met the covenanted stars that reminded him of his defections. Each breath brought him closer to Jerusalem where the final reckoning with Rome, with himself, lay. He had confided to Epaphroditus that his only authority to negotiate a new pact with Rome was from a handful of powerful nobles on the *Sanhedrin* Council, a minority among the fractious extremists who were drawing their country into open revolt against Rome. He had not dared to inform the same man that no one, not even his father, knew that he was returning with a Roman wife.

He heard Lucia's even breathing puffing beside him and he became calm. As a child he had suffered from nightmares, foretelling doom. He would run barefoot down the cold hall to his mother and lay between her and his snoring father. Once, when he was nearly six, his mother's gown had opened and he soothed himself at her bared breast.

Cautiously he undid the ribbons of Lucia's robe. Like two chicks the small, round flesh nestled each against the other, the pink nipples beaks. He cupped one in his palm and gently kissed it. Then he began to suckle on it like an infant.

Lucia stirred. Her mouth closed and he heard her teeth grinding. "No," she moaned, as Joseph pressed her knees apart. "First me." She wrapped her arm around his neck and pressed her breast hard against his mouth.

Before Joseph fully understood what had happened, she tensed, then groaned into a sigh. "Now you," she said, guiding him into her.

"But I never touched you."

"Your teeth did."

"That's not natural," he said, as much amazed as he was aroused.

"Any form of love is," said Lucia, as he shuddered and squealed so loudly, she had to cover his mouth with her hand. By the time he rolled over, she was already sleeping. He wondered if his thoughts of drowning while making love were also natural.

He could not sleep. The odor of the Nabatean camels and the cry of the jackals soothed him. He rose and searched among his bags. Epaphroditus had given him Apion's *Chronicles of Egypt*, a treatise which disparaged the Jews of Alexandria. "If no one corrects his lies, his shall become the recorded history of your people," said the counsellor when he gave the volume to Joseph on his departure. Joseph pushed the text aside and withdrew a scroll, his own journal and what he knew was to be the true history of the Jews. Under the clutter of stars he wrote:

for the jew falling in love with a gentile is a catastrophe. being a small, obdurate race, we must hold ourselves inviolate — a people alone. how do i explain to lucia that if roman law declared us wedded, according to the laws of moses and israel, we are not yet man and wife; that she still would have a tortuous process of conversion before her. yet i cannot accept that the plunging of the head into the mikva pool or the cutting of the foreskin can of themselves inject the pain and sense of mission that is the life-blood of our people. perhaps only in judea can a jew be created.

He did not record that he was already married to another.

With his head pillowed on a flat stone, he thought of Hagla's fuller breasts and her nipples, dark as grapes: how she would lie unmoving as he usurped her body.

"You sleep lightly as a good soldier should," said the legate Titus approaching. Joseph hid his journal in the folds of his tunic.

"I fear what the day will bring."

"Then you should sleep under the cover of the sun and let the stars record your destiny. I, too, keep a kind of diary, an unrecorded dialogue with myself."

"You know, Titus, that the helmsman tried to kill you."

"Or you."

"It doesn't really matter. We represent the same authority."

"Only my own."

"Still sufficient reason for the helmsman to kill you. The dagger he threw is the mark of the Sicari, the most zealous rebels in Judea." Joseph was thinking of Eleazar ben Yair, his childhood companion whom he had first met at the Essene settlement in the Judean desert at the foothill of Masada and who was now the leader of the Sicaris. He wondered who would be the victor if these two men ever did battle.

"And under whose authority do they prevail?"

"The Lord of Hosts. Their only sovereign."

"And yours?"

"His moral Law. The Emperor is my temporal lord."

"And when you jumped overboard?"

"I'm not sure. Maybe it was only to save myself."

"At such moments the act is the only truth."

"The suction of your cape forced my reaction. It drew me down to you."

"So there's your sovereign," laughed Titus. "The lavender cape of office."

He walked over and petted the rump of a camel who stamped his hoof in the muddy stream. "Your animals seem as disgruntled as your people. Where are your horses?"

"I thought I made that clear to you in Rome. An old interdiction. From our holy books. They are rarely used."

"And in war?"

"Jews fight best on foot without any mediator between them and God's land."

"Not even chariot races?"

"There is a small hippodrome in Jerusalem. The race you invited me to in Rome was the first I'd ever witnessed."

"That was an interesting one. I tried to outguess my enemies. With your help, I think I have."

"And whom do you consider your enemies?"

Titus laughed. "That too is a guessing game."

"The crisis in Judea is no game. We do not have the luxury of space afforded Rome."

"Let's wait and see how my plan develops."

"It shall be presented to the proper authorities."

"And will they approve?"

"Your guess is as good as mine."

Titus smiled. "I see we understand each other."

"But you understand Lucia Paulina better than I do."

"We're both Latins."

"You knew my wife. Knew her before I did."

"As well as she has known me. She is the epitome of Roman womanhood. Loyal, obedient, ambitious."

"Contrary qualities."

"All women are contrary."

Joseph stepped closer to Titus. Though of medium height, he was a head taller than the legate. "If I am correct, ambition begins in bed and ends in a bathtub full of blood. You failed those who supported you."

"Those who thought I supported them."

"Am I to think the same?"

"They were impatient. We Flavians have the patience of your camels."

"Emperors are elected from the west. Never from the east."

"Rome is not Greece. We are not compelled by geography."

"We Jews are."

The camel nozzled Titus, who tore a tuft of grass from between two stones and fed the animal. "I like your terrain," he said. "It's ideal for battle."

"Our land is blessed with a variety of texture."

"Let's hope that you and your supporters are as flexible."

"Our purposes differ. The road to them is the same. That is one definition of possibility."

Titus wiped his hand on the camel's rump. "Tell me, why did that helmsman try to kill you?"

"I should think that a Roman legate is more worthy of a Sicari blade. They kill Romans for distraction."

"And Jews?"

"For treachery," said Joseph, walking back to where Lucia slept.

Joseph woke Lucia and told her that they were leaving for Jerusalem immediately. "A half million Jews are gathered in the city for the festival. The whole country knows by now that the XVth Legion has arrived. What's worse is that they are heading in the direction of Jerusalem. This fact alone will unite the people in the cause of the rebellion. History is the most volatile element in Jews. They bear witness. They remember what Pompey did to the Holy City with the same legion."

Obediently Lucia gathered her belongings and followed Joseph through the Nabatean camp. He was amazed at how well she rode a camel.

They were passing through Samson country: another Jew, thought Joseph, who had married a heathen and made peace with Israel's enemy. Huge pellets struck them as they reached the mountains. Hail in the month of *Tishrai* held portents of evil times. The ice balls were the color of dust.

As they came over the first crest, the clouds broke, heaving up an intense dawn. All the villages they passed were empty and Joseph urged the camels into a canter.

"Look!" cried Lucia, the first word she had uttered since they had stolen the camels. Four bodies were nailed to the horizon. At their crossed feet lay piles of excrement, which meant that they had been crucified within the past twenty-four hours. The bodies stood in a circle, their ages and sexes already obliterated by vultures. Joseph sent his camel into a gallop.

Like a signet Jerusalem lay sealed to the earth by the sun. The surrounding valleys lay shattered and the late autumn grasses sagged like burned candlewicks. Along the Tyropoeon Valley, which rent the city in two, olive trees and cactus bushes stood petrified against the translucent sky. Steadying himself in final expectation, Joseph squinted into the sun, making his eyes tear as he caught the blare of gold across the snow field of marble — the Temple of the Living God. He slipped off his camel and fell to his knees, kissing the earth and declaring thanksgiving for having been brought home safely and in peace from the far corners of the earth, upright, to the city of his salvation. He was ready now to meet Jerusalem on his own terms.

As he rose he saw the opaque mirror of the Salt Sea and perched high above it like rock tablets the Fortress of Masada.

He rode on, Lucia following hard behind him. At the outer city wall, he stopped before the Gate of the Essenes, knowing that at this hour his friend, the centurion Metilius, would be the captain of the Roman guard that manned the south walls, affording them smooth entry into the city.

"Who stand below?" called the sentry on the wall.

"Joseph ben Matthias, Councilman of the *Sanhedrin*."

Before Joseph realized that it was not in Latin that he had been challenged and that the guard was a Jew, the gates swung open and two men bearing daggers at their sides dragged him off the camel and into the city. One of the men was the helmsman of Jaffa.

10

CHAPTER II — THE TWO FACES OF JERUSALEM

By noon Joseph was released from jail. He made his way through the unusually crowded streets of the Upper City, seat of noblemen and high priestly orders. In three days Jerusalem had doubled its population as pilgrims from all over the country as well as from abroad arrived for the *"Hag,"* as the Festival of *Sukkot* was popularly called, to celebrate the fall harvest and pay hommage to the Lord for having sheltered their forefathers in booths on their exodus from Egypt. Joseph felt a stranger in his own city.

He entered his palace and a maid hurried to relieve him of his dust stained tunic. When she reached for his leather pouch, he pushed her away brusquely, then strode into his chambers. From the pouch he took out a stylo and vial of ink and placed them on his writing table. Then, very carefully, he extracted the tightly bound scroll of his journal. He undressed and stepped into the *Mikva* set on the terrace overlooking the Temple compound that rose to the east across the Tryopoeon Valley. The maids had been trained to keep this large marble bath filled whether he was at home or not. He slid into the water warmed by the sun and groaned with relief as his body went limp, making him feel as if each of his limbs was disconnected. When he closed his eyes, a ball of fire burned in his brain.

Joseph let his head slip under the water. He opened his eyes and saw his red hair swiggle around his face Medusa-like. Two puffy eyes, whose color he could never identify, reflected back at him, and his lean hairy body floated like a corpse. Jumping up to a sitting position, he remembered Lucia. He shook the water out of his ears and saw that he had an erection.

"You're back," he heard his wife say. "I didn't think you'd have the courage to return."

His erection wilted. He did not turn to the archway where Hagla was standing.

"And did the priestesses of Rome prophesy well for your city?"

"Judea needs verification more than harlot prophecies," answered Joseph. He knew that his wife hated Jerusalem as he loved it.

"You were lucky to be released from jail. Your city's citizens now kill before they pass judgment."

"I assume my brother has some say in who lives and who dies."

"In Jerusalem one can assume nothing any longer."

ii

Joseph had met Hagla ten years earlier when she was thirteen and he seventeen. They had glanced at each other shyly for the first time while standing under the *hupa* marriage canopy. From the beginning things went wrong. Joseph had been too unsure of himself to assert his authority over so young a girl who had never dared to view her own body. After the marriage celebration, the couple retired to Jericho where for two centuries the House of Jehoyariv, Joseph's father's family, had traditionally gone on their honeymoons. Upon arrival, Hagla had immediately bolted herself in the palace nuptial chamber. After three days of pleading, Joseph finally convinced her to let him in. He found her lying stiffly on a carpeted sofa, still in her wedding gown which covered her arms to her fingertips and the rest of her body to her toes. She did not utter a word.

For a long while Joseph gazed down at the frightened child, hesitating what to do next. The movement of her ringed hand in order to tuck a wisp of hair that had fallen loose from her shawl aroused him and he dared to kiss her. Still feeling her small clenched teeth against his tongue, he had fumbled with her gown only to find when he opened it that her legs were rigidly folded. Forcing them apart with his knees, he tried to insert himself into her. In desperation he raised her clasped legs above her head while she screamed as he penetrated her sinfully in the way he had learned among the Nabateans. Hagla had been the shame of her parents because she was unable to conceive.

iii

"And has the great emissary Joseph ben Matthias succeeded in bargaining away his people's freedom?" Hagla asked as she looked down from the terrace and on to an arbor in the back garden.

Her intuitive guess over his doubts about the pending revolt had come to make him fear her, and more and more he avoided going to her chambers as the feeling grew in him that making love had become her form of revenge. There were times when he gasped with shame while she, like a hibernating python beneath him, lay without twitching a muscle. The thought brought on another erection.

"You can have Raya," she said, looking down at him. "I'm unclean."

Joseph sighed. She was still playing her little games. "That arouses me more."

"Pig," she snapped.

"I meant Raya. I've been gone more than six months."

Hagla walked up to the bath. "I've petitioned the courts against you. Just for that reason."

"You're the one who continues to offer her."

"It's the way you take my offer."

"I have nothing to fear from you," said Joseph, catching her real meaning.

"Every man has something to fear from a woman. Being devoured."

"That's just what you've failed at," said Joseph bitterly.

"A woman's failure is her husband's."

"I can't be blamed for the ignorance of your upbringing."

"I was young enough to be taught by a real man."

Suddenly Joseph wished that he were in the desert with Eleazar and among the silent praying Essenes. Raya, his wife's handmaiden, was from the desert, too, and never failed to satisfy all his needs without recrimination. Hagla relished blaming others for every mishap in her life: her barrenness, her war with God, His people, His city. Once he had caught her with the *teraphim* idols, the kind the half breed Syrians who dwelt among them worshipped. He had come home early after the evening *tamid* sacrifice at the Temple and found her standing before a small makeshift altar lit by two black tapers between which stood a clay goat statue and a larger pale blue limestone one. She had opened her robe and half kneeling let her blood drip between her thighs into a salver filled with salt and a few stalks of wheat. Joseph had grabbed her and forced her to the floor, penetrating her through her own oblation. Like her ancient Samaritan progenitors, she still needed an image for supplication.

"Within a few days, we may all be dead. What is it you want?" asked Joseph.

"To devour you," she shrieked, coming closer. Joseph stood in the bath and covered himself with a sheet. Hagla was slightly taller than he. "To destroy you as you have me with your corruption."

"The evil you accuse me of is perfectly normal. Perhaps in your city, in Sebastia, with its pagan traditions, the act of love for the sake of love has been corrupted into sin."

"Your methods are an abomination."

"Before whom? Your *teraphim*?"

"You shall be defeated. Tomorrow on the field of battle. The Romans shall devour you."

"The Witch of Ein Dor. I'm no King Saul. I do battle with no one. Nor have I sinned in the eyes of *my* Lord. Between man and wife, all ways are considered acts of love."

"Then you're ready to defend yourself publicly?"

"That too is part of the corruption of your inheritance. The love between a man and a woman is a private matter."

"Your proud family, princes in Judah, Oh how they and their

precious Jerusalem would like to hear what you do."

Again Joseph thought of Lucia. "Another part of your sickness," he said.

"Sin is sin no matter who performs it. I intend to denounce you before the *Sanhedrin* as a sodomist."

"I'm a priest. I can only be accused in a court of my peers."

"Your father, do you want me to denounce you before him?"

"And make an old man despise himself?"

"I intend to make the whole nation of Jews despise you." And glancing once at the shimmering city, she disappeared through the archway.

Back in his writing chamber, Joseph found Niger of Perea, his kinsman and aide.

Niger, whose hair was brighter red than Joseph's, embraced him. "It's good to have you back."

"I'm glad that finally somebody thinks so. First I was arrested. Then my dear wife —"

"Arrested? Who dared?"

"Sicaris. They just released me."

"They burned one of our storehouses yesterday. We retaliated by stampeding their livestock out of the city. They must have blamed that on your return."

Joseph shook his head in disgust. "If we continue fighting each other over supremacy of this city, the Romans need only sit back and wait for us to destroy ourselves. Let's hope there's no trouble in the next few days."

"Cestius Gallus' XIIth Legion is scorching the land. Not that it matters any longer," smiled Niger. "I think our forces are about to unite."

"What forces?"

"Simon bar Giora in the south, John of Gishhala in the north and Eleazar ben Yair and the Sicaris. Here, this just arrived from bar Giora." Niger handed Joseph a dispatch which he unfolded, his fingers trembling more than usual.

EMMAUS ON FIFTH DAY OF SUKKOT. WE'LL
BUST THE ROMAN'S BALLS AT EMMAUS.

"My dear wife," said Joseph, "predicted that tomorrow I shall be defeated on the field of battle."

"We beat the enemy there once. We'll do it again."

"I'm no longer sure who our enemies are. But if there's going to be a battle, it shall be fought according to my specifications. I shall join you and our retainers at Emmaus at sunset."

After Niger left, Joseph examined his face in a mirror. He hid it quickly when Raban Johanan ben Zakkai, President of the *Sanhedrin* entered and sat down at Joseph's desk. He kept tapping his cane against the tiled floor. "Catastrophe is upon us," said the dark faced white bearded sage.

"Isn't it always," said Joseph, wiping his hair. "I carry some hope from Rome."

"Rome is not our catastrophe. It is our own stiff necks." He leaned forward on his cane.

Joseph had known the old man since childhood and never before had he heard his voice tremble. His Pharisaic mind worked through reason and moderation. Superlatives were honed into truths through sarcasm or some humorous parable whose butt was always an excitable interlocutor. Joseph had studied under this casuist, noted for gleaning ethical aphorisms from the poetry of the Bible. For him each word and letter of the sacred text was a brick to be cemented into a house of The Law. With a select few, Joseph had sat at the feet of this great scholar beneath the old terebinth oak outside the Gate of the Essenes and gathered crumbs off his lips as he expounded that only through evolution of The Law could their people survive. He used to say: "If thou hast learnt Torah, ascribe not any merit to thyself, for thereunto wast thou created." For ben Zakkai there was little difference between the Sicaris, who mistook the concept of God's chosen for superiority, and the Romans, who could not comprehend the passion for balancing one word against another.

"*Ahm segula,*" he said. "The Chosen People only because we chose The Law as it has chosen us."

"Is that how one survives?" Joseph had asked.

"Say not *how,* but *why* one survives. That too is part of being chosen."

"And should we not go out into the world and share that *segula,* that peculiar treasure?"

"Like oil, *segula* becomes thin when spread."

"Does not that make us exclusive?"

"Privilege makes one exclusive. Having been chosen entails only obligations."

Joseph had learned the same order when living among the Essenes, the difference being that they saw their constant as death. Only in such finality could one absorb godliness and enter the cycle of creator and created. Ben Zakkai quoted Torah. Bannus, the wise Essene, sought the distortions of the sun.

"The Romans are on their way to destroy Jerusalem," said ben Zakkai.

"You have always taught that Torah and not place is our survival."

"Have you not yourself chosen Jerusalem above the highest joy?"

"So it is written."

"A figure of speech. What is Jerusalem? What is Torah without people?"

"And without land, shall we be the same people?"

"In time is where eternity lies. Never place. That is the meaning of the Ineffable Name. It is why we shall never perish from the earth as others have under the burden of newer civilizations."

"Rome? Are they not accordingly God's agents at the moment? to punish us for our transgressions?"

"The power of Rome is as false as the movement of the sun," said the President, again tapping his cane nervously against the floor. "They might overwhelm our land. Never our national memory. For we Jews are the hands of time."

Joseph walked out on to the terrace and saw a black cloud rising above the storehouses and drift over the *Mikdash*, the Temple. He came back and stood by his writing desk. He heard the old man wheeze. "What you're saying is that we must surrender our sovereignty to preserve The Law."

Ben Zakkai rose with the agility of a younger man. He tapped his cane once. "Eretz Yisrael without Torah is like a body without a soul."

"Akiva says that a people without land has no will to survive its own destruction."

The old man waved off Joseph's remark. His gnarled fingers were spotted with ink like a schoolboy's. "Land is merely the vanity by which God tempts us."

"Eleazar ben Yair believes that death holds the final victory."

"The most abominable sin. Nevertheless it must be used for the moment. We must use his obsession to stop the others."

"Perhaps the age demands a sacrifice."

"Christian nonsense. History holds no hostages. Those so-called heroes of our people must be stopped. If they are allowed into the city in force, the rabble is ready to worship their false doctrine of hope. Not only Jerusalem but all Jews will be doomed."

"And the offer from certain Romans I sent you?"

"Irrelevant until we get our own house in order. Until we halt the rebellion and again the *Sanhedrin* governs. You must go at once to ben Yair. Forestall him. Prevail upon him not to join the others. Keep him away from Jerusalem."

"And how, Raban, does one prevail upon Eleazar ben Yair?"

"Masada. Help him die for Masada."

When the President of the *Sanhedrin* left, Joseph sat at the desk.

He could not explain to ben Zakkai that to Eleazar, he, Joseph, must first win the privilege of dying: for Masada or Jerusalem. Nor would he accept the fact that only *Torah* — The Law — could save the eternity of Israel. What if, as he believed, their salvation lay in Rome? What if Eleazar ben Yair could not be forestalled? What if God had not chosen Israel?

He sighed as he fingered the edge of his journal. As always when he touched the scroll, hesitation evaporated. If he succeeded in blocking Cestius Gallus, he could have it both ways: with Eleazar and with Titus. Here upon the parchment of his life he could unravel any contradiction. Create enemies in others' image; raise heroes in his own. What greater pleasure than to ascribe the deeds of others to himself? change history by recording it to his own advantage? At this point fantasy and reality became confused in his mind. He would hold them fisted in his quill, shuddering until he spewed them up in relief out of the ardor of his imagination, then fall back trembling.

He wrote:

> *power makes truth relative. those responsible for the world order must see that it never remains static; that leadership and idea must constantly change. let them be aware that the sustenance of an empire is older empires. if rome is to survive her greatness, she must continue to soar, else she might find herself curled inward, devouring her own entrails. now that the frontiers to the west have been closed by the sea, only to the east lie vast open borders. Alexander understood this idea of movement, and but for his petty generals, would have moved beyond the indus, sustaining greece even unto the present as the greatest empire ever. the CONSTANT EMPIRE.*

Joseph liked the phrase. "Constant empire," he repeated to himself aloud.

> *herein lay the mistake of the jews who thought that in discovering a universal truth, they too, though a small people, could perpetuate a realm. but they had misunderstood the concept, which for them could only mean GOD, thus ossifying his omnipotence by adhering to his first revelation to them. b'reshit was the first word of the law and for that they had to pay a price no other people ever would. loyalty to the beginning: denying that the god of hosts had indeed mollified his own image, as the prophets foretold, into the living god, while they, his people, still clung to his inchoate warlike visage. if, then, the jews wish-*

ed to make war today, they would have to do it in their own name, like the romans or the germans or the britons and not behind the arcane shield of a holy ark. and that meant that like all other people they either had to win or be eradicated. the century of rome had taught that only power was inviolate.

rome itself, as lucia's father had warned, was enveloping itself in its own national error: TERGIVERSATION. no longer can it afford the luxury where poison chooses a new emperor and suicide his successor. to meet its fate, rome must replace its haphazard form of governance for that of a true dynasty. if this is so, then at the moment who controls jerusalem can be more decisive for the empire than who rules in rome. this is our new identity.

As an afterthought, he added:

raban johanan ben zakkai understands the jewish constant.

CHAPTER III — THE SECOND BATTLE OF EMMAUS

i

Mounted on a black Arabian, Joseph watched the XIIth Legion wind in an endless column eastward toward the slopes of the Judean hills where he and four thousand of his retainers waited. Yesterday's pale sky had divided itself into pillars of clouds causing the Roman army to appear and disappear in their shadows. First came four squadrons of cavalry, followed by two thousand elite guard, plus six regiments of the line which made up the complement of the famous legion. Behind it, in similar order and number came the satellite kingdoms of the east. Hordes of Syrian auxiliaries, including work battalions, mule teams and bearers hauling heavy weapons and siege machines brought up the rear.

Ever since the days when he and Eleazar ben Yair had played at war using the battles of their people as their script, and the rocks and boulders of the desert as their armies, Joseph had desired to lead men in combat. Eleazar always won these mock wars, and in frustration Joseph would throw down his wooden sword and declare: "No. It wasn't like that at Ziklon. Not like that at Megiddo, or at Jabesh." And Eleazar would stand silent and victorious. "You didn't do it as it said in the book," Joseph would reprove him. "In the book my side always won."

Once Eleazar turned around and pointed at the sun. "Let's fight for Masada," he said. "That's in no one's book."

Since then Joseph had read the tales of Aristablus, how Alexander the Great marched across Africa and Asia guided miraculously by two snakes and two crows. Later, like all Jewish princes, his father had enrolled him at the Antioch Roman military academy in Syria headed by the very general he would now meet in battle. There he had studied strategies and memorized the diaries of Hannibal and Ceasar's *Commentaries*. "Repetition," Cestius Gallus had taught, "is the secret to Roman victory."

Joseph had continued his studies while in Rome, on his recent mission, during which he had fallen ill with river fever. By good fortune his host was defense counsellor to the Emperor Nero, affording Joseph access both to Epaphroditus' excellent library on the art of war and to his daughter, Lucia, who nursed him back to health. It was then that he concluded that duplicity and cunning had won more battles than the numbers and the courage of men. Eleazar ben Yair had meanwhile remained among the Essenes, probing the wilderness for its weaknesses and its strength.

Joseph's battle plan now, however, did not grow out of alien concepts or chronicles, but from Simon bar Giora's note. Always needing the verification of history, Joseph chose to emulate the greatest general in the annals of his people. In a forgotten manuscript, *The Book of The Maccabees,* which Bannus the wise Essene had once made Eleazar and Joseph read, there was a detailed description of how Judah the Maccabee did, in effect, kick the Greeks in the balls in the same field of battle and thus save Jerusalem. Being a more cautious general, Joseph would insure his victory through duplicity as well.

Among Cestius Gallus' bravest troops were the Golan Royals, soldiers of a Roman satrapy northeast of Judea ruled by Queen Berenice, scion of the Maccabees and mistress to the legate Titus Flavius. Although Cestius Gallus knew that the Royals were descendents of the Babylonian exile half a millenium ago, like other Romans he could not conceive that like all Jews, they too had a special loyalty to the eternity of Israel and its God; that no matter where they lived or for how long, they still turned their eyes in hope and in prayer to the holy city of Jerusalem.

Like Judah, Joseph had divided his force in three. Simon bar Giora and his Idumeans waited above the pass at Shaar Hagai to the south of Emmaus and on the main road to Jerusalem, while he and his cavalry, mostly carriage horses since good mounts were always scarce in Judea, stood ready to charge down upon the Romans, surprising them so that Cestius would be obliged to send his own cavalry charging uphill followed by his Elite Guard in order to prevent a rout in the undefended town. The two opposing cavalries would clash at the plateau half way down from where Joseph sat. He would then swing north, drawing the Roman horsemen after him and lead them around the pine forest were Niger and five thousand of Jerusalem's militia would spring from behind and cut them off. Meanwhile, Simon would race down to Emmaus, defended only by the auxiliaries and the satellite kings with their half trained cohorts, and destroy the heavy weapons and supplies needed for the conquest of Jerusalem. At that point Joseph would turn back and make a stand. Cestius Gallus, seeing that Emmaus was aflame, would be compelled to acknowledge Joseph's successful strategy — in Joseph's eyes it was no longer Judah the Maccabee's — and come to terms without further waste of men. Joseph's one fear was that the zealousness of Simon bar Giora, who was not under his command but who had consented to join him, might carry them to extremes and kill too many Romans.

As Joseph had forseen, the Romans paused at Emmaus in order to refresh themselves at its famous springs before they began the twenty mile ascent to Jerusalem. So confident was Cestius Gallus of his force that he saw no need to rush his attack, especially when he knew that the Jews would be preoccupied with one of their holy pilgrimages. Like most Romans, the Legate of the XIIth Legion believed that the Jews would rather pray for their victories than fight for them.

Unknown to the Jews under Joseph's command and to Cestius Gallus was that Joseph's success was insured by conspirators in Rome who foresaw in his victory against their own countrymen a means of ridding themselves of the profligate Emperor Nero. It was why Joseph watched with satisfaction as the Golan Royals moved imperceptibly to the left flank of the other Roman troops who were frolicking in the baths of the deserted town.

ii

The plan was conceived six months earlier in Rome, toward the end of Joseph's illness. He had been forbidden to drink or bathe in any Roman waters but those of the *caldarium*. Each day he would go to the baths near the Circus Flaminus and follow the usual routine of sitting in the steam room as long as he could bear the heat, then he would hurry to the cooling room, gasping as he finally emerged into the hall where he sat shivering, wearing only a loin cloth.

One day Joseph entered the baths and was immediately blinded by steam. Someone had left the door open to the *caldarium* and vapors filled the changing room. As Joseph groped his way to the connecting door, he heard a man counting. "23...24...25...26...." Vaguely he made out a figure seated on a bench and scratching his elbows. From the *frigidarium*, on the opposite side, a figure entered moving like a faded shadow. "27...28...29...." The man looked up, the air now beginning to clear.

"Lucia Paulina," he said calmly. "What a pleasure to find that your ingenuity works even in public baths."

Joseph made out a young woman approaching the man, her bare bosom almost touching his sunken chest.

"I carry a message to you," said the woman. "From my father."

The man reached out and ran his palms across the pink nipples, firming the breasts. "And why couldn't the First Counsellor to the Emperor tell me what he has to say instead of sending his beautiful daughter?"

"Epaphroditus is under house arrest. He trusts no one but me."

"House arrest would appeal to me more than my own Caelian jail. That is till you appeared. How did you manage to enter the men's baths?"

"The legate of the XVth Legion lacks imagination."

"Former," said the man, touching the small of her back. "As a prisoner of the state I am allowed one bath a month."

"Have Calpurnia and the children visited you since the Emperor had you arrested?"

"She's pregnant again."

"She has the passion of a rabbit."

"At the moment so do I," said the former legate as he ran his hand below her left ear where Joseph knew she had a beetle colored beauty mark that had always disgusted him.

"Perhaps I should alert my mistress, the Queen of Golan," said Lucia Paulina.

The man laughed. "Berenice is not Roman. She doesn't know how to obey orders."

"You underestimate her Jewish heritage. She could be Empress of Rome someday."

"She has no such ambition."

"But you do."

The man drew her against his body. "Only in what has grown firm through a month's incarceration."

Joseph admired the coolness of their movements under the oppressive heat of the steam room.

"Your towels, Sire," called the attendant coming toward them. Lucia picked up a bucket and poured water over the hot bricks to her side, covering the chamber in a new cloud of steam.

When the steam cleared again, the attendant was gone and Lucia was wrapped in a robe. The man stretched his bare toes and squeezed them between Lucia's. She took up the bucket and this time poured cold water over his pock marked shoulders. The steam cleared.

"Perhaps that's what Rome needs," laughed the man.

"My father is a free man," said Lucia. If you race tomorrow in the Circus Falminius, so are you." Lucia walked toward Joseph, who retreated behind the door. "I shall signal you Rome's wishes. Whether to win or lose the race."

This time the man threw water over the hot bricks. "Rome," he said, hunching back into his former position, "never loses."

Lucia hurried by Joseph who was blotted out by the steam. He waited till he was sure that she was gone and then entered the *caldarium*.

As if expecting him, the man looked up. "Come sit here," he said. "It's about time we had a dialogue."

Joseph hesitated. Adjusting his loin cloth, he sat beside the stranger whose broad shoulders were covered with acne. He had the bowed legs of a horseman.

"My name is Titus Flavius," said the man in Greek. "At the moment I'm in retirement, thank the gods." He raised a bucket of water and poured it over his head causing a cloud of steam to cover him.

"There are moments," continued the stranger, "when one chooses to retire and in that way, like you, the fates shelter him from the public eye until the right time. For example, if you were in Jerusalem now, you'd either be crucified for chasing the procurator out of the city, or garotted by your own people for opposing the fanatics who recently perpetrated that act which has rent the city into civil war."

"You seem to know more about what's going on in Judea than I do."

"And from what I gather, you as much about Rome. Queen Berenice believes Rome and Jerusalem are compatible. Do you?"

"For Jerusalem's sake, I hope they are."

"Then you can still be crucified."

"Or garotted," said Joseph.

Titus smiled. "If I, for example, should still be in command of the XVth Legion as I was till a few days ago, I would be hanging from the Forum upside down with only my hair touching the ground."

"What if the fates chose now to keep you in obscurity?"

"Fates can neither push you to power nor deny it to you. The course of our lives is established long before anything or anyone can push us to our doom."

"Then you know the direction your life will take as well as its end?"

"Let's say I respect the course. The end then becomes merely a matter of obedience."

"That's strictly a military point of view," said Joseph. "The space I occupy in what you call the course of life interests me more than the time allotted to me. How I do is more important to me than the result of my doing."

"Then Rome's taught you nothing," said Titus. "Fortune and energy: there's your true sense of fate. Link it to the discipline of office and you have the real secret of Roman power. It's how a little town straddling seven hills subdued all the others surrounding her. She could obey orders. There was a man once, a father, who killed his only son for winning a battle against orders."

"We had a king who ordered the same. The people saved his son."

"The quickest way to disaster." Titus handed Joseph a pitcher of water and he sprinkled a few drops on his hairy shoulders.

"Here, give it here. It's for shock, else you lose the curative value.

Like war." And he poured the water over Joseph's head.

Joseph gasped. "Have you been ill as well?"

"Let's say that what's brought you here has also brought me. For more ways than you imagine."

"I'm here on orders of a Roman physician," said Joseph defensively. "For a Jew a bath is merely part of his ritual."

"Your people who live in the desert make much more of it. I'm told they're hardy warriors. Are they among your followers?"

Joseph was taken aback by the switch in tone. He did not like losing control of a conversation. "Why should that interest you?" he asked, forcing himself to look directly into Titus' eyes.

"A good soldier likes to know something about his possible adversary."

"Judea is part of the Roman Empire."

"Being only a part is what makes you a possible adversary."

"I should think that your loss of command makes your probable adversary right here in Rome."

Titus farted. He rose and walked into the adjoining room and returned with a flagon and two goblets. "Here, have some good Tuscan wine. It's good contrast to the sweat."

Joseph saw that the gesture was merely a maneuver to gain time. He pressed his last point, this time speaking in Latin. "The conspiracy, the recent one against Nero, how much of it was controlled by the military?"

The change of language threw Titus off balance. "If the military had really been implicated, it would have succeeded."

"Meaning the Emperor still has the support of the generals?"

For the first time since they had begun their conversation Titus hesitated. Joseph noticed how his chest was already sagging and that his genitals were shrunken.

"Not the right ones."

"Carbulo?"

"Carbulo's a nothing."

"Tiberius Alexander?"

Titus shook his head. "Tiberius Alexander has gone about as far as a Jew can under any emperor."

"He's no longer a Jew."

"A serpent doesn't change into an eagle merely by apostasy."

"Cestius Gallus, Governor of Syria?"

"A man worn out by his own limitations."

"He and Tiberius Alexander control the east."

Titus rose. He came so close that Joseph could feel the heat of his body. You're a graduate of the academy of Antioch," he said. "Offensive or defensive?''

"I've never been tried."

"You ask the right questions. Infantry or cavalry?"

"Infantry. Our country lacks the horseman tradition."

"Silas of Barnea is a fine horseman. Do you know him?"

"A general in Queen Berenice's service."

"He fought with me in Dacia. How would you like a command in my legion?"

Joseph wiped the sweat from his eyes. He liked this soldier's quick mind and how he sparred not to find weakness but the strong places. "You just told me you lost your command."

"I also told you that authority is a matter of luck. I've always been lucky."

"You might be sent to Judea."

"You didn't answer my question."

Joseph had felt at that moment as he did before he made love. Only one other man had the same effect on him: Eleazar ben Yair. "I'm a Jew," said Joseph. "Judea is my country."

Titus waved his hand. "Makes no difference to a good soldier."

"Is Silas a good soldier?"

"Can't kill Jews. Can you?"

Joseph's heart pounded making breathing difficult. "Can you kill Romans?"

The only sound now was the condensed steam dripping off the clay pipes.

"Haven't had the opportunity," said Titus Flavius. "If you accept my proposition, we might very well have to kill both."

iii

Joseph's horse snorted as the sun broke momentarily through the clouds revealing the Romans lying half naked around the pools of Emmaus. Only the Golan Royals remained mounted. He looked up at the pine forest on his right and then, his hand trembling, he withdrew his sword. All he need do was to brandish the blade, turning it to the sun, and Judea would be free, and Rome have a new emperor.

Joseph kicked his heels into his horse, who sensing the insecurity of the rider, began side-slipping awkwardly down the mountain. By the time Joseph reached the plateau, he could hear the frenzied trumpets of the Romans. He waved the sword over his head and shouted: "Follow me!" as he wheeled about dashing north along the mountain shelf.

The Roman cavalry rode up diagonally, faster than Joseph had anticipated, almost cutting off the Jews before they could reach the forest. Joseph's thighs sweated as they rubbed against the wet haunches of his mount. Fearfully, he turned and saw the sun dimming in the thickening mist that was rising over Emmaus. Simon bar Giora must have begun firing the Roman camp. Brighter than the sun, the moon hung over the Valley of Ayalon, and Joseph was sure that the Lord of Hosts had once again given them this day before their enemies.

At the head of his men, Joseph dashed into the forest, the Roman cavalry on his heels. When he reined in to turn and face the enemy, he saw that the forest too was shrouded in fog and that he could not tell Jew from Roman, horse from tree. Slashing his sword to the right and left, he struck a tree, and a branch crashed in front of him. His horse reared up and for a moment the whole battlefield whirled around him in confusion.

The fog lifted. Joseph was surprised to find a tall man in a green helmet talking to Niger at the edge of the forest.

"Joseph!" declared Niger. "We thought you were dead."

"What happened?" asked Joseph, who had fallen off his horse.

"Everything went wrong. The fog interfered with your strategy," said Niger with the same enthusiasm he had shown before the battle. "Simon never attacked. He never saw your signal."

"He's a liar. I rose in my horse and brandished my sword so that even the Angel of Death shuddered."

"You were already in the fog. No one saw it," said Niger.

"I saw it," said the man in the green helmet who looked like an ancient Assyrian prince, his beard square and gray, falling down to his armored chest.

"Who are you?"

"Silas of Barnea, Commander of the Golan Royals."

"Where in God's name was that devil?"

"By now I suspect he is half way to Gaza," said Silas, who exhaled on each phrase he spoke, giving his voice a tone of resignation. "His scouts reported that the XVth Legion had crossed the border from Egypt, invading what he considers his domain."

"Titus Flavius," nodded Joseph. "They come to greet him as their commander."

Silas exhaled deeply and waited.

"The fool," declared Joseph angrily. "It was all planned."

"What was planned?" asked the Golan commander.

"Everything. Your moving to the left flank was the signal to me that Titus, supported by the legate Tiberius Alexander, was marching on his own special pilgrimage to Jerusalem."

"Cestius knew nothing of this?"

"True to his nature, he hesitated to support a daring scheme."

"What scheme?" demanded the commander of the Golan Royals.

"The appointment of a new emperor in Rome. Nero is dead. Drowned in a bathtub filled with his own blood. We Jews might yet get to appoint the next Roman emperor."

"What scheme?" repeated Silas, again inhaling deeply.

"Titus, not bar Giora, chose Emmaus as the way for the Flavian ascendancy over Rome."

"And we are part of this plan?" asked Niger astounded.

"Right after *Sukkot,* when the city gets back to normal, I was to greet the XVth Legion at the gates of Jerusalem."

"That's treason," said Niger.

"So is his presence among us according to bar Giora," said Joseph nodding to Silas.

"And now?" asked Silas. "What happens now?"

"By disobeying orders, bar Giora has allowed Cestius Gallus to advance on Jerusalem, and he, not Titus, shall have the power to decide who shall be the next Emperor of Rome."

As they rode back to the city, Joseph noted that the sun and the moon had not changed their positions. He remembered that in their childhood games, Eleazar ben Yair had also won the Battle of Emmaus.

27

CHAPTER IV — THE FLEXIBLE FORTRESS

Back in Jerusalem Joseph took up his journal.
He wrote:

darkness. the fires of the pilgrims burn eyes into the horizon. having failed in our strategy at emmaus, the romans are confidently moving north of the city, jerusalem's most vulnerable side. cestius gallus believes that because of sukkot we shall be preoccupied with god, especially on the last day when one hundred thousand jews shall be jammed into the half mile square of the temple compound for the final sacrifice. his attack, i am sure, will commence on the sabbath, when normally we do not bear arms. that allows me two days to convince him that since the legates of the west are unable to unite behind a single candidate to replace the dead nero, for once an eastern legate has a chance to be elected emperor of rome. only he, as governor of greater syria, has thus far withheld his support for flavius vespasian, commander-in-chief of the army of the east. winning him over would allow both his twelfth legion and titus' fifteenth to enter jerusalem together not as victors but as saviors and allies, welcomed by johanan ben zakkai in the name of the supreme council of the sanhedrin. my only fear is bar giora. and no word from titus.

He looked up and saw that Raya was standing in the doorway. Once in the desert, Joseph had wakened with the sunrise and not three feet from him three Bedouin sat crosslegged in black burnooses while they smoked the Nabatean honey that made their eyes dilate. Like her people Raya had a way of appearing noiselessly and waiting until she was observed. She held a jug in her small brown hands. Without looking at him, she set it down near the terrace door. Joseph reached for her hand as she rose to go. With his free hand, he lifted the jug and poured a few drops over the girl's palm. Then he rubbed it against the clay jug. "Raya has forgotton the ways of the desert," he said. "She should know that if the *jarrah* isn't wet, it will not sweat with the morning sun and cool the water inside."

He set the jug down. Still holding her hand, he ran it across his face. She had been a child the first time he had lain with her and she had hardly covered his loins. Hagla had lied that she was pregnant and would no longer allow him into her chamber. Instead she sent her new maid whose chest was hard as a boy's.

28

"You've grown to be a woman," said Joseph.

The girl bowed her head. Joseph led her to the couch and drew her down upon him. "And who have you been enjoying since I've been away?" he teased.

The girl shook her head. "Only you, Sire."

"And your little friends, the kitchen maids, haven't they taught you how to amuse yourself?"

"I enjoy only you, Sire."

Joseph undid her bodice and her small, dark breasts fell to his mouth. The girl hovered over him without stirring. Joseph rubbed his teeth across her nipples, biting them gently. Lucia's were light and pink though not so firm. Hagla's had already begun to sag. The thought of Hagla made him spiteful and he bit harder. The maid did not flinch. He slid from under her and like a dog, mounted her from behind, his fingers clawing at the bristle between her legs as he penetrated her safely and endlessly. Long ago he had convinced himself that this way was not sinful so long as it was done with a woman. He had not enjoyed himself in this manner since the last time his wife claimed she was with child.

She left as silently as she had entered. When he awoke it was morning. Beside him he found a finger of Nabatean honey and the two-faced idol, Janus.

ii

From the top of the Psephinus Tower at the northwest corner of the Outer Wall of the city, Joseph and Silas of Barnea watched the swiftly evolving battle for Jerusalem. Silas explained how Cestius Gallus was following classic offensive tactics.

"Ballista stones in clusters at one target, followed by flaming arrows will begin the attack. There they go! heading for the *agora* on this side of the city. If I am correct, next will be the Ophel Quarter. The Romans always seek out the heart of a city they attack. When they hit the Antonia Fortress, you'll know that they've found it."

"That means the Temple," said Joseph. "Cestius Gallus is too clever to attack the Temple. Besides, there's a Roman garrison still in the Antonia. The official Roman presence in Jerusalem."

"The Centurion Metilius managed to get a message to us when we were still in Jaffa a few days ago. He said that he was more a prisoner than a presence in the city. If by tomorrow we refuse to surrender, you can be sure that Cestius will begin firing the Temple."

"Attack the Temple and every Jew will become a Sicari."

"He is a Roman general. He enjoys desperate battles." Silas looked up at the gray skies. "By this afternoon he will storm the Outer Wall we are standing on. Then dash across the sparsely populated new Bezetha Quarter behind us. By nightfall he will be prepared to assault the Antonia. When he is sure that we are really desperate, he will attack the Temple. It is the way every Roman commander is taught to conquer Jerusalem."

"You mean they actually learn to conquer this city?"

"Every city. They have a strategy for Alexandria, for Susa, for Petra. For every city in the world including Rome."

A stone crashed against the parapet and splattered Joseph and Silas with chips of brass and iron. Another whistled overhead and landed in the tower courtyard behind them raising a cloud of dust that spread slowly in ripples across the darkening sky.

"Any news from Titus?" asked Joseph.

"The battle is fierce at Gaza. Bar Giora is reported to have counterattacked."

"You should have stayed with Queen Berenice."

"If Jerusalem falls, I want to be inside her walls."

"That's just how Jerusalem will fall. Fighting for her inside. Traditionally Jerusalem defends itself outside her walls."

"Bar Giora fixed that at Emmaus. What are our alternatives?"

"Forays," said Joseph. "That's the next stage, if we follow history. Quick sorties at night against the enemy camp. Burn his supplies. Harrass him ceaselessly."

"All that will do is force Cestius Gallus to use his contingency plan. He is a very patient and meticulous commander."

"What contingency plan?"

"Siege. Walls of circumvalation. Starvation. Fire. That is also, I believe, in Jerusalem's tradition."

A cluster of bolts whizzed overhead. Joseph crouched lower behind the parapet. Silas leaned over and spat down on a black goat that nibbled on the malva grass growing out of the wall. On a boulder nearby, a Bedouin sat ignoring the gathering battle.

"Sieges are long drawn out affairs. He may not have the time," said Joseph.

A squadron of Roman cavalry cantered across the crest of Mount Scopus, their banners taut in the breeze. "The general has arrived at his headquarters," said Silas. "The attack is about to commence. Go down yourself and convince Cestius to hold off for twenty-four hours."

"And if Titus should not arrive? And if bar Giora spoils our plan again?"

"Use your imagination. Show the Governor of Syria that if he does not join the Flavians now, he will be left in the cold."

"And after twenty-four hours. If Titus should fail?"

"Rain," said Silas. "No one can do battle in those autumn rains. Maybe there will be a miracle and God will hasten the first rains that we pray for on *Sukkot*." He brushed the dust off his tunic and then carefully stepped off the rampart.

iii

Joseph sat on a sofa in a stone hut on the slope that looked down upon Jerusalem. Trumpets and bugles competed with the thumping hoofs of horses. Joseph believed in miracles — miracles against the Canaanites, miracles against the Jebusites, even against the Assyrians. Not against the XIIth Legion. God, he was convinced, was on the side of Rome.

For the piece of Nabatean honey Raya had left him, he had gotten the Bedouin goat herder to exchange clothes with him, which was how Joseph managed to get to this hut, headquarters of Cestius Gallus. The Roman sentries had let him roam about the camp, and only when he approached a centurion of the Elite Guard did Joseph flash the centurion sword from under his cloak which he had earned at the military academy in Antioch, revealing who he was.

Waiting for the general, Joseph wondered how much Cestius really knew about the broader plans of the Flavians: of their desire to establish a family dynasty rather than a lifetime emperorship as had been the custom till then. Titus himself had been ambiguous about his plans once Jerusalem was peacefully occupied, in this way keeping his options in Rome and his commitment to the Jews open. But what if Titus had misjudged Cestius Gallus? What if he was a more decisive man than the younger general supposed, and he moved against Jerusalem immediately, an easier and so much more dramatic a confrontation than the one Titus now faced down at Gaza against the toughest Jewish commander, placing himself in the position before the Roman Senate that the Flavians coveted? The thought of switching allegiances did not bother Joseph. He did, however, feel his usual frustration at again having his life controlled by the destiny of others.

The sleeveless sheepskin jacket he wore smelled of piss. The hut itself had the pleasant odor of melons. Looking around, he saw himself in a mirror hanging above a small table crowded with vials and jars. Since his sojourn in Rome, he had kept his beard shaven which dulled the color of his eyes. A half rolled map lay on the floor and a familiar gown was draped over the chair.

A tall, broad-shouldered man, whose frame showed that he had once been thinner, entered the hut. "We've been expecting you," he said, painfully unloosing the straps of his armor. Cestius Gallus rubbed his sides between the iron plating. "I'm too old for games. Any kind of games. This armor cuts like a woman's girdle must." He leaned over stiffly and poured wine into a glass. He drank it and filled the glass again. He did not offer Joseph any. "You fought well yesterday," he said. "Used your men and terrain properly. But never underestimate the knowledge of your enemy."

"I am not fighting an enemy."

"Gorgias lost the first Battle of Emmaus because he underestimated your Judah fellow."

"Don't Roman generals always underestimate their opponents?"

"Only in that we're sure we'll win. Your first battle yesterday?"

"Against the Roman army, yes."

"That wasn't the Roman army you fought. Only Syrian auxiliaries," the Governor of Syria and commander of the XIIth Legion smiled. "I think you know about them."

"They were generaled by a Roman. Yourself."

"I saw your strategy when you wheeled about too quickly on the plateau. You should have ridden right up to Emmaus before turning and feining retreat."

"That meant climbing back into the forest. My cavalry was not of the best quality."

"The complexity of battle is that the commander always has two choices."

"The ground fog confused the whole front."

Cestius drank quickly. "Excuses are usually prepared before one loses a battle."

This was not the man Titus had described to him in the bath back in Rome. "Silas implied the same thing."

"He can't handle more than a regiment. Neither can you."

"We were underequipped. You saw that."

Cestius Gallus shook his head. What was left of his hair was gray. His upturned nose broke the curve of his bald head and kept his face handsome. His teeth, however, were worn down and discolored from many years of wine drinking. "Simon bar Gioras," he used the Greek pronunciation, "He can lead an army. He had less equipment than you."

"He failed in his objective. His orders were to burn your camp."

"You forgot what we taught you at the academy. The flexible fortress."

Joseph was pleased that the governor remembered him. "I don't recall the term."

"A Roman camp is laid out so that it's self-sustaining under just such possible surprise attacks as you planned. Even our temporary encampment at Emmaus. To move forward or backward, and like a walled city, cover all sides. It's the advantage we have over Jerusalem." Cestius Gallus emptied his glass and refilled it, smacking his lips. "Once, outside of Lyons, in a place called Vienne, we captured a vineyard. I was a boy then — arms bearer for Germanicus. Maybe sixteen. And I discovered how easily courage can be had through the top of a bottle." He raised the flagon. "It too makes one self-sustaining in battle."

"Simon bar Giora is a cutthroat and a bandit," declared Joseph. "He's fired with the passion of a convert. His father was an Idumean. We lost the battle because he disobeyed orders."

"Not passion, patience. The best quality in a combat leader. Once we saw your ruse, we waited for his move. He didn't lose his head. He outwaited us."

"He took off before I even moved down the mountain. To block Titus Flavius outside of Gaza."

Cestius Gallus played with the edge of the map that lay curled on the table. "And have you decided whether you want him to succeed or fail?"

"If he succeeds he'll be back inside those walls soon after."

Cestius drank the remainder of his wine. "That's why I'm here."

"Attack the city and the Jews will make war till the end. Jerusalem is an idea. You can't defeat that."

"And Emmaus?"

"That was fought over only for the sake of Jerusalem. The last time that happened Jerusalem won."

"That's your trouble. You fight last century's battle today. Most generals are insecure enough to need the authority of history. Judah the Maccabee was original."

"Defeated his opponent under similar conditions."

Cestius Gallus sucked on his glass. "Rome can be defeated many times and still be the victor. Judea cannot. Lose once and it will take a millenium before you're ever given a second chance. That's why I mean to catch you before your idea of Jerusalem spreads. That's another Roman strategy. I shall occupy your temple and teach you the lesson Pompey did not."

"A few chieftains who control a handful of followers do not a rebellion make."

"They kill Romans. Refuse the Emperor's gift of sacrifice in that temple of theirs. They attack the cities of the Decapolis who are allied to us. John of Gishhalav even dared recently to raid the seat of the procurator in Caesarea."

An officer entered with a message which the general read as he tapped his fingers against the empty flagon. "Instruct Caesenius to advance according to plan," he said bending over to sign the order. "And get them to bring more wine."

"You mean then to carry on?" asked Joseph.

"We attack in fifteen minutes."

"And if the city holds?"

"Then we'll lay down a siege. It's already planned."

"You hardly have time. Vespasian is in Acre with the Vth Legion," lied Joseph. "Tiberius Alexander and Titus are on their way to the city from Gaza. You must change sides. Roman sides."

"Vespasian is an old antagonist of mine. We've risen in rank together, almost always at each other's expense. Seems to be happening again right here." He raised his empty glass and turned it impatiently. "If Vespasian is here, it's for his own purposes. Not for Rome's or yours."

"I've never met the general. His son is a friend."

"He's a better soldier than his father. Though not so cunning."

"Cunning enough to know that only you stand in his father's way to the crown of Rome."

"By subduing Jerusalem?"

"Before she is ready to be subdued."

"And who decides when a city is ready to surrender?"

"In this case I do."

"I've already handled you at Emmaus."

"Like you I fought with my retainers and the rabble. My Syrians."

"And with whom do you propose to defend Jerusalem?"

"Titus Flavius and the XVth Legion."

Cestius nodded. "I believe he would. It's a brave man who can fight against his own people."

Joseph remembered Titus' words about killing Romans. "Exactly why I ask for twenty-four hours. Tomorrow at the Great Altar of God, Titus and I shall deliver Jerusalem to you with timbrals and song.

A boy entered with a flagon on a tray. Cestius Gallus poured wine in his glass and was about to drink when he noticed another glass. "Ah, you can join me now," he said pouring wine for them both.

"It's too early for me," apologized Joseph. The general added a little more to his glass before setting down the flagon. He then stepped out of the hut and looked down upon the city. The sun winced upon the brass horns on the four corners of the Great Altar that rose in the center of the Temple compound. "There's a sacrifice tomorrow," said Cestius Gallus, his back to Joseph. "I believe you're a priest. Signal me from that altar by waving your sword as you did for bar Gioras."

"I have never performed the sacrifice."

"It's about time you did."

"Swords are forbidden in the House of the Living God."

"Whatever you use to read the entrails."

"The slaughtering implement. For an unblemished calf and seven yearlings."

"What a waste of omen."

"If Titus arrives you won't attack?'

"You wave that implement if he does. Then I'll make up my own mind."

"It's a wise man who chooses a side before that side itself is chosen," said Joseph. "The chosen then owe him a debt of gratitude. A soldier who has served Rome as long as you have should be rewarded."

"By whom? With what?"

"There are many sinecures that a man of your stature and patience deserve."

"Legate of Britain? My back can't take the dampness. Gaul? I drink too much wine already."

"I come to offer you one further possiblity."

The Legate shook his head slowly. "Possibility at my age comes only from my inferiors."

"There are those who feel you've been unjustly imposed upon."

"Only those waiting with their own impositions," said Cestius walking back into the hut.

"Proconsul of Rome," Joseph offered casually. "The first in line of rule after the emperor."

Cestius shook his head. "That's not Vespasian's way." The Legate raised the dressing robe and touched it to his nose, then let it fall to the floor. "I've been a soldier for forty-two years and with few successes. The mopping-up general is my title among my peers. When they appointed me the Governor of Greater Syria, I knew no one else wanted the position. By then I had already seen the limits of my ambition and I began to tire of the one authority through whom ambition succeeds. My own. Then I met a lady, a young lady, in Rome, after the great fire, and I let my vanity rule for one last time. I rose to her like a young buck who knows only the roe and the hunter's arrow. I flattered myself into thinking that I could change her nature, make her see the logic of my life; show her the austere beauty of the field soldier's existence."

"She's bewitched you too," said Joseph, shocked at his own realization that it was Lucia Paulina about whom the Governor was talking.

"Only young men can be bewitched by women. At my age I'm able only to have the privilege of caring for her. Watching her —" he waved his hand at the dressing table, "scenting herself. Her little intimacies. Putting on her armor. That's enough to make me forget the aches of old battles and vanities."

This was no flaccid man, as Titus had described him. In a few phrases, Cestius Gallus had shown Joseph the limits of time.

"Lucia," he continued, "is one of that strange breed of women created to rule. Because of her birth, however, she lacks the credentials."

"Epaphroditus was one of the most powerful men in Rome," Joseph objected.

"Her adopted father. Lucia is an enigma. Ambiguous even in her passions: That's what's fascinating about her."

"Aren't all women?"

The legate shook his head. "Only among Roman nobility. Other women do not calculate their emotions. They're truly passionate."

"And you prefer Lucia?"

"Most weak men do. We're afraid of passion."

Outside trumpets blared once again. The hut shook from the clap of hoofs of the passing cavalry. Cestius Gallus again walked out holding his wine glass up to the sun that had momentarily reappeared. "That officer who was just here brought me a message. Simon bar Gioras has routed Titus and Tiberius Alexander at Gaza. By tomorrow your so-called bandit will enter Jerusalem."

"I'll stop him."

"He's a Jew," said Cestius, pouring the wine to the earth then smashing the glass against a stone.

Joseph thought of what Titus had said about killing Jews. "You're a Roman. Titus was ready to kill you."

The commander of the XIIth Legion strapped on his armor. "The rewards of a soldier come in the instant of clarity he's given. Mostly in defeat."

"Then if what you said about Lucia is true —"

"Her decision, I think, will depend on what happens out there."

"Whoever wins?"

"Or loses. With her one never knows.'

Joseph had not dared to mention that according to Roman law

Lucia Paulina was his wife.

After Cestius Gallus left the hut, Joseph lay on the sofa. He reached for the flagon and sipped some wine as he watched cloud pile upon cloud, churning the sun. He saw a boy standing knee deep in the snows of Mount Hermon. He was holding an arrow fixed to a bow. A vague father restrained his hand as a roe gracefully leaped across the horizon. Blood dripped in the snow. Joseph closed his eyes and felt the wine burn in his stomach. He was sure that only a miracle could save Jerusalem.

CHAPTER V — FATHERS AND SONS

The night was beginning to fade when Joseph slipped into the city. Pilgrims were already swarming toward the Temple compound, their faces startled by the blasting furnaces of the smith shops where, despite the holiday, men worked at forging arms. The pilgrims themselves bore an assortment of weapons signalling that the ban of these on the Temple Mount had been rescinded. A boy, pulling his grandfather with one hand, his other grasping the leg of a chair, hurried by. The old man had a donkey's jawbone tucked in his waist. Joseph crossed the Tyropoeon Valley and headed for his palace.

His father hurried into Joseph's chamber. *"Barukh boakha!"* Blessed be thy coming!'' he declared and fell to his knees.

"Barukh hanimtza," Joseph returned the greeting, embarrassed at seeing the old man humble himself. When he tried to help him up, Matthias waved him aside, getting to his feet with difficulty. Joseph embraced him, tasting the familiar cardamon odor on his father's lips. He had not seen him in over a year.

"We've missed you. Our estates are in chaos since you left for Rome." Matthias shook his head. "Truly a bad year. You must go out as soon as the holiday ends and reorganize things. The stewards report poor crops. The olives are blighted and the lack of rains last spring is taking its effect on the vineyards. Added to all our troubles is the mass movement of the peasants either to the city or into the desert, lured in both instances by false prophets of disaster."

Joseph's father spoke as if there were still choices. As with all old people, the worry of rising to life each day had distracted Matthias from the imminent doom of the Holy City. Nevertheless Joseph was overwhelmed by the flow of words. Having lived alone in recent years and more or less retired from public life, Matthias hungered for listening ears.

"You're thinking of the Christians," said Joseph.

"Apostates. Who would have thought that that mad Pharisee and his followers would grow at the expense of our woes?"

"Merely transitional. As any faith derived from despair. Once we resolve our conflict with Rome, they shall disappear like all such sects."

The old man nodded without really listening. As he aged he had lost patience with the voices of others. His sense of tolerance that had made him the most respected priest in Judea and to whom all the different factions looked up to had soured toward those who disagreed with him. Once he had been the conciliator of disputations, spiritual and temporal, known for his uncompromising honesty because he refused, as had become customary, to purchase the necessary votes in order to be elected High Priest. But his own retreat from power had not made him relinquish the hope that his eldest born would someday come to that true eminance and stand alone before the Lord in the *Mikdash* — His Holy Place.

To insure Joseph's success, he had groomed him carefully, making him avoid choices that would pit him against those who could hinder his becoming their family's first High Priest. He used to say to him: "Understand. Never choose." and he had meant it even in the conflict between Rome and Jerusalem.

Thus he had raised Joseph in the way of the *Kohanim* priests, though never failing to point out to him the rigidities of ritual. His basic education had been placed in the hands of Johanan ben Zakkai, President of the *Sanhedrin*. Yet he always admonished Joseph to be wary of the traps of pure Pharisaic logic and how they might instead of strengthening God's purposes circumvent them. He had even insisted that Joseph spend time among the Essenes and learn from the wise man, Bannus, how the capriciousness of man could be subdued only by the study of trees in a storm and the immutable seasons of the desert. "The wilderness is a place for contemplating God outside the vanity of man," Matthias had told his son before sending him to the oasis of Ein Gedi. "A place where reason is qualified by the riddle of the stones."

When Joseph had returned from Ein Gedi, his father had encouraged his new interest in Greek and Latin civilization. He had even consented to let him go among the pagans and attend the Roman military academy in Antioch. For, to Matthias, the many faces of man were as much a part of the laws of nature as was a sense of justice and the love of God. Joseph had once cursed his father for teaching him equivocation.

"From all over the land," said Matthias, holding tightly to Joseph's hand as he led him under an arbor, "men come to me seeking advice in these angry times. My counsel is old and can no longer resolve the swift events of the present. The time has come for you, my *behor,* my eldest born, to take up the family sceptre."

"Then you'll consent to my officiating at the last *Sukkot* sacrifice this morning?"

Matthias had not expected so quick a response to his hopes. "That can wait, There will be many ceremonies for you to perform in your life."

"It's imperative that I perform this very morning."

The old man, who a moment ago spoke so urgently of giving up his responsibilities, suddenly became reluctant to part with the little power he still held. "As you can see, I am already dressed and anointed. Any change in the ceremony will cause more tension. The Romans are at the gates."

Joseph persisted. "We can change garb in a moment. You yourself can anoint me. Jerusalem's fate may rest in your decision."

Matthias straightened his miter in a gesture Joseph recognized as one his father made when his mind was set. "The disruption of the order of service is more dangerous than any outside threat. In moments of crises, let worship sustain the children of God. As always, in His Temple in Jerusalem."

"There was a time when we had no Temple at all," said a young man in a white robe who entered the garden. "For seventy years we survived without the *Mikdash* and even longer before."

"I am speaking to your brother. Your elder brother. Please leave till we are done." Turning back to Joseph, Matthias addressed him as if in answer to his younger son's challenge. "Land and pride must be tempered by the way one contends with God. This is what must be taught over and over to the children of Israel. Once, two thirds of our people abandoned the place which He commanded. They set rival altars to Jerusalem in Bethel and Dan, molding golden calves and anointing unsanctified kings. Where are those ten tribes today? Only Judah survives because we priests, our ancestors, preserved an order of life which was the equivalent of the order of God."

"I must speak with Joseph," said Mati, interrupting his father. "It's urgent."

"The seventy years of then," persisted the old man, "could well be seven hundred in our own age. If ever the Temple is destroyed again, by the time it could be rebuilt the whole concept of such worship might be an anachronism."

"Joseph," continued Matthias. "We are priests, chosen by God. No family had ever been so sanctified. It is why the sons of Aaron have always held the destiny of our people. The Maccabees, *Kohanim* of the fifth order, rescued the nation from alien hands. Only when their progeny turned dedication to God into a thirst for power and went the way of all conquerors did they push the nation on to the threshhold of disaster where we now find ourselves. They forgot that they were the golden link between the kingdom of earth and the kingdom of heaven. Through us as their paragon, the nation of Israel prevails. Beware then of those — Jew or gentile — who might try to cajole you out of your inheritance."

The jeweled miter of Matthias glistened, and the palm trees beyond the garden swayed in the breeze. Joseph was so tired he almost wished that his father would remain adamant and refuse his request. Lucia, he thought, would just be going to bed with Cestius Gallus.

"Joseph. I must speak with you. Alone," said Mati.

"*Aba*" said Joseph softly. "Let me have a word with my brother. He seems upset."

"He thrives off upset. He and his Sicari traitors," the old man fumed.

"Have we gone so far as to consider a Jew a traitor because he wishes to preserve his existence?" asked Mati.

"Existence is not so simple as your cutthroat friends make it out to be. To exist today, no matter how distasteful for Jews, means reconciliation with Rome," said the old man, his voice trembling in such a way that for a moment Joseph thought he was listening to himself.

"My pledge is only to God. He is the sole emperor," declared Mati. "You taught us that."

"Nonsense, Mati," said Joseph embracing his brother and rubbing his short red beard. "By the way thanks for your intercession in winning my quick release from jail upon my arrival from Rome."

"I had nothing to do with your arrest or release."

Joseph dropped his arms to his side. "You knew I was arrested."

"For trafficking with the enemy."

"You've grown taller than I in height but not in intelligence. Know you that all actions are controlled by the positions in which we find ourselves. That is God's will. Now if you'll let me finish I'll be with you in a moment."

"Bar Giora has just taken over the defense of the city. He wants every available man on the ramparts, including those under your command. He doesn't want any sacrifice ceremony this morning."

Matthias reeled back and fell into a chair, his miter rolling between his legs. "Never," he said hoarsely, a dazed look in his eyes. "Never but when the Temple was gutted by Nebuchadnezzer has the *tamid* sacrifice been cancelled since the exodus from Egypt."

"*Al kiddush Hashem.* In the name of the Lord," said Mati. "Once we defeat the Roman, we shall celebrate with a hundred *tamid* lambs."

"I must go," sighed Matthias.

"I'll go instead," said Joseph, picking up the miter.

"The *ephod* lies inside, in the study. So does the oil and the slaughtering implement," said the old man, unable to rise.

Mati followed after Joseph. "They'll kill you as soon as you step up on the altar. Bar Giora knows you've had contact with Cestius Gallus."

Joseph slipped on the *ephod* and then grabbed the leather case that held the slaughtering implement. "The performance of the *Sukkot* sacrifice can do more to stabilize our situation, to calm the people, than anything in bar Giora's power. "Cestius Gallus has promised me," lied Joseph, "not to attack the city."

"He's already begun the bombardment of the Antonia. That leads directly into the inner Temple courts. By the time you get to the altar, we will have attacked the Roman from their rear. Up the Tyropoeon Valley."

"He's set on destroying us all, your bar Giora," said Joseph, pushing his brother aside as he rushed out.

In his head he recorded:

the passion of the jews for freedom prepares them for anihilation.

CHAPTER VI — HEAVEN'S BOW

i

The *Sukkot* festival was the most joyous of the three pilgrimages up to Jerusalem. The week celebration always began with a procession to gather myrtle twigs at the village of Motza, just west of the city. These and some willows would be inserted into small pouches on the sides of the *lulav*, a palm branch, which together with the *etrog*, a golden citron, made up the symbols of the holiday. Two supplementary ceremonies took place during the *Hag*. One was held on the evening of the first day and called the Joy of The Water Drawing when men and women danced out to the Brook of Shiloah and gathered water for use in the Temple. The other was performed on the last day, when the Levites sang special hymns so that the coming rainy season would be plentiful and make the fall harvest abundant. Usually the *yoreh* rains fell within a few weeks of *Sukkot*. When the rains came and in what quantity would decide who would eat and who would starve, who would live and who would die more than all the breast-beating and penance done on *Yom Kippur* which preceded *Sukkot* by a few days.

Joseph hurried across the Xystus Square, his tinselled *ephod* and the tiny silver bells along the wide sleeves of his tunic clinking as he entered the Temple compound. Coming through the Inner Court, he noticed how meager were the piles of skins left by the pilgrims from the animals they had sacrificed during the week long holiday. These were customarily left to the citizens of the city for their hospitality, since The Law forbade any direct payment. He entered the Court of the Priests and in the readying room washed his hands and feet in the copper basin before walking out toward the Great Altar. He wondered too who had arranged his release from the Sicaris.

Joseph was always shocked at the splendor of the Temple. The harsh white buildings softened by the gold domes, which made the limestone glitter like marble, stood in contrast to the pastel blue colonnades that together were blinding even under a cloudy sky. Long ago the rabbis had declared: *He who has not seen Herod's Temple, has never seen a beautiful temple in his days.*

Like fire embedded in a block of ice, the Great Altar rose thirty feet high with its unhewed, whitewashed stones that according to law had never been touched by iron. Thousands of men in long striped holiday kaftans circled the Altar. So great was the press of worshippers that they overflowed through the great Corinthian bronze Nicanor Gate and down its fifteen marble steps into the Women's Court where both sexes were permitted. The women were dressed in white and their heads garlanded with fall flowers. On this last day of the *Hag*, people were momentarily more preoccupied with the *geshem* rain prayers which followed immediately after the sacrifice than with the rumored attack by the Romans. Eyes looked up at the skies in hope that the Lord in his munificence would not only stave off the enemy but would make the miracle of the rain come true. For every Jew knew that in times of war, more than arms, water was Jerusalem's weapon of survival. On rare occasions, just as the Levites raised their voices in psalm, the heavens would darken and rumble as lightning streaked across the horizon, followed by a rain that fell upon the joyous multitude like arrows, which was exactly what *yoreh*, the name of the first rains described.

Over to his left, Joseph glanced at the vast stone stage upon which stood the glowing facaded *Mikdash* through whose open portals a cloud of frankincense filtered. He made out the Table of Shewbread and the seven branched candelabrum that stood in the *Dvir,* the holiest of holy places in the Temple compound. In a distance he heard the booming of the catapults and the crashing of stones. Smoke still rose from the Bezetha Quarter where the Syrian auxiliaries continued their looting. Almost in front of him loomed the Antonia Fortress, built by Herod in honor of Mark Antony. He wondered whether Metilius and the Roman garrison were still in the fortress. On top of the altar, two acolytes were washing blood and ashes from yesterday's sacrifice down the ducts that drained under the city, and he felt heartened by the stubbornness of his ancient *Kohanite* order. His father was right. The day the Temple rites ceased, Judaism would die. Just to be certain, he felt for his sword which he had hidden beneath his priestly robes.

Joseph was startled by the sounding of trumpets. A priest handed him a *lulav* and *etrog* which he held in one hand. Slowly he led a procession of priests up the altar ramp that was lined with Levites in blue silks, while the multitude broke into hymn. Above the voices, Joseph heard a strange chant.

> Woe to the House of Boethus;
> Woe to their cursing.
> Woe to the serpent hissing.

The House of Boethus was an old priestly family who had recently been accused of pilfering the Temple Treasury in order to purchase the high priesthood for a member of its clan. They were of the first order of priests and cousins of Joseph on his father's side. The priests urged Joseph forward and he moved up the ramp. Again he heard the chant.

Woe to the House of Boethus.

His brother's warning came back to him. These were bar Giora's supporters mixed among the worshippers reminding him of his own defections. When he reached the top of the altar, the Levites raised their lyres and broke into song.

Atta horeta la-daat —
Unto Thee it was shewed
that the Lord is God.

Joseph waved the *lulav* high in the air, then brought it down, beating the palm branch against the altar which the people below began to circle seven times, then moved on through the Nicanor Gate where they were greeted by a procession of maidens shaking tambourines. The voices of the multitude repeated seven times.

Ana Adonai hoshiya na —
We beseech Thee, O Lord, save our souls!

the priest and Levites responded each time:

Praise be the Lord for He is good!

My people appear civilized, thought Joseph, only when their minds are numbed in repetitious praise of the Lord. He understood why their ancient leaders, Moses and David had led them in battle chanting hymns to the Lord of Hosts. Remembering the ordered squadrons of the XIIth Legion forming north of the city, he saw how similar were the rites of God to those of war.

I call upon the Lord in my distress;
The Lord answered me and set me in
large places,

Joseph intoned. And again the people chanted:

Ana Adonai hatzliha na —
We beseech Thee, O Lord, send us
prosperity!

A half dozen priests now hurried up the ramp and set a bullock, one ram and seven lambs of the first year and without blemish into the wood locks of the altar. Joseph withdrew the slaughtering implement from its case. Again he heard that other chorus.

> Woe to the House of Boethus;
> Woe to the serpent hissing.

He stepped forward and raised his *lulav* and *etrog* with its crown-like stem held up, and shook them to the four winds. To the west, Jerusalem looked like a cracked dome crowned by silver mountains of boulders. The crack was the Tyropoeon Valley where cheesemakers dwelt and where at any moment the forces under bar Giora and those under Cestius Gallus would clash for control over the Temple of God. He looked out upon the arched bridge he had crossed earlier to enter the Temple compound and saw the Serpent Pool, one of two water sources for this riverless city which through the long summer lived off subterranean wells and stored rain water for which he was now praying.

To the north he saw the Tower of Psephinus, one hundred and fifteen feet high, from which the guardians of the city could see as far as Caesarea on the Mediterranean coast, and where he had stood with Silas only yesterday before going to plead with the Governor of Syria. He followed the wind swept olive trees, to the east, bordering on the great cemetery that sloped down into the Valley of Kedron where for a millenium Jerusalem buried its dead. Southward he saw the hovels of the Ophel Quarter home of the poor and discontented masses who had fled the Roman repression in the Galilee. Nine hundred years earlier a young king of Judah had conquered these hills from the Jebusites and named them for himself, the City of David. In a distance he recognized the blue and gold banners of Titus' XVth Legion. Sixty miles beyond stretched the Dead Sea like a second sky and walled in by the shadows of Masada. As he raised the slaughtering implement in signal, he swirled about. Joseph thought he was falling.

ii

The first time he had seen the desert fortress was when he was fourteen years old, after the terrible Passover riots provoked by the Procurator Cummanus. Twenty thousand Jews had been slaughtered during that pilgrimage, and many of the noble families had begun an exodus from Jerusalem that was to continue unabated till the present time. Matthias had refused to leave, but thought it prudent to guard his eldest son from the snares of the fanatic Sicaris who were already winning over young aristocrats and others to their cause of rebellion. He had sent Joseph into the Judean Wilderness to the wise man, Bannus, where he would be safe and could continue his studies.

By the time Joseph had arrived at Ein Gedi, the last rains had fallen and the small Essene commune was overgrown like a jungle, its waterfalls gushing so loudly he had to shout to be heard. Bannus told him that within a month the waters of the stream they lived along would dry to a trickle and the falls would drip in silence. He warned Joseph not to roam too far from the oasis without water and to be wary of the desert sun.

On his second day among the Essenes, an olive skinned lad whose black hair hung in two ringlets, one over each ear, accosted him. Eleazar ben Yair was a year younger than Joseph and he immediately challenged him to climb to the top of the Fortress of Masada.

They had followed the coast of the Dead Sea for twelve miles, moving southward across stones and pebbles the color of tar. By noon Eleazar, who had hardly spoken to Joseph, was out of sight. Joseph kept twisting his ankles on the uneven stones and after an hour had to stop to take off his boots and cool his toes in the sea. The water was near boiling. Half dazed he watched two lizards fornicate. His nostrils burned from the smell of salt and his tongue tasted of ashes.

After a while Eleazar reappeared. "It's worth it if you can make it," he said, taunting him with encouragement.

"I'm thirsty," said Joseph, his lips blistering and gray.

Eleazar picked up a few pebbles and handed them to him. "Suck on these. "They'll keep your spit wet."

"You didn't tell me it would be so hot. And my feet. Look at my ankles."

"It gets smoother near the mountain."

"What's so great about up there that we have to go?"

Eleazar shrugged. "It's there."

"It'll always be there."

"No it won't," said Eleazar and he moved on.

For a while Joseph watched him, using his lean form to gauge the distance between himself and the fortress that wavered in the heat. A mist had risen over the Lashon, the peninsula that protruded like a tongue from the opposite shore from where Moses once saw the land inherited by these boys. A cloud of dust was blowing toward Joseph and he became frightened. He hobbled after Eleazar.

It was late in the afternoon when he caught up with Eleazar who was standing by a rock, his white prayer shawl over his head.

"How far yet?" asked Joseph.

Eleazar didn't answer. Only his lips moved. Finally he bowed and stepped two paces back. He had been praying.

"What are those black clouds gathering across the sea?" Joseph asked.

Eleazar tucked his prayer shawl into the rope around his hips and continued on toward the mouth of the wadi that led inland between two sheer mountains.

"I thought we follow the sea all the way?" said Joseph.

The sky darkened. To the west lay an endless chain of black domed hills. The sun flattened and turned the color of sand.

"I'm going back," shouted Joseph, who had again fallen behind. Two brown goats scampered up the mountainside. Above the wadi, on the crags, a brood of vultures sat humped and patient. Joseph hurried on.

The wind became stronger carrying with it dust and tumbleweed which bounced along the wadi bed chasing after them. Earth and some stones loosened from the sides of the mountains. The sky pressed upon their heads distorting the boulders into a herd of beasts. A shriek tore through the wadi echoing into a clap of thunder.

Both boys turned and saw a marble wall crashing down upon them. Eleazar clawed his way up the mountainside, climbing and slipping at the same time. Joseph froze as he saw the wall turn into a tidal wave devouring the whole wadi. By the time he began to run, his legs were no longer on the ground. He felt himself being lifted, soaring higher and higher, certain now that he would scale the mountain. He thought if only he could learn to breathe again, he would be safe.

He was sure his chest had collapsed when he discovered that he was pressed against a wall of a cavern. The water had followed him inside, gushing white as it quickly reached his waist. With a last effort, he grabbed on to a ledge and pulled himself up. The roaring waters plugged his ears so that he could feel his heart beat in his temples. He knew that he was breathing.

He lay panting on the ledge as he stared up at Eleazar who was cautiously breaking off a piece of quartz from the cavern wall. A streak of light fell upon a jackal sheltering two bald pups. The jackal crouched back snarling, showing uneven fangs. Just as Eleazar raised his hand, the beast leaped, missing Eleazar and landing in Joseph's arms. Blood and saliva trickled through his fingers as Joseph tried to pry loose the jaws tightening on his forearm. Eleazar fell upon Joseph and the jackal and slit its throat with the sharp edge of the quartz. The jackal shuddered and rolled over dead. It smelled like the sheep in the Temple slaughterhouse.

Eleazar tossed the corpse into the water that had by now reached the ledge. He picked up a quivering pup in each hand and smashed their heads against the wall. Then he raised himself to a higher shelf, wiggling through an opening at the top through which the light had fallen on the jackal.

"What happened?' asked Joseph, panting as he now lay on his back above the cavern.

"The rains are falling late this year," was all Eleazar said. They both lay in silence watching the stars explode above the Fortress of Masada.

The sun burned into Joseph's arm waking him. He saw where the jackal's teeth had pierced his skin. Blood and hair were encrusted in the wound and he could hardly move his fingers. Eleazar had vanished. The only hint of the tidal wave was a stream trickling in the wadi. He peered into the opening and saw that the cavern was still full. Reaching down he washed his wound with cool water, then splashed some on his face and nape. When he looked up, he saw a steep path that snaked up to the fortress. The vultures still brooded.

The legionnaire on duty at the gatehouse immediately noticed Joseph's arm. "I suppose you don't want an unclean Roman to touch you too," he said swinging forward on the rope stool that had been leaning against the wall.

Joseph looked at his arm without answering.

"Your friend," said the legionnaire in the strange accent Romans had when they spoke the language of the Jews, "he's got some bad cuts. But he wouldn't let me touch him. Pretty crazy for you kids to come up here at this season. Think you'd know about those flash floods."

"Flash floods?" said Joseph, letting the soldier take his arm.

"You aren't from around here, are you?"

"Jerusalem. Just visiting."

"Well, it's a bit late for rain, but it can happen. They start around your way, in the hills of Judea, even further north. It can rain up there around sunset and a half hour later we have flash floods down here in the wadis. Especially in that dried riverbed below where you were. Your friend should know better. I've seen him up here many times. Besides, he took you up the hard way. West Gate is the real way in."

"We must have been washed half way up here."

"Just about," said the soldier, spreading some yellow balm on Joseph's arm. "We watched you till you disappeared into one of the reservoirs. You're lucky to be alive."

"Reservoirs?"

"Those big cisterns carved into the side of the mountain. You can't see them from this side. When the water rises from the canyon, it floods them. It's what keeps Masada alive during the dry summer."

"What legion are you with?"

The Roman smiled at Joseph's imperious tone. "Tenth. On detached service to this elevated hell."

"Must be dull for a line legionnaire."

The soldier shrugged. "The place gets into your blood. The last outpost of the Empire," he said with pride as he held Joseph's hand very gently and sprinkled some powder over the balm. "That should do it. May be a good idea to rinse it in the sea on your way back."

"What about the madness?"

"I wouldn't worry about that. The jackals here are pretty clean. There's little here to contaminate them."

"A whole cave full," said Joseph, suddenly feeling the need to tell what had happened. "Eleazar and I fought them off for an hour. They almost killed him."

The soldier looked at Joseph skeptically. "Strange. Usually there's only one family to a cave."

"At least ten of them," persisted Joseph. "And big. Big as bears."

The legionnaire leaned back on his stool, letting his back rest against the gate wall, his feet perched on a scalloped ballista stone.

"Where did my friend go?" asked Joseph.

"Probably to the market. Tuesday's market day. The Nabateans come up from Petra and Avdat to cheat us," chuckled the soldier. "And spy."

Joseph thanked him and then walked inside the fort. A high, white, stone wall with many even taller towers ran around the flat top of the mountain ending at a small pastel colored palace on the north end. On the walls a dozen sentries paced like sleepwalkers. Last night's storm had left a large puddle in the middle of the fort where women now knelt filling jugs with rain water. A few chickens pecked at the wild tufts of grass that grew in scattered patches. Daisies poked out of the wall crevices.

An old woman crumbled wheat between her palms into a black kettle from which the acrid odor of goat's milk rose. "You've come with Eleazar," she said. "And what have you brought for *savtah*?"

Joseph was puzzled. "What did Eleazar bring?"

"This piece of quartz," said the old lady, holding up the stone with which Eleazar had killed the jackal.

Two children, their bare feet gray with dust, squatted nearby as they carefully laid out strands of straw in an oval shape. They smoothed down the inner surface with their palms before taking two clay jars and dumping six black insects into the oval.

"You have scorpions this high?" Joseph asked, watching them hone their stingers on their backs.

The woman waited until two legionnaires passed. "The Wilderness is filled with strangeness. Yesterday a python was found sleeping in an eagle's nest above the reservoir."

The milk odor made Joseph weak. "I have a copper. Give me some milk."

The woman laughed, her flat breasts shaking beneath her white robe. "What use have I with a copper?"

"What use do you have for a piece of quartz?"

The woman laughed again. "For a mirror."

"Since when do Essene women allow themselves the vanity of a mirror?"

The old woman frowned. "To catch the heat of the sun, you fool. For fire."

The woman stirred her wheat and milk with a stick. "What's that on your finger?" she asked.

Joseph raised his wounded hand with difficulty, and when the woman saw what he wore, she bowed and kissed his priest's ring. She then gave him a cup of milk and wheat and a *davla* fig cake. She told him Eleazar was in the synagogue.

As he turned to leave, he saw the boys light a twig from the old woman's fire, then ignite the straws that surrounded the scorpions. Joseph was fascinated by how each boy prodded a scorpion with a twig. As the straws smoked, the scorpions scurried. They crawled first to one side of the oval and then to the other, their stingers desperately searching for something to strike. Finally the largest one hopped into the air, then rushed frantically around the lighted straws before poking its stinger between its crusted back and head, stinging itself dead.

"The one whose vermin lasts longest wins," said the old woman laughing again.

One of the boys looked up, his dark eyes glinting at Joseph. "Sometimes we do the opposite. The one who stays alive, he loses."

Joseph followed the west wall passing the Roman barracks and the main gate to Masada until he came to a synagogue that rose in the wall. It was faded ochre and was unfinished. He crouched through a small opening and found himself in a blue room. He stepped into a footbath, then out into an open auditorium with stone tiers on either side. In the center were six marble posts about waist high, each with a large urn beside it. Two fat scrolls on wooden rollers leaned in a niche against the north wall. The sun baked the tile floor and burned his bare feet.

Eleazar stood by a post near the wall. Once again he was praying. Through an embrasure Joseph saw a few clouds in the sky splattering the hills with mauve shadows. Almost below them was Ein Gedi and not much further beyond lay Jerusalem. Above its walls, protruding like a jewel in a crown, stood the Temple of God.

A shadow drifted over the fortress toward the roofless synagogue, making Joseph shiver in the momentary shade. It was a cloud shaped like a gigantic bird floating overhead. Suddenly the wind changed. For an instant the cloud hung in midair before it flexed its yellow claws. "The eagle," gasped Joseph, falling on top of Eleazar.

iii

The arrow that had struck Joseph up on the altar pierced his arm where years before the jackal bite had scarred it, and he was knocked down into the arms of his brother who cushioned his fall. "You're lucky," said Mati. "If the Roman hadn't gotten you the Sicaris would have. They are more accurate."

But Joseph was not listening. He saw that the altar and the surrounding portals were ablaze. "Fire," he shouted, as the explosion of catapulting stones burst around him. "He's attacking. Cestius Gallus is attacking Jerusalem."

"Began just as you were hit."

Up on the altar the priests in their falsetto voices sang:

> Surround us, O Lord,
> with pure and holy radiance of Thy glory
> that is spread over our heads as an eagle
> over the nest stirreth up:
> and bid the stream of life
> flow upon Thy servant.

And the Levites:

> Thou who causes the wind to blow
> and the rain to fall.

And the maidens:

> With joy shall we draw water
> out of the well of salvation.

Joseph scented the earth. He heard the clap of thunder. Two fat drops of rain splashed in his blood.

CHAPTER VII — THE BLOOD OF A LAMB

The wound was superficial and by the next day Joseph was out on the ramparts, watching the Romans retreat to the coast. The miracle of the first rain continued.

"The people," said Niger standing beside Joseph, "think the rain is a a sign that God has not abandoned Jerusalem. They've surrounded the Antonia and demanded that Metilius and his men surrender."

The Centurion Metilius had been in the same class as Joseph at the academy in Antioch. Being Roman and of a wealthy family, he did not have to work so hard as the Jewish cadets did. His lack of leadership ability had destined him to garrison duties such as the one he held now at the Antonia. Little did he ever imagine that his own legion would abandon him to the Jews.

"Not a very smart idea," said Joseph to Niger. "Metilius will be useful when we negotiate with the Governor of Syria." They descended the stone steps that led to the gate of the fortress where a group of armed citizens milled around the already occupied Antonia courtyard. Metilius stood among them beside Joseph's brother.

"How's the arm?" asked Mati.

"Stiff," said Joseph. "Are these your men?"

"I'm negotiating the garrison's surrender," answered Mati, scraping mud off his sandal with the edge of his sword. "The centurion has accepted our terms."

"Honorable ones," interposed Metilius, his eyes avoiding Joseph's.

"Honor for a Roman officer," said Joseph, "is never to surrender."

"No choice. They've threatened to set the Antonia aflame."

"Threats are just what soldiers are created to prevent."

"Our supplies are down to a day's ration. Now that the governor has failed to relieve us, we've got to accept terms. Fair terms," said Metilius nodding to Mati. "Very fair."

"And under whose authority do you act as negotiator?" Joseph asked his brother.

"Mine," said Simon bar Giora stepping out of the east tower. His mustache arched like the scimitar that hung from his waist.

"What authority do you have?"

"Commander of Judea South. As of now."

"And who might I ask is commander of Judea North?"

"You, if you fight for it."

Joseph looked disdainfully at the dust covered, dirty robed chieftain. "Unless you act as you did at Emmaus, for which you're still accountable, there's no further need to quarrel with Rome."

"I mean John ben Levi of Gishhalav in the Galilee. He's just raided Zippori and that, he thinks, gives him claim to your command."

"Both your actions can only exacerbate the situation. The rains have made Cestius Gallus vulnerable. Free this garrison and we can begin serious negotiations with the next ruling party in Rome."

"Too late," said Mati. "Victory is a great unifier. The whole country is up in arms."

"We've already surrendered," said Metilius. "We have General bar Giora's word that we'll be allowed to march out in regular formation unharmed."

"With your arms, I presume?"

His answer came when he saw Metilius' men being led out from the tower. They stacked their arms, then lined up in the center of the courtyard. Even in surrender they moved in perfect order.

Through the corner of his eye, Joseph caught bar Giora's men drawing their swords. "Get Silas," Joseph ordered Niger. "Get him immediately." He then drew his own sword and stepped out in front of the Romans. "You men, follow me!"

The Romans looked at their commander who in turn looked at Simon bar Giora. Simon withdrew his scimitar and grabbing the legionnaire nearest him, hacked off his head. In an instant the other Jews set upon the unarmed soldiers and began to murder them.

Joseph lunged at the man at his right. It was his brother. Luckily a pain shot through his wounded arm and he staggered against the wall, his sword still held aloft. He saw Silas and a contingent of his Royals hurry into the courtyard, but when they saw bar Giora, they halted.

"Charge!" roared Joseph, as he tottered out to place himself between the unarmed Romans and the Jews. The Royals did not move. Joseph let his sword drop, the blade clanging against the stone court. Transfixed, he watched how the legionnaires died without a struggle and in silence.

When the slaughter was over, Joseph, still dazed, turned to his brother. "And him?" he cried hoarsely, raising his sword so as to bring it down on Metilius, who had stood without protesting the massacre of his men.

Bar Giora whacked Joseph's blade so hard that the sword flew from his hand. "Don't you worry," he said. "We've got something better waiting for him." Then he and Mati marched Metilius off between the corpses. Silas and the Royals followed behind.

When Joseph reentered the Temple compound an hour later, he saw thousands of men and women massed near the altar in the Court of the Israelites where a stage had been temporarily erected just below the Nicanor Gate. On the stage in a makeshift throne, his arms and legs set in wood locks, sat Metilius with the same bewildered look as that of a beast ready for sacrifice.

Niger joined Joseph without saying a word. They watched as people joked and displayed a holiday spirit that belied the past few tense days. Near them, a man with one eye half sewn closed, the other a faded blue and without a pupil, kept jumping up in order to get a better view as though he could really see. An old hag, indifferent to the ceremony, pushed him away as she searched the ground. She picked up a crust of bread and bit into it with her toothless gums. A youth at her right grabbed it from her mouth and tossed it high into the air. She cursed him as she scurried off in search of the lost treat.

"It's really hard to believe this," said Joseph. "A public execution in the Temple. They must have all gone mad." After what he had just witnessed at the Antonia, he was not so shocked as he thought he should be.

"Circumcision," said Niger. "Metilius was given a choice between dying with his men or converting."

"A Jewish bread and circus," said Joseph, really shocked this time. "It's not a public rite. Certainly not one performed in the Temple."

Metilius sat in the stocks, his legs stretched out before him and his elbows locked behind him. For modesty's sake his bare thighs were half covered with a white cloth. His back sweated through his Roman tunic.

When Mati, dressed in a long, white, priest's robe, approached the stocks, the people broke into cheers.

"He's become a fanatic. Like all Sicaris," said Joseph to Niger.

"To be a Jew today is to be a fanatic," said Silas, who came and stood beside them.

Half facing Metilius and half facing the multitude, Mati raised a brimming silver goblet of wine in one hand and a small gleaming daggar of the Sicaris in the other.

> For this throne of Elijah —
> May he be remembered,

he declared. And the people responded:

> Blessed art Thou O Lord our God,
> King of the Universe, who has
> commanded us to make our sons
> enter the covenant of Abraham
> our father.

And the people roared: "Amen!" and broke into dance with timbrels and horns as young virgins sang hallelujahs while strewing flowers around the groaning Roman. Finally, the excitement of the ancient ceremony had reached Joseph. His feeling of a moment earlier had been washed away as he looked up and saw a cluster of grapes engraved in the center of the Nicanor Gate, the ancient insignia of Israel. And he felt his own blood leap in the glory of the covenant of the Living God.

Some of his retainers recognized Joseph and lifted him on their shoulders. Soon a procession formed behind them as they moved toward the stage. "*Tipah! Tipah!*" the people shouted. "Let Joseph ben Matthias be blessed with the *tipah!*"

Joseph heard the cheers thumping in the beat of his heart as he was raised to the stage. Half dazed, he waved back to the people, hearing only the bleating of new lambs being readied in the Place of Slaughtering behind the altar for the evening sacrifice. As Joseph knelt down and set his mouth to the new Jew's groin in the ancient rite of *Timpat Dahm,* he wondered what Lucia would have to do in order to be converted a Jewess.

"Long live Joseph!" roared the people. "Long live free Judea!"

Joseph grinned down at the multitude, his teeth still washed with blood.

CHAPTER VIII — DEFEAT AT SHAAR HAGAI

i

In his dream, he wrote:

my father wakes me and i follow his legs to the temple. the darkness chatters in my teeth as i watch the dawn separate the city from the sky. the city walls leap like lions, and inside the court of the priests, i smell dung soaked in blood. my father dresses me in a stiff, white robe that chafes my chin. my scalp itches as he anoints my curly hair with oil, then sets a miter, a small replica of his own, upon my head. my breath is weighted by the silver breastplate hanging from my neck. outside, the antonia fortress desecrates the dvir with its shadow. levites pray as they hurry across the courtyard. my father climbs the ramp of the great altar where the gold lampstand raises the sun. my father unsheaths a long knife, the blade is like the swell of the sea. he runs it across his morning tongue. the law, he says, declares that the slaughtering implement be without blemish so that the animal sacrificed dies instantly and without suffering. my father runs the blade along my tender tongue. i begin to cry
— don't be a coward.
— behold the fire and the wood, but where is the lamb for the offering?
— i said don't be a coward.
— aba, why do the widows weep behind the sunrise? why in the evening do they grasp at the gloaming? why do they weep for the burnt offering?

His eyes opened and he looked up at Hagla. Metilius' circumcision had become confused in his memory with his initiation into the rite of priesthood. In the journal of his dream, he had denied being repelled by the slaughtering implement, and that it was his brother Mati who had slit the throat of the Sabbath lamb whose bleating was muffled by his own screams as he watched the blood trickle, then flow down the drains below the altar and into the bowels of the city. He wondered if the Sicari dagger used on Metilius was also without blemish.

"It's the anointing oil," he said to Hagla, as he scratched his nape vigorously. "It always affects my skin."

"I'm leaving the city," she said. "For Sebastia."

"It's unsafe. The Syrians are killing Jews there."

"The Syrians are our neighbors. I can deal with them."

"Only when we're winning."

"According to your brother, we've just had such a victory."

"My brother," said Joseph scornfully. "He believes miracles go on forever."

"This does," she said tossing down a sealed parchment. "Till death do us part."

As soon as she left, Joseph climbed out of bed, and still naked, sat at his writing table. Hagla had left him a writ summoning him before the High Priest that afternoon. He had two choices to escape her action: to accept bar Giora's challenge and try to take command of the north, or to leave Jerusalem in search for Titus. He pushed away the writ and glanced at his journal. To his amazement the dream he had just had was all recorded on the top sheet of papyrus.

He added.

my first memory is sitting in the sand planted with sticks in a circle around me like a cage. the sun deflects the shadows into a wheel, turning perpetually. they make me sleepy. a stench softly swaddles my body. i cannot crawl free.

ii

It was still raining when Joseph made his way out of the city. The Outer Wall ran with water, in many places loosening the stones. Some of the embrasures had collapsed and the whole west parapet, the farthest advance the Romans had made, had toppled into the Valley of Gihon. The burnt out Temple porticoes tapered like decaying teeth. Only the *Mikdash* glistened, defying God's miracle.

Overnight, the mountains had become cluttered with flowers. The path he followed was sodden, and along its sides clusters of soft lipped cyclamens trembled in the breeze. Anemones overwhelmed the slopes and the air tinkled with the bells of goats and sheep that appeared from nowhere now that the earth had once again become bloated. Jerusalem had never seen such a deluge.

At the village of Motza, four miles outside of Jerusalem, he caught up with the Romans. Chariots were slogging through the mud, while the cavalry stood glued to the mire. The land was rutted and wherever Joseph passed, he saw the work battalions struggling to extricate the weight of war from the sucking earth. Command countermanded command and shouts roared into curses as a Roman legion and its baggage tried to discover an order for retreat.

He found Cestius Gallus seated alone outside his tent. When the general saw Joseph, he reached for the flagon at his side. There were no glasses.

"This is madness," said Joseph. "Let me guide you safely back to the coast."

The general drank from the flagon. "The Fulminata needs no guarantors. We've been checked by cloudbursts before."

"Not in the Judean Mountains. Here it can happen again in an hour. Stay out of the valleys even though they're easier to move in. Keep along the horizon."

Cestius looked up at the white sky, then at his legion struggling through the mud. Sergeants and centurions trudged back and forth trying to keep the ranks in order. The horses moved more slowly than the men. "My equipment's too heavy. We're moving out through Shaar Hagai past Bet Horon and then down the Valley of Ayalon. My scouts report the way is still passable."

"One more flash storm and that whole wadi will be gushing with water," Joseph warned.

"The other way we'll just slide down the slopes. All the terraces have been washed away. The Syrians say the omens predict sun at least till this evening."

"Unpredictable. I've been living in these mountains all my life and I could have sworn that this year the rains would not come at least for another month."

Cestius pulled off his boots and washed his feet in a basin of cold water. There was no sign of an orderly. "By the way, my compliments to your men. They fought better than I had expected."

"They had God on their side."

The general drank more wine, then picked at the calloused sole of his left foot.

"Lucia," Joseph asked, "is she with you?"

"Disappeared. She's done her work well."

"Then it wasn't the rain?"

The general wiped his feet with the edge of his robe, then slipped back into his boots. "Let's say that battles have many sides to them. Like women."

"Didn't you see my signal?"

Cestius Gallus did not look up. "All we saw was you hit by a stray arrow."

"I waved it. I swear I waved the slaughtering implement."

"That makes two you lost. You claimed the same at Emmaus."

"I saw the XVth coming up from Hebron. I saw the blue and gold of the Apollonaire Legion before the arrow hit me and I waved. I waved."

Cestius rose and strapped on his sword. "Doesn't really matter. Titus was ordered by his father to forget Jerusalem. Vespasian has taken over my command."

iii

From above Shaar Hagai, Joseph watched the long line of the XIIth Legion retreat through the water soaked pass. Tenticles of grapevines curled down as if to ensnare the troops below. As Cestius had predicted, the skies cleared and the sun hung in sparkling balls off the tree branches. It had taken the Romans nearly a week to approach the coastal plain. Along the ridges a few cavalry men half-heartedly guarded the flanks of their weary comrades. One horse slipped and rolled into the wadi, its legs kicking in the air while its white mane turned red. The rider, who had fallen off, tried to chase after his mount but became stuck in the mud and stood helplessly with his arms outstretched like a scarecrow. Another soldier came and checked each of the fallen horse's legs. Finding one broken, he stripped off the saddle bags before pointing a lance at one eye and plunging it through the beast's head. A stream of urine ran down between the legionnaire's legs. As if the killing of the horse were a signal, thousands of armorless men with short swords drawn appeared on the ridges on both sides of the wadi and charged down whooping and howling upon the Roman forces. To his left Joseph saw that the pass leading out to the coast was blocked by uprooted boulders behind which Jewish bowmen began to cut down the disciplined column of slow moving legionnaires. Over on his right Joseph spotted Simon bar Giora dashing down at the head of his men who rolled and slid down almost gleefully upon the trapped Romans. The XIIth Legion inexorably trudged on, never once breaking ranks.

Joseph cut diagonally in front of the charging Jews, and brandishing his own Roman centurion sword, screamed at them to stop the treacherous attack. Like a man drugged, he half ran half slipped down the wadi where he saw the Jews pour their vengeance upon the enemy. Corpses lay in the pass and the hands of the wounded reached up to him, their bodies half drowned in the mud.

Ahead of him and racing down from the north ridge of the wadi, men with prayer shawls tucked about their hips cut a path through the Roman column that began to bend and spiral back on itself until it snapped. Now the discipline of the Fulminata that had once spearheaded Rome's victory against Greece at Pydna cracked as legionnaire fell upon legionnaire, each trying to save himself from the swift striking swords of the Sicaris led by Eleazar ben Yair. He had the same look in his eyes as when they were boys and had sneaked behind the boulders surrounding a Jewish village and watched how the Roman soldiers methodically killed each man, then each boy. And believing that for the Jews there was an interdiction for the maimed to enter the Hereafter, they cut off their genitals and stuffed them up the corpses' rectums. They then proceeded to the leisure of rape.

"Why don't they kill themselves?" Eleazar kept repeating as he pounded his small fists, leaving circles of blood on the sharp rocks. "Why don't they cut their throats, bless God and die?"

And Joseph knew that somewhere in that slough of blood Eleazar ben Yair was in his own distorted hate wreaking vengeance not on the Romans, but against those villagers who years earlier had not died decently by their own hands.

The Jewish attackers worked swiftly though disorderly, hacking through the Roman lines. Many Jews fell upon their opponents, pressing their heads into the ground, drowning them in mud. A Roman cavalry officer emerged from the melee, dashing toward the blocked pass. He found an opening through the boulders and led three squadron of horse out to the wider valley and down to the coast. Just as he came through, an arrow caught him in his left thigh pinning him to the haunches of his mount. The horse reared up throwing the rider in the air and over the boulders. By the purple sash on the officer's sword, the same he had once seen him wear as he drove his chariot in the Circus Flaminius, Joseph knew that it was Titus Flavius.

Looking up, he saw the Jews gleaning the weapons the Romans had abandoned. They were also gathering their dead. Jews never forsook their dead, but saw that they received burial according to The Law. Nor did they do as the pagans did, desecrate the enemy dead. They left that to the vultures and the jackals. Despite the successful attack, Joseph knew that the bounty of war would not be measured in this wadi but in the future number of corpses throughout the Jewish nation. And as always, finally, in the destruction of Jerusalem.

His brooding was checked when Niger ran up to him. "I knew I'd find you here," he declared with his old enthusiasm.

"Are you alone?"

"With our retainers and Silas's Royals. He ordered us out."

"Once I heard that Cestius Gallus was bogged down, I decided to attack with whatever forces were available," lied Joseph. "Ben Yair's were available."

"That's what I told Silas."

"And what did he have to say to that."

"He said that if you were out there, you'd be with the Romans."

"I'm not so sure I shouldn't have followed his advice. Most of the Romans managed to escape through the pass thanks to bar Giora's sloppiness. The price of victory is not yet paid for."

"But they left their weapons. Look at all those arms!" said Niger slapping a catapult sunk in the mud and covered with brown leaves, very similar to the one Joseph remembered that had ornamented the atrium leading to the pool at Lucia's palace in Rome. "There's enough here to lick the whole damn Roman Empire."

iv

He had first met Lucia while she was swimming in the pool in her father's palace just off the Via Aurelia. After paying his respects to the old counsellor, he had come out of the library through a colonnaded walk that ran around a pool. A girl was backstroking languidly, the sun tracing her movements through a large overspreading tamarisk tree. In the center of the pool stood a bloodstone pillar around which a bronze viper curled. The girl had spun about and grasped on to the pillar. Her toes flexed like claws.

"Do you like to swim?" she called up to him. Her hair was tied to the top of her head and hung in ringlets of gold. She did not smile.

"I have no bathing robe," answered Joseph.

"Neither have I," she said kicking her feet in the air so that her white bottom flashed in the sun. She swam up to him and hung on to the pool ledge below where he stood. "I'm taking a party tonight to the Mulvian Bridge. Bianca and others will also be there. You're invited."

"And who are Bianca and others?"

"Jews. Rich Jews. Queen Berenice stays at their palaces."

"I'm related to the Queen of Golan," said Joseph.

"Every Jew in Rome is related to the Queen. Jump in and I'll race you."

Two peacocks approached the opposite edge of the pool and pecked at the water. Their turquoise feathers were the same color as the girl's eyes.

"I'm waiting," she said, and she grabbed his ankle and pulled him into the pool.

Joseph struggled till he got to his feet, then quickly combed back his thin hair with his fingers. "Don't ever do that again," he said, climbing out of the water.

The girl stood up and grasped her hair from behind and wrung it out. Her breasts bobbed along the water line.

They both burst out laughing. "How do you expect me to swim in this wet, heavy robe?" Joseph said.

"Take it off."

Joseph looked around, then quickly disrobed and dived into the pool. When he surfaced he saw that the girl had swum to the far end. She had her mouth in the water and was making gurgling sounds that frightened the peacocks into fluttering their wings. He swam awkwardly toward the girl. "You're Lucia, aren't you? The counsellor's daughter."

"In Rome first names aren't used so freely as in the provinces. Even among equals."

"I'm not your equal. I'm at least ten years older than you."

"Then you're much older than you think."

"How old are you?"

"Twenty...I'll be twenty on the Twelfth of Xanthicus."

Joseph swam after her as she floated on her back. Their thighs touched cooly. "You're really nineteen then," he said touching his lips to her bare shoulder. "In my country you'd already be a mother of three."

"Peasants marry when they're capable of dropping. Like animals. How many children does your wife have?" And she arched her body until she summersaulted backwards, resurfacing at the deep end of the pool.

Joseph swam up to her and held her around the waist. Her fingernails cut into his wrists. They floated out to the center of the pool and Lucia began to drift off. He pulled her to him and sought leverage at the bottom of the pool with his toes. "This is very awkward," he sputtered, his mouth filling with water.

"There's no comfort in love," she said, scissoring her legs around his hips.

"You make me feel a solicitor."

"Isn't that what you really are?" And she pulled him down with her to the bottom of the pool.

Joseph surfaced gasping for air. He grabbed the edge of the pool nearest to him, his stomach heaving uncontrollably as he tried to catch his breath. With much effort he lifted himself out of the water. He was comforted by the warmth of the tiles. When he finally sat, he saw Lucia sprawled naked on sofa beneath a russet canopy. She was feeding grapes to the peacocks.

"They're known to be vicious," said Joseph, standing and covering his body with his wet tunic.

"No one's vicious when they're properly fed," said Lucia biting into a grape and letting the juice trickle down her chin.

"Then I'm still vicious."

"So am I," said Lucia flinging a handful of grapes against the tamarisk trunk. The two peacocks waddled off to fight over the fruit.

"Let's play house," said Lucia, the sun turning her lashes to gold.

After, they lay in each other's arms for a long while watching the shadows crawl into the iris beds along the base of the colonnades. Lucia kept wiggling her toes as she played with a medal that hung from a chain around Joseph's neck and rested in the hair on his chest. "From the emperor," she said. "Which one?"

"The Governor of Syria. When I was a child."

"Cestius Gallus?"

"At the time it was Tiberius Alexander."

"The Jew."

"An apostate. The present Governor of Egypt."

"Give it to me."

Joseph shook his head. "You haven't earned it yet."

Lucia pushed him away with her feet and stood up. "Have you?" she asked, and she leaped into the pool. A moment later she surfaced and wrapped her legs around the pedestal. A white dove landed on the head of the bronze viper.

v

It was dark when Joseph and Niger rode into bar Giora's new headquarters at Gazara on the coastal side of the pass. They could see the timorously flickering fires of the Roman camp set up again at Emmaus. The watch calls of the Roman pickets echoed throughout the night, and the activity in the camp foretold that Cestius Gallus was planning to fight his way out of the trap. Joseph resigned himself to the final massacre of the XIIth Legion.

He came by piles of weapons that were being neatly sorted and stacked. A convoy of mules, already packed with weapons, was slogging its way along the mountain crest toward Jerusalem. Bar Giora stood arms akimbo so that his mustache and scimitar curled at the same angle as he watched Lucia Paulina instruct his men how to strap captured catapults on to the backs of camels. Joseph was not surprised. He wondered if it was Lucia's will or God's torrent that had won the first battle of Jerusalem.

She came to him as the cry of the Roman fourth watch echoed across the wadi that once again gushed with rain. Joseph leaned against an abandoned stone thrower and for a while they both stood like gods as they watched the tatters of that afternoon's battle snap in the wind.

"You seem an expert at dismantling weapons," said Joseph.

"My father. I grew up with the verifications of war."

"I saw his genius for weaponry in Rome."

"The ram. It was I who named it *Viktor*."

"And for whose victory this time?"

Lucia sat down in the mud and leaned against the wheel of the stone thrower.

"You've been among the looters," said Joseph.

"Among the defeated. First among the defeated."

Joseph found a piece of armor plate and sat on it beside her. "It was you who convinced them to release me from jail."

"Eleazar ben Yair. He gave the order."

"He hates my guts. Always did."

"I asked him."

"First Titus, then Eleazar, then Cestius Gallus. Finally you come to me."

"You have the order confused."

"How did you get to Eleazar ben Yair?"

"The Sicari. The helmsman of our lighter in Jaffa. He took me to him."

"But why? How?"

"I showed him a message I bore to his leader from Rome."

"It seems we both bore messages from the enemy."

"Mine was from the Sicaris."

"In Rome?"

"The commitment to this country goes beyond your Jerusalem."

His desire for her became mixed with disdain. "Don't tell me about commitments to this country."

She stared at him and, almost sarcastically, replied. "Wither thou goest —"

"Cestius Gallus?"

"The same commitment."

"Then it was you who convinced him to abandon Jerusalem."

"A Roman legate listens, then makes his own decisions. I take credit for nothing."

"He loves you very much," said Joseph. "So do I."

Across the flowing wadi activity in the Roman camp increased. Shouts and commands rang through the wet air and the earth trembled with the anxiety of animals.

"Catastrophe excites me," said Lucia as she pulled him down upon her by the chain about his neck. The pain he felt linked them. "It makes me part of the battle." She drew him into her and their limbs became entangled so that Joseph felt he was being swallowed.

The mud sucked their bodies together and he could no longer tell who was on top of whom. He moaned as he lost the rhythm of his movements, Lucia taking him over the crest of his own capacity. And he marvelled at her control, how no matter when he let himself go, she was riding the same wave, crashing down with him upon the coasts of passion.

"I'm starved," she said, and she extracted some bread and a bottle of wine from her side bag. "The real loot." She tore rapaciously at the bread with her teeth. Joseph refused any nourishment and watched as she rinsed her mouth with wine in the Roman fashion. And it came so that he remembered the two faced god, Janus.

To his surprise the sun rose the next day on a nearly abandoned camp. Cestius had outwitted them. Having left four hundred men as decoys, he slipped out of Emmaus with ten thousand of his regulars and made his way to Caesarea. In their frustration the Sicaris charged into the near deserted town, killing all of the Roman rear guard. This time they cut their heads off and carried them back to Jerusalem on their javelins. Or was it more in the course of Titus Flavius' strategy the new commander of the XIIth Legion?

Watching the macabre carnival, Joseph wondered how long before Rome sent its armies against the perfidy of Jerusalem; before the cauldron of war would again seethe from the north, finally invoking true prophecies of disaster? The legate Cestius Gallus was right: you do learn more from defeat then from victory.

He knelt to the ground, shrouding himself in mud, forcing tears to wash away his filth. He beat his breast attempting to excoriate the vision that now rose before him: himself fornicating in the Temple of God. Not for Titus. Not because of the rains, Not even Hagla's curse, his corruption, but the scapegoat of his own failures — Lucia — would be the Nemesis of Jerusalem.

He rose. He saw the Essenes already in a distance turning southward instead of following the others up to Jerusalem. And in his contrition, he wondered why Eleazar ben Yair had decided this time to join the profane rebellion which had nothing to do with his peculiar faith in the God of Israel.

Then he remembered that the village they had once watched being destroyed was an Essene settlement not far from where he now knelt, and that the Roman soldiers had been from the XIIth Legion. He knew now that Eleazar would return to Masada, descry the heavens and seek with envy the souls of his dead in the eye of the sun.

Part II
MASADA

*Of these tracks one leads
from the Lake Asphaltitis
on the east, the other by
which approach is easier,
from the west. The former
they call the snake, seeing
a resemblance to that reptile
in its narrowness and
continual windings; for its
course is broken in skirting
the jutting crags. One
transversing this route must
firmly plant each foot
alternatively.*

Bellum Judaicum — Josephus

CHAPTER IX — SERPENT AND THE EAGLE

i

His guides took him as far as the charcoal mountains that wavered across the Judean Wilderness. They bowed to him as he kissed their camels in farewell. Then the Bedouin turned back the way they had come two days earlier along the green wadi north leading to Hebron. The sky was clear, almost white. Joseph drank from the gourd they had left him. The water tasted of earth. He cast a stone on the mound raised by the guides against evil spirits, then set out at a quick but measured pace hoping to reach the Essene settlement at Ein Gedi before dark. The slopes were so steep that he had to lean back in order to control his footing. The soles of his feet burned from the flat bituminous stones that hissed as they rolled out from under him and into the canyon below. The air smelled of brimstone and salt.

At the top of the last mountain, the sky turned blue, colored by the waters of the Dead Sea. Three times a day the waters changed hue, and even before the sun began to set, he saw by their marble tint that the day was waning. In a distance a broom tree brushed across the horizon. A cactus bush exploded out of the loam. Bloated melons hung from the cactus, and knowing that he would miss the evening repast at the settlement, he chose a fruit. In Jerusalem the children would tie a tin vessel to a pole, reach in and cup it over the melon, break it off, then scoop it back without coming close to the bush. Having no cup he broke off a forked twig from a nearby acacia and with it spiked a fruit, drawing it out from the amidst the paddle leaves that were thick with thorns. Without touching the green fruit, whose tinge of rouge showed that it was ripe, he gingerly cut lines in the skin, peeling it back so that the hundreds of invisible and infectious prickles would not powder his fingertips. The melon itself was pale orange with a center like a mouth filled with bloody teeth. The fruit was too mealy and cloying, and he threw half away. Instantly a swarm of gnats attacked it. Joseph drank again from the gourd, the water parching his mouth with sweetness.

The sun suddenly flared against the domes of the Mountains of Moab, and he fell to the earth in terror as he saw the gloaming ignite the crest of Mount Nebo. And in that vision, he thought he saw the Temple of God collapse into ashes.

He lay upon the scorched stones trembling, unable to rise. The image of his father came to him as they walked the streets of the Ophel Quarter that was scattered with sheep dung, and by the Synogogue of

Freedmen in front of which he had scorned the worshippers.

After awhile he rose and continued down the path through the boulders whose fissures were tufted with shadows of grass and rock rose. The gourd hanging from his side clattered like a drum as he half slid, half trotted down into a gorge. Then he heard the flow of water.

Soon he came to a cascade that splashed into a pool. The water continued on in a trickle through a grove of wild jujube trees, then fell again into another pool two hundred feet beneath where he stood. The water had cut steps covered with moss, and he had to grasp the thorns that grew from the crevices to keep from slipping. The lower he descended the more the water roared, raising a spray that formed a halo around his head. He passed under a cavern dank with the smell of roots and stopped to watch a lizard that stood in his path. Joseph raised his robe and pissed on it, washing its dusty skin before it darted into the varicosed rocks. He felt the water rumble in his toes.

At the first pool, he sat down on a ledge and without taking off his sandals washed his feet in the cool water. He rinsed the blood off his hands, then plucked some thorns from his palms. He was about to splash his face when a dagger of sunlight pierced his eyes. Looking up he saw an object plunging down the gorge at him from where he had begun his descent. Half way down it became distorted in the mist and seemed to hang on to the moted light beams, before crashing into the pool. A second later a head of ebony hair, thick and curly, surfaced. With clear, unblinking eyes, Eleazar ben Yair stared at him.

Then he raised himself out of the pool and without a word Joseph followed him through another cavern and out upon a narrower ledge. Tucking his side locks behind his ears and securing his Sicari dagger between his knotted robe, Eleazar dived out between the canyons. Joseph backed away until he heard Eleazar hit the water of the second pool forty feet below.

Ten minutes later he found him, hardly wet, seated on the ground in a small grove. Eleazar was peeling the scales off a pine cone which he had smashed against a stone. He shook out the seeds and chose two, brushing the rest away. Then, with a smaller stone, he crushed these, extracting from them two golden nuts which he tossed into his mouth. A vulture screeched in the boulders above them.

Joseph realized that the companion of his youth was in a period of silence and that not till the sun set would Eleazar utter a word. Joseph raised the gourd to his lips, but it was empty. He walked to the edge of the pool and for a moment watched the bugs skitter across the water. He knelt and was about to drink when he remembered the Roman physician's admonition about river waters.

Eleazar watched him. The black beard he now wore added strength to his deformed chin which always made his lips curl in a permanent sneer.

"I've been warned against open waters," said Joseph in apology. "I caught the river fever in Rome."

Eleazar tossed a nut into his mouth. Joseph ran his fingers along his shaven face. Once only the truly Hellenized Jews went beardless; now many young Jews had begun to shave. Joseph had had his own beard removed on the day he arrived in Rome and since then had gotten into the habit of shaving every day. The Essenes continued to let their beards grow naturally, never even trimming them. Joseph once noted that Bannus wore no beard. Eleazar had scowled at him, wiping a hand across his delicately hooked nose. "God never gave him the capacity."

The sound of the waterfalls and the thickening shadows walled them in as the sunbeams drew light out of the grove. Joseph recalled how steep the final descent was and nervously looked up at the quickening darkness. Watching Eleazar break open another pine cone, he noted that his fingers still trembled when he worked carefully as they had when he was a youth. Joseph decided not to move until Eleazar did.

"I've come for Bannus' blessing," said Joseph, seeing by the way Eleazar glanced up at the setting sun that in a moment he would be ready to speak. "How is our teacher?"

Eleazar remained silent. Essenes felt that most questions were best left unanswered. Only their elders had the privilege of instituting conversation. When they were young, Joseph would talk through the night to Eleazar, reviewing for himself the day's discoveries, while his friend would lie on the mat across from him without uttering a sound. Joseph knew he was awake because he could hear him breathing unevenly, practicing as he did every night to hold his breath as long as possible. After one such long silence, Eleazar had turned to him and said: *I didn't swallow my spit once all day.*

Eleazar now pressed his two fists against his eyes and looked up into the sun. Bannus had taught that a pinpoint of light in a dark cave or a white wall was all that was necessary to clear the mind of distraction. He would have Eleazar and Joseph practice by setting a candle in the earthen floor of their cave and make them stare at it in silence. Eleazar learned to sit motionless for hours, his eyes half closed as he meditated with total concentration. Joseph would become restless and after a few minutes the rocks became distorted into voluptuous figures and his body would purr with the sound of the springs that flowed beneath them into the Dead Sea. Meditation gave him an erection, and often he would go out into the brush, and thinking of the dark-eyed Nabatean witch, he would rub himself in the green, parted lips of a blossoming desert apple, spurting into it his restless seed.

"You think you can beat the Roman?" Eleazar asked, rising.

"What Roman?"

"All of them."

"Right now I'm concerned only with one. Titus Flavius."

"All," persisted Eleazar. "Even at Masada."

Joseph waited. He was measuring his words because he already saw that Eleazar had spoken more than usual and that he would not spare him much more attention. "Why waste time on that rock?" he asked, watching Eleazar's lips follow his own, a characteristic common to many desert dwellers because of their not having much opportunity to speak.

"Masada," repeated Eleazar. "The place where I was born." He walked to the edge of the pool, where again the water began its cascade, and tucking his robe more securely under his belt, he raised himself to his toes and dived down into the last pool at the bottom of the gorge.

Joseph watched him sail through the air, scattering the vultures that floated in the abyss seeking their evening perches. He saw Eleazar hit the water a few feet from the stone in the center of the pool where the girls of the settlement were gathering the linen that had been drying in the sun. Some children playing near by waved to Eleazar as he climbed out of the water and disappeared into a copse. They then raised their eyes to where Joseph stood. The fear he had always felt for these strange Jews whose loyalty to God was veiled in silences now came back to him. He saw the vultures hunched like harridans waiting along the ledges of the gorge, and he looked away. A tree bent over the cascade and on it hung green, shrivelled bulbs shaped like oysters and out of which white fiber sprinkled with black seeds protruded. Sodom apples, Joseph said to himself, remembering the spent energy of his youth. He leaned over and squeezed one. Milk squirted in his face burning his eyes. He reeled back under the waterfall which sucked him off the ledge, his hands flaying as he soared out then down the gorge. This time the vultures swooped out at their prey who glimpsed the Fortress of Masada tumbling in the distance before he let the silence of his fall envelop him in retrospection. . . .

ii

"It's flexing its talons," Joseph heard Eleazar shout as they stood in the roofless synagogue of Masada. "Because it's found its prey."

Eleazar had interrupted his praying, the sun having become eclipsed by a wing shaped cloud that dived directly at the two boys. Joseph was knocked down by the rush of wind as an eagle, its yellow claws opening and closing, wheeled overhead and down the wadi below them.

"Look!" cried Eleazar, leaning half out of the embrasure in the wall. "It's heading for that cave."

Joseph squinted his eyes, flinching as he hardly dared to rise, and saw that half way down the chasm a python lay sunning itself at the mouth of the cave he and Eleazar had been washed into the night before during the flash flood.

Eleazar whispered. "It's a female because I've never seen one so big."

"There are eagles down here?"

"And serpents. He too must have been washed up by the flood."

"Serpents don't exist," said Joseph unconvincingly.

Eleazar's lips moved silently. Then he said. "The eagles fly low over what they establish as their territory. They seek food and enemies in the crevices of the canyons. Then they soar as high as possible and come swooping down. She must have spotted him earlier."

"But the noise. It sounded like thunder when it flew over us."

"Serpents are deaf. They only feel the vibrations from the ground. Look!"

Joseph could hardly watch as the eagle enveloped the unsuspecting python, its beak slashing a piece of flesh as large as a pomegranate from the thickest part of the snake. The python rolled over, flashing its pink belly, then snapped the rear of its body like a whip at the head of the eagle. But the eagle sprang back, then floated out across the canyon, its wings held stiffly in a long glide. The serpent recoiled into the cave, baiting the bird with its head that now stood upright, its forked tongue flickering in and out. The eagle whirred out of reach, gyrating its wings so that it hung in mid air. When it attacked again, the whole wadi thundered.

"Watch. She's going to try and beat it to death with her wings," said Eleazar.

Blood spurted from the side of the python and down the silvery cliff marking a shadow on the sun. Joseph waited until he was sure which side was winning before he made his choice. "The eagle," he now pronounced.

Eleazar dug his fingers into Joseph's arm. 'I said look!"

The python was hanging now around the eagle's neck and they soared across the canyon in wide circles. The serpent's forked tongue licked its own blood off the eagle's hump as they grasped each other in despairing love. Joseph was sure the serpent was smiling.

Then he saw the python tighten its grip around the eagle's wings, but the great bird managed to flutter free. The python fell on to a ledge below the cave where its blood still trickled from above, while the eagle rolled over rising high above the fortress, its talons flexing at the sun.

On its third dive, the eagle was stunned when the serpent shot out across the chasm and grasped it in a knot, drawing it back to the ledge. The eagle's wings desperately resisted the strangling hold of the serpent. Joseph was so engrossed in the battle that he did not feel Eleazar's nails still digging into his arm. The more the python squeezed, the more the eagle's stiff wings relented, each time the snake jerking its grip tighter. Slowly, like windless sails, the eagle's wings collapsed. Joseph began to doubt the power of eagles.

But the flying beast was no easy prey to hold on to, and suddenly it folded its wings so that it became hard to tell the serpent from the eagle. Her slick feathers made it easier for her to slip out of the death clutch, forcing the python to curl around and mistakenly bite its own nether part. The pain made it snap its coil so tight that blood burst from its under belly and from the eagle's eyes.

"Who's winning? Who's winning?" screamed Joseph, covering his eyes with his free hand, no longer able to watch.

"Once I saw a serpent swallow a sheep," said Eleazar. "And an eagle carry off a girl." He then turned and walked out of the synagogue.

Joseph leaned out of the embrasure as far as he could. The sun had covered the canyon in a pink glow. When the air cleared, he saw that both beasts had disappeared. He was astounded that in all that time, the shadow of the sun had not even crossed beyond the line of the serpent's blood.

CHAPTER X — THE SONS OF LIGHT AGAINST
THE SONS OF DARKNESS

i

Long before his father had sent him to dwell among the Essenes, Joseph had encountered them on the streets of Jerusalem. It was a time of seers and the capital abounded with black magicians who foretold the coming of the Day of Judgment. They preached that salvation lay in the desert, the only place where God still spoke to man. Joseph did not believe in the concept of doom nor in the new Jews, the Christians, and their ideas about the Messiah. But the modesty of the Essene sages, who sat silently in their tattered white robes, their bare feet stuck out before them as they contemplated the sun, had impressed him. Only when someone approached them would they drop their glazed eyes, nod their heads and raise a finger of admonition. "*Da!*" they would declare. "Know!"

Most Jews considered the Essenes saintly, and unlike the prophets of old, they bore but did not preach God's will. Their austere vision and not the mendacious one of the professional soothsayers had won them support in these times of fear and recrimination. Theirs was the *Fourth Philosophy* which professed that not even mortal risk, as the rabble called it, exonorated sin. It was through this belief that life and death were merely stages of existence to be followed by other purer phases that allowed many of the Essenes to join the ranks of the Sicaris.

Their silences were known to heal, making the lame believe they walked and the blind, they saw. Once, while wandering through the Ophel Quarter, Joseph had seen two women approach an Essene. One pleaded for a miracle to fill her barrenness, vowing like Hannah had to God, to offer her own child to the community of the Essenes. Lowering his eyes from the sun, the wise man pointed to the other woman who held in her arms a dying infant. "Her fruit," he said, "has wilted. Take it as out of your own womb and it shall flourish." Both women had turned and gone their separate ways. For few knew that among the tenets of the Essenes was one that disdained the vanity of procreation which to them was an act of uncontrollable passion. Their members were encouraged rather to adopt those less fortunate than themselves and to raise them according to their rule.

Most Essene settlements, called *Yahads*, were in the Judean Wilderness and always by water. They lived communally, usually in caves and off what God allowed to be sown, limiting their labor to bare necessities so that they might devote most of their time to meditation which for them was the essence of prayer. Two principles governed their existence: concentration and cleanliness. They would sit for hours concentrating on an object — a pinpoint, a pebble in a pool, a candle in a cave — until their minds were clean as their bodies which they bathed as often as possible in the waters of the Jordan or the Dead Sea. In this way they recaptured the vision of God that had once again become precious in the land.

Together with meditation and bathing, fasting became their substitute for the rites of sacrifice, and they felt little obligation to make pilgrimages to the Temple of God. It was in fact in the Essene settlements that the synagogue first became the central place of worship for the Jews. Although their extreme asceticism and their arcane rule which they gleaned from secret books was held somewhat suspect by the academicians, they followed The Law itself according to the teachings of these rabbis. Many a Pharisee student would come and live for a time among them, though few could withstand the rigors of their code.

Because of their piety and will, they made light of danger and believed that death with honor was the equivalent of immortality. It was why, among other reasons, they required two years of novitiate before they would accept even their own children into their community of saints — an initiation period long enough to prove one worthy of having been created in the image of God.

Joseph had first arrived at Ein Gedi on his fourteenth birthday, in time to see a group of Essenes leading Eleazar, shrouded in white and with a prayer shawl over his head, out of the oasis and into the Wilderness. A week later Eleazar returned, his body barely clothed by the fringes of his *talit*. As he walked by, Joseph saw that he was covered with boils the color of the sea and that puss ran from his eyes. His lips were parched like dead flowers and his hands trembled and were swollen with sores.

"Where in God's name have you been?" Joseph asked, thinking that he had gone again to Masada.

Eleazar, still capable of raising scorn in his voice, answered hoarsely. "*Maaleh Ha-akrabim*, the Ascent of Scorpions."

Joseph saw that his beard had grown to manhood.

For many days after Joseph avoided Eleazar and at night he dreamed the horror of his destruction. He could not comprehend how this holy community which preached passivity could condone sending a thirteen year old up into those desolate heights where only sage and scorpions grew. Bannus had taken three years to answer this question. "He chose his own inchoation," he said. "From the Ascent of Scorpions, he could contemplate the forbidden *Hor Ha-har*, where both your own and his ancient proginator Aaron died."

After that Joseph decided to leave the settlement of the Essenes and return to Jerusalem.

ii

The habit of ten years earlier came back to Joseph as he rose into the light of no sun and made his way to the *Mikva* where anyone coming from the unclean world must bathe before having any contact with the community. The bath was in a cave measuring forty *selah* according to law and filled with water not drawn from the earth. Since the Wilderness was dry during most of the year, the rule had been interpreted by the great Rabbi Hillel to mean, "part of the water and not all of the water." Most *mikvas* were divided in two, with one section on a higher level filled with pure rain water and the other, the real bath, filled with well water. Joseph slid gingerly into the lower pool and reached up and unplugged a hole in the separation allowing the rain water to trickle in, giving sanction to the ritual bath. According to the custom of the Essenes, he submerged himself completely beneath the surface for as long as he could hold his breath. The water was cold and stagnant.

Joseph lay in the pleasant heat of the stone slabbed entrance to the cave and let his body dry in the rising sun. He closed his eyes and spots danced in his head. He concentrated on the largest light, almost gaining the full purity of its whiteness, when it became distorted into the face of Hagla. Slowly he exorcised her from the light and conjured Lucia.

Whose side was she on? In which bed was she gaining courage at the moment? He remembered her lust at the Mulvian Bridge outside Rome. He also remembered the book she read each night before going to bed because her father had told her that the heritage of the Jews was as essential to Rome as the matter of Greece.

"My favorite is *The Book of Judith*," she said one morning to Joseph after they had struggled with love.

"That is not truly of the Bible," said Joseph.

"Deborah then."

"You choose strong women."

"I should like to lead men in battle." Her eyes tightened, creasing her translucent skin. "Or cut off their heads while making love." Joseph thought of scorpions.

Always, among the Essenes his mind seethed with ideas, making him abandon preconceived plans. The burden of the sun made him heavy with prophecy as the pinpoint of light in his brain now expanded into the fortress of Masada. Joseph opened his eyes, refusing to be goaded by the obsessions of others. He rose and slipped on a coarse robe, hiding the medal he always wore around his neck upon which was a graven image.

The settlement was already busy at its chores. Before a long stone table, women were preparing the first meal of the day. Old ladies, like shadows, moved about the commune gathering weeds and what little kindling they could find, while by the pool, maidens squatted filling jugs with water. Along the shores of the sea, the men stood in muted prayer. Essenes were forbidden to speak after the sun sat high and raised the scent of salt.

Joseph walked by the cave in which half a dozen men in threadbare garments sat by candlelight dipping quills in inkpots and drawing slowly and meticulously upon scrolls. After the synagogue and the *mikva* bath, the scriptorium was the most important place in the *Yahad*. In the two centuries of their existence, the Essenes had become renowned for their *Torah* scrolls which had found their way to all corners of the earth. It was in this cave that Joseph discovered such Apocrypha texts as *Jacob's Dream, The Damascus Testament,* and *The Book of Jubilees.* One, entitled *Enoch*, dealt with the geneology of angels and demons and the secrets of dream interpretation. Joseph had read here that the sun and the moon were chariots driven by the wind, and that falling stars were really sinful angels. One text was considered as holy as the books of the Bible and forbidden to laymen. Only Essene wise men were permitted to read the scroll of *The War of the Sons of Light Against The Sons of Darkness.*

Across the Dead Sea the horizon wavered into purple mountains. Joseph saw Eleazar come among the men by the sea who all wore prayer shawls and phylacteries strapped black upon their foreheads and left forearms. The water washed their bare feet, and they raised their voices once to the sun as if the world were newly created.

Beneath a fig tree a group of children sat in a circle and recited in unison: *"B'reshit bara Elohim,"* while a young tutor nodded approvingly as he continued the phrase with ". . . the heavens and the earth?" During his earlier stay, each morning his day had begun in the same fashion with this opening passage of the *Torah.* What shocked now was that after the responsive reading, they all took up staffs carved from willow branches, which though thick were still moist and green, and began to thrust and parry at each other under the guidance of the same tutor in what Joseph recognized as a simulated spear and lance exercise of infantry combat. The settlement resounded with the clap of wood.

Joseph looked up at the cascading water and saw a goat skipping from one crag to another, following the rhythm of the spreading daylight, and he smiled, proudly recalling his daring plunge the night before down the gorge. He no longer remembered that he had actually lost his footing.

When the full circumference of the sun crossed the horizon, he knew it was time for first food and he went and joined the others at the stone table. The women, who ate later, set before each man a bowl filled with a mash of ground figs and wild wheat. One woman, her hands white with flour, distributed small, flat loaves of bread. The meal was exactly as he had remembered it, for the Essenes never varied their diet. Two acolytes sat on the ground eating from the same bowl. They received no bread. From the state of their robes, Joseph could tell that they were near the end of their two year initiation period and would soon qualify as members of the community. Essenes wore their clothes until they were in shreds and only when their shame became exposed were they issued new raiments. Each new member was given an ax which he wore at his side like a sword. A few days after Joseph had arrived at Ein Gedi on his first visit, his stomach had become upset. His tutor had handed him a small ax and explained that it was to be used to dig trenches for sanitary purposes. One Sabbath Eleazar caught him shitting, an act forbidden on the holy day. Joseph had suffered terrible pains because Eleazar followed him till sunset, making sure that he would not sin.

A young woman came by with a jug of milk set on a flat, woven disc on top of her head. Despite her bloated belly, a rare sight in an Essene commune, she walked tall and lightly like a roe.

"You're Shlomit," said Joseph.

The woman acknowledged the fact by lowering her eyes.

"Don't you remember me? I'm Joseph. Joseph from Jerusalem."

The young woman backed away.

"We used to play together. And Eleazar. How you'd dare us to hold snakes by their tails and dip our heads with our eyes open into the Salt Sea."

They had discovered a pepper bush once, and she had taunted the boys to walk through it. Eleazar, of course, plunged in and out without warning Joseph what might happen if the exposed parts of the body contacted the plant. Joseph kept looking at the dusty haired girl whose eyes reflected the mountains across the sea. Then with a flourish of his hand, he pushed his way slowly through. Eleazar and Shlomit giggled as his eyes became inflamed and his hands turned to fire.

"Cross your arms over someone who hates you," said Shlomit, becoming frightened by Joseph's swelled face. His eyes tearing,

Joseph raised his hands over Eleazar's head.

For three days and nights Bannus prayed and fasted so that Joseph would not go blind. In punishment for their foolish prank, Eleazar was made to sit a full day once a week facing the sun until Joseph had healed, while Shlomit was ordered to care for all Joseph's needs.

Joseph recovered quickly but feigned illness in order to have Shlomit continue to nurse him. One day she appeared and as usual began to anoint his arms with the balm Bannus had prepared from limestone powder and the milk of the Sodom apple, since oil was banned for bodily use among the Essenes. The sun's heat had penetrated the cave and the huge flies that came from across the Dead Sea whirred around their heads. Joseph lay motionless watching the rising movement of her new breasts as she kneaded the ointment into his ankles. Her braided hair had unravelled and fallen in her face. "Higher," he said. "Up to the knees."

The girl obeyed moving her hands beneath his robe. Joseph felt her hot fingers in the hair of his calves as she nodded back and forth as though in prayer.

"Higher," he insisted, and for a second her eyes filled with hate before she pushed away his robe and anointed his knees with the white pasty balm that smelled of sorrel.

"I said higher," repeated Joseph, raising his garment so that his body was completely exposed.

Shlomit had been a willful girl, an orphan as many of the Essene children were. She had been the only creature found moving after the Romans had razed the village of her birth near Emmaus because the elders were unable to collect the special tax placed on their meager crops. An Essene couple had adopted her, but her beauty and contrariness made it hard for them to control her fiery blood. Bannus had even exorcised her but to no avail. The women of the settlement had rightly predicted that she would be the type to have her own children.

She had looked at Joseph's nakedness without shock. She had seen the goats pissing and little boys dueling with streams of urine. Joseph grabbed her wrist. "There too," he said. "I touched myself there and it burns badly."

Shlomit accepted it as part of her penance and rubbed Joseph's groin. His body stiffened and he began to squirm. Through the cave opening, he could see Eleazar, his eyes up at the sun and his lips moving in prayer. Shlomit thought that Joseph was writhing in pain, until he groaned and then spent in her brown fist. She licked her fingers, sure that this too was part of her contrition.

iii

"You're married," said Joseph to her, as she tilted the jug and poured milk into his bowl.

The young woman brushed aside her still braided hair and said nothing.

"Who's the fortunate man to have won such a beauty?"

"Eleazar," she said, her eyes flashing up though she kept her head bowed.

Joseph sat down at the far end of the table where most of the younger men were already seated.

After a priest said grace, the men leaned toward their bowls. They ate in silence and with a concentration as though each morsel was being preserved in a special part of the body. They used their fingers to gather the food, leaving some at the bottom of the bowl for the animals, thus avoiding an act of gluttony. They would not eat again till darkness.

On his way back to the cave assigned to him, he spied a lone figure lying upon his back in the sea. From the clothes made of bark and leaves which were neatly piled on the stony shore, he knew the man was Bannus. At first Joseph backed away, fearful to meet his old teacher. From behind a tannery, he watched the wise man reading a scroll while he floated, the salt in the sea being very dense. Joseph had often seen children walk upon the waters.

Finally Bannus came out and dressed without drying. He walked along the shore to his cave which was isolated from the rest of the *Yahad*. As if it were understood, Joseph followed behind.

Bannus had not aged. His bald head, however, was covered with more freckles than Joseph remembered. Someone had informed Joseph that the wise man was ending a month's fast this morning and that he had not spoken a word in the same number of days. The Law held that fasts were from sundown to sundown, but Bannus disliked rushing penance and always extended his until the following sunrise.

An orange taper, stuck in a crevice of the cave wall, dripped upon the floor. As in all Essene abodes, a quill, a mug of ink and some parchment lay on a raised, flat stone. Joseph sat on the ground and watched Bannus take a few green almonds from a pouch hanging near the candle. He bit into the fuzzy, green rind of one and chewed it slowly, sucking in the juices. Then he broke the shell and extracted the nut, peeling it with his fingernails until it was white and glossy. He split the nut and carefully chewed only half, cleaning his teeth with his tongue before he ate the remaining part. In this manner he finished seven nuts, then rinsed his mouth with water from a clay jug that stood sweating at the entrance to the cave. He ate one date then rinsed his mouth again. Never would he mix his food nor would he eat anything that did not grow wildly. He came back and adjusting the candle, sat down beside Joseph. He was ready to listen.

"I've come, *Raabi*, for your wisdom about survival."

Bannus always spoke in epigrams or in silences. He chose now to say nothing.

"The question of survival," said Joseph, "has been pushing me to action. I'm losing my freedom of choice."

When Bannus closed his eyes, Joseph knew that this time he would speak. His face was powdered from the sea salt. "We can absorb no more than a single idea concerning existence. There is a need for penetration." He spoke as if there was no relationship between what was asked and what was on his mind. It took days to sort out his wisdom.

"Time runs swiftly. The Roman is at our gates ready to spring at his destiny. Only we Jews dare to stand in his path."

"Ask yourself," said Bannus, his eyes still closed, "about living and dying."

Joseph never quite understood the Essene concept that the beginning and the end of the human cycle were more essential than the reality of living. To them all birth was accidental and existence merely custodial till the coming of the Messiah. "By definition a question holds two parts. It always entails an answer."

Bannus smiled. "Only questions. The rest are merely reactions."

"How can we ask when once again death stalks our destiny?"

Bannus prepared another almond. Though he ate sparingly and fasted regularly, he was not thin. With his bald head and his eyes shut, he could have been an idol made of ivory, or a corpse. "The infant wails. Why? It is his only freedom."

"Why then does the Almighty impose choices upon us? Even His law commands *do* or *do not*."

"Of our own making. If He is one and all, how can there be choices?"

"Evil? Good? War? Peace? Are these all one?"

"Is not my friend another man's enemy?"

It was Joseph's turn to remain silent. He tried to concentrate on the light of the candle, but its shape and color reminded him of ben Zakkai's eyes. Bannus was letting him answer his own questions, though the answers were not those he had come to seek. The shadow on the cave wall brought Joseph back to his fears. "Last night," he said, his voice trembling, "I fell from heaven. And as I fell I prophesied disaster. How one day the sun shall cast a shadow instead of a glow."

"Spittle and earth. It's the serpent," said Bannus shutting his eyes more tightly so that his face became old. "It devours the sun."

"A scene I witnessed as a boy at Masada. With Eleazar. A python entwined about an eagle, and they were fornicating in each other's blood. Out of the cornucopia of their strangulation, the voice of the sun blared at me: LET US MAKE MAN!"

"The sun is the wrong timepiece. It lacks motion. GOD. MAN. MATTER — in that order. After that in any order that is needed."

Abstractions confused Joseph. He had to read them or write them before he could work out their sequence. "First God. Are there any rewards for worshipping him?"

"None. The veritable satisfaction."

"And when he stands by and lets us destroy ourselves?"

"To reach Him is impossible. Dying is the only striving toward His perfection."

"Like Isaac."

"Like Abraham. His was the closest victory over matter."

"But God came to his rescue."

"He came to God's. *Rahamim*. His only mercy."

Joseph rose. "May I borrow some paper and ink?"

Bannus pointed to his utensils.

"But why do you write on black parchment and use milk for ink?"

"The milk is the juice of the Sodom apple. The parchment is papyrus from the Nile. Together they remind me of our designation."

From the mouth of the cave, Joseph could see across the Dead Sea to the mountains upon which Moses must have contemplated the same problems before God commanded his disappearance. Joseph saw also to the south the Fortress of Masada and far beyond where Aaron had last ordered the stammering words of his brother. In a scroll Epaphroditus had given him, Joseph read that as a young man, before seeing God, Moses had led the armies of Egypt against Ethiopia. To surprise the enemy, he took the way of the desert and not the Nile. This route carried him through the breeding ground of serpents of strange aspect. Some were even winged. To combat these Moses had arks made of the bark of papyrus and took these filled with ibises which he knew were the serpents' deadliest enemy. The war had lasted ten years.

"*Raabi*, tell me, who won the battle between the serpent and the eagle?"

For a long while Bannus stared at the candle and Joseph thought he was going into the trance of meditation.

"Neither. It's the law of nature."

"And our battle?"

"All talk of the future turns into the past."

"History records us as the loser."

Bannus rose and handed the scroll he had been working on to Joseph. "Battles can only be lost. It is the only answer to survival."

iv

In his own cave, Joseph dipped the quill into the stone jar with the milk of Sodom apples, the same liquid that had squirted into his eyes last night and blinded him, making him tumble into the pool beside the settlement.

He wrote:

bannus says that since abraham was ready to sacrifice his son, his only son, out of submissiveness to god, he had actually performed the command. he had absorbed the order — GOD, MAN, MATTER. after that he was privileged to follow those in any order he wished. by declaring, therefore, for the war of god against rome, i too am given the right to follow my own commandment.

He was discovering a sanction for hypocrisy. He wrote on:

the essenes have solved the problem of duplicity. through a complex rule, they have established a simple way of life. take their belief in the Lord. GOD, being one, all-perfect, the beginning, the middle, the end of all, cannot be perceived by MAN who lacks the power to conceive an all-perfect concept except through MATTER. but if GOD in his magnitude is unperceived, how then can we understand his works. for us, therefore, GOD is uncreated, and positive attributes such as duty, generosity, humility are merely man's imperfect understanding of what could just as well be greed, dereliction and arrogance. if i sin, i create my own punishment: fast or stare at the sun. if i feel distressed at my incompatibility with the universe, i dance, creating my own sphere of happiness. say then that good deeds are merely a deflection of my own bad conscience or the other way around. i create. GOD is uncreated.

He was pleased with the dexterity of his mind. The white ink and the black scroll tricked him into believing that he had understood the wise Essene. In his need for heresy, he failed to see that priests were practical men who made matter real for others through symbols, in this way simplifying what *is* to what already *has been*. To the ascetic, reality itself was a symbol. The rebellion meant nothing more to Bannus than another form of concentration. Courage had no connection to cowardice, enthusiasm was no defense against depression; gratitude held no recompense in submission. For the Essenes life and death were merely compensating vanities for the flaws of mortality. So if God *was* uncreated so was man. Long before others, the Essenes had learned in the obeisance of the sun the gyrations of the earth. For them gravity held no ambiguities.

He wrote:

each millenium demands new prophets in order to cleanse the past. the question is: does the past remain the past even when manipulated? maybe that was why bannus wrote with milk on black parchment. and what he meant by the need for penetration?

He read:

wars of the sons of light against the sons of darkness
(Extract)
THERE TOO THE KING BUILT A PALACE ON THE WESTERN SLOPE BENEATH THE RAMPARTS ON THE CREST AND INCLINING TOWARD THE NORTH THE PALACE WALLS WERE STRONG AND OF GREAT HEIGHT THE FITTINGS OF THE INTERIOR WERE SUMPTUOUS AND MANIFOLD INCLUDING COLONNADES AND APARTMENTS AND BATHS ALL SUPPORTED BY COLUMNS TWENTY CUBITS HIGH AND WITH WALL AND FLOORS OF VARIEGATED STONES MOREOVER THE CELLARS WERE DESIGNED WITH BINS WHERE HUGE SUPPLIES OF CORN OIL AND WINE WERE STORED AS WELL AS A VARIETY OF PULSE AND PILES OF DATES THAT BECAUSE OF THE HEIGHT OF THE CITADEL WERE UNTAINTED BY THE FOULNESS OF THE EARTHBORN AND THE CORRUPTION OF THE AIR BENEATH THESE WERE THE GREAT CISTERNS CUT INTO THE ROCK OF THE FORT IN ORDER TO CATCH THE MEAGER RAINFALL WHICH WAS SENT UP THROUGH AN INTRICATE WATER SYSTEM IN ORDER TO IRRIGATE THE FRESH VEGETABLE GARDENS IN THE PALACE COURTS ONE OF THESE POOLS COULD ONLY BE ENTERED THROUGH

A SECRET PASSAGEWAY BEHIND WHICH WAS A CHAMBER FILLED WITH ARMS SUFFICIENT FOR TEN THOUSAND MEN IN ADDITION TO SUPPLIES OF UN-WROUGHT IRON BRASS AND LEAD THIS SECRET CHAMBER WAS SHELTERED BY NESTS OF SCORPI-ONS ONE OF WHICH HAD TAKEN IN ITS STINGER THE BLOOD OF CLEOPATRA QUEEN OF EGYPT WHO HAD INPORTUNED THE TRIUMVIR ANTONY HER LOVER TO SLAY HEROD AND CONFER UPON HER THE THRONE OF JUDEA

CHAPTER XI — THE NEED FOR PENETRATION

i

Fourteen hundred feet high, Masada dominated the surrounding canyons and moonlike craters. Below lay the caravan route from Arabia going north to Syria and west toward Jaffa and the Mediterranean Sea. Though legend insisted that it was this dolomite rock mountain where David hid from Saul, it was only centuries later under King Herod that it was inhabited and converted into an impregnable citadel now garrisoned by two hundred Roman legionnaires, who guarded this most southern outpost of the Roman Empire in Asia.

Despite his military training, Joseph felt as exhausted as he had on that first trek with Eleazar thirteen years earlier, and found himself drinking too often from his gourd. It was dark when they reached the foot of Masada. Most of the men split off and moved toward the eastern slope, while Eleazar, Joseph and four others turned down the wadi cutting along the north side of the fortress. Eleazar had not spoken a word all day.

Eleazar ben Yair was born among the dead. His grandfather, an owner of pomegranate groves near Cabul in the Galilee, had been dispossessed by the Romans from his ancestral lands for sheltering a handful of Jewish brigands. Instead of drifting south to Jerusalem and becoming a beggar on the overcrowded streets of the captial as most did, he took to the hills around Jotapata with his retainers and other ousted farmers, and trained them into zealous fighters. They became notorious for their raids against the Romanizing Jewish nobility and the occupying forces of the XIIth Legion. Like his Maccabee namesake, Judah the Galilean swore his men upon the scroll of the Torah and the short daggers that they had all used to prune their groves and vines to the oath: NO KING BUT GOD, thus founding the Sicari movement.

After a long period of successful hit-and-run operations throughout the country, Judah was ambushed in the Judean Wilderness by Syrian auxiliaries and was compelled to retreat to Masada where to his surprise, instead of finding friendly Essenes, he was met by a regiment of Roman regulars on escort duty to Tiberius Alexander, the then Procurator of Judea, resting there for the night. The next day the local Essenes returned to find Judah, his son-in-law Yair and his daughter dead, with the infant Eleazar at his mother's breast.

For the next fifteen years Eleazar was raised by Bannus at nearby

Ein Gedi. One day Eleazar came upon a legionnaire at a watering hole not far from the *Yahad*. Having decided that his hatred had incubated long enough, he broke the rule of the Essenes and killed the soldier with his bare hands. From that day on, Eleazar ben Yair prided himself that he had slain at least one Roman for every day he himself had lived.

ii

For two days they hid in a cave in the wadi and waited, Joseph assumed, for reinforcements. Twice daily Eleazar handed out a handful of carob and a few black olives. On the third afternoon, when the others lay dozing, Joseph was attracted by a light reflected on the cave wall. Eleazar had seen it too and immediately signalled back with a piece of mica on to the embrasure high up on the west wall of the fortress where Joseph figured the synagogue stood.

"What's all that?" asked Joseph.

"Our people. Up in the fort."

"But I was told that they abandoned it last week, after the fighting in Jerusalem."

"Not *our* people. They've lived there for two hundred years," said Eleazar, pointing with the withered blue nail of his thumb up at the eastern section of the wall. "Over by the great *mikva*."

"And the Romans trust them?"

"Everyone trusts the Essenes," answered Eleazar, smiling or sneering, Joseph could not tell which.

"That was a signal?"

"To take Masada."

"Just like that."

With the same piece of mica, Eleazar sketched an outline of the fortress. "Simple. Market day is Tuesday. Tomorrow. Before dawn our men come up the snake path to the east, which is our usual way in. Here." He made a mark. "Where the *Yahad* is. The Roman trust our people from Ein Gedi as well. They know our custom to pray at dawn. As always our men go directly to the synagogue over here." He tapped the mica on the opposite end of the diagram, and Joseph looked up at the wall in the fading light.

"Only this time," Eleazar kept tapping, "bar Giora and his men are with the others. They quickly occupy the storehouses, the quarry, the synagogue, cutting off the north section of the compound. At which point we meet and take the rest of the fort."

Bannus must have divined that bar Giora would join Eleazar in taking Masada. In giving Joseph the forbidden scroll, he was in effect approving the plan to nullify the union of the two chieftains, knowing that if Herod's arms cache existed, the two men would quarrel over its possession.

"How did bar Giora get into Masada?" asked Joseph, checking that the scroll was still tucked beneath his tunic.

"Last night, from Beersheba. He joined our people in meditation, which is also nothing strange to the Roman up there."

"How many men do you have in the fort?"

"Maybe thirty. Plus those we sent up the snake path coming for the market, and the six of us."

"Against two hundred seasoned legionnaires?"

"About the right odds to make it interesting. That's why I brought you along. Once we take the central area, the guards manning the walls will be neutralized."

"Neutralized? A Roman fort is organized with reserves in each of its parts. Everyone of those thirty-eight towers along the wall is a fortress in itself. Besides, Larcius Lepidus never surrenders."

"He already has," said Eleazar, raising the piece of mica and flashing it across the wadi. A spot of light shimmered upon a hole in the cliff halfway up toward where Herod had built a small palace. It was a similar cave to the one where Eleazar and Joseph had once been washed into by the flash flood and where the eagle and the python had fought. "As soon as it's dark, our people will let down ropes for us to climb into those cisterns below the palace. Up there, on those walls, we begin the defense of Jerusalem."

It was exactly the spot described in the *Wars of The Sons of Light Against The Sons of Darkness.*

iii

They waited for the night to fall. Joseph kept walking to the edge of the cave and coming back, always meeting Eleazar's gaze. After three days together they had exchanged few words. Eleazar spoke only when absolutely necessary. Even as youths, when they played games, which was what they were doing now, thought Joseph, he had wondered if Eleazar truly believed in the rule of the Essenes or whether his extremism stemmed from his love for trial and adventure. He had always preferred to learn by discovery, while Joseph's greatest pleasure was still in observing others. Maybe that was what had brought him back to these peculiar Jews who endured mountains and ate flowers and talked to God through the rays of the sun.

At a young age, Joseph had discovered that if he was not a coward, he had a cautious respect for the many ways his imagination ascribed to dying. Dare and challenge became confused in his mind with the knot in his bowels and the itch he always felt on his nape during moments of tension. To suppress these he had set a false foundation to his character, imposing upon himself the facade of a man who feared nothing. Because of this the tests he endured were often exhausting, causing him to collapse in a fever which would exonorate his failures. Thus, for him courage became twisted with cunning, making him prefer as heroes men like David who chose to dance in the shelter of other's sacrifices rather than like Saul, to fall upon his own sword.

He sweated. He caught the intense eyes and fanatic cheekbones that followed his pacing. Eleazar's face resembled Mati's, and his square frame reminded him of Titus.

Tonight, thought Joseph, he will try to defeat me.

As he watched the wadi fill with darkness, an incident came back to him which emphasized this fear, and now he wished he could change the ending.

Eleazar and he had been sent by Bannus on retreat beyond an oasis called Ein Avdat in order to seek revelation. They were to spend a month eating only what grew naturally, praying and meditating without squandering time on survival. Going south they passed innumerable natural stone fenced mesas that looked like measured off graves, and when they reached the crater called Makhtesh Ha-gadol, Eleazar dashed up the steep Nubian sandstone slope and by the time Joseph followed, his companion had already raced down into the cavity formed aeons ago by the earth's hesitation and where it had devoured itself in its own lava. The sun scorched the air, drawing out of the desert a hot wind that howled ceaselessly. All around them piles of stones shimmered like resurrected dead. The razorback, circular ridge where Joseph stood rose like a wall and the cairns spaced about it were magnified into turrets. He felt himself a conqueror gazing down from a cemetery upon a burnt out city with Eleazar its last survivor.

Eleazar climbed out of the crater and held up two square, black stones. He pushed one under Joseph's nose. "Flint," he shouted above the wind. "God's gift to sinners."

They had followed the dry riverbed of Zin through an inhabited oasis where the people lived off goat herds and a little terrace farming. The villagers were gathering their produce to take to Avdat for marketing and were busy loading sacks of fruit and wheat over camels and donkeys which were linked together by colorfully embroidered twine. A few goats, their bells tinkling impatiently, skipped nervously at the head of the caravan. Joseph and Eleazar watched two men press an immense stone hammer into a trough filled with olives. A third man filled the oil that dripped from the drain into two jugs. He tied one on each side of an ox, then slapped its rump making it join the other beasts. Joseph told Eleazar that he had read about Avdat; that it was a city filled with beautiful buildings and statues. Eleazar told him that the Nabateans were uncircumcised and that going there was sinful.

The boys drew close to a group of herdsmen in sleeveless sheepskin jackets, and to some camel drivers seated in a circle and partaking of a meal before departing. Their fingers were greasy and they washed them by squeezing grapes between their palms. A girl jumped into the circle and began to sway from side to side to the clapping of the men's hands. She then drew two smouldering twigs from the fire and holding them like horns to her head, she leaped out of the circle and danced around the boys, her bracelets clicking. The next thing Joseph saw was Eleazar dancing after her, holding on to one edge of a handkerchief she held out as she drew him toward a gully.

Before running after Eleazar and the girl, Joseph snatched a few olives lying in the dirt and stuffed them into his pouch. He came to a pond which was larger than the pools at Ein Gedi and had narrow trenches that flowed with muddy water, irrigating the nearby rows of pomegranate bushes and gnarled vines whose melons weighed them to the ground. A palm stood in the middle of the pond with clusters of dates, like beetles clinging to its trunk. The girl and Eleazar lay in one of the trenches beneath a tan goat, each with a teat in his mouth, pressing the udders as they sucked out the milk.

The girl rose and pointed up the gully made of sharp ledged layers that rose on each side and from which short horned ibexes looked down upon them. "Here," she said. "Show it to me here."

Eleazar hesitated before raising his robe and tucking it into his belt. Then he plunged into the pond. Looking up at the sun in mid sky, Joseph understood that it was time for bathing. He slid into the water after Eleazar.

An ibex approached the opposite side of the pond and munched weeds and drank water at the same time. The girl sat on a rock overlooking the pond and watched. "You bathe with your clothes on?" she asked.

"And you?" called Joseph.

"They never bathe," said Eleazar, climbing out and walking toward the fruit bushes.

At the sound of a splash, Joseph turned and saw the ibex, one leg raised in anticipation, its head cocked to one side. Ripples faded at the edge of the pond. Joseph called to Eleazar who was staring into the sun. The girl was gone.

Joseph dived into the pond and swam below the roots of boulders that reminded him of the tunnels he and his younger brother traversed beneath the city of Jerusalem. Pink pebbles sparkled, the same color as the girl's eyes. He shot up out of breath, panting. "She's disappeared." Then he heard a giggle and he saw the glistening curly hair of the girl among the papyrus reeds further up the gully.

The girl looked beyond Joseph to Eleazar. "Tell him I want his stone."

For a moment Joseph didn't understand. "What stone?"

"His. The black one that smells of fire."

"Here's mine," said Joseph, digging out the stone Eleazar had given him from the crater.

Eleazar came and stood before the reeds. He took out the other stone and held it up. The girl backed deeper into the papyrus reeds. Then, as if hypnotized by the stone, she came forward scattering a cloud of red and black birds with white tipped wings high up the gully. She waded through the rushes, her hands holding one of the two twigs which now smouldered with green smoke. Unlike the boys she had plunged into the pond robeless.

Joseph stood bewitched, while Eleazar instinctively brought two fingers in a V to his eyes to cover her shame.

"Give me the stone!" she demanded.

With his free hand, Eleazar tossed the black igneous stone into the water. Instantly Joseph dived in again and fetched it. When he surfaced he saw Eleazar, eyes still covered, swaying as the girl waved the twig under his nose. "Breathe deeply," she said. "Breathe as deep as you can, then swallow. She then reached down and grabbed the stone Joseph held up to her. She knelt beside Eleazar who now opened his eyes.

"He was afraid to go down into the *Makhtesh*," Eleazar giggled, the corners of his mouth hinged with green spit.

"Anyway, what's the difference between one stone and another?" called Joseph.

The girl cupped her hands beneath her breasts in order to give them more fullness. "His is holy," she said softly. "The four corners make it holy."

Joseph knew nothing of Nabatean stone worship. He watched with amazement as the girl ran her green stained tongue, like a priest before sacrifice, along the edges of the stone. Then handing it to Eleazar, she guided his hand down making him force the sharpest edge between her legs. Blood trickled down her thighs and she fell back upon a patch of grass pulling him on to her. "Nabatean honey," she whispered. "Made for dancing with the god."

"Serpents," cried Joseph. "The crater was filled with millions of scorpions and serpents!"

But they no longer heard him.

CHAPTER XII — THE CONQUEST OF MASADA

Darkness fell. Only by the sound of the breathing around him did Joseph remember that he was now in a cave opposite Masada. He was still thinking how the Nabatean witch girl would not dance with him after she had finished with Eleazar, when he heard pebbles falling into the wadi.

"The ropes are down," Eleazar whispered, "Follow me!"

Outside the stars gave shape to the men and the mountain. They found the ropes dangling stiff and hairy. After yanking a few, Joseph chose the one that hung beside a young Essene whom he remembered as one of the acolytes from Ein Gedi. On his other side, Eleazar was running his hands up and down his rope. He told them that the ascent shouldn't take too long but warned them to pace the climb without pausing unnecessarily. He pointed out that there were many crags and crevices that they might utilize as steps. All Joseph could make out was a tumescent protrusion about five feet above him. The cliff was sheer, going straight up to the stars.

As an infantry cadet, he had been trained for forced marches, climbing and descending all kinds of obstacles. He had borne these trials well until it came to hauling himself up a free hanging rope seventy-five feet long, using only his hands. He managed to make it about half way up when he lost his grip, sliding down and burning his fingers badly. Finally he had bribed Metilius to take the test for him, the payment being a night with Joseph's Jewish orderly.

Joseph touched the damp wall with his hand and saw that it was slippery. Even with the use of his feet and resting along the way, it would be difficult to climb the four hundred feet to the cisterns of King Herod. He heard the scraping boots of the men who had already begun their ascent. Hanging with his full weight from his rope, he tugged at it once more, then taking a deep breath, he began to climb up to Masada. His throat felt as if he had swallowed a ball of thistles.

Fearing that he might lose the others, he began to pull himself up too quickly. He felt secure beside Eleazar and tried to keep pace with him, but soon it took all his energies just to raise one hand. After what he estimated as a long enough spell, he found a crevice with his toe and half rested. When he looked down, he was surprised that he was barely twenty feet from the ground. He sweated and was breathless. At the academy they had warned them always to save enough energy for the descent which could be as hazardous as the ascent. Eleazar never briefed them about failure.

A tug on his rope from above spurred him on and he moved more steadily hand over hand. He breathed more evenly, but soon his fingers went numb. One foot slipped and his body jerked, causing a pain to shoot across his shoulders. His sense of gravity became confused and he thought if he could only float on his back and rest awhile, it would all be so easy. Again someone tugged on his rope.

He found a footing in a crag and the blood came buzzing back to his fingers. When he raised his gourd for a drink, his foot slipped. The stars flashed below him and he thought he was tumbling. He gasped with relief when he realized that he had glimpsed a reflection of the sky in the waters of the Dead Sea.

Someone passed him on his right and, encouraged by not being last, he moved on. At one point he could see four climbers and they seemed hanging from a gallows. He grasped the rope so tightly that for a moment he thought he was no longer holding it. The hairs on the rope stung like cactus burrs, but the fire in his armpits urged him higher.

He was afraid to look up or down. He became giddy, even sang to himself. He thought he was climbing a ladder to heaven and froze when he saw eyes glowing at him from each nook and crack in the wall. Slits slithered and the higher he climbed the louder did the breeze hiss. He remembered that the crevices held nests of vipers and he swung out in horror. The wall had become his enemy and his savior. He shivered and sweated, his fear confusing the day and night air of the desert. Then he saw four golden eggs catching the starlight. He reached out for one, and biting off the top, he sucked in the egg. He pulled himself higher.

To further distract himself, he thought of names of places he had visited, then of old classmates, of women he had loved; of the order of the Temple sacrifice. His mind slipped quickly to those whom he had once known and the different ways they had crawled to the grave. A favorite aunt came to mind, one he had long since forgotten, who baked cakes filled with poppy seeds that used to fill the spaces of his teeth. His father said that she had been a nervous child and that she had tumbled into the Valley of Hinom when the terrace of her house collapsed. Joseph wasn't sure now whether she had not been pushed by his uncle. Or maybe he was confusing all this with his mother.

He wondered if the Nabatean witch girl had by now grown fuller breasts, and if she still worshipped the stones of Petra; whether the mark of circumcision made a man of Metilius. He also remembered another stone god. He almost thought about Hagla.

The stars now drew into the shape of Lucia. They were lying beside the Pool of Israel and the pendent around his neck had fallen between her breasts.

Lucia said: "I want the medal."

He said: "It's the navel of the world."

Tiberius Alexander had given him the medal at a farewell banquet in his honor hosted by Joseph's father. In a few parting words, the late Procurator of Judea had warned the Jewish elders that "the stubbornness of your people, their insularity, strengthened by the certitude that there was only one God and that He was theirs, will be your destruction."

"Your Uncle Philo," said Matthias, "sees a reconciliation between Rome and Jerusalem."

"My uncle has never felt the weight of the sabre against his groin," said Tiberius Alexander.

Joseph had been proud that for the past two years a Jew had been the procurator, but Mati had insisted that he was a traitor. Joseph had slapped his brother and said that a Jew can never be a traitor.

Rome had been clever in appointing a former Jew to oversee Judea. The Jewish nobility trusted him, and in their innocence, he had robbed them of the little independence they still retained at the time. "Trust me," he would say, and then, through some ingenious slight of hand, he would take away a little more of their sovereignty. Only the Sicaris hated him and for that alone Matthias had continued to have confidence in the general. He had even brought forth his two sons that evening so that they might partake in the Roman custom of receiving a gift from the departing ruler of their country. Despite his hatred of the heathen, the seven year old Mati could not resist the tunic clasp with the emblem of the XIIth Legion on it, a legion that would one day kill him, which the general gave him and which at the time he commanded. Tiberius Alexander was about to pull off a second clasp when Joseph shook his head and pointed to the medal that hung from a chain around the procurator's neck.

For a moment the guests were silent. Then Tiberius nodded. "If you answer one question."

Joseph kept his fleshy lips tightly shut, his eyes never leaving the medal.

"Now then, where is the center of the universe?" asked the Procurator of Judea.

They all listened intently as if the nine year old's answer would settle the direction of history forever.

"Nikolas of Damascus says Delphi is the navel of our planet," said Joseph, tucking his long robe behind him and bringing one foot forward in what he imagined was a Ciceronian stance. "Raban Johanan ben Zakkai, however, teaches us that Jerusalem is *tabur haaretz.*"

"And you, little man, I asked you where *you* thought the center of the world was?"

Again all eyes centered on the curly headed lad. Defiantly, he raised his robe so that one hairless calf of his leg showed. "Rome is the nexus of the present," he declared, "the vortex where time and space join."

Before the astonished guests, Tiberius Alexander pulled the chain off his neck and hung it around that of young Joseph. The medal was the same one Lucia had tried to take from him while they made love beside the Pool of Israel.

As he climbed higher, Joseph still did not know why he answered as he had. Nor could he explain how an apostate had become his model to follow.

He remembered that it was the same Tiberius Alexander who had killed Eleazar's whole family just above them, on top of the Fortress of Masada. Joseph forgot now whether he was climbing or descending. Like a noose Tiberius Alexander's amulet hung about his neck. Hanging men, he was once told, stiffen all over before they die, and as if in verification of his doom, he felt himself in erection.

Like a spider on a pin, he kicked, trying to regain the security of the wall. Desperately, he swung himself forward, clawing the cliff with one hand, and he held on. He prayed for a torrent to fall upon Jerusalem, gush down the wadi below him and raise him on the wings of its fury into the mouth of a whale.

A body fell past him. The idea that one of the others had failed cheered him on. Then it came to him — and slowly — how the man had fallen without uttering a sound.

"Eleazar," he cried, trying to remember on which side of him his friend had been. He kept incanting his name, hoping in this way to be able to hear the silence of Eleazar's scream.

In his many visions, Joseph had once seen how Eleazar would die. Against a wall. His feet stretched stiffly before him. Eyes at the sun. Holding a dagger smeared with his children's blood. And he, Joseph, inciting him to plunge it into himself because he had thus already prophesied. *DA!* In another world a jackal howled.

"Shut up and give me your arm." A hand hauled him into a cistern, and by its dryness he knew it was Eleazar's. Joseph's fingers were wet with blood.

"Three," said Eleazar, taking down a torch from a crevice in the wall and holding it diagonally as he counted those who had climbed safely. "Two more than I expected."

Joseph tossed a stone into the cistern which made a splashing sound. "It's filled with the late spring rains. We'll have to swim."

"Swim? There's a stairway leading up to the palace," said one of the other men.

Joseph walked to the edge of the cistern. The stars were fading. "To the arms chamber," he said pointing at the water.

"What arms chamber?" Eleazar asked.

"Why we came."

"Masada. We came here to take Masada."

"With Simon bar Giora?" Joseph let slip out slyly. "You know that the *Sanhedrin* has appointed him commander of the whole Negev?" He wiped the blood off his hands on a piece of silk he carried inside his tunic. "And that includes Masada."

"The flowers and the birds and the people of the Negev have nothing in common with Masada," said Eleazar. "Nor does the taste of its waters."

It was getting light and Joseph saw his shadow reflected in the cistern waters. "He'll never let you keep it," he warned. Eleazar was occupied with coiling the ropes they had used in the ascent and didn't answer.

"He'll let you bleed for it," insisted Joseph. "Then take it away from you or even destroy it. I have the same problem facing me in the north with John of Gishhalav."

"The Galilee is of no interest to me. Neither is the Negev."

"Be logical for once. Disunity now can destroy our cause."

"It's you all who have lost the logic. Besides our causes are different."

"Today there is only one cause: survival. Bar Giora like John would rather fight other Jews outside their clans than Rome."

One of the men signalled Eleazar, who had by now made three nooses out of the ropes.

"According to Raban Johanan ben Zakkai, you've signed a treaty with bar Giora and John," said Joseph. "They'll let your men die and take credit for taking the fortress."

This time Eleazar really sneered. "Dying," he said, "is the same as winning."

Eleazar and one other man disappeared up the stone stairway, while a third followed slowly behind. A grace of starlings floated out across the wadi searching the dawn. Joseph wondered how long he would have to hold his breath under water.

Plunging feet first into the cistern, then tumbling backwards, he sank to the bottom. The light was eerie and distorted, the stones making them appear as large as those of Jerusalem's walls. He could discern the mosaics of a deer and a lion, both standing on their hind legs and guarding a russet medallion. THE OPENING IS ON THE SIXTH POINT OF THE OCTAGONAL STAR, Joseph's mind had recorded from Bannus' manuscript. He counted from the left letting his fingers grope along the wall.

No opening. His chest tightened. Bubbles rose above him like the rope he had so desperately clung to on his ascent to the fortress. He heard something splash behind him and he panicked. Perhaps some mysterious creature guarded these waters? A cramp knotted his stomach, and he let out his breath causing him to surface like a corpse.

Holding to the edge of the cistern, he looked out through the opening and saw clouds expanding over the Dead Sea. When he went down a second time, he followed a streak of light that broke through a crevice in the wall. He grasped a stone and pried it loose, then breast stroked through the opening. Behind him something gurgled. He let out his breath and surfaced, only to bump his head against a ceiling. The new chamber he had entered was filled to the top with water. He was sure he had swallowed his tongue.

A moment later he stood in a third chamber, having been sucked through a hole in the ceiling. He stood knee deep in water, and coughed. Blood trickled from his nostrils. He dragged himself out of this pool and on to a stone landing. For a long while he lay there panting, thinking he was under the city of Jerusalem.

When he sat up, he saw piles of dates pressed into squares as large as bales of hay. Thousands of spears, lances, javelins and axes lined the walls. Swords bound like sheaves of wheat, and daggers as numerous as dragons' teeth covered the tiled floor. Bows and quivers filled with arrows stood in the corner of the chamber. The biggest surprise was the ballista machine and a dismantled catapult, including many stones stacked in small pyramids. Interspersed between casks of oil and wine lay sacks of lentils which had burst open. Joseph rose and walked about slowly, running his fingers through meal and bushels laden with grain. Clay pipes encircled the floor of the great chamber. There were no scorpions.

Herod's caldarium, thought Joseph, eating a date which tasted like soured wine. He was already thinking how to get all these supplies out and up to the Galilee. Then he remembered Eleazar had told him that Larcius Lepidus had already surrendered.

He found a ladder tall enough to reach an aperture half way up one of the walls. Two Romans sprawled drunkenly in the next room, their necks bound with the climbing ropes. From here Joseph could see the whole compound and that the sky had turned a glowing orange.

"Sand storm below," said Niger, coming to meet Joseph.

"What are you doing here?"

"Silas had a feeling you'd need help. Half the men who came up with the Essenes are ours."

Joseph took a swig from his gourd. He was irritated that Niger had been sent to watch over him.

"Wind's been blowing for three days," said Niger with his usual exuberance. "It begins to drive you crazy."

Outside Joseph heard squeals and giggles intermingled with shouting and singing coming from the bathhouse which stood fifty yards away from the palace. Eleazar was waving from the rooftop to a group of Essenes who were rolling leather bound urns toward the bathhouse entrance.

"Roman officers," said Joseph. "They always bathe before roll call."

"And their women," added Niger, smiling.

Joseph helped Niger roll one of the urns. He was surprised how light it was, having assumed that it contained oil to fire the key postions of the Roman garrison. The orange haze and wind made caution unnecessary. Atop the walls of the fort a few guards somnambulantly patrolled the walls.

Just as they set the urn before the entrance, a nude figure approached and was about to address them when one of the Essenes, who had sneaked behind him, slit his throat with a dagger. The Roman, obviously late for his bath, walked on as if nothing had happened until he collapsed before the door. Steam filtered out of the bathhouse shaping genies as it was whisked up by the wind.

Niger untied one urn. Together with the Essene who had just killed the Roman officer, he tilted it over, at the same time pushing open the door. Hundreds of scorpions fell out, jumping and darting one over the other and into the bathhouse. They dumped the second urn at another entrance. Some of the scorpions climbed over the dead Roman. The missing scorpions, thought Joseph. Those mentioned in the scroll.

He followed Eleazar, who jumped off the roof and ran toward the west wall. At each tower a Roman guard with his head hacked off, his mouth drooling green, was smiling. Eleazar hurried ahead, making sure to lock each tower.

The synagogue still had no roof, and the marks Eleazar had scratched on the wall the day the eagle attacked were still clear. Sixty armed men waited while Simon bar Giora pared his toenails with his bloody scimitar. The Essenes prayed silently facing Jerusalem.

"This is a synagogue," said Joseph to bar Giora.

"The Romans fucked in it," said bar Giora without stopping.

Eleazar sipped from his water skin, then handed it to Joseph who drank a swallow before passing it on to Niger. "Up here, you must keep drinking," said Joseph. "The body dries quickly because of the salt in the air."

When the Essenes finished praying, their eyes greeted Eleazar. "The citadel," was all he said.

Bar Giora reached for the water skin and squeezed out a mouthful. He rinsed his mouth, then spat out the water, splashing some on Eleazar's sandals. "The snake path," he said. "It's the only way to get the arms out of the cistern. And I mean to have the whole lot."

Joseph realized that the splash and gurgling noise that had followed him beneath the cistern had been one of bar Giora's men.

"By the time the Nabatean honey wears off those heathen in the towers," continued bar Giora, "we'll be half way to Gaza where there's real fighting going on. The XVth under Titus Flavius is back again. Reinforced and cutting across our borders."

"The worst thing is to split our small force. If we break for the gate, the Romans will believe that we're merely raiders," suggested Joseph, agreeing for once with bar Giora. He would argue with him about the possession of the arms after they were out of Masada. "When they see us retreating without a fight, I doubt they'll even leave the shelter of their towers and that way we won't take any casualties." He did not add that neither would the Romans, which concerned him very much.

Eleazar didn't wait for Joseph to finish. He walked out, not even bothering to see who would join him.

"He's looking to die," said bar Giora. "Like all of them. He's always looking how to die. They're walking into a trap."

"Masada isn't worth it."

Simon bar Giora wiped his hand across his mustache. "For you, asshole. He's doing it just to dare you."

Joseph hurried out in confusion. He almost caught up with Eleazar, when he saw what Simon had meant about a trap. It happened that while they were waiting in the cave below the fort, that a small fire had broken out in part of the south citadel. The Roman commander of the base, having no other available quarters, had to move fifty men to an unused columbarium, also built by King Herod as a tomb for his non-Jewish mercenaries stationed here, and which faced the citadel. Joseph and the few men who had joined him stopped short when they saw that up ahead Eleazar and his Essenes had already been spotted by the Romans and were caught in a crossfire between the citadel and the columbarium. Unless bar Giora joined Joseph now and came to Eleazar's rescue, he and his small force would quickly be wiped out. Doing that would, however, convince the Romans that this was no ordinary raid and cause them to attack in full force.

"What's that villa out there, opposite the columbarium?" Joseph asked Niger.

"The Royal Dwelling. For guests."

"I mean who's there now?"

Niger hestitated. "Officers. Roman officers and their Nabatean whores."

Joseph nodded. If he could get into that villa, he might save them all from disaster. It would also be his chance to break the shaky compact between the two chieftains. "Follow me!" he ordered calmly and ran across the compound toward the villa. He felt sure he would succeed because he was improvising.

As he had hoped, the building was empty, the officers and their women all being in the showers. Clothes lay strewn in abandoned intimacy, and the acrid smells of fornication lingered above the odor of sand. In one corner stood a few standards of the Xth Legion.

"Aim at those embrasures facing the columbarium," commanded Joseph. "When I shout down to you, fire away." Then grabbing one of the standards and pulling off a white shawl from one of the Essenes who happened to be with them, he dashed up to the roof of the villa. He had just enough time to hang out the standard with the prayer shawl tied to it, when the screams began to rise from the bathhouse. The scorpions had begun their own attack.

From all corners of the fortress naked men and women hobbled and ran about howling and moaning. When the soldiers in the citadel and those in the columbarium saw their officers panicking, and then looked up at the roof of the villa and glimpsed their standard bound by a Jewish shawl, they became convinced that their forces had been routed. In ordered formation they marched out of the buildings, surrendering to the astonished Essenes with Eleazar who were already making peace with their Maker. For once Joseph felt that he had won a contest over his most formidable challenger.

The wind stopped suddenly, revealing two hundred Romans naked to their waists, seated in the center of the fort, their hands clasped beneath them. Behind them a long caravan of mules, brought up by Eleazar, was already loaded with the arms cache of King Herod and ready to move out. Bar Giora came up and challenged the Essenes in charge of the mules. His men circled the caravan.

"Those arms go with me," said Joseph. "For the northern campaign."

"You found them," said Simon. "Now you'll have to fight for them."

"You're spoiling our victory in your usual divisive way. Leaders such as John and you will make Rome victorious without her fighting at all."

"Like you at Shaar Hagai," taunted bar Giora.

"And you at Emmaus. And John at Caesarea. Sometimes I wonder about your true loyalities."

Simon's hand went to his scimitar. Joseph stepped back and saw that Eleazar was watching. Again he caught the flash of a dare in his friend's eyes.

"No king but God!' declared Simon.

"David was a king. So was Agrippa."

"And his daughter is a Roman's whore. From your family."

"My blood is pure. I can't say the same for yours." All the Jews about knew that Simon bar Giora was from a converted Idumean family which was what his name meant.

"The pure Jew doesn't exist," said Simon. "If he did he'd be like those shit smelling Arab whores sitting with those Romans."

"Some of us have ancient blood that's been civilized through service to God."

"Spoken like a true priest of Israel," said Simon picking his nose and wiping his finger on his burnoose.

"The unity of Israel rests in the House of Aaron."

"Horseshit. I'd rather have a hundred Sicaris then all your vain oblations and fat calves."

"We've had enough of your civil wars, your disobeying orders," said Joseph. "The *Sanhedrin* has ordered you south. Masada is Eleazar ben Yair's domain. These arms are mine and his."

Simon drew out his scimitar and half the men surrounding them did the same. The Romans looked on disinterestedly. As if they were already dead. Joseph signalled to Niger and immediately the other half of the men in burnooses stepped forward and drew out their swords. "These men are mine," said Joseph, and turning to Eleazar. "It's you now who must choose."

Eleazar shrugged. "All this matters little. God demands a simple place for those chosen to take his stand. *Maoz tzur yeshuati* — fortress rock of my salvation."

"You really believe that if Jerusalem fell, this rock, as you call it, would be worth defending? You think that the Romans, with their patience and power can't retake it if and when they wished?"

"The next conqueror of Masada, " said Eleazar, "will see me dead first."

Eleazar's bluntness shocked Joseph. Suddenly Bannus' phrase

became clear: *the impossibility of reaching divinity.* This was what the Essenes believed drove men to the perfection called God. And if for them the road to divinity passed through Armageddon and through there to the Messiah ben David, then their sacrifice meant human sacrifice, the final victory of man over matter. For them, then, the rebellion was not a choice but inevitable, and Eleazar being here at Masada meant a commitment not to survival but to national destruction. It was the peculiar cycle of Jewish history repeating itself, and which had to do exclusively with Jews and their Creator. Matthias, his ancient progenitor, father of the Maccabees, those earlier zealots against Greece, had in a similar moment in time raised the cry at Modin, *me l'Adonai elai — who for God, follow me!* The trouble was that Eleazar ben Yair's covenant was with the god of death. Joseph wondered now who really was the victor in their constant battle: he or Eleazar?

"And the arms?" asked Joseph.

Eleazar nodded to the caravan. "Yours," he said, turning his back on Simon. "All of them. For now."

"And the Romans?" asked Niger.

"They've formally surrendered," said Joseph, "respecting us as a recognized fighting force. We shall follow the law and allow them to rejoin their regular unit at Machaerus."

"What law?" demanded Simon bar Giora. "Ours says: 'Remember what the Amalekites did unto thee!' Destroyed our women and children and sick and maimed."

"Only men and whores," said Eleazar, passing the water skin to bar Giora. "That's all they've got."

"I've guaranteed them their lives," Joseph lied. "As a priest in Israel, I've given them my word."

"Then we'll take it back for you," said bar Giora, rinsing his mouth and this time squirting out water at Joseph's feet.

"They'll fight again later on," said Eleazar. It was his way of acknowledging Joseph's act at the villa. The fate of the Romans would have to be awarded to Simon bar Giora.

The Sicaris had meanwhile herded the Romans and the Nabatean whores along the east wall. Their limbs leaked with puss from the scorpion bites and some were still retching from the poison injected into their bodies. The smell of excrement and vomit would haunt Joseph for the next three years. He spotted a ranking officer and without letting the others see, he questioned the prisoner about Larcius Lepidus.

"Gone," said the officer. "The lady Lucia Paulina arranged his release."

Joseph had to move off before he could find out how, because the Sicaris were shoving the prisoners on to the wall of the fort overlooking the Dead Sea.

"When it's dark," said Joseph to Simon. "At least do it after dark."

"What's the difference?"

"So they don't see how deep the drop is. A man shouldn't die in fear."

The sun set slowly mitigating the struggle of the sands and the sea. Below, the anvil tongued peninsula faded into the waters that now rejected the color of the sky. There was darkness in the mountains. Joseph felt sure that if ever the Sons of Light would do battle with the Sons of Darkness, it would have to be up here.

Long after the second watch, Simon gave the order to push the Romans two at a time off the ramparts. The drop was so deep that half way down their screams were silenced.

Dawn rose. Across the horizon the Mountains of Moab discreetly appeared as a talon of vultures screeched down from the cliffs at the carrion splattered on the rocks below. Joseph found Eleazar standing on the ramparts. He had conquered this fortress in order to further isolate himself, knowing that whatever the outcome of the rebellion, victory was already his.

Part III
JERUSALEM

Thereupon the principle citizens assembled with the chief priests and the most notable Pharisees to deliberate on the position of affairs, now that they were faced with what seemed irreparable disaster.

Bellum Judaicum

CHAPTER XIII — YEAR ONE

Joseph returned to a jubilant Jerusalem. He was greeted with hosannas and hallelujahs, and declared GIBOR YISRAEL, Hero in Israel. Niger had exaggerated Joseph's part in the rout of the XIIth Legion, and the citizens welcomed their native son as a conqueror. Joseph did nothing to dispel these honors. Five thousand three hundred infantrymen, one fourth of the Fulminata, plus four hundred and eighty of its finest cavalry had been killed at Shaar Hagai. And then there was Masada.

Jerusalem celebrated for seven days and nights. Trumpets blared insistently across the hills and valleys as buglers of Bezetha called to pipers of the Ophel Quarter, all framed by timbrels and lyres of the Levites on the Temple Mount. And the mountains skipped like rams and the hills like lambs. The sea fled, once again; the waters of the Jordan trembled. And Jerusalem exalted, for there was light and gladness and honor throughout Judea.

He was pleased when the populace bowed as he passed, offering up kraters of wine and bowls of nuts and dates in his honor. Children stopped at their war games and ran to him with honeyed citrons made from the *Sukkot etrog*. The maidens of Jerusalem, robed in the colors of the sun, abandoned all modesty as they danced and swirled their skirts above their knees, kissing him while teasing the other fighters who were still adorned with Roman helmets and armor that they had plundered. And he smiled sadly at their innocence. He told no one of the message from Titus that awaited him.

Mati stood in the laver in the priests' readying room rinsing his feet. "I've been waiting for you," he said. "So have they all out there."

"Ben Zakkai is distraught. He believes the people are being tricked, fooled by the stupidity of that attack on Cestius Gallus and Masada. Vespasian will punish the XIIth Legion's cowardice and then he'll return here in a fury and avenge their shame. It's the Roman way."

"You were there," said Mati, stepping out of the laver without wiping his feet. "You've accepted the revolt."

"Its inevitability. Not its success."

"Less than a month ago, when you returned to Jerusalem, you told me that Rome, the whole empire was in turmoil. Rumors say it will be in a state of anarchy for a good year. That gives us time."

"Time for what? To destroy ourselves still further?"

"What if the chaos in Rome lasts longer than a year? Say two years?"

Joseph sighed. "We easterners always believe that time is on our side. We refuse to understand that unlike us the Roman army has its own momentum and can fight on despite the politics of the Palatine Hill. While Nero plotted Claudius' murder, half of Germany was conquered."

"This new emperor, Galba, what do you know about him?"

"The autumn flowers will outlive him."

"And who will replace him?"

"Vespasian maybe. It all depends."

"On whom?"

Joseph shrugged. "On the Roman Senate. On us."

"Rome no longer has anything to do with us."

The new assertiveness of his younger brother made him a stranger. Suddenly Joseph saw him dead. "But we have everything to do with Rome. Rome is the world."

Mati turned silent as he usually did when they argued.

"This so-called victory celebration, what happens after it?" asked Joseph.

"The *Sanhedrin* has divided the country into six districts, in the same fashion as Gobinus did a hundred years ago, with a general over each whose job will be to fortify his area and recruit and train troops for the coming war with Rome. Silas has been appointed commander of all forces. I am his adjutant."

"Merely a rumor."

"Confirmed," said Mati. "By the *Sanhedrin*."

"You're assuming the whole country is ready to fight."

"After Shaar Hagai and Masada, bar Giora, ben Yair and you left them no choice."

Joseph could not help but be flattered to be included among the two commanders most feared by Rome. The chorus of thousands singing psalms of thanksgiving that rose from outside did not allow him to dare think of the true consequences of his brother's words.

"Bar Giora has been named commander of the south," continued Mati. "Including Gaza."

"A good way to keep him away from Jerusalem."

"You have been given the two Galilees plus the city of Gamala."

"A good way to keep *me* away from Jerusalem." Despite his insinuation Joseph saw immediately how his new appointment, now officially confirmed, fitted well with Titus' plan. The command of the north included Jotapata. "And Eleazar ben Yair?" asked Joseph.

"John the Essene, his second in command, has been given charge over the Valley of Ayalon and Jaffa. To keep the coast open to Jerusalem."

So Bannus had signalled to raise the sword and sing hallelujah. The wise Essene had offered his own son John to join the full rebellion. Or was it rather as ben Zakkai had claimed: Bannus' way of teaching them all how to die?

The trumpets sounded in the Court of the Israelites. "It's time to go," said Mati. "The people are waiting."

Outside Joseph met Silas, the new *Aluf* of Judea. They had to struggle through the throng who crowded around them in order to kiss the hems of their garments. The Temple compound was so crowded that even the burnt porticoes and roofs of the colonnades were dangerously packed with people. A flame simmered upon the Great Altar where the duty priests, having no room below, lined the ramp as they waited to assist at the sacrifice. By the shadow of the post on the Antonia, Joseph saw that it was beyond the time for the noon offering. He saw Mati climb up to the altar, the slaughtering implement in its leather case under his arm. Again he wondered what special occasion was being celebrated.

Niger embraced him at the Nicanor Gate. Joseph bowed to the President of the *Sanhedrin,* and other dignitaries who stood in a semicircle around him. Johanan ben Zakkai sat beneath the arch and leaned somberly on his cane. He ignored Joseph's nod as his lips munched on a prayer. In wood racks on each side of the gate stood the captured standards of the Fulminata Legion.

When Joseph appeared beneath the arch, the multitude roared:

Ahm Yisrael hai!
The nation of Israel lives!

Joseph waved to them with both his hands. Silas stepped forward and waited for silence.

"The eternity of Israel never lies!," declared the new commander. "On this third day of *Marheshvan,* by the grace of the Holy Name, blessed be He, in the holiest of cities, in the place where He commanded —" his voice droned in the same tone he had used a moment ago while speaking to Joseph. "By the powers vested in me as *Aluf Yisrael,* I declare *HERUT YISRAEL!*"

The people broke into wild cheers, swaying back and forth in their attempt to jump and dance. Over and over they chanted: *H-E-R-U-T Y-I-S-R-A-E-L!*

Silas stared down at the joyous multitude. He did not smile. Behind him, up on the altar, Mati drew the slaughtering implement across his tongue, then slit the throat of a red, unblemished bullock as Niger sounded one blast on the black, fluted ram's horn. At the blast of the *shofar,* Silas dipped his hands into an urn, and raising them above his head, declared: *Bet Yaakov lekhu ve-nelkha!* House of Jacob come let us go!'' and flung fistfuls of coins over the heads of the throng, then led a mass procession through the bronze gates toward the Great Altar.

The people surged up the marble steps circling Joseph and the others, dancing arm in arm around them. As when Metilius was circumcised, Joseph lost his head. His hands rose unwillingly and his fingers snapped as he intoned in a high, priestly chant.

> This is the day the Lord made;
> Let us rise and rejoice.

Then leaping into the air, he clicked his bare feet twice, swirling around.

> *Hodu l'Adonai ki tov* —
> Praised be the Lord for He is good.

And the multitude bowed their heads and responded.

> *Ki l'olam hasdoh* —
> His mercy forever and ever.

Joseph was jostled as the people shoved toward the altar. Between his toes he felt one of the coins Silas had tossed out. He picked it up and turned it over and over in his fingers. Its newness brought him back to sanity. One side was engraved with a *lulav* palm branch, symbol of the *Sukkot* festival, and with the words SHEKEL YISRAEL. The other was inscribed, *Shana Rishona L'herut Yehudah* —Year One to the Liberation of Judea. He read it as an epitaph.

CHAPTER XIV — ROOTS OF THE CITY

Before he entered the cave under the Ginnot Gate in the Outer Wall, Joseph stopped to rinse his face with the water trickling down from above. The deeper he moved under the city, the more filled he became with premonitions of failure. Joseph hated penetrating surfaces.

Jerusalem had been built on the ruins of earlier cities on the same site through whose subterranean foundations and buried streets King David had once infiltrated when he conquered it from the Jebusites and declared it the capital of Israel. Later, the last of his ruling progeny had tried to escape through its labyrinthine tunnels from the rampaging hordes of Nebuchadnezzar, first destroyer of the City of God.

Bats hung motionless from the leaking roots of the city. Small grooves cut into the elephantine walls channeled the waters into puddles making Joseph's sandals squeak. In places the ceiling was so low that he had to crouch nearly to the ground in order to move forward.

He passed through numerous chambers, some glistening with aquamarine limestone, others hung with stalactites. Finally he had to crawl through an opening which widened into a large grotto ending at a pool twenty feet wide. He waded across the sludge that reached to his waist. The water had the same sweet smell of the Tiber below the Mulvian Bridge in Rome. Not till he stood on the opposite side of the pool did he recognize the squat figure of Titus Flavius sitting on a shelf that stuck out of the wall, his bowed legs swinging in time to the blood dripping off the ceiling.

"Through blood and fire Judah fell. Through blood and fire it shall rise again," quoted Titus. "You think so?"

A shaft of light shot down upon Joseph through a small aperture at the top of the grotto. At that moment he was certain that no matter what he did, no matter what all the Jews did in Judea and elsewhere, the fate of their people lay in the hands of this man who looked more like a porter from Thessalonika than a legate commanding a Roman legion.

"Rising and falling," said Joseph, "occupy the same time and space. The action is merely relative. Besides, the blood trickling down is from the morning sacrifice. We're directly below the Temple's drainage system. All the altars are above us."

"So you whipped Cestius," said Titus, bending over and scratching his toes through his sandals.

"The rains did."

"Or maybe Lucia?"

"Or you. You never entered Jerusalem."

Titus chuckled. He picked up a chip of limestone and drew some scratches on the wall behind him. "It wasn't worthwhile. Not at the moment."

"The people think they've defeated Rome. They've declared their independence. The revolt will spread."

"Further than you realize. To Rome. Nero is dead by his own hand."

"I know."

"Galba has been elected Emperor."

"So the west wins again. And your plan?"

"The time and place were wrong. That's why I didn't come to Jerusalem."

Joseph sat beside Titus. Something in the Roman nature made them less than honest. Calculating. He remembered Lucia's strange revelation to him at Shaar Hagai about her other loyalties even in Rome. Cestius Gallus had said she was an enigma. Ambiguous in passion. "Calculating." Titus too, like Lucia Paulina, thought Joseph, would control the destiny of his people.

"I've come to recruit you," said Titus. "In preparation for the right time. It's you who have to choose the right place."

"Maybe I already did?"

"Shaar Hagai was superfluous."

"I meant Masada."

"Superfluous. Like Galba, the Senate's compromise between Vitellius and my father. I'm here to see that their next choice is more permanent. That was why I joined Cestius."

"You never left Hebron."

"I did. My legion did not. I joined the route at Shaar Hagai. Got them through the pass, in fact."

Joseph nodded. "I thought it was you. But what has all this got to do with Judea?"

"I'm here to show you how to help us win the crown."

"Us?"

"We Flavians, and for you a free Judea under Queen Berenice." Titus signalled one of his aides standing in the shadow of a torch and he approached carrying a large map of Judea. "Flavius Vespasian is disembarking in the north. I join him at Acre. He needs one clear victory to convince the Senate that he has the qualities of an emperor. You're going to give it to him."

"I told you I won't kill Jews."

"Romans." Titus spread the map. "Choose a spot in this radius," and he drew a circle with a stylo. "You have till spring to build your forces so that they're worthy of fighting us."

"What legions support you?"

"For the moment my Apollonaire, Larcius Lepidus' Tenth —"

"What's left of it."

"Maybe the Twenty-Two," continued Titus ignoring Joseph's remark.

"Against a force like that, there won't be any victory but a rout. What am I supposed to use for arms?"

"Cestius Gallus left you plenty. It was on my advice that he abandoned his weaponry and saved men." Without a blink, Titus added. "Then there are those of Masada."

Joseph would not admit that the latter were still not under his control. "Still only half of your logistics."

"You know the terrain. That makes the other half."

"Other than when I was a cadet at the academy at Antioch, I've never been north of Tiberias. Besides, only here in Jerusalem, can your father win laurels worthy of emperorship."

Titus shook his head slowly. "Jerusalem's out. Too bloody. I know what this city means to you Jews."

"What you're suggesting then," said Joseph, "is a limited rebellion."

"And suppression. Once Vespasian is emperor, Jerusalem has nothing to fear."

"You guarantee that?"

"In a conspiracy nothing is ever guaranteed. You should know that."

A gambit such as Titus was suggesting was filled with hazards. Once an action was instituted, certainly between nations of unequal power, unwritten commitments suddenly turned into coercion. What Titus was demanding of him was to write the future of his people from the perspective of the Palatine Hill instead of the Temple Mount. Where, for example, would Judea be once Titus won and then refused to give back the independence taken from her by that same Rome sixty years earlier?

"In the matter of the Jews nothing can ever be guaranteed either," said Joseph.

"You can fight as hard as you wish," said Titus. "It will be your blood."

"And if we win?"

Titus laughed. "Then maybe the Senate will elect you Emperor of Rome."

Joseph tossed a stone into the pool whose water had turned rust color. "The Levites must be washing the altar."

Titus bent over the map. He slapped it with the back of his hand.

"Choose your battleground."

The largest city within the circumference of the circle Titus had drawn was the capital of the Galilee and known for its treachery. "Zippori," said Joseph. "Big enough to win glory for both of us."

"Zippori's out. We've made commitments to her."

"The only other city in this circle worthy of three Roman legions is Acre. You have that already."

"Any place. Time is more essential than the name. One quick overwhelming victory will win us the support of the other legates in the east who are fence-sitting, and in that way secure a political base for us in the Senate against Vitellius and the west."

Joseph shook his head. "These others are villages. Unknown worthless villages."

"So was Actium once. So was Marathon. Together we'll make one of them famous."

Joseph leaned closer to the map and searched more carefully. He saw Cabul, one of the most beautiful cities in western Galilee until Cestius Gallus had sacked it on his way down to Jerusalem. Then he recognized a name familiar from biblical days, a city built by Joshua. "Here!" declared Joseph. "I'll make my stand at Jotapata."

Part IV
JOTAPATA

Is life so dear to you,
Josephus, that you can
endure to see the light
of slavery?

Bellum Judaicum —
Josephus

CHAPTER XV — CHIEFTAINS OF THE GALILEE

It was late autumn when Joseph and Niger, his deputy, together with a battalion of his retainers journeyed north to take command of the Galilee. Except for winters spent in Tiberias as a child and his year as a cadet at the military academy in Antioch, Joseph never travelled north. He did not like the Galileans who, like the Idumeans in the south, had been converted by the Maccabean conquerors a century earlier. The fanatic loyalty to their new faith had made them accept unquestionably the tenents of the Sicaris. As a priest of the first order, Joseph always conceived of these northerners as barbarians whose ancestors, including his wife's, had forsaken the City of God for the golden calves of Dan and Bethel. In their turn the Galileans distrusted the Judeans, feeling inferior to their ancient brethren who had kept the Covenant, while they had sinned and fallen upon evil ways in the eyes of the Lord. No doubt their new piety and patriotism was a consolation for their renegade history.

Since the defeat of Cestius Gallus and the conquest of Masada, the country had found a new unity. Jews had taken control over cities in which they held the majority and had driven out whatever Roman and Syrian garrisons were there, together with the gentile population, some of whom had been living in the country since the days of Alexander the Great. Within a week after he had left Masada, Simon bar Giora had occupied Jaffa and Ashkelon, thus giving Judea a strong southern line of defense running from the Dead Sea to the Mediterranean coast and blocking any quick Roman thrust against Jerusalem at least till spring. Joseph's task was to do the same in the north.

News from abroad was not so joyous. In Alexandria riots had broken out and the Syrians and Greeks of the city rampaged through the Delta Quarter where more than a million Jews lived. Tiberius Alexander, the apostate Governor of Egypt, refused to allow the Jews to defend themselves and thousands were slaughtered. In Rome, tensions mounted against the Jewish citizens after news arrived of Shaar Hagai and Masada. There, however, the Praetorian Guard, knowing that one disorder led to another and that there was enough anxiety already in the capital over the appointment of Galba as emperor, protected the Jews. To show their appreciation, many Jews reaffirmed their loyalty to Nero's successor. Nevertheless there were those who chose to support their brothers and secretly set sail for Judea to join the revolt. At Shaar Hagai Lucia had said to Joseph: "Whatever happens in Judea must affect the Jews throughout the Empire."

To gain support in the north, Joseph advanced slowly like a conquering hero. The arms he had been awarded at Masada impressed the local warlords who quickly threw their support behind him. Wherever he stopped he performed the rites of sacrifice, so that like his forefathers, the Maccabees, he was greeted like a king.

The winter grasses were already wavering in the cold sun when he approached the great Plain of Jezreel. Beyond, the mountains of Galilee were half covered with snow. Here was the north country where seasons had difference. Through the Valley, which divided the country from the arid south, armies had marched since the beginning of War: north, south, east and soon, he knew, from the west. To his left loomed the camel humped hills of Megiddo where history lay buried in its own rubble. He glimpsed the elevation of Moreh where Gideon had defeated the Midianites, and to the east Mount Gilboa where Saul and his sons died upon their own swords rather than surrender to the Philistines. Ahead, like a gigantic turtle's back, stood Mount Tabor from on top of which Deborah marked the end of the Canaanite rule over the land. And Joseph felt secure in the patrimony of his people.

Outside his tent he picked dates off a cluster on a branch. He squeezed the stone out of the fruit and slid the meat into his mouth. Unlike Jerusalem's they were thick skinned and cloying. He washed their sweetness down with milk so cold that it made his teeth ache.

He thought of Lucia. Had she returned to Cestius Gallus in his defeat? Or had she gone back to The Golan to serve Queen Berenice? And how had she secured the release of Larcius Lepidus from Masada? As always whenever he was reminded of her and the questions she aroused, the answers he evolved never failed to surprise him. He was sure that Lucia was in Acre with Titus where he and his father, Vespasian, were gathering for battle against him. No one but Raban Johanan ben Zakkai, President of the *Sanhedrin,* knew that the only war Joseph would give the Flavians would be a victory which they needed to achieve hegemony over the Roman Empire. And only Joseph knew that Lucia Paulina would make war against them all.

To organize his forces, Joseph called a council of Galilee chieftains to Tarichea, on the southern end of Lake Gennesaret, the only city in the region to accept his credentials as the new commander of the north. Together with Niger and Hanan ben Zevi, the mayor, he sat in the synagogue on the lake's shore and contemplated the half wild chieftains who sat facing him on a long bench. A few candles stuck in the earth floor lit the room whose small altar faced toward Jerusalem. The room smelled like an animal pen.

The men wore sheepskin coats with puffed sleeves and hats of the same material pulled over their ears. Unlike the Judeans their beards

118

were never cut but plucked and therefore grew in bristles. Their speech was guttural and sounded more like that of the Syrians. Before their reconversion to Judaism, the Galileans had mixed freely with Assyrians, Phoenecians, Samaritans and even the hated Greeks, giving many of them emerald eyes and flaxen hair. Mostly they were herders and mountain farmers. They worked their own land, living simply and worshipping God in the same manner. Though they accepted the Temple as the seat of God on earth, they preferred to worship in small groups in their synagogues.

For more than one hundred years these northerners had been fighting Rome and were first to suffer any punishment meted out by the various governors and procurators. It was among these fiercely independent peasants that Simon bar Giora and John of Gishhalav were raised. Not far away Judah, named the Galilean, Eleazar ben Yair's grandfather, had founded the Sicaris.

Joseph knew that the Galileans resented taking orders from Jerusalem, and even after the defeat of Cestius Gallus, they thought more of their own raids against Roman centers at Caesarea and Acre or the cities of the Decopolis than the recent victories in the south over the most renowned Roman legion. He was also aware of the rivalries among these chieftains now seated before him, rivalries he hoped to exploit in gaining the support of most of them. As if in warning, he spied Justus of Tiberias, a member of the *Sanhedrin* and an old antagonist from his student days under ben Zakkai.

Joseph's *shalom* was not acknowledged by the chiefs who sat as in a court of judgment over him waiting to be convinced that they should accept his leadership.

"Let me say to you," Joseph opened, "that I come not as an intruder but, if you will, as an arbiter in any internal conflict you might have so that we can quickly get on with the matter of war. Jerusalem, as you well know, has bled unnecessarily because of such strife. The Galilee can learn our lesson and conserve its energy for the coming struggle with Rome."

"We've handled Rome well enough till now," said Justus, huddling into his quilted burnoose, the kind worn by noblemen during the winter months. He and Hanan ben Zevi were the only city representatives at this council. The huge amethyst Justus always wore hung out of his cloak.

"That I know. But for your efforts we might not have had the victory we had against Cestius Gallus."

"Cestius Gallus is a chicken hearted commander. He razed our villages but refused to fight us in the open spaces," said a man who stood behind the others.

"What matters," said Joseph, "is that you gave us the time to unite our forces. That's what this winter will give you. Once the rains stop, the Romans will be upon us."

"The Roman is always upon us," said Hanan whose chin was so deeply cleft that the skin showed through his graying beard. "It's the traitors among us who refuse the levy of men and gold we need, and cause our defeat."

"We pay our own levies and use our own men. We need no city folk to tell us how to defend our land. Neither from Tarichea, Tiberias or Jerusalem," said an elderly chieftain who patted down his fleeced boots.

"And we need no succor from bowmen in the night," said Justus condescendingly.

"On the lake. Every time the Roman comes near Tiberias, you take to your boats and flee across Gennesaret."

"Having the only naval force in the area, it's wise strategy," answered Justus, drawing out a handkerchief from his sleeve and wiping his lips as he spoke, a gesture that had always repelled Joseph. But the quibbling among the chiefs suited his purpose and for the moment he remained silent.

"Fish livered," declared Hanan. "Where were you and your great navy when we, your closest neighbors, were attacked by the Tribune Placidus? Our men fought with their backs to the lake allowing the women time to wade out to your boats to be saved, and you refused to take them on, fearing Roman reprisals. Two hundred of our wives and daughters faced God and drowned themselves."

"I came," said one of the chieftains. "We did our best to relieve you."

"That you did, Jonathan. You and John. By then the only thing left was to fish out the bodies."

"John ben Levi is crafty," said Justus. "He knows how to win support with the least effort."

"It's how he hides his pride," said a young man whose accent sounded foreign. "He likes to fight the Roman his own way." The man's nervous blink cautioned Joseph.

"A dozen Roman heads a month," mocked Justus. "That's about his quota."

"The Romans have lots more heads to spare than we do," said Hanan.

"John's a true patriot," said Jonathan. "He heads our best raiders."

"But does he truly understand the consequences of insurrection?" asked Joseph. "Do any of you?"

"He's a peasant," said Justus. "Like the rest of you. Your patriotism goes as far as killing trespassers."

"Peasants," said Jonathan angrily. "You're lucky we still bring you produce."

"And that we can still buy it," retorted Justus. "Besides we have a lake filled with food."

"Fed by the flesh of our women," said Hanan. "While our fishermen sit by idly unable to sell their full catch because the gentile cities of the Decopolis have been forbidden by Rome, their protectors, to deal with Jewish rebels."

Joseph shook his head slowly. "I see you have the same divisive problems we have in the south." And smilingly he added. "It's true then what they say about Galileans; that they would rather wait and be attacked on their own ground than send aid to a neighboring village under fire."

"We've preserved our liberty through our own means," said Jonathan. "We've fought our battles without help from anyone."

"It's not you who need the help. It's Jerusalem — why they sent me up here. By an unfortunate accident we defeated a crack Roman legion. That act affects your struggle, makes it a hundredfold more difficult, as it does ours. No longer are we engaged in small actions. The day of the ambush and foray are over, ended with the defeat of Cestius Gallus. From now on we shall all be called upon to pay for the luxury of independence. Because of its geographical position, the Galilee will bear the brunt of the first Roman counterattack. You are the main line of Jerusalem's defense."

"Bearing such burdens," said the elderly chieftain whose white beard touched his lap, "doesn't frighten us. It's in the nature of our people to carry them. Even God's."

Joseph shook his head "Such attitudes are fatalistic and contrary to our Law. Suicidal, and can lead only to total destruction. Every nation must learn its limitations. That is the real road to survival."

"Israel survived because we surpassed our limitations," said the young man.

To calm the tension, Joseph turned to him and asked. "Your speech, it's not Galilean. Where are you from and how are you called?"

"My name is Shevah," said the young man blinking, "and I come from Rome."

"You seem familiar to me. Have you been in the country long?"

"Long enough to have killed my first Roman."

"Then you've returned to Judea permanently? That's rare isn't it for a Roman Jew?"

"With fifteen hundred eager fighters," said Hanan. "The *Bnai*

Golah."

Joseph again remembered Lucia's revelation to him. He had not heard of these new volunteers, Sons of the Diaspora, as they had named themselves. Like converts, they could be overzealous and dangerous. He looked at the sullen chieftains seated along the bench. He would have to speak more simply, keeping to the formalities these primitive tribesmen understood. They were stubborn patriots who would rather die than win. Nothing outside their mountains and forests existed but God above. If he could at least keep them pacified until he was strong enough to impress them that he and no one else could keep them free. He spoke slowly. "I come to you as an equal. Unpaid, unheralded, perhaps even unwanted, to help prepare you to face the mightiest force ever gathered against us. Before that lake out there begins to brim with spring, the Roman, filled with vengeance against our meager victory in the south, shall pounce upon you. I desire nothing from you but your known bravery. I offer you my own, and with God's grace perhaps we might prevail, be it through blood or the bread and salt of peace."

"The enemy knows only one peace," said Shevah. "Roman peace. And that mean hanging us all upside down."

"At the moment," said Joseph, daring to hint at what he really hoped for, "They may need us as they once did Judah the Maccabee, as they needed Herod and more recently Agrippa the elder."

"It's Herod's sins that we pay for now," said the old chieftain.

"Each of us pays for his own sins," said Joseph, turning to look out the small aperture where the stars glittered on the weapons these warriors left outside so as not to desecrate the synagogue.

"And how does Prince Joseph ben Matthias plan to convert the Roman into a Jew?" asked Justus. "Or is it the Jew into a Roman?"

"Through the discipline of fighting men. Even more than fortitude, Rome respects discipline. In our new found unity, they shall learn to respect us, not only to fear us. I ask for your trust, your faith. Send me your men. Let me train them as their bravery merits into the army of our emerging state, as the Army of the North. The Army of the South and the Army of the Sharon have already been formed. Let them come — all of you — to our camp at Cana, set up by the noble Niger who stands at my side."

"A new Barak ben Avinoam," chided Justus. "And who might I ask is your Deborah? No thank you. Tiberias will raise its own levy when necessary and care for itself. Our walls are strong. I built them myself."

"So's your lake," said Hanan.

"Tiberias needs no help from the likes of you. Nor do they ask any advice from Jerusalem the golden."

"Perhaps you're contemplating your own deal with Rome, like Zippori, our erstwhile capital?" asked Jonathan.

"Zippori is not the capital of the Galilee," retorted Justus indignantly, this time wiping his whole face with his handkerchief. "Tiberias was named so by Agrippa the elder himself."

"In that I assure you his daughter, the queen, concurs," said Joseph.

"Only because she wants our city's wealth," said Justus. "The prestige of our famous baths. Wants us as her capital."

"And why should you object to that? Why shouldn't the Golan again be part of Israel? Wasn't Damascus once King David's summer capital?"

"No Idumean, not even Simon bar Giora, comes near our land," said the old chieftain.

"So John rules the Upper Galilee, Hanan the Lower; Justus, Tiberias, Jonathan the Western and you Naim and you Dabaritta," said Joseph losing patience, pointing along the bench at the querulous leaders.

"Tiberias is a whore and so's Zippori," declared a large man wearing an open sheepskin vest who stood in the doorway. He had more hair on his chest than on his head. "What have you got for us, Priest?"

Joseph knew immediately that his new antagonist was John ben Levi of Gishhalav, unofficial commander of all the Galilee and notorious raider of the Roman bases throughout the country.

Like many of the Jewish rebels, John ben Levi had been orphaned by the Romans when his father had been killed during the sacking of Gishhalav, his native city. John, a boy of twelve, turned smuggler, an ancient and honored trade among the border people of the north. Instead of dealing in holy oils and wines as was customary, he became the chief of an arms smuggling ring which invariably drew him to the rebel bands of the Galilee. The more he attacked the Romans and their Syrian puppets, the more did he win recruits to his own band from these rugged mountain dwellers among whom he had been raised, and from the lower classes in the cities of the valleys and the plains. While Joseph was fighting in the south, he had attacked Caesarea, causing the Procurator of Rome to flee to Antioch. He too had been named *Gibor Yisrael*, hero in Israel.

Joseph was disgusted by the curly hair on John's chest and how his jacket opened down to his navel. "The seventy-one members of the *Sanhedrin* have commissioned me to take command of the north. I carry enough arms to make the Galilee a true first line of defense."

"That buys you nothing, Priest."

"I also have the support of Queen Berenice," Joseph lied. "Her army is ready to fight at our side once the rains stop. Meanwhile they have offered to train you all secretly so that when spring comes we shall be a united force which even Rome might consent to negotiate with instead of surpress."

"A whore as well," declared Shevah, jumping to his feet. "That queen of yours is a whore."

"Once we had a queen worthy of the throne of Judea," said the old chieftain, moving over to allow John to sit. "Alexandra. My father used to speak of her as righteous."

"There are those who feel that Queen Berenice holds the hearts of her countrymen as well," said Joseph. "Who believe that she is the true inheritor of her noble father, Agrippa."

"Whore," repeated Shevah. "She stays more in Rome than in Judea. All our troubles started with the cursed Idumean family of Herod."

"Her blood flows also with that of the Maccabees," Joseph reminded him.

"I'm not convinced," said Hanan, "that our troubles didn't start with them."

"Look, this is no time for history lessons. Let's be frank. You need my help." The chieftains showed no reaction to Joseph's bluntness. "Without me," Joseph went on, "you can't ever succeed. No doubt, you're brave, dedicated, but ignorant. Rebellion for you amounts to killing a handful of Syrian auxiliaries or raiding an isolated encampment of legionnaires."

"Caesarea was no camp," said Jonathan.

"Saved your ass," added John. "Yours and bar Giora's down in Shaar Hagai."

"That is true," said Hanan. "The fact is that Vespasian was about to hurry down to Cestius Gallus' relief. John made him turn instead to Caesarea."

"If you really believe in rebellion," said Joseph, addressing himself to Hanan, "then it's a full Roman army that we all must be prepared to face." He had often used this tactic. As a student at Johanan ben Zakkai's academy, he would seek out a potential ally or at least a man of open mind and cater to him with his eyes and smiles in order to win tacit support from him against a true adversary. Joseph sensed immediately upon entering the synagogue that Hanan would support him. "What if I asked you, any of you, to tell me how many Roman regiments are in Syria? in Egypt? How many regulars? How many auxiliaries? work battalions? How many legions, for example, could

Vespasian field during the next six months?''

"A Roman legion is only a Roman legion," said John, breaking into a hacking cough that brought sweat to his brow. The cough made him vulnerable.

"And three? Reports say Vespasian has at least three legions," said Joseph. "Are you ready for that?"

"Winter is upon us. That plus our raids will wear them down," said Jonathan, handing John a jug of water.

"The many stars and warm nights portend a mild winter," said Hanan.

"You got rain for Jerusalem on time," said Shevah. "God will see to the snows of Galilee."

"Or even," persisted Joseph, keeping to his one line of argument, "are you even ready for each other?"

"These," said John, "are ready for me."

"And after the Galilee?" asked Joseph. "Are you ready to fight for the rest of the country? For Jerusalem?"

John raised his eyes at Joseph without moving his head. "The rest of the country is nothing. The prophet said the seething pot faces north and that the harlot of Jerusalem is fickle. There's only one place to fight the Roman. Here!" and he pointed his index finger into his palm and along his life line. He had small hands for a man his size. "Lose the Galilee and you lose the whole country."

Jeroboam, the founder of the kingdom of the north, must have felt this way, thought Joseph, when he tore away the ten tribes of Israel from the House of David in order to set the people apart from Jerusalem. "Lose Jerusalem," said Joseph, "and you lose the Jewish nation."

"Four cities," said John. "Zippori, Tiberias, Gamala and mine, Gishhalav. After that fall down upon your sword and die."

"Zippori is a whore," declared Jonathan.

"Tiberias is no better," said Hanan.

Before Justus could protest, Joseph added. "Other cities can be more crucial. Never let Rome choose your battleground."

"We'll beat him bad once. Fast," said John. "We'll bust his back on real cities."

"John's right," said Justus, toying with his amethyst. "Rome will break its bones on my cities. I built the walls of Zippori, Gamala and Gishhalav as well. No one can penetrate them without me."

Jonathan shook his head. "In the wadis and on the mountains; the small redoubts. That's where we'll take the Roman. They know how to deal with organized uprisings, established rebellions: with cities and walls. Fixed points are what Rome's strategy is all about. It's bands of fighters in forests of stone and with God that make men free."

"Both ways," said Joseph feeling that sudden surge of enthusiasm that always rose in him at moments of decision. "We need demagogues, you John, men who grow out of the people's grievances who will finally make Rome helpless. But for all that we must train, train your bands, the Sicaris, into a disciplined force."

"You can't train a Sicari," said Eleazar ben Yair, who entered now and squatted at one end of the bench beside the others. "You're born one."

"With arms," said Joseph hiding his surprise. He avoided Eleazar and looked at the man who had entered with him and who was dressed in the robe of a judge. "You can make anyone fight well. Feed a soldier, give him God and a clean weapon and he won't understand the possibility of dying."

"Bull shit," said John, disregarding the sanctity of the building they were meeting in. "Every man, so long as he's alive, knows about the possibility of dying."

"Do you?" Eleazar asked, looking directly at Joseph.

Joseph's neck burned and he had to control himself from scratching it. "My lords, for the past hour you've been proving my point. You do need an arbiter. Let's isolate your disputes and see what can be resolved and what cannot. An Essene teacher of mine and Eleazar ben Yair's," he nodded to his companion who kept staring blankly at him, "used to say: 'solve what is soluble and soon the whole conflict resolves itself.'"

"That's right," said John. "What's soluble right now is those arms, the ones you got from Masada. You're in my territory. So they're mine."

"Eleazar ben Yair is here to witness whose they are."

"Ask him," said John.

Joseph turned to Eleazar who rose and walked to the man in the Judge's robe. "Jesus ben Sapphias, chief magistrate of Tiberias, he'll tell you."

Jesus ben Sapphias stepped forward and unrolled a scroll. "In the name of the district court of Tiberias, I charge you, Joseph ben Matthias with the breach of the holy matrimony contract as signed by you according to the laws of God, Moses and nature." The emphasis on the last word already verified what Joseph had suspected. Hagla had preceded him north and opened the case against him in Tiberias, a city which had always been antipathetic to the nobility of Jerusalem.

"I don't think my private affairs," said Joseph, hearing the tremor in his voice, "have anything to do with the conduct of our war against Rome."

"You have till sunset on the Sabbath hence, to appear before me," said ben Sapphias, "and to answer the charges. Your wife abides in Tiberias."

"I am a priest and shall face only a court of priests."

Ben Sapphias raised his ring of office. "So am I. Of your same order."

The elderly chieftain from Nain rose. "Gentlemen, the time for the morning *Shema* is upon us." And turning to the south, he began to chant softly the first prayer of the day. It struck Joseph that all his antagonists' names in the Galilee began with the letter *J*. So did God's.

CHAPTER XVI — ROME AND JERUSALEM

i

Because he felt that the outcome of the trial would decide who commanded the Galilee against Rome, Jesus ben Sapphias with the approval of Justus ben Piscus, Mayor of Tiberias, ordered that Joseph be judged publicly in the municipal stadium. Joseph refused to appear, insisting that any case against him be held privately. The judge overruled him and held court with the accused absent from the dock. The jury consisted of the chieftains of the Galilee, including John and Justus. Every seat in the stadium was occupied.

Alone in the family villa, Joseph awaited the verdict. He refused to believe that after the heroic events of the past year, including his adventures in Rome, that he might very well be convicted. Nevertheless the ominous barks and screeches of hyenas and bats coming up from the swamps of the Jordan valley made him restless. He knew that the sentence according to The Law for his crime was death by stoning.

On the third day of the trial he woke in a sweat, hearing the wailing of voices in a distance rise and grow threateningly louder. Before he had a chance to slip on his sandals, Niger pushed his way through the barricaded door, giving Joseph a glimpse of the screaming multitude moving against his house.

"Guilty," said Niger. "On all counts."

"What counts?" declared Joseph angrily. "Does a married man have to give account of how he makes love to his wife?"

"Our laws are not so corrupt as Rome's. Even when lying with a woman, one must be aware that the eye of God is upon him."

"Then you accept the verdict without hearing me out?"

Niger rested his hand on the hilt of his sword. "The court has ordered your arrest."

"John, did he vote with the others?"

"The vote was secret. I assume in such cases the verdict is always unanimous."

Joseph paced the long room. He picked up the quill he had been using, and like a dart flung it at the wooden plaque over the hearth. It was his commission as a centurion in the Roman army.

"You really think all this is fair. You really think that it was not staged: to be rid of me, trap me by giving me command here, away from home," he said coming so close to Niger he could smell his own breath against the other's face.

"There were also reports about you in Rome," said Niger. "Shevah, the blinking one, reported how you got sick in Rome. About the synagogue."

"Lies," Joseph sputtered, pacing more quickly. "It was the river fever. Because of those Roman Jews. They live by the river and it's filled with death."

Niger was embarrassed by Joseph's hysteria.

"My men," said Joseph, "they won't stand for it."

"They've been ordered to join John's units."

"Eleazar?"

"He leaves for Masada at sunset."

"Then there is no one to stand for my honor?"

"Only yourself. It's why I insisted on bringing you the verdict."

"You're mad. You're all mad," declared Joseph as he peeped through the closed shutters at the thousands waiting for him to appear. He stepped back and drew Niger's sword from its sheath. "As a soldier and a priest there is only one way to teach them about dying." He grabbed the hilt with two hands and pressed the point of the sword against his rib cage.

Niger grabbed Joseph's arms. "The *Sanhedrin*," he said, "has suspended your sentence. Until further investigation John is to take command of the north."

"Do you think I'm guilty?"

"No."

"Will you still serve under me?"

Niger hesitated then nodded. Joseph ran a finger along the blade of the sword as he used to do to the slaughtering implement up on the Great Altar in the Temple courtyard. Unlike his brother he had always feared to use his tongue in testing the blade. He slipped the sword back into the sheath and unbuckled it from Niger's waist. Then he smeared his face with ashes from the hearth and hung the belt with the sword around his neck and walked out to face the people.

Only the lapping of the lake waters disturbed the silence that fell upon the multitude. Ten yards before him stood the Galilee chiefs, among whom was the blinking leader of the *Bnai Golah*. Joseph remembered now where he had first met Shevah.

ii

Having established himself at the palace of Epaphroditus off the Via Latina, Joseph decided to pay his respects to the elders of the Jewish community. On his way he paused on the top of the Palatine Hill, and in the bright sun, he grinned down upon the city of Rome.

Not truly a walled city, Rome expanded endlessly, her streets bustling and bedecked with flowers melding into the surrounding hills. Only on the three pilgrimages during the lunar year was Jerusalem so crowded and even then hardly ever so gay. Everyone seemed on a permanent holiday. As he came off the Palatine, the streets widened, emptying their polyglot masses into the Forum Romanum. There were Africans in colored robes, bearded Syrians in black caftans and tarbushed Parthians. But most fascinating for Joseph were the giant, honey-haired men from the north whose wild eyes darted furtively from laden shops to the abundantly piled stalls as they bumped into others without a word of apology. They wore short leather skirts and their muscular thighs were hairless. Two unescorted young ladies, flirtatiously twirling their parasols and brazenly returning his look, passed Joseph who stopped at a stand to examine the unfamiliar fruit. The sun was as warm as Jerusalem's.

"Go on, taste it," said the smiling vendor. "Just arrived from Tuscany. First of the season."

Joseph felt the strange fruit and hesitated before he bit into it. His mouth tasted of sand. He shook his head and instead purchased a pomegranate which he had to admit was as juicy as those around Acre but not so sweet. He tossed the rind into the flowing gutter marvelling at how the Romans allowed such a waste of water. The streets, he noticed were paved with flat cobblestones and not the large unevenly laid slabs they used at home. Passing a shop he saw through the raised shutters men reclining in chairs and having their hair cut. That was when Joseph decided to get his beard shaved.

The synagogue of Rome, where he was sure to meet the elders, was a miniature of the Temple in Jerusalem. On its facade in large Hebrew letters were the words

LO YANUM VELO YEESHAN SHOMER YISRAEL
He That Keepeth Israel Shall Neither Sleep Nor Slumber

Joseph entered the building through a narrow courtyard where he washed his hands and feet in a large basin as was the custom of priests. He then walked through a passageway out into a small amphitheater. The ten tier stone seats were already filled, including those on the left partitioned off for women. A marble lectern stood in the center of the theater and on it lay a scroll. To the right was a large puce urn on which the Hebrew letter מ was scrawled in black and into which the Jews of Rome continued to pay their *maaser* tithe to the Temple in Jerusalem. Two men sat on the other side, one with a lyre and the other with a brass horn. A seven branched candelabrum was engraved on the wall behind them.

Joseph introduced himself to the man at the lectern.

"*Shalom, shalom,*" declared Judah Hakohen, head of the Roman Jewish community. "We've been impatiently awaiting your arrival for more than a week."

Before Joseph could make his apologies, others gathered around him and kissed his priest's ring.

"These are members of the community of Israel," said Judah, seating Joseph beside the musicians. "All of whom can still recall memories in the land of our fathers."

For a moment Joseph had a vision of the immense Temple in Jerusalem stripped bare after having parcelled out its splendor in order to sanctify these growing communities of Jews in the Diaspora.

Without warning Judah looked up from the lectern and began reciting.

The heavens declare the glory of the Lord...

The congregation rose and bowing their heads stood without uttering a sound. The music and Judah's chanting spread a veil over the open synagogue. Above, a smear of cloud lay across the altar of heaven. Joseph thought he was sitting in the holy Temple and that at any moment the High Priest would mount the Great Altar, take up one and then the other of the yearling lambs kept for the sacrifice, slit their throats, then sprinkle the blood upon the congregation. He regretted his visit to the synagogue.

"Why do you live so close to the river?" Joseph asked as they walked back to Judah's house. "I've been told that it's an unhealthy part of the city."

"Our settlements in the Diaspora are focused around the house of worship," answered Judah. "As you know the custom is for synagogues to be founded upon waters."

"The river also affords a natural barrier for keeping the uncircumcised from at least one side of our community," added the man to Joseph's right.

"You mean there's a safety problem?"

"In times of strife and uncertainty, we are the first to suffer."

"But you're all Roman citizens," said Joseph.

"Once you leave Judea, you are considered a Jew first. Besides, whatever you do over there," Judah nodded as if Jerusalem was just beyond the hill at the Forum, "we pay for over here."

"So all Jews of Rome are in contact with each other?" asked Joseph.

"Until recently, yes. Lately, however, because of the troubled times, they are drifting northward. We already have substantial communities in Umbria, in Liguria, even as far north as Helvetia, Gaul and Belgium. Next week I take my first journey up the Rhine along which many of our brothers have settled."

"But why do you remain here?" Joseph asked the question that had long bothered him. "I mean away from home?"

"Those of us living in the Diaspora quickly discover the flaw of our nation. As a people at home, we are contentious. Alone in exile, we are too anxious to please. Ready to sell our patrimony for a pittance of approval by those we think worthy of emulation. Patience weakens our capacity to withstand indulgence and decadence. Only in suffering have we achieved strength, condemned by others into the dark caves of posterity."

"But surely if you will it, you can return?"

Judah sighed. "After seventeen years, it's difficult to pick up and move again." The others who followed behind them nodded dolefully.

"I intend to return within a year," said a youth who blinked nervously.

"Yes, yes," said an old man. "It's nice to think so."

The dwellings they passed were crowded one on top of the other like those in the Ophel Quarter of Jerusalem, except that here they ended at the banks of the Tiber instead of sloping into the Valley of Kedron.

"Some of us who live beyond the Forum think that you who live down here exaggerate our problems," said a man dressed in the toga of an aristocrat. "Many say that with gold we can buy the protection of Rome. Especially from those of the Flavian Party."

"The only safety," said the young man, "is the safety of the sword."

"It's not us that they're anxious to bait. It's that they confuse us with the Christians."

"Then it's our duty to defend them," said Judah. "In times of crisis we are both vulnerable to Rome's whims."

"Times of crisis for Jews can only be measured by events in Judea," said Joseph. "Whether we like it or not all Jews, Rome's included, shall live and die as Jerusalem does."

"There are those among our wealthy brethren who blame the arrogance of Jerusalem for our troubles," said the aristocrat. "Each time there's a threat of rebellion in Judea, we in Rome and elsewhere in the dispersion suffer."

"Its just such divisive talk that will destroy us," the other man said angrily.

Joseph was beginning to understand that not only was life in Rome different from that at home, but that the Jews of Rome were different, with their own problems. He had often heard of the troubles of Jews living in Alexandria, in Antioch, even closer, in Caesarea, but only now, listening to these voices of the Diaspora, did he suddenly understand their constant insecurity. Eleazar ben Yair was right. A people without a land, has no will. Not even about their own destruction.

The whitewashed courtyards, the trellises heavy with grapes and the comfortable odors of coriander mixed with the sweet smell of dung reminded Joseph of the villages around Jerusalem. "All of us," said Judah, "are interested in news — fresh news from home."

"Everything. Tell us everything," declared the young man, his heavy lidded eyes quivering with excitement.

"Everything, young man," smiled Joseph, "is a boast I'm incapable of making."

"Of the war," he said, leaning closer to Joseph.

"What war?"

"The revolt."

Joseph shook his head. "The Jews of the exile have two choices. They can either continue to raise the *maaser* tithe which is desperately needed in these times of economic hardship or they can come home and partake of the more difficult task of living the decisions they wish to be a party to. It's easy for you living here to talk of war and rebellion when at this moment Jerusalem is concerned about how to feed its doubling population and control the serious unemployment problem."

"Most successful revolutions," persisted the young man, "come as a result of hunger. Not for the love of freedom."

"You must excuse my son," said Judah. "Living here has made him overzealous in his patriotism. Part of it, I suppose, is that we look to you to end our exile."

Suddenly Joseph wanted to escape and be among strangers. "Only you, Judah, can shorten your exile."

That evening Joseph had been invited by Lucia, Epaphroditus' daughter, to join her and some of her friends on an excursion to the Mulvian Bridge. They had sailed down the Tiber on barges spread with cushions. Slaves served platters laden with stuffed partridges circling speckled lobsters, with silver spokes of trout forming a wheel jutting out from their still flexing claws. Swirls of kelp entwined with sea urchins lay tossed like streamers across it all. Other trays were piled with pink and white asterisks of prawns sprinkled with parsley and planted with slivers of limes all rimmed with crisp brown larks. Between these stood large sweating jugs of wine, and nearby, under a canopy of silk, two naked men, as black as the skies, hovered over a kettle and stirred a thick, green mixture. One man held a lighted skewer which he dipped into the liquid making it glow amber. He would then poke it into his white mouth and taste the ash formed on the tip, after which he would pass it on to the guests lounging about, and then prepare another.

Nabatean honey, thought Joseph somewhat surprised, as Lucia who was lying at his side handed him a skewer. She ran her free hand along his chest and he covered it with is own "Try it," she coaxed.

"I've had the pleasure before," he said, guiding the skewer into her mouth. Lucia closed her eyes and sucked gingerly on the ash. Joseph felt her body shudder. In a distance and still flickering with life, he recognized the Jewish Quarter stretched on a tongue of land that lapped into the water like the Lashon on the Dead Sea opposite the Fortress of Masada.

Lucia took another skewer and this time Joseph let her ease it between his lips. "My," she said, "you swallowed it fire and all."

"It's the way I was taught," said Joseph reaching for another.

A thin barefooted woman leaned toward them. "I want him," she said pointing at Joseph. She was slightly drunk.

"This is Bianca," said Lucia. The girl fell across Joseph's lap as the barge bumped against a wharf. Everyone jumped up, leaping over Joseph and the two girls as they hurried ashore. Bianca pulled Joseph up and he drew Lucia after him. Together they hopped off the barge.

Joseph was happy. He had always preferred the company of women, feeling safe in their presence and satisfaction over their flatteries and flirtations. "The desire to be loved," Bannus had taught, "is man's highest vanity." Perhaps all men's actions, thought Joseph, are taken because of their craving for affection, and power itself was merely another side of desire.

Hundreds of fires dotted a cleared field across which throngs of people converged on an arena carved out of a hillside. Everywhere hawkers shouted and music whistled. Children raced in and out of the crowd as they chased each other with abandon. Two little girls, splitting sunflower seeds between their teeth watched from a boulder where they sat, their bare legs hanging just above the bodies of a man and a woman thumping frenzily against the earth. Further on a group of old men, their eyes and lips painted, danced naked around a fire. Women moved through the crowd soliciting men with their bared breasts. The smell of sweat cut a layer through the sharp odors of garlic and burning flesh.

Joseph became separated from the girls and he entered a tent where people were watching a belly dancer performing to flutes. The girl was bedecked with tiny cymbals on her wrists and ankles, a baby python wrappped around her bare midriff.

He had to push his way into the next tent where a goat wearing a tiara of glass stones around his horns and a purple band around his neck stood tied to a ladder decorated with bunting. A man in ballooning pants banked a fire, while a woman with warts on her face the size of walnuts and with eyes of a toad pranced around the circle of watchers. Her loose breasts shook to the rhythm of the tambourine she held out, already half filled with coins.

Suddenly the man cracked a whip over the fire. The woman dumped the coins into an earthenware pot and then, untying the goat, she began to swirl around the fire, slapping and jangling the tambourine. At first the goat followed her, his snout rubbing against the flounces of her patchwork skirt. When the man cracked the whip again, the woman skipped up the ladder and stood balancing herself on a board that lay across the top like a see-saw. Now the goat began to mount the ladder. Each time the man cracked the whip, the goat climbed another rung. The woman rocked back and forth, furiously whacking the tambourine.

When the goat reached the top, the woman fell to her knees, then summersaulting once, she stood on her hands balancing the board exactly across the top of the ladder. The whip cracked and the goat hesitated. This time the man whipped the beast's legs, and after trembling momentarily the goat strained as it stood on its hind legs, setting one on the slippered foot of the women. At the next swish of the whip, the goat leaped up balancing itself with two legs on one of the slippers and two on the other.

The crowd stood hushed. The man poured liquid on the fire making the flames leap higher than the ladder, silhouetting the woman and the goat against the tent sides. He then moved among the people, and holding out a beggar's cup, received the final tithe for the act. Joseph tossed a coin into the cup without taking his eyes off the woman who still stood on her hands. Her hair had fallen over her face and her skirt was tied around her naked hips.

Again the man cracked the whip and the crowd groaned as the goat bent its head, its green stained whiskers disappearing into the spangled hair between the woman's legs.

Joseph turned to the man standing beside him and with much effort asked where they were. The man grinned at him and opened his mouth to show his mutilated tongue. Joseph's throat burned with thirst.

He found the girls under an aquaduct where the stench of urine was so strong it made his eyes tear. "Where are we?" he asked. Lucia stuck another ash in his mouth and they moved toward the hillside. Bianca laughed. "In hell, man, created by royal decree. And a better one it is than Hades." She slipped her hand through the crease in Joseph's robe. "I want you." she said, blowing a toy horn in his face. For no reason, Joseph began to cry.

"This isn't the Temple in Jerusalem," said Bianca. "Further down, nearer the river, you'll get a better view of where mighty Rome gets the jism in its blood."

"More than what I've already witnessed?"

"You haven't seen anything yet. In the hollow down there," said Bianca, pointing into the arena, "man's natural inclination to evil is set free."

The hillside was jammed with spectators sloping down in rows to the oval at the base of the arena. Men in leather aprons covering their bare chests were pounding posts along the perimeter of the arena. Torches burned holes into the night.

"The Emperor," said Lucia, "comes here regularly. In disguise."

"Filled with self-pity," added Bianca. "Dressed as a beggar and allows himself to be beaten and spat upon by anyone. In his gayer moods, he appears with a band of thieves and bawds who follow him like the snakes that guarded his cradle at birth, and with them he tyrannizes the noblemen who come down from the city to relax by orgy. Occasionally, when he's truly starved for affection, he rapes Christians — men and women — who live beyond the bridge out there in those hovels. If we're lucky you'll witness this favorite game of the Emperor. Everyone joins in."

"But how will I know him?" asked Joseph, his lips going numb.

"If you perform as you're expected to, he'll find you."

"And this, all this?"

"The Mulvian Bridge. Where Rome hones its discipline on perversity. Without this," and Bianca stretched out her arm, "there would be no Roman Empire."

A roar rose as the men in leather dragged out a scraggly band of about fifty men, women and children, chaining them to the posts, then tying their arms to crossbars. Though they squirmed in agony, their moans were drowned out by the howling voices of the crowd. Joseph felt sick.

A man bearing two wine skins like kidneys, one on each hip, thrust the nozzle between Joseph's lips and squeezed the skin. "Here you go. Ointment for your female stomach." Joseph gulped the wine, much of it running down his neck and over his robe. His thirst was unquenchable. As he handed the man a fistful of coins, he saw clouds pursuing him.

He was seated now in the amphitheater. Lucia and Bianca kept passing him wine from a decanter into which they dipped the little ash balls of Nabatean honey they carried. The heads of the girls now merged in Joseph's eyes and at times he thought they took the shape of Hagla. He leaped up and roared with the other spectators when wild beasts charged into the arena.

His mouth was filled with tongue. It was wet and sandy and he swallowed it whole letting it hang down his gullet. He didn't know which of the girls he was kissing.

Below, the beasts stalked the crucified victims. They were cumbersome beasts and even in the light of the many torches, Joseph could not identify them. Finally, as though trained, each stood before one human and roared.

Joseph focused on one beast and one human. The animal lumbered toward a dark haired girl and poked one paw at her, then the other. Each stroke tore off more of the rags she wore. Then the beast reared back and gazed at the naked child.

The other beasts did the same to their victims, clawing them until they too were naked, then began to taunt them, dancing before them, hugging and biting them obscenely. As they jumped and grunted, some proceeded to shed their manes though their bodies remained covered with skins. Joseph saw that they were human. Some produced whips and lashed at their victims. Other poked fingers in their eyes. One woman climbed up a cross and sat with her bare bottom on the shoulders of a bound man and defecated on his face. A man whose tiger skin dragged like a tail from his waist exposed the penis of his victim, manipulated it until it stiffened, then bowing, he pressed his mouth to it. He bit it off and stuffed it into the man's mouth to the roaring approval of the spectators. Someone below Joseph shouted: "Now let's see him piss. Make the Christian piss blood!"

Bianca or Lucia, he couldn't tell which, urged him to go down into the arena. All pointed excitedly at a man still masked straddling the girl. The crowd cheered in time to his jerking movements. Joseph's beast wore the head of an eagle.

"Let's get us one," cried Lucia. "Let's get us an old mama!" and she and Bianca climbed down tier after tier into the arena, holding their gowns high so as not to trip on them. In order to help them down, the spectators lifted them over their heads. From all the tiers people surged into the arena.

The eagle now was at the girl's breasts, fighting with a woman over them until they compromised, each taking one. The girl squirmed causing her bound wrists and ankles to bleed. Suddenly she shrieked and a silence fell across the amphitheater as the crowd saw blood spurt from one breast. Bianca grinned up at the spectators with the girl's nipple stuck between her teeth. Joseph rolled over the heads of the spectators, following the girls into the arena. His hands were already covered with blood.

When he awoke, the sun was shining. A fly crawled across a white mound that rose on top of him. He watched as it cautiously disappeared into a valley of flesh. A woman in deep sleep, her huge ass exposed, obliterated him. He pissed.

After much effort he wiggled out from beneath her and vomited into the river. Bile snaked out of his mouth and into the current. Along the bank many people lay sleeping, still stuck in fornication. Joseph washed away the vomit from his face and drank a few gulps of water from the river. He thought the sun had orbited in his eyes.

He staggered up a dirt road along which all the houses were shuttered. His robe was in tatters and he tried to cover his exposed body, but the effort again made him gag and spit air. Next, he found himself sitting in a theater scattered with torn parchment. A black spider leaked across a seven branched candelabrum. Joseph's head thumped against a step as he rolled on to the tiled floor. He remembered the Sabbath.

He lay sweating, listening to the distant howls of jackals. Walls squeezed close, raising an immense fortress around him. Thunder roared between his temples, and he saw himself running, his feet not touching the ground. The scent of the earth penetrated his eyes, while from behind, torrents of water came crashing after him. "Eleazar," he whimpered. Looking up, he saw Shevah standing in the doorway and blinking at him.

"Rome's in turmoil," said the son of Rome's Jewish community's leader. "Generals, senators, counsellors are being rounded up to quell the most serious conspiracy since the death of the Emperor Tiberius. Lucan is dead. Piso is dead. The Regent of Rome is dead."

"Seneca the wise?" Joseph backed against the wall as if Shevah was about to strike him.

"Drowned in a bathtub filled with his own blood."

"And Epaphroditus?"

"Hangs upside down beyond the Palatine in the way of a traitor."

Joseph slid down on the bed, his sagging body showing through the open neck of his sleeping gown. Only now did he realize that he was in his own room in the palace of the dead counsellor, Lucia's father.

"And were you aware, also," said Joseph breathing heavily, "that I nearly died?"

"Ever since our quarter was attacked."

"The Jewish Quarter attacked? When?"

"On the day we first met. That very night. They came from that den of sin, the Mulvian Bridge, looking for Christians. They say the Emperor himself was among the vandals."

The room smelled of fever, and Joseph wished the walls were covered with objects. The panic he felt was familiar. Often as a child he would lie in his bed in their winter villa above Tiberias feeling the heat strangle him as it rose with the dawn out of the red hills of Perea. About to run barefooted to his parents' room, he would see the sun struggling through the mist over Lake Gennesaret and being lifted on its ambiguous beams until he would sight the first palm tree, then the serpentine valley of the Jordan river. And he would know that he need not fear for the coming of the day. "Go on," said Joseph.

"They mistook our quarter for that of the Christians who live beyond us, and in their drunken and drugged frenzy sacked our homes and raped our women."

"The synagogue?" asked Joseph, shaken, as he tried to verify his clearing memory. "Did they desecrate the *Bet Knesset*?"

Shevah's eyes met Joseph's. They did not blink. "That was where I found you."

"Liar!" declared Joseph, forcing himself up again. "I was already collapsed with the fever. My hosts say they found me down by the river."

I found you lying in the synagogue. There was a man with you of high military rank."

"Tell me exactly what happened at the synagogue."

"The man with you blocked the mob's entry. It was hardly damaged."

Joseph sighed with relief. "And then what happened?"

"The mob moved on up the hill and the man carried you away in his chariot."

Joseph slid down on his back. "Forgive me. I've been very ill. Your news seems to have put me in a state of relapse."

"The fever affects people in different ways."

"I recollect only crumbs of the whole affair."

"It was you who led the mob to the synagogue," said Shevah. Then he turned and without farewell disappeared down the corridor.

iii

Joseph walked to the edge of the terrace. For a long while he stood with his head bowed, the sword hanging from his neck. Then he looked out at the mass of Galileans gathered before his villa.

"I know that you are all pleased to have cause against me. You all accuse me. Vilify me. Shame my family. I know I am sinful. Who among us is not? Each of you has his hidden cache of guilt as I have mine. But I swear to you under open skies that for what you judged me, I am innocent."

Joseph waited until the wave of muttering died down.

"Despite this, I accept your verdict and humble myself as no man ever has before the community of God. If you think I am guilty, I say amen! You believe that I have transgressed The Law, amen to that as well. But if you question my loyalty to our country, I will take this sword that hangs in sign of humility about my neck and before your very eyes plunge it through my heart."

The murmur rose louder as a woman rose. She waited till the noise subsided.

"I am Judith bat Ephraim, a child of the Roman exile," she began.

Joseph's lips fell open.

"I have come back to be with my people, to fight side by side with my husband, Joseph ben Matthias."

The voices rose in a tumult. Joseph could not believe his ears.

"As spouse to Joseph, his most recent beloved, the priority of matrimony is mine. It is I and not Hagla who shall mother his progeny. I, not she, who am already with child. His son, which for five years God denied her."

Lucia paused and the multitude remained silent. Covering her head with a shawl, she bowed to Joseph. "I am your humble mistress."

Taking Joseph by the hand, Lucia Paulina led him back inside the villa where they found Eleazar ben Yair.

"The arms," said Lucia, not surprised to see him. "Let us keep the arms."

Joseph was still dumbfounded.

"They're the only card we hold," said Niger, "to win over the Galilee."

Eleazar did not answer questions. He spoke out of necessity. "I'm going to watch you," he said to Joseph. "She will be my watchdog over you. Your only exoneration."

Niger lit a fire after Eleazar departed. He told Joseph and Lucia that the Queen's Royals had taken over the city. "Just in case the ruse fails."

"What ruse?" asked Lucia, her shawl now tossed over her shoulder, revealing short hair. "I have slept with him. I bear his child. The Law says that is marriage."

"Our law. Not Roman Law," said Joseph.

"I am in Judea. Here there is only one law."

"For Jews," said Niger.

Lucia took the sword from around Joseph's neck and strapped it around her waist. "For me," she said, "there is only one law."

"Eleazar ben Yair," said Niger. "It was he who saved your head. He ordered me up here. He wanted to test you. See your reaction to death."

"Suicide," said Joseph. "His lifelong obsession."

"The way of the Essene. You reacted as he would have. Otherwise, despite the Queen and her Royals, despite, Judith here, he would have killed you."

"You're wrong," said Lucia. "It was I who convinced him to come here and see for himself."

"You?" said Joseph. "You convinced Eleazar?"

"I and Bannus. He gave Eleazar his approval."

"Bannus believed you? That you were my legal wife?"

"My father was converted by him on his last trip to Jerusalem. Your father was witness to the ceremony."

CHAPTER XVII — FAMILIAR SPIRITS

i

Joseph was convinced that to win the support of the chieftains he would have to join them in battle. And to fight Rome on the Galileans' terms was the last thing he wished to do.

To reconcile this dilemma, he sought a breach in the fierce wall of these warriors' opposition to him and found it among the city leaders of the north. Justus of Tiberias, though a contemptible man, was Sophist enough to understand the precariousness of the situation. Justus had been educated in Rome, and though not of a priestly family, he was of the new class of wealthy who had many connections throughout the empire. He had even been a scribe and adviser to the court of Berenice, but because for the moment his ambitions clashed with hers, he cast his support behind the powerful families of Tiberias and other cities who distrusted the Queen of Golan.

Though both were educated to see Rome as a protector of the Jews, Joseph chose to remain in Judea where he received the usual eduation worthy of a prince, including attendance at the military academy at Antioch in Syria. Justus, coming from a less hierarchical and secure background, was sent to Rome by his father in order to gain there the prestige their family lacked at home. Justus, who was a few years Joseph's senior, had returned home a sycophant and a Romanizer. His studies had been primarily in history and architecture. It was he who had finished building Tiberias, and adding its now famous baths, modelled on those he had visited in Europe. Joseph, as was expected of his class, waited to be called to serve.

Whenever they met in Jerusalem, they would argue over the role of Judea in the world. Justus unquestioningly accepted the vassal position of the Jews to Rome, while Joseph, having the perspective of a priest with a longer link to the heritage of his people, held a more positive though still pragmatic view that Judea was a pivotal area which under certain conditions could affect events more than its power merited. It was in the precariousness of such a position that he saw its permanence. If God had exaggerated the promise of Israel, he had also not set them on the crossroads of the world merely as a parade ground for the glory of others. Once or twice Israel had even managed to surpass itself: in ancient times under King David and more recently under Alexander Janaeus, the first Maccabee king, who had grasped on to the tatters of Greek power before Rome stripped it away from his sons. But Joseph understood these as exceptional epochs. By nature the Jew was a foreshadower of others' greatness or doom. If the Jews were chosen as The Law said they were, it was for prophecy, not for conquest. Ben Zakkai used to say in his academy which Joseph had attended, "Judea must surpass its humanity as a paragon to nations." Epaphroditus had expanded on this idea to Joseph in Rome when he declared that the mission of the Jews was to be the fulcrum of power, always remaining constant beneath the see-saw of destiny. The trouble was that Judea could never agree on what was good for itself.

Though he had been much discouraged after the fortuitous defeat of Cestius Gallus, coming north had given Joseph renewed hope to set in perspective Judea's place in the cycle of history. And that meant helping Titus crown his father Emperor of Rome here in the Galilee.

However since he distrusted Justus, Joseph had to turn to a lesser leader who was more reconciled to Joseph's theories of survival. As they strolled through the marketplace of Tiberias along the shores of Lake Gennesaret, Hanan ben Zevi listened to Joseph explain how the Galilee alone could save the whole blessed land of Israel.

"They won't join you," Hanan finally said, as Joseph picked up a silvery bleak by its tiny fin from a pile that lay on the cobbles. "Their concerns are contained in the framework of a week. From the end of one Sabbath when they take up their arms to the beginning of the next when they set them down."

The quantity of produce he saw surprised Joseph who had become used to the shortages in Jerusalem's agoras. The market in Tiberias was similar to those he had seen in Rome and not divided according to product as in Jerusalem. Here everything was laid out more neatly and the stalls were made of stone instead of the wood and rag sheds of those at home. The smells of the lake dominated, and instead of the sides of lamb hanging from black hooks and dripping blood on to the street, gray waters heavy with scales clogged the narrow gutters that ran into the Gennesaret.

"Fresh from the midnight catch," cried one vendor.

"It smells of Friday," said Joseph as they walked along the shore covered with black stones.

"Only today is Monday," said Hanan. "These are from last week's catch. The revolt is slowly strangling the lake economy. No markets. Another problem you must face."

In a distance Joseph spied the mountain villages, some already covered with snow, which he knew were controlled by the chieftains whom he had met a week earlier and who had no allegiance to no city.

"John's the only one they really trust," said Hanan, sensing Joseph's thoughts. "On his way down to Jerusalem, Cestius Gallus sacked those villages and scorched their forests. I offered what help I could, but they didn't trust me since I had declared my loyalty to the *Sanhedrin* which they felt was solely concerned with Jerusalem."

"We had a civil war on our hands. Still do. Jerusalem is divided between those loyal to the rebellion and those who are undecided."

"Even after the *Sanhedrin* voted for independence?"

"Frankly the *Sanhedrin* is its own worst enemy. Many among its members voted for freedom reluctantly, fearing the masses. Fearing John and Simon bar Giora. The only man who had the courage of his convictions was Raban Johanan ben Zakkai."

"How did he vote?"

Joseph looked across the lake and saw a fisherman struggling with the net he was hauling in. "He didn't. He prayed during the whole ceremony."

A donkey fitted with a hempen saddle strapped about its upper rear legs trotted by as a man whipped it with a twig. Hanan and Joseph had to back against a shed lined with casks. A hand grasped Joseph's and offered him a castor. "Holy oil, my lord. Wine too, blessed by my own lips." The ignorant country priest had failed to notice Joseph's ring of office.

"It's their only livelihood," said Hanan. Lately there are few public sacrifices and the tithes are not paid." Hanan nodded to a few passersby and then dropped a coin in a blind man's box. "Look at this *shuk*. Once it was the pride of the lake, teeming with as many people as fish. My own city, Tarichea, is in an even worse state."

"That could be turned to our advantage," said Joseph, expressly using the plural. "I'm convinced that if we are to succeed in organizing an army, we'll have to rely on the cities."

"Your suspension as commander gives the Galilee a further excuse not to support you."

"You do. Niger does. The Royals. I think ben Yair will."

"Then you intend to carry on as before?"

"What we need is an army, a real army to impress Rome," answered Joseph nodding enthusiastically.

"They'll march through us like bees through a honeycomb."

"Bees pause to make honey." He was tempted to tell Hanan about Titus.

Hanan stopped and turned to him. "What kind of army do you think you can raise to impress three imperial legions of more than sixty thousand men?"

"One hundred thousand Galileans would be about enough."

"Even if you can muster half that many, which is inconceivable, you could never train them by springtime, less than four months away."

"For what I have in mind, they won't need much training. Just their presence in the right place at the right time will be decisive." Joseph walked on past the stands packed with the famous Gennesaret, thread-lipped barbel and tilapia whose fins looked like Babylonian peacock fans. Green leaves separated the fish whose upturned eyes scrutinized him the way Hanan did.

"Decisive for whom?" asked Hanan.

"For Vespasian," Joseph dared. "He's desperate for the fame he will never win fighting John."

"You won't get a hundred kernels of wheat out of those mountain people. Their bands consist of fifty, maximum a hundred men."

Hanan had not taken up Joseph's hint. "Zippori and Tiberias, how many can they supply?"

Hanan shook his head. "Justus controls Tiberias. He'll give you nothing till you give him something."

"If Tarichea — you — join in mass, it will force Justus' hand."

"We've been in competition with Tiberias for nearly a century. They'd be more interested in supplying your troops than joining them. They can't lose that way."

They passed a fish basin made of slate in which a school of large mullet splashed. Joseph was surprised to see Lucia up ahead casually conversing with a tall man in a burnoose. "I mean to purchase supplies for my troops only from families that give us three men each as soldiers," he told Hanan. "With the largest population in the area, Tiberias will grab at the offer. So will Zippori."

"When they surrendered to Cestius Gallus to save their city and lands, on his way down to Jerusalem, they gave him their crops and swore new allegiance to Rome. That's why they had no representative at our council in the synagogue."

Lucia and the man moved along one of the wharfs while Hanan stopped to examine some ripe walnuts that were mixed in a bin with sorrel and dry beans. "Winter crop's been bad," he said, lifting a wrinkled apple from another bin. Beside this stall stood an almost perfect pyramid of pomegranates. A barefooted girl squatted behind them, her eyes raised to the sun. The black robe she wore was torn, revealing tanned, sturdy legs. Her feet were long and narrow and her toes shaped perfectly.

"Justus can still wait you out," said Hanan. "Controlling a city as large as Tiberias, he's in the best position to deal with Rome or even John."

"He probably will. With both at the same time," Joseph smiled.

They walked on as Joseph thought aloud. "Assume that in one way or another we are able to raise a substantial army. We know that we can't match the professionals of Rome, but I have reason to believe that Vespasian isn't interested in obliterating us. At least not yet." Joseph paused to see if this time Hanan was following his line of reasoning. He went on. "The domestic instability back in Rome makes him need us as much as Julius Caesar once did when he wished to win power away from Pompey. It's a rare moment in history when a mighty empire needs an ally as insignificant as we."

"The Herod principle," said Hanan. "You hinted at it a moment ago."

"The Herod principle," nodded Joseph, relieved that Hanan finally understood him. "He too started here in the Galilee. He too acted as a pivot which brought success to Antony and later Augustus, as Agrippa brought power to Claudius. We might just be in a position to create a new emperor for Rome."

They had reached the end of the wharf where a few camels stood. Colorfully woven and tasseled sandbags laden with dried fruit and bolts of linen were slung over their humps. Behind them stood tall Abyssinians holding ivory tusks, some already shaped into necklaces and bracelets. The smell of fish and spices that spilled out of the sacks lying at the feet of the camels made Joseph sneeze. He was surprised to see that these Africans were also selling arms.

A boy came running up to Hanan and informed him that two Jewish fishermen had been caught dealing in unclean lake food, and that a crowd threatened to toss them and their catch into the water.

"This is what they like to fight over," said Hanan to Joseph who was watching the breeze ripple Lucia's gown. He noticed that she was again dressed in the fashion of Rome. "It's been happening more and more lately."

"Support me and I'll temper their querulous talents," said Joseph.

Hanan sighed. "It's a dangerous game you play."

"The declaration of Judean independence was the most dangerous game of all. It could lead to our annihilation."

Hanan hurried off with the boy without answering Joseph. Joseph followed Lucia, wondering who it was she was with. He had not seen her since yesterday when she professed to be his wife, but Niger had informed him that she was being watched by spies of Justus. Strolling with a strange gentleman in Nabatean garb could be incriminating for a married Jewish woman. She strode like a Roman *puella*, as though the world were a carpet in her boudoir. Again the image of the god Janus crossed his mind.

"Josephus," called Lucia when she spotted him. She had not used his Roman name since they had arrived in Judea. "You understand the language. Buy us some trinkets."

"They are made of the shells of unclean lake creatures and are forbidden to be worn or sold."

"You ate them in Rome," said the gentleman.

"You Romans have an expression for that, I believe," said Joseph, recognizing the man as Larcius Lepidus, Commander of the Xth Roman Legion, whom Lucia had rescued from Masada.

Larcius Lepidus bent down and scratched his toes through his sandals. Without saying a word to Joseph, he winked at Lucia, then jumped into a waiting boat manned by two Golan Royals. His hair was the color of boulders.

"What in God's name is he doing here?"

"He's visiting with Queen Berenice."

"Doesn't he realize the danger?"

"Danger is his utmost pleasure. That's why he crossed the lake."

"To see you?"

"We are old friends. No. To see Justus ben Piscus."

"The Mayor of Tiberias? It reeks of treachery."

"Eleazar ben Yair thinks that treachery is rife in the Galilee."

"You act more like your Roman self. Reminding me who you were."

"But never forgetting what I am." Her short hair made her eyes bulge and reflect the setting sun.

"Just now your eyes glinted like a fanatic Jew."

"Perhaps fear has made us all into fanatics."

"In this country fear is something you learn to live with. Like your bowels."

Lucia pulled her shawl about her shoulders and over her head. Joseph did not know whether she did it out of modesty as they passed a group of women in black or because the breeze rose across the lake. They stopped at a fish stand and Joseph picked out some bleak and four bloated tilapia. From the corner of his eye he saw the barefooted waif hold out a pomegranate, the juices trickling through her fingers. "From Jotapata," she hissed at him. "Still blood red, untouched by the blight."

ii

Joseph took Lucia to the lake shore after dark, to the spot where he and his brother Mati used to go when they were boys, sneaking out at night from their villa instead of going to sleep. He carried the fish he had purchased earlier as well as a bottle of wine. They made their way through the thick wild vines and palms that drooped into the swamps at the effluence of the Jordan. He bore her across the river and followed the south shore of the lake until they reached a boulder hanging over the water. The moon was full and the lake so clear they could see the fish wiggling just below the surface.

"Let's swim," said Lucia.

"First you owe me your lie," said Joseph catching her as she was about to dive. He forced her to her knees, bending her back until she sprawled on the rock. "This time it's my turn to win," said Joseph.

Lucia touched his nose with the tip of her tongue, then kissed him. "You have an ugly mouth," she said, drawing him toward her. "It's what I most remember about you."

The earth was warm and smelled of brown rivers. He was angry how once again she had taken control of his passion.

"Let's eat," he said, pulling himself away.

"I get hungry after," she said. But Joseph was already gathering driftwood for a fire. He unwrapped the bleak from a damp rag and then the tilapia packed in mint leaves. When the fire breathed evenly, he set a flat stone upon it and waited until it glowed. Then, leaving the tilapia in the leaves, he lay them on the stone where they sizzled. The bleak he dumped into a clay bowl and filled it with olive oil, then sprinkled all with thyme, letting them simmer over the fire. He propped two flat breads near the stone and tended the fire with a green twig. An owl barked in the swamp.

"Who taught you to cook?" Lucia asked.

"All priests must cook. For the sacrifice."

"Do you like fish?"

"Not really. It's the idea of it all that I enjoy."

"You feel that way about everything you do?"

Joseph stirred the embers. "What we have in common. How did you get Larcius Lepidus to surrender Masada?"

Lucia looked out across the lake. "By saving his life, of course."

"I can't accept that. The commander of the Xth Roman Legion does not leave his men behind."

"He didn't. Most of his legion is here. Across the lake at Gamala with the Queen."

"Two hundred and fifty-eight men. He sacrificed two hundred and fifty-eight Roman legionnaires. Very unlikely."

"Titus Flavius ordered him to."

"Titus has not the rank to order him."

"Vespasian. His father."

"You're lying as you lied about being with child by me."

"It saved your life as well."

"A lie like the first one."

"How can you be sure?"

"You have a bad memory. The last time we made love was during the battle at Shaar Hagai. You cannot know yet."

"There was another time. Earlier."

Joseph shook his head. "I'm not a Roman. I don't take such things lightly."

"In Rome. At the Mulvian Bridge."

The breeze changed direction and turned warm, now coming up from the desert. Joseph shivered. "Your other self. I still don't believe it."

"*Your* other self. By the Tiber in the synagogue. After you drank the bad waters."

"The Roman synagogue?"

"Some day I would like to make love in the Temple," said Lucia and she walked to the edge of the boulder.

"Sleeping with me doesn't make you my wife."

"Judah HaKohen says for some Jews it would. Especially since I bear the child your wife could not."

"He is head of Roman Jewry. Here in Judea, no."

"Bannus, the wiseman confirmed it."

Joseph stood up.

"He blessed me and named me Judith."

"My mother's name. Did you know?"

Lucia shook her head. "I chose it to bear witness to my own conversion. I intend to do as she did."

"And who shall be your *Holofernes*?" Joseph mocked.

She did not answer. "Larcius Lepidus is regrouping his legion at Gamala. Vespasian intends to cross the Galilee and meet up with him here, then together with the Xth Legion and the Queen's forces, move south and attack Jerusalem from Jericho."

"Madness. At this time of the year the Jordan valley is a jungle. Besides Queen Berenice's Royals are committed to me."

"He's taken her as his mistress."

"Larcius?"

"Vespasian. He and Titus share everything."

"And which one do you intend as *Holofernes*?" repeated Joseph, this time taking her more seriously.

But she was gone, plunged into the lake. Joseph lay on the warm boulder looking up at the mountain of the moon. He listened to the memory of his brother frolicking in the water with the other children, diving for coppers that Roman legionnaires, then stationed around Tiberias, would toss to them. Joseph had always stood apart, remembering their father's admonition against such Galilean vulgarity.

A voice now called to him: *"Joseph!"* and he jumped up answering, *"Hineni! I am here, Lord."*

"Fear not the sheaf of your destiny. For soon you must make war upon mine enemies."

The fish leaped at fireflies that skimmed the lake. Joseph walked into the warm waters and swam slowly, feeling the cold current in his ankles. Even in his youth, the voices he heard were always his own.

Lucia was sitting on the cobblestone boat landing across the lake and combing her hair. Above them hovered the statue of Janus, set there by the Emperor Tiberius for whom the city was named.

Joseph sat beside Lucia, the warmer drops from her body dripping against his. The moon faded across her face distorting her mouth. Like the vestal virgins he had seen in the Temple of Jupiter in Rome or among the harlots of the Baal on Mount Carmel, she was communicating with the constellations.

"Witch of Ein Dor," he whispered to her. "Who shall win the battle of the beasts?"

The embers of their fire across the lake raised and lowered the heavens. A wildcat screamed, silencing the cicadas. The lake lay like a scorched plain.

She took his hands and drew him down clasping her thighs about his waist. For an instant the moon reappeared shrouded in a cloud. Joseph caught sight of the Roman god above them as Lucia slid with him into the water. Then he knew that it must be an omen: that the battle between Rome and Jerusalem was now raging between them and that he could only save his city, his people, by destroying her. He would have to carry her beyond her capacity as she had once done to him and as she had done to Cestius Gallus and Larcius Lepidus. If only he could reach up and hang on to the blade of the moon that now cut swiftly through the clouds and catch her — lead her to the place and the time of his own passion. He slipped his hands beneath her and raised her high so that her legs spread in a V like a priest's fingers held up for benediction. Then he penetrated her as he knew she would despise, holding her and finally grunting. "Now you've given me of your true self. You've finally made love to me as you have to no one else."

"To myself," she hissed. "I imagined I penetrated myself."

They struggled, each trying to devour the other. He felt pleasure as she winced and he gained hardness in her pain. Suddenly the face of Hagla spewed hate at him, trying as she always had to deny him the extravagance of his lust. "Raya," he moaned. For only the maidservant let him love completely, uncalculatingly, like a gazelle in the wilderness plundered by a jackal.

Dazed, he saw that he had spent himself on the earth. Sitting once again on the boulder, her arms locked about her bare knees, eyes heavenward, Lucia was quivering with the energy of the moon. He no longer cared that he had again been vanquished.

CHAPTER XVIII — A ROMAN CENTURION

Throughout the winter Joseph waited at his headquarters in Cana for word from Titus. He refused to be goaded into the raiding tactics of the Galilee chieftains who for the most part ignored his presence and continued to acknowledge the leadership of John of Gishhalav. Those who had joined Joseph's forces, such as the Tarichean militia, trickled back to the warmer climate of the Jordan Valley, having suffered unduly from the unexpectedly severe winter in the Galilean mountains. Only the Bnai Golah, with nowhere else to turn, remained steadfast in its determination to learn the proper use of arms. Under the regiment of professional Royals that had been assigned to Joseph by Silas, they trained hard and uncomplainingly. Niger imposed a harsh Roman discipline upon them, never letting them stand when they could be walking, walk when they could be running. He saw to it that their tents were pitched in the valley and that their training and maneuvers were up in the mountains so that they were always climbing. He even insisted that they run to the daily synagogue services and bathe in the icy streams of Sakhne that ran with islets of snow. Not to be outdone by his aide, Joseph put them on half rations. "Let one day a week be a fast day," he ordered, "so that when the time comes, they will be fit to withstand anyone — Roman or Jew."

Niger was too naive to catch the nuance of that last phrase.

"It all depends on negative stamina," continued Joseph. "No one has ever defeated Rome in open combat. Siege had been the Roman way of victory. To overcome such a tactic required men capable of enduring on a handful of figs or a tuft of malva grass; fighters with an indifference to the stench of their own blood."

But all these brave words did not lessen Joseph's fears. Rumors kept filtering in from different sources foreshadowing disaster. Jerusalem, with whom his relations since his trial, had remained unclear, refused him the men and gold for which he kept pleading. He had even tried to convince John to join forces with him and build a well trained army so that by spring they could meet the Roman onslaught and contain it. Joseph never let on that with such a disciplined force, he could more readily control the coming battle to his own advantage. Instead of heeding Joseph, John had conspired with Simon bar Giora. Only the matter of Jerusalem stood between the union of their forces.

Zippori, a few miles from Joseph's camp, and its large storehouses of wheat remained his one hope to survive through the winter and check the disintegration of his army. In order to win their support, he sent a deputation there, hinting of his relationship with certain Romans which if all went well might change the whole course of the revolt. But the elders of Zippori refused to commit themselves and like the name of their city, sat like hawks, secure in their fortified nest and in their own unwritten pact with Rome.

It was nearly Passover now and the snows on Mount Hermon and Mount Canaan refused to flex their claws. Joseph brooded. All day in his headquarter hut he felt his fortunes sink in proportion to the growth of those white mountains which rose taller and more ominous each day. Beneath his great burnoose, his body was damp and his nostrils stuck with frost. As always, any despair led him to think of all his failures, and he allowed himself to languish in self pity. He daydreamed of his stay in Rome and shivered in its heat. He saw himself priest to the secretly professing Jewess, the Empress Poppaea, through whom he could have influenced the fate of Judea more than by being stuck here in the slush and sleet of the Galilee winter. But then he remembered that the Empress was six months dead and that he too would have been lying at her side, strangled in her poisoned entrails. He recalled the orgiastic games at the Mulvian Bridge and he became angry at such privilege.

Lucia rose before him and he groaned. He thought of lounging at her side by the pool in her father's house where the light dripped off the overhanging tamarisk. But the palace no longer existed. And Lucia, too, became part of his adversity.

He allowed the voice of his father to wail into his memory. *High Priest in Israel. The Urim and Tumim beyond the contention of the sword.* Joseph blinked away the blood and fat of sacrifice, sure that soon the Temple of God would stand only in mausoleums of prayer. Instead he girded himself for the final leisure of self pity: Eleazar ben Yair. He saw him perched like a hawk (or was it a lizard) on his own rock from where he refused to allow victory or defeat to indulge his pride, knowing that so long as Masada stood, he would live.

Turning away from the snow-capped mountains, he saw a youth in a short tunic standing in the doorway.

"I am Eleazar ben Shamia. My men and I are ready to join you." The name, Joseph knew, was already legendary in the Galilee.

"From where?"

"Jotapata. It's of no signficance."

"Every Jewish settlement has significance," said Joseph becoming wary. "In principle we should defend every inch of our sacred soil. Your men, are they all as young as you?"

"Most have beards," answered the youth sharply. "Except for the women." Joseph had heard that Galilean women bore arms beside their men. "And the others, have they changed their minds?"

"We are all pledged to John ben Levi who sits in his town under another attack."

"Gishhalav is covered with even more snow than we have here. The Romans would never attack so fortified an area under such conditions."

"An attack of the cough. He suffers in his lungs. Especially in the winter."

It was hard for Joseph to imagine that the robust and barrel-chested man whom he had argued with a few months earlier was so seriously ill that he could not lead his men. "An excuse. I make no apologies for waiting, for planning my attack."

"You've waited too long. Tiberias has just fallen to the Romans."

"Larcius Lepidus?"

"And the regrouped Xth Legion."

"The Macedonian is moving up the Jezreel Valley as well," said Hanan entering the hut with Niger.

"How did all this news come to you?"

Eleazar ben Shamia stepped aside and drew in a barefoot girl whose feet were encrusted with mud. "She just came from Tiberias." By her skeletal feet Joseph knew it was Lucia.

"She has no right to be here," said Joseph controlling his anger.

"She's a member of the Liberty Fighters," said ben Shamia. "She joined my unit on her own."

"So you do use them," said Joseph shaking his head. "You really use women."

"As they wish. They have an equal share in freedom."

Joseph walked to the far end of the hut. He toyed with the scroll of his journal that lay on a bale of hay. "What objective can we attack?" he asked. "How dare we face two Roman legions?"

"Catch the Roman before he takes Zippori," said the youthful commander. "Without supplies their stomachs will freeze with hunger."

"Zippori has a compact with Rome."

"We have enough men, and with the arms ben Yair gave you," said Lucia, "we can take Zippori."

Joseph resented how they all called the arms taken from Masada Eleazar's.

"Zippori will collapse before nightfall," said ben Shamia.

"It's a walled city. We need a plan to take her."

"Eleazar ben Yair knows all there is to know about taking walled cities," said Lucia.

Joseph walked by her as though she were a stranger and stood under the hanging icicles above the doorway. "It's snowing again. The Galilee is not the Wilderness of Judea. It is now the end of *Adar* and it's still snowing. A bad omen."

"All omens are bad if you read them badly," said Lucia.

"The snows will force Larcius Lepidus to move into Zippori more quickly."

"His equipment is cumbersome," said ben Shamia. "We can move faster. Attack Zippori and the Galilee is yours."

"And if not?"

Eleazar ben Shamia brushed by Joseph followed by Lucia. "You'll lose your command," said the youth. "John ben Levi has already demanded of Jerusalem to declare him irrevocably General of the North."

He must have dozed because when Niger came rushing into the hut, Joseph sat up with a start and gasped, "Eleazar!"

"Silas," said Niger and handed Joseph an ostracon. Joseph tore off the oil paper cover and glanced at the thin stone tablet. He shook his head. "I wish it was. We could have used his troops."

"By the way," Niger grinned, "We've got us a Roman. That should give us some intelligence on the whereabouts of Larcius Lepidus and what he's up to."

"Has he been interrogated?"

"He gave only his name, rank and city of birth. James and Levi are with him at the moment." The mention of his bodyguards gave Joseph to understand that pressure was needed to coax the prisoner into talking.

"I found this among his belongings," said Niger, tossing a medal at Joseph.

Joseph turned it over a few times. "Not Larcius," he said. "Vespasian."

"He's in Antioch, isn't he? Two hundred miles north."

Joseph nodded. "This medal," he said flipping it back to Niger, "is the insignia of the Apollonaris. A soldier of the XVth Legion wouldn't be this far from his base. What city did he say he was from?"

"Acre."

"Acre? A Roman born in Acre?"

"I think he said that's where he came from."

"That's not the same thing. Not the same thing at all." Joseph walked outside.

The sun came out crystalizing the snow. Water trickled into the valley. By evening it would pick up speed, gushing southward, blasting its way past Jerusalem and down through the wadis below Masada. The ice cracked under the weight of Joseph's boot. "The prisoner," he said, "came from Acre. What if this time the Romans were debarking their troops there and are about to swoop down Jezreel made secure by Larcius Lepidus," and remembering what Lucia had told him, "then head south through your Perea, recrossing the Jordan at Jericho and attack Jerusalem from the east?"

"It's never been done. You told me that Vespasian is a cautious man."

"Only the Apollonaris is Titus' personal legion. He's the only man daring enough to slug through the mud and attack Jerusalem from that side a month before the rains stop."

"Leaving his whole northern flank here in the Galilee exposed?"

Joseph reentered the hut. He creased his brow as he raised the ostracan and read the chiseled message carefully. "Maybe, like me, he believes Jerusalem holds all flanks within her walls. Even his Roman flank back in Italy?"

Niger was confused. "What's the message read?"

Joseph pushed the stone slab around to him.

THE FOLLOWING ACCUSATIONS HAVE BEEN
CHARGED AGAINST YOU BY LORDS
TEMPORAL AND SPIRITUAL OF THE DISTRICT
OF GALILEE:
A) ILLEGAL USURPATION OF POWER IN THE
GALILEE THROUGH BRIBERY.
B) CONTACT WITH HERETIC CHRISTIANS IN
CANA WHO OPPOSE THE ESTABLISHMENT OF
A FREE JUDEA.
C) PLOTTING SECRETLY WITH THE QUEEN OF
GOLAN TO OPEN THE NORTH AND THEN THE
WHOLE OF OUR SACRED SOIL TO THE
ROMANS.
IT IS THEREFORE INCUMBENT UPON ME TO
ORDER YOU TO RETURN IMMEDIATELY TO
JERUSALEM TO GIVE TESTIMONY BEFORE THE
COUNCIL OF THE SANHEDRIN CONCERNING
THESE CHARGES. IN YOUR ABSENCE JOHN
BEN LEVI OF GISHHALAV HAS BEEN
APPOINTED COMMANDER OF THE GALILEE.

Joseph noticed that Niger read with his lips as Eleazar ben Yair did.

"But these allegations are false," declared Niger.

"Truthful only in that we now know who our enemies are. Each charge lays witness to another who is conspiring against me."

"Justus and John," said Niger. "The fight this evening at Zippori will surely convince them of your loyalty. Including Jerusalem."

"Rome," said Joseph opening the long coat he was wearing. Niger was shocked to see that he was dressed in the uniform of a Roman centurion. "This is why I'm defying the *Sanhedrin* and all the chiefs of the Galilee," said Joseph. "Instead of Zippori, I ride at once to Acre and at least find out if the last charge is true. To that charge only Titus Flavius holds the answer."

CHAPTER XIX — THE PRIVILEGE OF JERUSALEM

i

It was still raining when Joseph sighted the coast. The mist that rose out of the sea deepened his forboding. He had been sent north to unify the Galilee in preparation for a war he had never believed in and which he was sure would bring only devastation to the land. In the hundred years since Rome had moved eastward more than two million Jews had emigrated or been killed. Joseph sensed that his present journey would be the last opportunity to save his people through helping to crown a new Roman Emperor, perhaps even a Jewish Empress, making Jerusalem the second capital of the world. After five month's absence, he yearned for the Holy City and realized that he loved it more than the whole ancient land of Israel. It was why he had been giving serious thought of surrendering himself to the privilege of Jerusalem.

Dressed as a Roman centurion, he rode into Acre and announced that he carried a message to Titus from the legate Larcius Lepidus.

The commander of the XVth Legion was working on some papers and did not look up when Joseph entered. Titus lay on a sofa, his naked body half wrapped in the same blue and gold cape he wore the day he raced in the Circus Flaminius, the stakes: his head against the Emperor Nero's. It was then that Joseph realized the Berenice was in fact the mistress of a potential Emperor of Rome.

ii

The sun burned pleasantly through his thinning hair as Joseph followed the crowd to the circus. The excitement of the Roman day reminded him of Titus' offer in the caldarium twenty hours earlier and since which time he had dared to think of attaching his fate to Rome. Thinking that he could if he so desired have a command under Titus made him take special pleasure in being jostled by strangers.

Standing in the tree-shaded entrance to the circus, he watched ticket scalpers hawk chains of coins hung around their necks, and banners with caricatures of the most popular drivers. A crumpled man under a shed sold Joseph some raisins mixed with hazel nuts that were piled on a counter. He strolled by a statue of Mercury where women in black, squatting on their haunches the way the Nabateans did back home, snapped their fingers silently, offering him evil eyes of glass.

At the gates people pushed their way inside stooping through the low archways into the arena. There were fewer people at the main gate and the archway was higher and carpeted. Joseph waited here as Titus had instructed him, watching half contemptuously, half fascinatedly, as carriages pulled up and unloaded elegant ladies and gentlemen who continued to chatter as they walked by him. Slaves followed bearing baskets of food and drink.

A gold-tipped gate swung open to the right and the crowd surged forward as a squadron of cavalry, twelve abreast, entered the arena. Behind them came columns of foot soldiers followed by auxiliaries and workmen carrying an array of weaponry. A centurion approached Joseph and saluted. "This way, Sir. To the games."

They entered a long tunnel streaked with light that came through the chutes leading up to the arena. The wet stones, splattered with animal dung, depressed Joseph and reminded him of the pens behind the Temple in Jerusalem. He followed the centurion past a man and an ox tied to a wheel that together they turned as they moved. "Water pump," said the centurion. "To keep the dust down on the track. One of the Emperor's new innovations."

Titus was looking out an embrasure in the chariot pit. Without turning, he dismissed the centurion and waved Joseph over to join him. Together they watched the attendants sweeping and sprinkling the track.

"Lane Two is our best," said Titus' pacer who joined them.

Titus was staring at the Emperor's box that by now was filled. "He's a good horseman," he said.

"Spiculus?" asked Joseph.

"My pacer. Fought at my side in the Rhine campaign. He's the key figure in a race. Knows the track. The nuances of the opposition and above all the changes of the wind. We ride today for the first time under Nero's new rules. I must say they are fair. There's been too much fixing of the races."

"Makes your choice harder."

"Easier. Just let my horses do the betting." Titus turned to his pacer. "I'll ride Three," he said.

The Circus Flaminius was the largest track in Rome, built by the conqueror of Greece. From the elegant, canopied boxes to the sloping standing sections for the plebians on each end of the stadium, there was not an empty space.

"It's where you should be," Titus said to Joseph. "With the real fans and in the sun."

"I've been invited to the Emperor's box."

"A distraction. They eat too much."

"The Emperor hasn't arrived yet," said Joseph glancing through the embrasure. He saw Lucia Paulina leaning back on one of the dining sofas, her mouth plucking at a cluster of grapes that she held up in her hand. Above him he heard the rumble of feet.

Titus ran a fingernail along the rump of the horse nearest to him, deliberately drawing a line of blood. Then he walked back to one of the empty animal pens and strapped on his armor. The smell of lye and dung made Joseph wince and he was relieved when the warning trumpet sounded, signalling the beginning of the spectacle.

"You can stay here," said Titus. "What follows is a mere formality." He hurried out and Joseph remained in front of the embrasure.

A second trumpet sounded and Joseph saw a squadron of cavalry, their horses caparisoned, trot out on to the track. Near the public stands, they split into two columns, each turning outward in opposite arcs like a burgeoning orchid, allowing a third column, dressed in magenta from their plumed helmets to their leather gaiters, to gallop out into the center of the circus. At their head and holding a blue standard with the gold number XV, rode Titus Flavius into the odorless sun.

He cantered up to the royal box and saw Epaphroditus standing slightly stooped in the box below Lucia who still lounged on the sofa. Beside her sat Tigellinus, Nero's hatchet man who had recently replaced Titus' uncle as commander of the Praetorian Guard, Rome's garrison troops and makers of emperors. To the First Counsellor's left, his head bald down to his ears, stood Mucianus, imperator of the most powerful Ferratti, the VIth Roman Legion under whom Titus had first served as a centurion. The Emperor had still not arrived.

Without hesitation, Titus wheeled about and with the rest of the cavalry behind him, their arms clanging and their banners snapping in the breeze, he dashed around the ivy covered wall of the *spina*, an island cluttered with obelisks and statues in the center of the track. At that moment, Nero, dressed as Aeneus, his favorite disguise, and with a wreath of fig leaves on his head, arrived with his retinue. Unperturbed, Titus completed the traditional three circles around the arena. Then, without acknowledging the Emperor's nod, he thrust his standard at Lucia, who caught it in midair and slipped it into a rack, letting the flag of his former legion hang over the circus. Titus whirled about so close to the box that his horse scraped its flank against the embankment. He rode through two columns of cavalry who brandished their sabres as they roared: HAIL LEGATUS! the multitude echoing the cry as the horsemen charged back through the tunnel and under the stands.

"I must go," said Joseph as Titus dismounted. "They expect me at the royal box."

"I'll join you," said Titus. "I have time before my race. I must pay my respects." He removed his armor and Joseph noticed the grease stains on his white tunic. He smelled of animal hide.

They walked back through the tunnel and by the pump wheel. "A quick pee," said Titus, and Joseph followed him into the urinal.

"Titus!" shouted a cropped, prematurely gray-haired man whose black burnoose was pulled over his groin.

"Larcius. You old fart."

"I did that before you entered. Just hoping for a piss."

"Not the old gift of the gods again?"

"First for the thirst, then we drink for pleasure," laughed Larcius, splashing against the wall so hard that he splattered Joseph's bare legs.

"What in Hades brings you to enemy country?"

"That was quite a show out there, tossing your colors to the beautiful lady instead of to Emperor Fat. You sure saw to her neutrality."

"Lucia Paulina is never neutral. She bears no colors but her own." Titus nodded to the burnoose. "He always dresses like the enemy he is presently fighting," he said to Joseph. "Especially when he's not fighting them." Then turning back to Larcius. "Do you know her?"

Larcius winked. "The other night we discovered we had mutual enemies. She was the one who told me you were in jail."

"So you're the signal she promised me. The other day in the baths. But I thought you were beyond politics and supposed to be guarding the outposts of the empire."

"Its asshole. Masada. Where the sun speaks only to the sand and both only Hebrew. I came to polish up my Latin and admire the low slung carriage of Roman *puellas*."

"Another form of defense," said Titus.

"It's been long since I've savored a Sabine peach."

"Lucia Paulina of late prefers the bearded burrs of the cactus melon. She's been entertaining a Judean prince," said Titus.

"A man of many coats, as his people name him." Larcius did not address Joseph. "They believe he's here by order of Cestius Gallus," said Larcius.

"Joseph, meet Larcius Lepidus," laughed Titus. "And how is the Governor of Syria's constipation these days?"

Larcius met Joseph's equivocal glance then went on to talk to Titus as though they were alone. "Still afraid to fart and take chances. Jerusalem and the red desert to the south give him gas."

"Meaning you."

"And the Jews. He sends his love."

"To me or to Lucia Paulina?"

"How many times have you had her?" asked Larcius, dropping his burnoose to his ankles.

Titus pissed extravagantly. "Lucia Paulina has *you*," he answered, his straight hair falling across his narrow forehead.

"The devouring kind. I like that."

"I see the wine still goes straight to your balls."

"Haven't had a drop since my last piss."

"You'd be wasting your time with her."

"Nothing like finding out. Right now, I go to pay my respects to her father. He has many admirers in Judea."

"And the Emperor?"

"Not even among the auxiliaries."

Above them they heard a long rolling rumble. "Must be the artillery display," said Titus.

"That's what I really came to see. I'm told they'll be showing some new heavy weapons."

"You always did prefer the fights to the boredom of horses."

"I'm becoming a real Jew. I like humans more than animals."

Titus shook himself vigorously and turned to his friend. "An old cavalry man like you?"

"Lately my piles are acting up," Larcius mockingly confided. "I dream I'm sleeping on horseback. Maybe if the Emperor wills your losing, he'll make you a gladiator. That's the usual punishment for losers, isn't it?"

"Spiculus is his present favorite."

"Then why don't you make a gladiator out of him?"

"As you say, only if the Emperor wishes it."

"I'm told he likes surprises."

"Not being a soldier, he's unpredictable."

"Has no need for counting," laughed Larcius.

"Likes to surprise himself more than his enemies. His rewards and punishments are extemporaneous and without logic."

"Then maybe that transvestite in clown's clothing will punish you by sending you to join me."

"The weather out there makes me itch."

"Only in Jerusalem. Where I'm stuck the one thing worth scratching is your cock. Besides, the Salt Sea is good for syphilis."

This time Titus laughed. "It hasn't been diagnosed as such yet."

"There's an old wiseman my officers tell me. He lives in a cave not far from our base at Masada. Cures them of homesickness, they claim. Homesickness, cactus juice poisoning and the clap. Nabatean honey they call what he gives them. Cures everything. How would you like a legion in the east and do some real fighting?"

Joseph was impressed by Larcius Lepidus' change of pace, his switch from joking to the serious talk of war. It pleased Joseph that Larcius had placed Titus in the same category that only yesterday, in the baths, Titus had placed him.

"Don't be fooled by this man," said Titus to Joseph. "He's the only person I know who can sketch an intricate battle plan and carry it out impeccably even when his skull is numbed with wine. We once went to a whorehouse in Lyons and while we awaited our pleasure, he explained to me where Mark Antony had gone wrong at Actium, presenting his own plan after we left."

Larcius Lepidus and Titus Flavius had been boyhood friends, both growing up among the stoic terrace farmers of Umbria. Their families were not aristocrats, but followed the tradition of offering one son each generation to the legions of Rome. Larcius and Titus cut their first wounds on the glazed plains of the Belgium winter. Until recently they had climbed the ladder of military rank at the same pace, Larcius being the luckier, having been sent east as legate of the Xth Legion to guard the shores of the Salt Sea in southern Judea where Arabs and Nabateans, with Jewish extremist encouragement, had been nibbling at the coasts of Roman earth. Because of Nero's fear of the army, he made it a principle to exile his popular generals to the outposts of the empire where unceasing war contained their ambition. Galba in Gaul, Ortho in Britain and Vitellius in Germany. There remained the Flavians whom he feared most because of their lack of ambition. Being a master at neutralizing rapacity, he was inept in the face of loyalty. He suspected anyone who raised Rome above his own highest honor.

Larcius Lepidus was a daring and colorful soldier and did not object to being banished from the intrigues of the capital so long as he was allowed to play at war. At most, his ambition was to die in battle. Titus was more rational. If he ever thought of his future, it hung on the premise that the sun would rise. At the age of thirty, both generals had risen quickly so that each had time to tarry over living and dying.

"Take a legion against your Arabs?" said Titus.

"Against an army that never surrenders."

"Do they fight as well as the light eyed Celt?"

"Different. They believe they have god on their side."

"Which one?"

"That's it. They only have one."

"Your Jews again."

"One specific Jew."

"Eleazar ben Yair," said Joseph. "Leader of the Sicaris."

"The most zealous of the Jew rebels," said Larcius to Titus, still ignoring Joseph. "He understands about winning."

As they walked to the royal box, Joseph wondered if Larcius Lepidus was not the signal Lucia had mentioned in the baths. Was he too part of the conspiracy, or was he speaking as a soldier who never thought of the possibility of losing?

The commander of the Praetorian Guard was first to greet them. "Hail Titus, son of the most noble *mulio*," called Tigellinus. "What odds are you giving on today's funeral?"

The Emperor sat in the middle of the box on the sofa beside Lucia and in front of a table. Larcius climbed over Tigellinus and sat next to the girl on his right.

Four bare chested mahogany slaves were setting gilt platters laden with food on the table. Three pheasants lay on one, circled with oysters in their shells, and pink baked apples, a walnut stuck in each, were pierced by the beaks of the game. On another lay slices of blood-black boar meat garnished with watercress and artichoke leaves shaped into the imperial eagle. Two silver palavers brimmed with mounds of caviar mixed with chopped chives and cream the color of gravel. Numerous water buckets with half a dozen bottles of cherry-red wine sparkled in the sun. Before a third platter could be set down, the Emperor snatched a buttered biscuit with a goose liver on it and swallowed it whole. Then turning as slowly as the water wheel Joseph had passed earlier in the tunnel, he grinned up at them, pieces of liver swiggling between his teeth. "Titus ben Vespasian," he sang out mockingly, his jowls glittering with fat. "I see you've met our honored guest, the noble Josephus ben Matthias, son of the most distinguished priest of Judea. We have a special event, too, planned for him."

Titus bowed stiffly. He was clumsy with graces.

Joseph was startled when he looked out and saw six dromedaries race by — Nero's surprise in his honor. Titus was impressed. Are they any good in battle?" he asked. But Joseph was watching the Emperor fondling Lucia and ignored the question.

After the third time around, most of the spectators lost interest in the camel race and they too began to eat and drink. In the plebian stalls one man was standing on his head and trying, with the encouragement of his drunken companions, to drink from a cask of wine. Elsewhere people shouted good humoredly to one another, some taunting their neighbors with the banners they held which represented the colors of the different drivers. Titus' blue and gold predominated.

"Do you think you can harness those camels to chariots?" Tigellinus asked looking up at Titus. "Your father should know all about that, having been raised around stables."

Joseph understood the reference was to the time Titus' father had been compelled to breed horses for the circuses in order to make good on debts accrued while he was imperator of the legions in Britain. The mad Caligula had refused to compensate the troops and Vespasian paid them out of his own pocket.

Joseph watched Titus for a reaction to this insult. Titus merely watched the Emperor raise a shell and toast Lucia with the juices of the sea. Joseph turned away in disgust.

"What! leaving already?" Tigellinus said when he saw Titus back down to the tunnel archway.

"Merely bowing to Lucia Paulina and the other ladies," answered Titus.

"Come down and meet Sidonia and her sister. Roman Jews from Rhodes."

"Jewish Romans," corrected Joseph, sitting down with Titus. His eyes vaguely followed the camel race.

"You people haggle over everything. Even words," said Tigellinus. "Here, drink wine in celebration."

"In celebration of what?" asked Joseph.

"Anything. Those camels racing in your honor. Or yours," he scowled at Titus. "By what authority did you lead the XVth in parade earlier?"

"By the authority that asked me. Its officers and men," said Titus, reaching for a free goblet and pouring himself wine.

The trumpets blared signalling the next race. Two chariots came out taking a ceremonial turn around the track. As they came by the royal box, the Emperor leaned over the balustrade and without rising waved a flag, approving the commencement of the race.

"Seems a long course," Lucia addressed the legate Mucianus, who sat on her right.

"Outside lane's the better. More maneuverability."

"You lose on the turns then."

"You can switch lanes," said Tigellinus.

"Not always," Titus answered abruptly.

"There goes number one's right wheel," cried Sidonia.

The outside chariot had come alongside the leading one and crowded it against the *spina* embankment causing it to crack a wheel and slow down. The attacker lost control of his own vehicle which now headed diagonally across the course. The driver leaped from his chariot just as it crashed against the stadium wall and he rolled over coming to a sitting position just below the royal box. The dirt masking his face made him look like a clown.

"Number two wins," Sidonia's sister cheered. "That will keep me in coin for the rest of our visit.''

"There are no bets on this race," Mucianus informed her. "This was run for those two boys to qualify as professional drivers. A master racer must sponsor them." He turned to Titus. "The loser was his pacer.''

"This isn't your lucky day," said Sidonia to Titus.

"Luck has nothing to do with racing," said Mucianus. "Guessing, in some cases, is more important.

Four bedraggled men followed the caretakers who again flattened, then watered the course. They mimicked the hoses by urinating in high arcs. Joseph noticed that Titus watched the clowns with the same concentration that he watched the camel race. Their performance came immediately before the main event.

Two other clowns rode out in dilapidated dung carts hauled by mules. One jumped off and pulling out a red bandana raised it, signalling the start of the race, and then jumped back into a cart which darted off in the opposite direction from the other. The clowns tumbled and jumped between the legs of the animals, and when they passed each other exactly in front of the Emperor, they switched carts. Only Nero and Titus laughed. Over at the chariot pits, Titus spotted one of the chariot drivers changing a wheel.

"Wine before wine is fine," declared the Emperor, offering a goblet to Lucia. "Wine after wine is a time to recline.''

On the final lap the mules became unhitched and galloped off causing the carts to career and crash against the *spina*. The drivers chased after their animals, mounting them backwards, and grabbing their tails as reins, they guided them out of the circus in a trail of dung.

"Tell us," the Emperor asked Joseph. "Do your camels shit as often as our horses?''

"I believe, Caesar, they follow the same habits.''

"I am told your people eat camel.''

"Apion of Alexandria also says you eat donkey shit," said Tigellinus, who was getting drunk. "Drink camel piss as wine.''

"I'm afraid the only wine allowed us is the sanctified wine from the Temple of God.''

Sidonia turned and with her elbow knocked Titus' goblet out of his hand. The wine spilled on his thigh and on her gown. She reached up and with her hand wiped his bare legs. "Shall we bet on you?" she asked.

"Your guess is as good as mine," answered Titus.

"But not quite so good as mine," corrected the Emperor, who leaned over and licked a red drop that hung between Sidonia's breasts.

"Women's blood," mocked Tigellinus. "That's what you Jew priests drink according to Apion."

"I'm a god," said the Emperor, pulling out one of Sidonia's compact breasts and lapping it with his gray tongue. "Now you, Josephus. Savor of the fruits of Rome."

"Rhodes," corrected Sidonia, holding out her bare breast to Joseph.

"If you so command," said the Prince to the Emperor, and reaching for Lucia's goblet took one sip of wine.

"And you shall join us tonight at the Mulvian Bridge."

"You compel me, Caesar, to be what I am not."

"The Roman way," persisted the Emperor.

"Perhaps you already are what you thought you could never be," said Epaphroditus, leaning on the balustrade and looking across the track.

"It's the texture of life here, Sire," said Joseph, turning to the old man whose hands never ceased trembling.

"The contrast," said Epaphroditus. "I fear we Romans lack the tension you are accustomed to in Jerusalem."

Joseph nodded thoughtfully and reached for Lucia's hand. "Even my own voice sounds different in Rome."

"That's your Jew accent," said Tigellinus.

The Emperor giggled.

"A wise man hears his own voice," said Mucianus, again glancing back at Titus.

"It is that I bear the brunt of priesthood."

"That's the trouble with you Jews," said Tigellinus. "Wherever you go you think you're responsible to that impossible god of yours."

Joseph watched the parade of heavy weapons. He recognized the catapults used against the walls of Lutèce, the quick-firers which he read had won Vienne for the Emperor Claudius; heavy stone throwers that Vespasian had flung against the Celt embankments along the Thames River. He knew these weapons also from the celebrations he had observed when the Romans liked to flaunt their invincibility before their possible enemies. Himself. But never before had he seen the one that some fifty slaves now hauled by on a caisson that reached as high as their box.

"The ram," said Epaphroditus. "Named *Viktor*." It was the largest breaching weapon Joseph had ever seen, and as if to verify what he was watching, he turned about and saw that Larcius Lepidus, though drunk was scrutinizing the incredible machine. Sidonia was sitting on his lap.

"Larcius Lepidus received the plans from my friend," Epaphrodi tus whispered in Joseph's ear, "the wiseman, Bannus, who resides in a cave by the Dead Sea. He discovered them in a place called Masada. Drawn by a master armorer of your own King Herod. I built it. Bannus forswore its use against Judea."

"Six by fifty," said Titus with a professional eye. "Will it balance?"

"To quote your friend Larcius," said Epaphroditus leaning closer to Titus, "it could bust through Nero's ass."

"Has it been tested?"

"Doesn't need to be."

The ram was now being drawn to their side of the arena and Joseph studied it more closely. "Could only be used on flat terrain. Fifteen degree angle, I'd say."

Titus looked at Epaphroditus. "Is that how you got back in the Emperor's favor?"

"Now you have to do the same for us."

"I serve only one ruler."

"Young man, you serve Rome. The matter of Rome. You have sacrificed much for her. We ask one last tribute."

"Mucianus' phraseology. You have a more original mind."

"Many support us. Perhaps too many. Each for the wrong reason. His own." Epaphroditus held his thin body tightly in his arms, a scroll between them stuck up like a horn. Like Joseph's father he always carried something to read. "Have you ever studied Zeno?" the counsellor asked Titus.

Titus grinned embarrassedly. "Not much time for reading in the service of Rome."

"A stoic philosopher who believed that the hand of time cannot be controlled. Merely placated, the only means for its extension."

"Philo taught the same," said Joseph. "It was he who taught me to take a chance with time. He used to say: 'Always carry reading matter and extend your life by at least a decade.'"

"Tiberius Alexander's uncle, wasn't he?" said Titus.

"Who is one of us as well," said Epaphroditus. "As are most of the legates of the east."

"For the wrong reasons, no doubt," said Titus.

"Reasons are static. At the moment we are united in movement. Present defined circumscribes the yeasty future." Epaphroditus glanced back with disgust at the Emperor who was kissing his daughter's ear. Tigellinus was forcing a finger down his throat, trying to vomit. "Doing is a form of life extended."

"His men are all over," said Titus. "In every one of the surrounding boxes."

"So are ours. Mucianus has seen to it."

"And is our Jewish prince among your men as well?"

Joseph said nothing.

"Related to kings and queens in the east and of the highest order of Jewish priests," said Epaphroditus. "Queen Berenice is his first cousin."

"A very passionate woman."

"And he a very passionate young man," said Epaphroditus patting Joseph on his thigh.

"So Lucia Paulina informs me."

"It is hard to talk here," said Epaphroditus.

"Easier than in jail," said Titus.

"The prince," said Epaphroditus nodding to Joseph, "is the key to our success."

Titus tightened the leather straps binding his wrists. "I'm a soldier of the west. Judea holds no interest for me."

"It must. We have reached the limits of power in the west. If Rome is to survive, she needs movement. Space eastward."

"And whom do you propose as the next Emperor of Rome?" asked Titus flexing his fingers.

"The sons of farmers. Breeders of horses. Loyal to themselves through the land. The Flavians: risen, not born into a dynasty of power."

Titus rubbed his strapped wrists against his cheek. "Right now my concern is out there. What directions do you have for me to keep my freedom?"

"One of Josephus' ancestors showed the direction. We never followed it properly. The Maccabees gave us the leverage we needed against Greece. When we armed the Jews, we signalled the death of the Greek's Syrian empire. This time it's the back of Persia, Parthia as we know it, that must be broken, opening the way to the Indus and beyond."

"There are more numerous people than the Jews," said Titus rising. "The Armenians, for example, who can be of greater service to us as allies."

"In numbers, yes. Not in spirit. The absolute dedication that the Jews hold is their staying power. Their endurance is the endurance of God."

"Larcius said the same thing a moment ago."

"He too is part of our present."

"Only his idea of the Jewish god is not so positive as yours."

"That god might yet become the instrument of greater conquest: the world. The concept of the Jewish god might form its own dynasty

and rule long after Greece and Rome and Parthia and the Goths fall
under its spell.''

Epaphroditus' intensity together with his calm manner of speaking
made Joseph wonder if old men still sweated. "You still haven't told
me," said Titus, "what I should do out there to win my freedom."

"Do you know why Nero has ordered this spectacle today, on the
Ides of March?"

"It's a holiday. For the sport of it, I suppose."

"The only sport left in Rome is the sport of assassination. Today
competition is over the Roman Empire."

"I rather thought of winning till you put it in those terms. What
makes you think I'm interested in controlling the Roman Empire?"

"Because power now is your only refuge."

"Lucinus Mucianus?"

"A dissipator like Nero. He squanders his talents on intrigue."

"You appear to be in the same business."

"But not for myself, for my pleasure. Rome. Mankind. Perhaps
for the god of the Jews."

"And who is your present client?"

Epaphroditus' lips hung on thin hinges of saliva forming in the
corners of his mouth as he spoke. "You, Titus. Finally you."

"Quick decisions give me indigestion. Rebellion is my ulcer."

"Tigellinus intends to destroy the Roman army. He has lists."

"I assume you are his number one target."

Epaphroditus shook his head. "I am no soldier."

"You've always supported us. Your inventions, your pleading for
more funds for us, the ram," Titus nodded toward the stadium. "As
you yourself said, the concept of Rome."

"First Mucianus. He heads the list, followed by other imperators
of the west. Perhaps then myself, the Flavians. Your father."

"All soldiers have fear."

"*Ecce.* A man who is afraid sees distinction enough in anyone
whom he fears. But like the Emperor, Tigellinus too was never a
soldier."

A chorus of trumpets announced the final race. Epaphroditus was
breathing deeply. He grasped Titus by his forearm. "Hear what I
have to say. Listen carefully, Titus Flavius. The plot is hatched. There
is no retreat. Half the people in the royal box are about to commit
murder. It all depends on your winning."

"A chariot race holding the future of Rome? I thought only Nero
took the circuses seriously."

"That is exactly the answer. When the darling of Rome, you,
defeat the Emperor's favorite, the stadium shall rise in pandemoni-

um. Not since that maniac fiddled Rome to ashes has the populace had a chance to season rage with audacity. Their rage. Your audacity. Our people shall move quickly. Mucianus' men sit in every box and stall in the circus. Even the Senate awaits in the eaves, having been called by me into emergency session to elect a new Emperor this evening. All we need is one moment's distraction. You."

"And if I fail?"

"You have never failed."

"There are chances in races."

"Win, or we shall all be hanging upside down in the Forum by sunset," said Epaphroditus.

"And Lucia Paulina, is she, too, involved?" asked Joseph.

"Young man, in Rome a beautiful woman has a choice we men never have. She can either be killed or made love to."

The trumpets blared in warning, and Titus rose. "I must prepare for the race." He sighed. "There are times when I think that I have experienced too much intrigue at the age of thirty and wish that I could again be a tribune, even a centurion, in the VIth where both Larcius and I had first felt the sting of metal." He smiled. "I remember once when Larcius and I crossed the Marne to make love to two young German wives whose husbands were off fighting for their own posterity. War, then, still had its compensations: looting, rapine honored as trophies of victory. Larcius Lepidus still fights at the side of his men, lays with the same women they do, relishes their rewards, while I have to content myself with racing before kings and foreign tributaries."

"Be certain," said Epaphroditus, "that Caesar rules by the luxury of whim. He would rather see Rome burn at the nod of his head than leave it rebuilt in memorial to himself. He prefers the Lucans and the Senecas dead than be outdone by their poetry. To surpass Caligula's madness and sensual pleasures, he has reinstituted the Mulvian orgies, where each night he performs some outrage with male or female."

"Lucia Paulina says sometimes with both at the same time."

"At the moment he proposes to enter a new arena. He has invited us all to witness his power to control victory."

"In a Roman circus?"

"Today, as soon as the last race is run, he intends to declare his divinity."

The spectators settled into silence as two men on white Arabians charged into the circus, meeting below the royal box and bowing before the Emperor. From under the sheds and lined abreast, six chariots moved on to the track. Wearing a gold helmet set deep on his head so that its rim came down to his eyes, Titus rode the outside lane. Unlike the other drivers, he stood slightly round-shouldered and held the reins loosely with two hands. Five chariots, including his own were painted white and trimmed with green. One was splashed in flames of red paint. As the chariots passed the royal box the Emperor waved a purple flag, starting the main event of twenty-five laps.

At first the chariots remained aligned, pacing each other. After a few laps one driver made his move, edging forward, followed by the others. Only Titus reined in and kept the steady pace he had set from the start. As he swung around the statue of Mars on the *spina*, Joseph noticed that the caretakers had forgotten to shut the water duct lid.

On the fourth lap, the two leading chariots came up side by side battering each other's cockpits. Although such a maneuver cost valuable time, it was a legitimate way to eliminate a competitor early in the race. As they rounded the sixth lap, one of the clashing chariots eased off and pulled away toward the sheds. It was rolling on one wheel only.

The red chariot now took the lead, cutting back and forth across the course, allowing no one to pass. Two drivers took up the challenge, sandwiching the red one between them, hammering it from both sides. Titus held back a few lengths behind. Titus came by the royal box and looked up at Larcius Lepidus, who was kissing Sidonia, while one hand was slipped under her sister's gown. Titus tightened his helmet. The red chariot, meanwhile, was ramming the chariots to its right and left trying to escape. The crowd roared as one of the chariots crashed against the *spina*.

As he came around again, Titus saw his pacer splattered against the bloodied statue of the God of War. In the red blazing chariot, now in the lead, Spiculus saluted as he raced by the royal box. Joseph's body rumbled with horses' hoofs.

Over on the *spina* a team of workmen was clearing away the chariot debris. Spiculus cut in front of Titus and challenged him. Titus eased back refusing to be baited. Only Spiculus, his pacer and Titus remained in the race. He was beginning to make up his mind.

Titus advanced and was immediately flanked by Spiculus and his teammate who forced him into the center lane. One of his horses turned its mane. Titus acknowledged the warning by snapping the reins against its flank as the two chariots smashed against his.

The placard above the pits flashed XIV. Always anxious with concentrating on the moment, Joseph distracted himself in his usual manner by composing a dialogue with the cause of his discomfort.

"It's because your father has no ambition," he addressed Titus,

"and why he suffers the venom of the fat pervert emperor and his henchman. Fearing no man, Vespasian allows others to fail."

"Who?"

"You. You will never allow yourself to surpass your father. You Flavians are obsessed with hierarchy.

"Strange remark coming from one of so ancient a family as yours."

"My father has the audacity of antiquity. He would like me to surpass him.

"Would you?"

Joseph chuckled. "I already have."

If Vespasian showed ambition, Nero would ship him off to the east where he sequesters all his gifted captains."

"The east may yet rule the west," said Joseph.

"You're as much a schemer as Lucinus Marcianus," said Titus. "Like him the arrogance of your blood flows with conspiracy. Like your ancestor, Herod and like his, Brutus, assassin of the first Caesar.

"You Flavians are soldiers of the line, unencumbered by history."

"Loyal only to whomever gives orders," Joseph could see the wise smile of Titus.

"It's time for the generous Vespasian to declare who shall give the orders."

Titus laughed at Joseph thinking his father generous. "And whom do you think should give the orders?"

"You," said Joseph rising now as he saw Titus move ahead of Spiculus.

"Is that your way to gain his generosity?"

"In my case generosity can only feed the love for my people."

"And ambition?"

"My tradition forbids self-serving."

Titus laughed deep in Joseph's soul. *"Lucia Paulina,"* he said, *"shall see to all your traditions."*

The race was coming to an end. At any moment Spiculus would break from his teammate and set his own pace for victory while Titus was still undecided. The plaque over the pits flashed number XVIII.

Titus advanced astride Spiculus. Did he agree that the fate of Rome was at stake in this race? Joseph was about to create a dialogue with Spiculus, but the professional racer's vapid eyes left no space for imagination. As if in answer to Joseph's question, Titus let his opponent inch forward. Unlike Joseph he was never one to keep an advantage unless it was vital.

His father would make a fine emperor, thought Joseph. Better than Epaphroditus and the others, he believed. Vespasian was a born soldier, a man of modest temperament, a genius for detail and relatively happily married, with all his energies committed to Rome. But the others would force payment for esteem. Conspiracy, like the phoenix, is born of its own intrigue. Vespasian was merely the pawn in the old nobility's struggle to regain power. He snickered thinking Titus could bring down all their plans by crashing against Spiculus and having the race end inconclusively.

But there had been an urgency in the rasping words of Epaphroditus. "It must be now," he had said, "or we shall all be hanging upside down in the Forum by sunset."

Sensing Titus' hesitation, his horses instinctively picked up speed. Unlike their master they had no choice. They were trained only to win. Five laps remained. Joseph saw that Titus was counting.

Pacing Spiculus' second, Titus again came alongside his opponent. Spiculus was talking to himself aloud, cajoling his team with soothing words and sweet whistles as he lashed at their backs. Titus seemed to cherish the silent moments of crisis and had told Joseph earlier how he had been shocked when once he happened upon Larcius Lepidus in battle and heard him chattering, thinking he was urging his men on. Only when he came closer did Titus realize that Larcius was whipping and scorning his own courage.

Now! now! now! you cunt. Do it now, chicken heart! Go! go! There, right into the boil of your own blood. You're a better man than you are, Larc. Personal. Make it personal. Hate. That man hates you less than you hate him. Yourself. So you will outlive him. Yourself. This is a personal battle, Larc. Always is. Not your men's. Not the enemy's. Not Rome's. Yours. The only way to win, Larc, is to get yourself killed.

Often, Titus said, he heard him growl, gnashing his teeth like a hound at bay, at the same time snarling and foaming. "The way he made love," Titus told Joseph. "Larcius enjoys two sports: war and women, and depending on whim, would turn down one for the other. Nothing else had meaning for him." So when Titus looked up at the stands and saw that his friend Larcius had left the circus with Sidonia and her sister, he smiled at Joseph who was thinking that at that moment Larcius was already lashing himself with vile words of love.

Coming around toward the royal box, Titus was in control. Joseph caught a glimpse of the Praetorian Guard jostling some dozen men whose clipped hair was combed down on their foreheads in military fashion. They stood with lances held high, and by their blue tunics, he recognized them as men of the Ferratti, Lucinus Marcianus' VIth Legion.

Everyone in the crowded royal box was standing. The food table lay turned over, wine trickling through the stone pillars of the balustrade and on to the track. Nero's wreath lay at Joseph's feet. Larcius Lepidus, who had reappeared, had his arm tightly enveloping the Emperor, while Mucianus was giving orders to his men. Nero was not struggling. Behind him, her hair snaking with sweat, stood Lucia, a dagger flashing in her fist.

Titus was passing Spiculus, who was still talking to his horses, when he saw that his opponent's wheel was heading straight for the open water duct. Reaching over his cockpit door, Titus slammed the cover shut with the back of his hand just as Spiculus' left wheel crossed over. Then he lost control.

Half crouched, his knees touching his chin, Titus rose like a tumbler, feeling himself lift out of himself. Then he came back. The reins strapped around his wrist urged his pulse as they pulled him down between the haunches of his team, his bare knees scraping against the track. The circus stood in silence. Joseph envied Titus, knowing that it was he alone who controlled his own capacity.

Spiculus' flaming chariot was two lengths behind Titus. From the eyes and teeth of the two lead horses, Joseph sensed that the race was over. If Titus could hang on to his team until the finish line and keep them at their present pace, he would win. The circus rules only called for the rider to finish with the reins in his hands. To keep aloft, however, Titus had to rein full in and this slowed his horses. Spiculus took the lead.

Bracing his feet in the team's aft traces and resting between them, Titus eased up on the reins. The horses moved out again without urging and quickly overtook Spiculus who was still shouting and whipping his beasts. He must have realized that there was only one way for him to win. As they rounded the last lap, he fell behind and stalked Titus' empty chariot. For the rules also held that there was no penalty for trampling an opponent to death. Joseph felt himself slipping with Titus between the sweating haunches of the horses. There was no longer any question of losing.

Blood trickled down Titus' face and Joseph moaned until he realized that it came from where Titus had earlier scratched the rump of one horse. The chariot slowed and Titus climbed back into the cockpit in order to greet the multitude who, because of the manner of his victory had only now broken into cheers.

Ironically, by not condescending, and defeating Nero's favorite without fearing the consequences, Titus had shown his loyalty to the Emperor, and at least for the moment had saved both their lives. The drama of his victory had turned the usual uproar into silence, not allowing the conspirators the pandemonium they needed to succeed.

Titus wheeled about in a tight circle, his hand stretched out in salute. "Hail Caesar!" he cried, the first time his lips had opened since the start of the race. The Emperor, grinning with approval, saluted back and as was the custom, took the wreath from his head and handed it to the guest of honor, the only other person left in the box. Without precedent and to the roar of the multitude, Joseph ben Matthias tossed it down to Titus.

iii

Titus looked up from his papers.

"I didn't expect you would begin your campaign until the dry season," said Joseph.

"The priests of Baal up on Mount Carmel say that these are the last of the rains. By next week we shall be in summer."

"Long ago such priests were put to shame on that same mountain by the prophet of God."

"Did he have anything to say about Tiberias?"

"Larcius Lepidus has sacked it. I know."

"Then maybe *you* are a prophet."

"I have," said Joseph, "been blessed with modest prophetic powers."

"And did these tell you that I was there with him?"

"You were at the Battle of Tiberias?"

"With the Queen and her troops as well as with Larcius. Neither knew I was there. I went as an ordinary legionnaire. I like to see the terrain I'll do battle over from all angles, especially from the angle of defeat."

"I should think that such a victory would have been proclaimed throughout the empire."

"You forget the Flavian hierarchy. My father wasn't at Tiberias."

"And his generosity?"

Titus rose from the sofa, his sword belt hanging over his protruding stomach.

"As you once said. It's been tempered by ambition."

"Do you always sleep armed?" asked Joseph.

"Always. At home and in the field." He lifted a glass pitcher and poured some pomegranate juice into a bowl. "I'm sorry. It's all I have to offer. My wine supply hasn't arrived yet from Egypt. But this is pretty strong. They let it ferment, these mountain people. Keeps them warm in the winter, they say."

"I come for your generosity," said Joseph refusing the drink. "My command has been taken away from me on suspicion of consorting with the enemy. You."

Titus drank slowly, sucking his teeth with his tongue. "Well, have you?"

"That's for you to say. It's a serious charge."

"From what Berenice tells me, you're just being made a scapegoat. This bar Gioras wants to occupy Jerusalem. He's offered John of Gishhalav your command if he supports him in Jerusalem."

"Then nothing's much changed in Jerusalem since I left."

"The Queen thinks that bar Gioras has the best organized fighting force in the country."

"Silas Barnea has. Trained in Rome. Together we can defeat you."

"Silas is dead. I killed him myself on my way back from Egypt. He fought well, but finally we broke the old fellow at Gaza. Me and the XVth."

"Then you didn't come from Rome?"

"The Vth and the XXIInd did. With my father. I've been in the Golan since I saw you last. With the Queen." He sipped more juice. "And Lucia."

Joseph raised Titus' pitcher with both hands and drank. His fingers trembled. "Silas was my last hope. Maybe yours as well. There is little room now for compromise. You'll have to wipe out half the country to win."

"I have no compunctions as you have about killing Jews."

"A pyrrhic victory. Like your father's at the Isle of Wight. A slow, lugubrious slaughter. Without stars to halo the crown of an empire."

Titus frowned. "Ortho's been assassinated. The Senate is about to confirm Vitellius as Emperor of Rome."

Joseph understood immediately that an old, weak man was about to be replaced by a strong one, the leading legate in the west.

Titus held the glass pitcher up against the light. "Looks like wine. Wish it tasted like it." He drank from the pitcher, then set it down. Picking up a riding switch, he whipped it against his thigh. "Your people have already humiliated us three times: the slaughter of Metilius' men and his circumcision, the massacre at Masada and worst of all the rout of the Twelfth Legion."

"I had nothing to do with any of those cowardly acts."

"You participated in all of them."

"In effect, so were you. You sanctioned your own defeats. You named these all superfluous."

"The situation has changed."

"And you?"

"As you ask. Generous.

Joseph felt strong. As in Rome, standing before the Circus Flaminius, he was ready to act out his own destiny and contend for power beyond the limitation of Jerusalem. Wasn't it Bannus who had said: *Never allow life to get in the way of your contingencies?* Titus still needed him. If Simon and John could make their compromises with each other for their self-aggrandizement, why should he not find his own salvation through Rome? He saw himself a viceroy to the emperor, a second Tiberius Alexander. Only instead of having abandoned his brethren, he would become their savior. What Joseph had refused to ask himself was whether among Bannus' possibilities was one about killing his fellow Jews.

Titus walked to the entrance of the tent. "The rains have stopped. The Priests of Baal were right. We've advanced our timetable. Orders have already gone out to the Xth Legion to by-pass Zippori. Before Vitellius becomes too entrenched in Rome, we need a victory." He lifted the pitcher. "In two weeks to the day, Larcius and myself under my father march against you at Jotapata as planned." Then he poured the pomegranate juice to the ground. It looked like blood around the Temple's Great Altar.

CHAPTER XX — THE BATTLE OF JOTAPATA

i

From the top of Mount Atzmon Joseph saw the Bay of Acre eighteen hundred feet below protruding into the Great Sea. Directly across lay the Carmel range where at this moment Vespasian was receiving the final omens for victory from the priests of Baal. Though it lay only a quarter of a mile away, he could not see the town of Jotapata.

To the south he watched the smoke rising from Zippori which the young ben Shamia and his Liberty Fighters, no doubt with the support of Eleazar ben Yair, had attacked while he was in Acre. Vespasian had been compelled to send units of the Vth Legion to relieve the city after a thousand of its citizens were killed and its storehouses razed. Why is it, Joseph asked himself, that whenever Jew fought Jew, they excelled beyond their own expectation?

A few patches of scabrous snow still clung stubbornly between the boulders half way down the mountain and glistened in the clear sky. The slopes were sprinkled with daisies, and pink dandelions trembled in the shelter of purple clusters of bramble. He could see that some of the boulders darkened into caves which Hanan told him tunneled into Jotapata. In peacetime these caves were used as storage pits for grain and fruit. Now rebel bands hid in them. The countryside was brushed with new grass and spotted with anemones like huge drops of blood.

Though Mount Atzmon dominated the valley, it had no strategic value for the Romans since Jotapata, hidden somewhere below, was out of firing range. The boulders, thought Joseph, were a much more logical first line of defense for the town. He wished he could have the cover of the pomegranate groves that lay between the town and the mountain, but the trees were just beginning to bud and his bowmen would not have the natural cover of the leaves. A stubble field lay where the Valley of Bet Netofa opened to the sea, a perfect site for the Roman camp. So engrossed had he become in the terrain that for a moment he forgot that he was planning for the defeat of his people.

To break his descent, he had to side-slip, loosening a small avalanche of pebbles. An exhiliration of starlings rose suddenly from the groves and whirled in a perfect circle across the valley. Joseph came through the boulders and stopped when he saw Jotapata, its walls like teeth stuck into the jaw of the rock plateau whose sides fell into precipitous cliffs. He knew that these walls were as thick as Jerusalem's, having been built and rebuilt many times since the days of

Joshua. Also, like Jerusalem, the town was accessible only from the north where a spur of another mountain made the ascent to the main gate less steep. The wind had not ceased to howl since Joseph had arrived at Jotapata.

ii

On the morning of the Fourteenth day of *Iyar*, Joseph and his forces entered Jotapata, and after taking over the west tower in the wall as his headquarters, he called together the town council and informed them that in less than twenty-four hours they would be attacked by three Roman legions. The councilmen were not surprised, having supported John of Gishhalav even before independence had been officially declared by the *Sanhedrin*. Because of his exploits in the south and even more because they believed that he was involved in the attack on Zippori, the city they most hated, the people of Jotapata welcomed Joseph. In his opening address to them he had declared that in the defense of their small citadel the whole nation of Israel would be named. Instead of causing them to panic as he had hoped and thus giving him full control over the outcome of the battle, the citizens immediately set about preparing for the siege that they had undergone so many times in their history. They took pride in the fact that the first Jewish general in more than a century had chosen their town as his base of operations. They had not heard that Joseph's command had been rescinded.

After a tour of inspection, Joseph felt assured that Titus' plan would go well. No other town in Judea, not even in the Wilderness, stood so open to attack as this fort where not a guard on its walls bore arms, nor had anyone bothered to ration the spring crops and water which wastefully overflowed in troughs. The staffless shepherds, herding their fleeceless young flocks up the mountain slopes, seemed to epitomize their own condition of lambs being led to slaughter.

Nevertheless, to show his commitment to the town's defense, Joseph had Hanan, a Galilean and fully trusted, appointed quartermaster, and instructed him to cut food and water intake immediately to one third. Benjamin ben Natan, the town's head priest, was ordered to temporarily cancel the tithe and to keep control over the slaughterhouse and water supply. Unlike Jerusalem, Jotapata had no natural springs inside its walls, and all water came from the cisterns filled with the last of the winter rain. These Joseph ordered sealed until each family used up its own supply gathered in troughs on their roofs. Together with Niger and Hanan, he inspected the walls and issued orders to narrow and lengthen the firing embrasures as well as raise a wood barrier on the town's vulnerable side against enemy bowmen and earthworks that might be imposed over the walls. Such precautions finally alarmed the citizens, which was exactly what Joseph wished to do, though he alone knew how superficial were his preparations in comparison to what his ancient namesake, "the provider," would have done in his place.

A delegation led by Benjamin ben Natan met him at the main gate on his way back from a last tour of the town's outskirts. "We thought, General," said the priest, "that it would be much wiser to evacuate the women and children into the surrounding caves so that they will neither be in the way nor in danger during the fighting."

Joseph was annoyed. "I was told that the women of Galilee fight beside their men."

"It is their own choice to make," said a gray bearded man.

"Men fight better," said Joseph, "when they know that they're defending their families."

"And the food, the extra food we shall need?"

Joseph waved the baton he carried. "There's enough food here to feed the whole of Jerusalem."

A more serious point of contention awaited Joseph at his headquarters. "Mount Atzmon," said Eleazar ben Shamia, who had entered the town secretly with his men through one of the tunnels, "it's got to be defended. It's the Roman supply route up from the coast."

"After Zippori I would think that you'd leave any strategy to me."

"I now command fifteen hundred men," persisted ben Shamia. "They take orders from me only."

An hour later scouts brought news that the Romans had moved out of their base at Acre. Glancing up at the hovering mountain, Joseph told Hanan and Niger to avoid all contact with the enemy until he gave the order.

When they left, he took up his journal. He wrote:

according to their manual, the romans take twenty-four hours to set up camp. we will attack them first with a small force outside the walls, enough to whet their appetites to take the town in one light counterattack. my men will hold. titus will be confused and want to attack more fiercely. his father, a more cautious man, will bid for a siege. after three weeks, starvation and death shall take their toll so that by the beginning of sivan, the romans shall be ready to scale the walls and take jotapata in a glorious victory, enough to impress the jews and the roman senate. lucia and myself shall celebrate the pentacostal festival and the coro-

*nation of vespasian and queen berenice at the temple in
jerusalem.*

And as an afterthought he added:

*any harassment of the advancing roman column by brigands as
at shaar hagai must be checked so that rome's legions do not
wreak vengeance upon us once they break through our defenses. it becomes necessary, then, to eliminate ben shamia and his
men before titus arrives.*

iii

Despite the continuing rain, a fire broke out in the main granary.
Joseph saw the possibility of a ruse to find a scapegoat. That night he
had James, his bodyguard, drop a Sicari dagger among the rubble of
the granary, and in the morning gave orders to round up all the Sicaris
in town. But by then Eleazar ben Shamia and his men had already disappeared.

Towards evening the guards on the watchtowers sighted the enemy
moving down the Valley of Bet Netofa. Joseph watched the approaching Romans with awe. First came the XVth Legion led by six
squadrons of cavalry. Along the mountain ridges on both sides of the
valley two thousand cohorts of infantry guarded their flanks. Behind
came the work battalions followed in the same order by the XIIth and
Vth Legions. Wherever necessary slaves quickly widened the valley
road to allow the war machines guarded by Syrian auxiliaries to move
through the mountain passes.

On dawn of the Twentieth of *Iyar,* the Jews massed on the walls and
were astonished to see that overnight the Romans had erected a
miniature city six hundred yards to the west of the town, at the spot
Joseph had guessed. And a great fear gripped the Jews of Jotapata.
Unlike the Greeks who first chose a battle site, the Romans preferred
to entrench themselves before attacking, convinced that logistics and
not terrain were the essence of victory.

From the embrasure in his headquarters, Joseph gazed down at the
mirage of the Roman camp, hardly able to believe its reality. He saw
the stubble field ordered into streets with rows of tents perfectly spaced. In the middle of the camp stood a square of officers' tents, the
center one, named *Praetorium,* was the headquarters of the commander-in-chief. Interspersed between the tents stood armories, forges,
stables, and food and water depots. There was even a marketplace behind which whores sat combing their hair in the first sun in more than a

week, while legionnaires already lined the lanes between the girls' tents. Near the officers' quarters, he saw an open air court gathered to ajudicate disputes among the men. A stockade ten foot high with twenty wood towers, each with a different war machine, surrounded the camp. The stockade had three gates and a fosse around it six feet deep.

Only when he recognized Hanan followed by five hundred armed Jews charging toward the enemy camp did Joseph snap out of the trance in which Roman efficiency had held him. He fumed at this breach in the war code where notes of challenge were first exchanged before battle commenced. The Jews barely reached the fosse when a barrage of arrows cut them down, forcing a quick retreat. A second wave, led by Niger, came charging out of the caves from the higher ground to the left of the Roman camp, while from the town walls the few catapults simultaneously released their missiles which fell short of the enemy, landing in the midst of Niger's men. Nevertheless the Jews managed to reach the fosse, leaping into it in order to take up closer positions against the Romans on the stockade. But the fosse was half filled with water and Niger's force was immobilized by the mud.

A third sortie swung out off ropes from the south cliffs of the town and landed in a part of the stubble field the Romans had not used. The screams of the Jews made Joseph realize that this area had been left as bait and that it had been sown with knife sharp bamboo sticks. Ben Shamia had convinced Joseph's most trusted commanders to strike before the Romans were prepared, hoping in this way to surprise an army that had never been caught off its guard. Next time, Joseph was sure, they would wait for his orders.

Despite all the miscalculations, the Jews climbed out of the fosse and over the stockade. Joseph found himself cheering as the cavalry of the XVth Legion dashed down the camp's main street attacking the foothold the Jews had established. In desperation some of Niger's men formed a human bridge, spanning the fosse in order to allow their retreating comrades to cross over and into the groves of pomegranates. A few streets from the battle, the lines of men in front of the whore tents continued moving, orderly and unconcerned.

After dark, Hanan and Niger retreated into town and reported that casualties were light and morale high. For the Galileans the advance upon the Roman camp was a victory, and they prayed in their synagogues, thanking the Lord of Hosts. Niger declared that his men were ready for another sally.

"I gave orders for no sallies. Neither yesterday nor now," said Joseph angrily.

"It's the only way they know how to fight. They're uncomfortable on the defensive."

"Another such mad foray and you'll be wiped out."

"They were magnificent out there. They'll endure."

"Not from where I witnessed it. It was the most disorganized battle I've ever seen. Do you know how many times the Romans have sucked fools like you into the same trap?"

Benjamin the priest entered. "We're ready whenever you are," he announced.

"That's just what the Romans want. They're trained to fight the same battle over and over again until they wear their enemy down. Then they overwhelm him with their full force."

"Ben Shamia insists on continuing sallies," said Benjamin. "He's a local hero. If he succeeds without you and your men, you'll lose hold over the town."

"Heroes don't win wars," snapped Joseph.

"Jotapata is only one battle," said Benjamin.

"A very crucial one," said Joseph.

"For you or the country?" asked Hanan.

Hanan had changed since Joseph had secretly visited Titus. "What do you mean by that?"

Hanan turned away. "Look," said Niger. "Let's try them at night. I'm ready to test how well their order holds up under darkness."

Joseph was no longer listening. Through the embrasure he saw that Roman troops had occupied the crest of Mount Atzmon, sealing off the town. Instinctively he flinched as the first barrage of ballista stones came flying into Jotapata. "It's for morale shattering," said Joseph. "For three days they'll pound us with stones interspersed with long arrows. At night they'll continue with fire. They never change their tactics."

"Then neither must we," said Niger. "Do I have your permission to strike through the caves?"

"Permission granted," said Joseph.

That night Joseph disguised himself as one of Niger's men. He wished to discover for himself what the Romans were doing on Mount Atzmon.

Once out of the caves, Joseph hid among the boulders until Niger and his troops disappeared into the moonless night. By the scent, he knew he was entering the pomegranate groves. Soon he was ascending the mountain. His breath came quickly and his supper seethed in his gullet. The few stars gave no light, making the mountain and the night merge into a black cloud. When he smelled the sea, he knew he had reached the summit.

Not to be silhouetted against the horizon by the line of torches that he saw coming up from the Roman camp, he skirted the western ridges of Atzmon until he was close enough to see two work battalions widening a path into a road that ran directly to Jotapata. Behind them a third battalion, harnessed to thick ropes, hauled a platform on wheels upon which stood a giant beast. In the dizzying wind, Joseph was ready to believe that the Romans had built a Trojan horse in order to trick the Jews into surrender. He crept closer, no longer afraid to be discovered, since the groans and other noises of the workers drowned out all other sounds. When a group of men held up their torches, Joseph reeled back at the sight of the ghostly face and grape colored eyes of the famous wall smashing ram.

He fell into a bramble bush from which a covey of crows flushed out. The voices of disaster pounded at him from the depth of the earth. Then he heard the howling of jackals.

iv

Joseph tapped his fingers nervously as he listened to Niger report what had happened during their attack on the Romans the night before.

"Like Samson. Five hundred jackals. Only this time their mouths, not their tails, were aflame with infection. And starving."

"Scorpions," declared Joseph. "Like at Masada."

"Foaming at the mouth with rabies. Eleazar ben Yair turned them loose on the Romans."

"You mean the work battalions."

Niger grinned, nodding his head excitedly. "Hundreds were bitten."

Joseph turned pale. "Idiots! Most of those were our own people, conscripted from the surrounding villages. Whom do you think the Romans use as their lackeys?"

"Some managed to escape into the caves," said Niger with dismay.

"And the ram?" asked Joseph.

"What ram?"

"The battering ram. Rome's latest and most powerful weapon of destruction."

"I know nothing of a ram."

"The one real benefit that could have been gained from such a raid and you ask what ram?"

"In any event our scouts report that the Romans are totally shaken by our ruse. They've had to double their sentinels and send out half a legion to track down the mad jackals. They're still roaming the mountainside."

"And in the meanwhile?" asked Joseph.

'You said time was on our side. It will take weeks now before they can attack us."

Joseph looked out at Mount Atzmon. And when they come, he thought, they're going to take every one of us.

By noon the Jews who had abandoned their villages began entering the town through the caves. The XIIth Legion, whose shame at Shaar Hagai made Vespasian place them on police duties, had been ordered to raze every Jewish settlement within a radius of twenty miles and not to hinder these peasants' escape into Jotapata. Not only did this mean more mouths to feed, but many of these Jews had also caught the disease of the jackals and would pass it on to the rest of the city.

In his journal, Joseph recorded:

there is always honey out of the lion's carcass.

That evening the Romans attacked in full force. For three hours the war machines pounded Jotapata with stones and missiles, while Arab archers smothered the skies with lighted arrows that streaked through the night like falling stars. Under their cover, five thousand men charged against the north wall. Their gold tipped lances and round shields identified them as Vespasian's personal guard.

"I warned you," said Joseph to ben Shamia. "The one thing the Romans despise is a break in the rules of war. From now on they will attack until they crack our defenses. Losses mean nothing. Kill a thousand, five thousand, and they'll send ten thousand fresh troops against us. It's not Syrians or scouting patrols you're fighting now, but the might of the Roman army. It's not only to punish us that Vespasian gives battle, but for his good name and maybe even his life."

At the north wall chains and bill hooks and grappling irons clanged and grated as the Romans began to mount the ramparts. The defenders were surprisingly calm, waiting until the soldiers reached the parapets before pushing them back to their death one at a time as if it were a game with its own rules. If Joseph had bothered to study the history of Jotapata or observed its ancient symbols, he would have been aware that it was engraved with attacks of this kind. Watching the defenders going about their task as if they were daily chores, he began to sense that he had chosen the wrong town to declare the destiny of the Flavians.

The fighting lasted through the night and the next day with endless waves of Romans trying to scale the walls, while behind them archers kept picking off more and more Jews. If he did not counterattack, Joseph would soon lose half his men at the north wall. Against his will he fell back on the old Jewish ruse. "Choose fifty of our best men," Joseph instructed Niger. "We've got to break up those Arab bowmen around the fosse."

"Eleazar has a way of attacking from behind," said Hanan.

"I've had my fill of ben Shamia's strategy."

"I mean ben Yair. Eleazar ben Yair."

"After sundown," said Joseph, "I'll lead the sortie myself."

From the mouth of one of the caves, Joseph watched with amazement as the Jews crawled halfway down the wall. Led by Eleazar ben Yair, they edged along a narrow ledge below the Romans from where they cut the rope ladders that the enemy had used to storm the wall. Fearing that they were losing contact with their camp, the legionnaires leaped off the ramparts to instant death.

Despite this success, as Joseph had predicted, the following day the Romans returned with double their strength, but the Jews, inspired by Eleazar's feat, met them at the main gate and drove them back beyond the fosse. The humiliation of the Roman professionals at being forced to retreat by half trained peasants hardened their determination. Without concern over their losses, they pressed the attack. The battle had become self propelling and even Joseph found himself caught in the momentum of valor. By evening, the Romans finally broke off the attack. Two thousand legionnaires and five hundred Jews lay strewn across the terrain between the enemy camp and the town gates. On the Third of *Sivan,* Vespasian decided that he had no choice but to lay siege to Jotapata.

Joseph ordered Benjamin ben Natan to cut rations again, hoping in this way to weaken the morale of the besieged. Ben Shamia, who with Eleazar ben Yair was now fighting totally independent of Joseph's command, immediately occupied one of the storehouses. "Siege has always been the doom of our people," he warned Joseph. "I intend to use as much food and water as my men will need in order to destroy the earthworks which the Roman is now setting up."

"My men are trained to withstand just such siege tactics," countered Joseph.

"We came north to fight," said Niger. He too had been arguing for more supplies. Rubbing his unshaven chin, Joseph reluctantly agreed. "Take one battalion of Royals and go out with ben Shamia."

Eleazar ben Yair walked into headquarters.

"So you've come to spy on me," said Joseph.

Eleazar's lips moved before he spoke. "On all of you. What you do here depends on how long I stay around."

"The men fight better," said Niger, "when they know you are here."

"You're not quite the observer you make yourself out to be," said Joseph, ignoring Niger's remark. "Certainly not after the night of the jackals."

"Not my idea. Hers." He turned around as Lucia entered. She was dressed in a white robe, the edges tucked around her belted waist.

"Cleopatra did the same once," she said. "It's good for morale."

"So did Samson," countered Joseph. "Only he died in defeat."

"No one ever dies in defeat," said Eleazar.

"It's not very hard to do what you did when you hold no responsibility but to yourself."

Eleazar pushed his side locks under the band around his head. Even in the half light of the small room his hair glistened. "I'm not convinced that you have the right attitude about the Roman."

"Exactly what I just said," ben Shamia agreed. "You abandon us when we no longer suit your purposes."

"This place is not worth fighting over. Makes my people nervous. Not worth it for Jews or for the Roman."

"Jerusalem? Would you fight for Jerusalem?"

Eleazar faced Joseph directly. "A place is worth fighting for only if it's worth dying for."

"Masada. The madness of Masada."

"The Lord demands that we die for His everlasting glory. It's in the order of things."

"Everlasting glory of the Lord is in dutifully worshipping Him under any condition and in any place according to The Law."

"Everlasting glory comes only when you die for him."

"It is written that God is a living God."

Eleazar leafed through Joseph's journal that lay half open on a work table. "Is that what you're recording?"

Their fingertips brushed as Joseph rolled up the journal. "The living part. All of it."

"As it is or as you'd like it to be?"

"Is there any real difference?"

"To other generations. Responsibility to how it really happened."

Joseph shrugged. "It happened before."

Eleazar looked out onto Mount Atzmon. "The responsibility to see that it doesn't happen again in the same way."

When Eleazar left, Joseph sat at his work table. For the first time he felt no desire to record anything. He was tired and could no longer stand the stench of his own body.

When he looked up he saw that Lucia was still there. "So you've now become a Galilean. A fighting lady," he said bitterly.

"A Jew. I pray. I eat proper food and have confidence in the Lord God of Hosts."

"And the child you bear? Have you chosen life for it?"

"My life. If I live I shall bear many children. I want a command in Jotapata."

Joseph stood and faced her. He was struck by how gaunt she had become and how her eyes dominated her face. He thought that in her new commitment she had abandoned her beauty. "If you remain in Jotapata, you'll take orders from me."

"I shall wherever I am. You are my husband."

"That point is still debatable. Nevertheless in Jotapata women do not have commands. There is other more essential work that men cannot do."

"Your wish?"

"The sick, the wounded, the dying."

"I've already chosen to be among the dying."

"*Aruhat bat ami.* Healer of our suffering. Not as a killer."

"And if I decided to join him?" Lucia nodded in the direction Eleazar had just left.

"You have much to learn about the paradoxes of Jews. He is married."

She released the edges of her gown from her belt and let it fall to her ankles. "So are you."

He knew that this time she was referring to Hagla.

The Roman earthworks kept growing higher, despite ben Shamia's continued raids. The one consolation in the youth's intransigence was that his sorties expended energy, and as the weather warmed, the water supply dwindled more quickly than had been calculated. Here again Joseph found a ruse which wasted water and at the same time ingratiated him on the town.

"More than food and manpower, we lack water," he told the elders. "Unlike Jerusalem, all you have are cisterns of rain water which my spies report Vespasian believes will last only till the end of the week."

"With care we have at least a month's supply," corrected Benjamin.

"Care doesn't seem to be in the character of Jotapata," said Joseph. "Nevertheless, I think it would be worth our while to squander some in order to prove to the Roman that any siege he intends will be as long and as arduous for him in the coming summer as it will be for us."

"What do you propose?"

Joseph turned to Lucia who stood in the shadows. "Lucia, let the women declare a laundry day. Let them hang their wash upon the parapets so that the Roman might see that water is of no consequence to Jotapata."

Everyone approved of the ploy. Joseph estimated that in one day half the town's remaining water supply would be wasted.

Toward sunset Jotapata's walls were shrouded in white with water trickling down their sides like runnels in springtime. Maybe, thought Joseph, he might still spend the Pentacost in Jerusalem.

The plan backfired when it rained the following day, replenishing the town's cisterns.

v

The sun came out waking Joseph to an unfamiliar sound. He reached out for Lucia, but she was gone. Through the aperture he saw mule teams led by a battalion of workers carrying saws and axes, moving toward the groves. A contingent of Roman infantry guarded their flanks. He scanned the sparkling trees which still dripped with rain and saw that in the two weeks of fighting, the leaves had thickened on the pomegranate trees. The laborers were felling the trees.

Suddenly a hail of arrows cut down the first line of workers. The others dropped their tools and fled. Even before they reached the camp, the cavalry was dashing through the muddy streets, out over the fosse and toward the groves.

"They've cut ben Shamia off," declared Niger breathlessly as he ran into headquarters. "He can't get back into town."

Joseph walked to the doorway and saw that the cavalry had surrounded the pomegranate groves.

"Why are we here?" Niger asked. "There's no damn strategic value to this town." It was the first time Joseph had ever seen his kinsman angry.

Joseph walked back to the table. "The mere investment of fourteen days has imposed strategic importance to Jotapata."

"Why?" cried Niger, pounding his fist on the table and on top of Joseph's journal. "Why should they be here? Why are we making a stand in this God forsaken town?"

It was time to let Niger in on his secret. "Because, my friend, the next Emperor of Rome shall rise from the ashes of Jotapata."

Niger failed to understand. "What difference does it make to us who the Emperor of Rome is?"

"Ask her," said Joseph, nodding to Lucia who entered with a tray of milk and honey, Joseph's usual breakfast. Niger stormed out without awaiting further orders.

When Hanan appeared and verified ben Shamia's desperate position, Joseph reached for his sword. "Order out the Bnai Golah," he said. "The only way to relieve the pressure on that stupid boy is to attack the Roman earthworks."

"They're already out there," said Hanan.

Joseph had trouble buckling on his sword. "Then get Eleazar ben Yair."

With three hundred of Eleazar's men armed with poles, Joseph sallied forth against the five central siege towers which by now had nearly reached the height of the town walls. Using the old Jewish skill of stick fighting, they drove off the Syrian guards. The whizzing arrows and the men dying around him excited Joseph. He was convinced that at least on this day and in this place, he was immortal. As at the circumcision of Metilius, a strange impetuosity gripped him, making him desire to be his own hero.

Only after setting four Roman towers aflame did Joseph come back to fear. He panicked when the Elite Guard turned away from ben Shamia in the groves and came directly at him. Titus was right. He was born on the defensive.

Back on the ramparts, he saw that his diversion had not freed ben Shamia to reenter the town through the caves as he had hoped, but that the young chieftain was advancing instead out of the groves against the enemy. Out of nowhere five squadrons of cavalry charged down upon ben Shamia cutting off his attack. By the time he tried to retreat into the groves, they were already in flames. The Xth Legion, under Larcius Lepidus, had under cover of night sneaked over Mount Atzmon on their way from the east and set fire to the groves of pomegranates.

It was past the fourth hour of darkness when a few Jews straggled into town. Five thousand defenders of Jotapata had been killed, among them Eleazar ben Shamia.

Joseph recorded the rout in his journal. He wrote:

today i set in motion the roman victory against us. the slaughter of innocents no longer allows me the dignity of surrender.

Like a penitent he beat his fists against his heart until it was hard for him to breathe. When he stopped, the pounding persisted, and he felt the whole tower tremble. Through the aperture he saw that the ram had begun the final destruction of Jotapata.

vi

It would not be that simple.

For unlike Joseph, the Galileans were used to Roman victories, and if, as they believed, there was no god but the Lord God, then Titus and Vespasian would indeed have to kill every Jew in these mountains before they could return to Rome. The slaughter in the groves did not break Jotapata's resistance. It brought instead every Galilean — some even from Zippori — swarming to the town like locusts during a *sharav*. Except John of Gishhalav.

Led by Eleazar ben Yair, the Galileans charged through the burnt out groves where, much to their surprise, they were met by the remnants of the Liberty Fighters and Bnai Golah, mostly wounded, who had been hiding for days in the surrounding caves and tended by Lucia. They joined the assault upon the Roman camp. Fearing that the Jews might conquer it, Vespasian had the ram moved back into the mountain pass. He then proceeded to set up a perimeter defense, contenting himself by bombarding the town with seventy-five weight ballista stones and with scorpion quick-firers and catapults. Neither victory nor time seemed to matter to the Roman general.

Again the Jews on the ramparts took heart from the courage of Eleazar ben Yair and his men and rushed out to join the advance. The brothers, Netira and Philip, who had been at Cana among the early recruits, led the charge against the tight column of the XVth Legion beyond the fosse, cutting a path of blood through it until they were finally stopped by Titus himself who had galloped out alone from the camp after shaking off the restraining hand of his bodyguards. He decapitated Netira, then, without lowering his sabre, he thrust Philip through.

"Kill me, Sire," cried Philip, "according to the rights of war."

Titus leaned over the side of his mount and spat in the Jew's face. Unable to stand any longer, Philip fell forward kneeling in the fashion of the gentiles, dying as he tried to hold in his entrails.

"Here, give me that bow!" Joseph beckoned to the man standing on the ramparts beside him. Titus glanced up and grinned as he saw Joseph set an arrow to the bow. He spun his horse about and cantered back to the camp.

Joseph lowered the bow without firing. He watched enviously as Titus leaped over the fosse and stopped just inside the stockade. A ballista stone came sailing over and like a bird seeking a roosting spot, it stopped in mid air, then headed to where Joseph stood. A man nearby dived at him and shoved Joseph down the parapet steps just as the stone landed.

"Shevah," said Joseph, as he was helped to his feet. "I thought you and the Bnai Golah were in the groves."

"Jotapata is my ancestral home. It's here that I intend to die."

The stone that had almost killed Joseph lay on the parapet. Shevah picked it up and to Joseph's astonishment, he heaved it beyond the fosse. It landed a few feet from where Titus still sat on his horse.

The wind increased its velocity carrying with it the smell of the sea. Then it stopped and for a moment they could hear the panting of the Roman horses by the fosse. Slowly the clouds grouped for a new direction as the sun paled. The *sharav*, thought Joseph. Soon there will be no water.

The desert wind drowned out the cries of the wounded who lay in the flat land between the Roman camp and the town gates. It took less than a day for the heat to dry their throats, confusing their voices with the barking of hyenas. Joseph decided that the time had come for a truce in order to give both sides a chance to bury their dead. He thought it best to go out himself and negotiate with the enemy.

After sending up the recognized truce signals, Joseph rode out toward the Roman camp. Wearing the plumed helmet of a legate, Larcius Lepidus, Commander of the Xth Legion, waited for him before the fosse. Joseph was momentarily confused when the Roman general addressed him in Aramaic.

"The dead are dead," said Larcius. "It's the living that concern us. Yours."

This was not the drunken legate Joseph remembered from the Circus Flaminius. "I am here for other purposes as well," said Joseph, remembering again Titus' remarks about the two sides of Rome.

"There's nothing more to discuss unless it's terms of surrender."

"I am Josephus," said Joseph in Latin. "I wish to speak with Titus Flavius."

Larcius Lepidus made no sign of recognition. His horse nozzled Joseph's, then jerked its head away. "So far as I know, all Romans speak the same language." He wheeled his mount around to return to the camp, but Joseph grabbed his reins. "I must speak with Titus."

Larcius whacked Joseph's hand away and drew his sabre. Then he grinned. "If that's your hostage, I agree." And he bowed to Lucia Paulina, who rode toward them from Jotapata. This time she was dressed in Roman garb with a *pala* tossed over her shoulders as she galloped side-saddle past Joseph and over the fosse followed by Larcius Lepidus.

Looking back, Joseph saw that the ramparts of Jotapata were crowded with Jews.

Titus appeared on foot from among the Arab archers who guarded the camp side of the fosse. "There's nothing to discuss," he said. "You've broken your vow again."

"Not I," said Joseph, dismounting.

Titus drew his sword. Behind him the archers stood at the ready. "No one gave you permission to dismount."

"We are in a place of truce. It's the law that we face each other on equal ground."

"The law of truce does not exist in rebellion."

Joseph leaned against his horse. "I am not in rebellion. Lucia exonerates me."

"This battle has already cost us seven thousand dead, the number of half a legion."

"And us more than double. I mean to go to Jerusalem and have the bloodshed stopped."

"Go where you like. But the battle goes on."

"As a priest I shall lead a small pilgrimage to Jerusalem for the Pentacost. It's a long established right. Once there, I shall recommend to the *Sanhedrin* that we surrender."

"The way your men fight, your only right is the right to die."

"It's the Sicaris' way. You once told me to join them."

"I didn't know they existed in the north."

"The movement was founded here. They go under various names though their purpose is the same."

Titus scratched the snout of Joseph's horse. "Vespasian is fed up. There's nothing more I can do."

"The battle that he'll soon win will be even more glorious than you and I ever planned."

"I don't believe a word of yours."

"Lucia Paulina is my word."

"It's no longer of any consequence. Vitellius has surrounded Rome. Had we been victorious sooner, my brother Domitian and my uncle would have won over the Praetorian Guard. As it stands, they and our kin are in danger of their lives."

"Let me go to Jerusalem. My report will convince those who have reluctantly supported the revolt to surrender."

"You haven't done so well locally. How do you hope to succeed in Jerusalem?"

"It's *because* I haven't succeeded here. Give me three days."

Titus kicked the ground and raised a puff of dust. "This is the worst climate I've ever suffered," he said. "It's affected my stomach."

Joseph smiled. "Jerusalem is pleasanter."

"You've fought well," said Titus without smiling. "Too well. My father is preparing for a long siege."

"But not you. You know that we're nearing the end of our endurance."

Titus took a piece of sugar cane out of his side bag and fed it to Joseph's horse. "Nice Arabian," he said. "I'm told these desert winds last fifty days."

"That's their total number throughout the year."

"How long will this one last?"

Joseph shrugged. "At this time of the year four days, at most five."

Titus slapped the horse's rump. "Till the wind changes. My last chance and yours. Then I assault the walls in force." Titus walked to the edge of the fosse. "Lucia as well." He jumped over the fosse and disappeared among the Arab archers.

Back in town Joseph called a council of all his commanders. Eleazar ben Yair came uninvited. Joseph explained about the pilgrimage and the permission to lead it.

"You're abandoning us," said Hanan. "For Jerusalem, as usual."

"Not so. The Romans believe I'm going for the *Bikurim* sacrifice. Instead I hope to return with a relief force. We'll attack the Romans from the sea."

"You're a traitor and you'll never come back," declared Shevah. "You intend to negotiate our freedom for your own high priesthood and hegemony over Jerusalem."

"The Romans have offered us a truce to make sacrifice to the Lord," Joseph lied. "Turning their offer down would be an insult to the Lord God of the Universe. Not to the pagan."

"You're a traitor," said Shevah, blinking wildly. "You've conspired with Rome, here and abroad. That's all that matters."

"Joseph has fought courageously here, at Masada and in Jerusalem," protested Niger. "I won't allow you to besmirch his name. If he's cautious, it's for our benefit. As Commander of the North, he's responsible for us all, including his wife."

"Let us compromise," said Benjamin the priest. "Joseph ben Matthias is our defender. Furthermore, it would be a great honor to have a *Kohen* of his rank perform the Pentacostal sacrifice here in Jotapata. Others can carry messages to Jerusalem for aid as well as our meager first fruits to the Temple for the pilgrimage."

Joseph saw no choice but to accept the suggestion. "I shall remain in Jotapata only if we refrain from battle until the pilgrims return. I warn you that without me, they have little chance of convincing the *Sanhedrin* to send us aid."

The commanders congratulated Joseph on his willingness to compromise and agreed to his terms. They then asked if he had learned anything new from his encounter with the enemy.

"Only that they have changed their strategy," he lied again. "Instead of taking the city by assault, they intend to lay siege until they starve us to death."

"We have enough food till the new year," said Benjamin.

Joseph nodded sadly. "There is also the matter of water."

For four days and nights the *sharav* droned, drying out the last of the rain rivulets that still ran down the town streets. Despite this, Joseph took these desert winds as a good omen. On the evening of the fifth day, the wind changed, but after a respite of less than an hour, another hot wind rose. Joseph hoped that the Romans hadn't noticed the short break in the weather. For the first time since his arrival at Jotapata he had a chance to review other matters than the rebellion. And it came so that he thought of Lucia.

Despite all that had occurred, her nature had not changed. From the moment he had taken her, or rather she had taken him, at the pool in her father's atrium through the madness of the Mulvian Bridge, even unto the last time by the shores of Lake Gennesaret she had remained the same willful girl whose commitments were only to a verification of herself. Titus had told him that she was not Epaphroditus' daughter but the illegitimate child of his wife, Lydia, by the Emperor Claudius, which made Lucia a direct descendent of Julius Caesar. Though Roman society cared little about origins, Lucia did, and had tried first through arrogance and shock and then through defiance to discover her true nature. Her mother had died in giving birth to her and had left her ambiguous. Of her real father she knew only through history and that he had the same birthmark she bore, except that his was on his genitals.

"By water," said Joseph. *"Why do we always make love by waters?"*

"For the sanctity of it," he heard himself answer her. *"I wish only to sanctify love."*

"Like Jewish synagogues. They are always set beside waters."

"I like to make love in holy places," said Lucia.

He had come upon her in Cana in a small synagogue, also by waters, a waterfall gushing with melted snow from the mountains.

"I told you once before," he said. "We do not kneel when we pray."

"The others do. I watch them."

"They are no longer true Jews and believe in the Nazarene. We bow to the Word and His ineffable name."

"Teach me to say his name."

"Only in the Holy of Holies, in the Temple on *Yom Kippur* the High Priest utters the Word and kneels."

"I would like to make love in the Temple of God."

She had been gentle and he found that he could not love her in the wild manner he enjoyed.

He was awakened by a messenger announcing that the pilgrims had been massacred. Stunned, Joseph ran out onto the ramparts where he saw Shevah handing out newly forged spears and lances to the men manning the walls. "It can't be," cried Joseph. "I was promised their going and their coming."

"You trusted the Roman," said Shevah. "You always did."

"This time it was not the Roman," said Hanan. "The Sicaris broke the oath to Titus." He came up to Joseph and whispered in his ear. "Eleazar ben Yair, together with his men, decided that they'd had enough of our bickering."

"We've never been united as we've been here."

"Ben Shamia was his man. You let him die. When John of Gishhalav didn't join us, he decided he'd rather die at Masada."

"Like you all," said Joseph angrily to Shevah. Then turning back to Hanan. "What has all this to do with the pilgrims?"

"Coming out into the Valley of Azochis, Eleazar ben Yair met what he thought was a Roman patrol and engaged them."

"That would not provoke Titus. Such incidents are bound to occur in a battle zone even during a truce."

"The patrol happened to be a hunting party of high Roman commanders. Flavius Vespasian was wounded by an arrow in the sole of his foot. This morning our lookouts reported a massing of all Roman forces."

Suddenly Joseph didn't care. It mattered little to him if he were fighting to win or to lose. Maybe he should have given himself up to Titus at the fosse? Again he asked himself about his alternatives and those of his people. Why are the choices so much more acute for us than for others? Why were we chosen in every generation? Is that our peculiar treasure: to be the crucible of history?

Climbing back to the tower, he saw the Bnai Golah huddled at the foot of the stairways leading up to the ramparts. The men all held pikes, the best defense against troops scaling walls. He no longer knew his priorities.

CHAPTER XXI — DUEL AT THE BREACH

i

He must have slept through the night and part of the day. He awoke leisurely, rinsed his teeth with a mouthful of water, then brushed his hair back with his fingers. He scratched his unshaven chin vigorously and ate a green plum. He felt refreshed. For the first time in a month of days his mind seethed with possibilities.

Ironically Jotapata had become a trap for the Flavians, while at the same time renewing Joseph's good name throughout the country. Of all the commanders selected by the *Sanhedrin,* only Joseph had prevailed against Rome. If he could now convice Titus to abandon Jotapata, reverse his plan and let the Jews be the victors, Joseph himself would march on Jerusalem, take over its command and as Herod had once done, also through the reputation he had won in the Galilee, deliver the captial peacefully to Rome, thus revitalizing Vespasian's claim to her crown.

Shevah's remark came back to him about wanting to be High Priest. Others in Judea and in Rome had thought the same. Maybe his father was right: that only Jerusalem was worth concentrating upon, the only place he and Joseph truly loved. Looking out on the already seared countryside beyond the Roman camp, he longed for the cooler air of the holy city; its silver rocks and lemon hills that fell away into the blue Salt Sea. Why not take up the sceptre of God's chief steward on earth and make Jerusalem his private domain? With Queen Berenice taking over the north, together they might bring peace to their country which, like a vessel in variable winds, had been floundering for more than a century.

His fantasies were quickly dissipated when he heard the more frequent whizzing of ballista stones and arrows overhead. As if to emphasize the Roman's negation of his hopes, Vespasian had ordered that the relentless barrage be intensified. Joseph was sure that the siege had been laid against him personally.

There were so many fires that no one bothered any longer to extinguish them. At night the town looked as if a candelabrum had been flattened across its surface. This one had many more branches than the traditional seven of the *menorah.* Walking along the south rampart one evening, Joseph felt the wall tremble beneath him. He recognized some of his Royals and asked a tall light haired lad if they had eaten yet. The man smiled and offered him a tear of bread and honey. Joseph thanked him and moved on to inspect his other troops. A crash sent him flying against the parapet, and when he looked up he saw the soldier to whom he had just spoken staggering, the crust of bread still in his hand. He no longer had a head.

ii

By the fortieth day of battle, the dead were no longer buried. They fell where they were hit, and their children, naked and bloated, clung to their corpses like maggots. Old men sat huddled together mumbling prayers, while women searched for sustenance among the rubble. One morning, on his way to check supplies, Joseph passed a donkey squatting in its own piss. Two little girls pressed their hands to the damp cobbles, then sucked their fingers.

At the town square he was asked to resolve a quarrel whether camel dung was edible according to The Law. Joseph did not venture out of his tower headquarters again until the Romans renewed their assault on Jotapata.

iii

Finally, the ram was again brought up to the wall. Two hours later the main gate of the town crumbled. To stem the breach, Niger organized a human wall, holding off the Romans till nightfall. Convinced by now that the Jews were intent on fighting to the death, Vespasian ordered his Elite Guard to dismount and widen the breach at all costs. Even before gangways were dropped, the Tribune Domitius of the Xth Legion charged into Jotapata over the corpses of the Jews. By now half the ramparts were occupied by Arab archers who gave cover to the entering Romans. Mounted Syrian auxiliaries brought up the rear, making sure that no Jew escaped alive.

Joseph could have escaped through a secret tunnel that led from his tower, but when Domitius scampered up the steps in his direction, Joseph took up the challenge and before the tribune could gain the rampart, he thrust him through with such ferocity that his blade broke inside the Roman's belly. Joseph pulled the tribune's sword from his stiff fingers, and tossing a leather bag holding his journals and a map of Jotapata over his shoulder, he leaped down from the tower. Gathering a company of Royals, he shouted: "Follow me!" and charged into the advancing Romans, wielding his new sword as if it were forged by the Lord of Hosts himself.

On seeing their commander dying, the Elite Guard hesitated. Joseph and his men pressed them back across the gangways by now slippery with blood. A regiment of wild Dacians moved into the breach.

Joseph quickly ordered his men to plug their ears so as not to be terrified by the war whoops these barbarians were noted for. Many of the Romans were unfamiliar with this tactic of their satrapy and became frightened themselves by the shrieking, and dropped their weapons and fled. For the moment the breach was sealed.

Standing on top of the rubble before the gates, Joseph addressed the Jews in a new ecstasy.

"Your fathers are about to be butchered. Your wives raped; your sons and daughters violated until their bowels explode. Let each man fight not to save Jotapata, but as if he were already avenging its fall."

Before Joseph could organize defenses for the next assault, a hail of flaming arrows struck the wood extension on the top of the north wall that Joseph had had erected upon his arrival. Instead of adding cover as planned, the wall collapsed over the defenders of this last section of the ramparts still in Jewish hands. The Romans clambered over the wall, while below a new wave charged through the breach. This time the attack was led by Titus who held aloft the battle standard of the Apollonaris Legion like an enormous skewer.

New planks were laid across the corpses as Roman and Jew engaged in hand-to-hand combat. Slowly the defenders retired over their own dead as the Romans pushed them back into the town. The Jews retreated up the winding streets as Titus led his men toward the synagogue. Much to their dismay, the Romans found the streets barricaded and manned by short bowed archers who again sent them back in disarray. Unknown to Joseph, Shevah had organized the women and children he found still alive and had them gather rubble, using it to link the many garden fences into a new wall against the enemy. Behind this barrier Niger and a company of men waited for the next attack.

"You see," cried Niger, his feverish eyes still holding their innocent look, "it can be done. Jotapata shall go down in history as one of the most heroic stands ever made."

Joseph looked with a mixture of pity and disgust at the gangrenous arm of the man who had been fighting by his side for more than a year. "At this point our hopes lie in its going down in Roman annals as their greatest victory."

Joseph entered the small tradesmen's synagogue where he had seen Lucia learning to pray and took out his chart. The Romans had already conquered two thirds of the town and were converging on this of dust. His father was wrong. No yearling nor bullock could save them now. He wished he had Lucia's capacity for prayer.

Outside, he walked along the line of men crouched behind the thickest part of the makeshift wall. Despite the sun their faces were gray, and they sucked on their tongues for dampness. They could no longer sweat. Nearby men leaned against the wall. They were either sleeping or dead. The time had come, he decided, to save himself.

Two possibilities lay open to him: to make his way through the back alleys and join the Syrian auxiliaries whose uniforms were similar to the Jews'; or to sound the ancient call to single combat, rarely used these days. Not able to get himself to join the hated Syrians, he took up the sword of the dead tribune, Domitius, and running its blade across his tongue, he sheathed it and strapped it to his waist. Then he drew out the broken *shofar* he had found in the synagogue and hurried to where the battle raged, knowing that Titus Flavius would be there.

He spotted the general leaping on to a stone fence in advance of his own personal guard. Pressing his lips to the ram's horn, Joseph blew the five notes of challenge. Titus, whose back was momentarily turned, faced about slowly, lowering his sword. Joseph climbed toward him his sword already drawn.

Titus easily parried Joseph's first thrusts, letting him tire himself. Joseph was a clumsy swordsman and Titus quickly took to the offensive in graceful slashes that belied his short, heavy frame. He drove Joseph into the already occupied *agora* and out of the sight of the Jews. Suddenly Joseph jumped back and raising his sword above his head, he brought it down hard into the ground. He fell to his knees and prostrated himself at Titus' feet in the ritual of surrender.

Titus swiped the tip of his sword across Joseph's head, cutting a lock of hair. "The next one draws blood," he declared. "Stand to and fight!"

Joseph rose slowly, his swollen lips trembling. "Nothing that's happened here has changed my loyalties. For me Rome is our only hope. Allied, we can continue to bring glory to each other."

Titus pulled Joseph's sword out of the ground and tossed it at him. "I once told you Rome has no allies. Neither do the Flavians."

Like a trapped beast, Joseph knew that he would have to strike quickly or flee. He retreated up an alley fending off Titus' methodical and hard hitting strokes. The Roman was too strong for him. By the time Joseph had been forced up to one of the makeshift walls that blocked the way, his arm was numb and his back twitched with pain. Again he thought of dropping his guard and baring his chest, but he knew that Titus would not consider it an act of cowardice to kill him.

Joseph's only choice was to fall upon his sword and die like King Saul, depriving this pagan from killing the Commander of the Jews. Grabbing the blade of his sword with both hands, Joseph pressed the hilt against the wall and pushed himself onto the point. Voices whirred in his ears and the sun fell upon his head.

"It's my side," said Joseph regaining consciousness. He was breathless and his hand was covered with blood.

"A flesh wound," said James.

"Where are we? From where did you come?"

"Our eyes never leave you," cried Levi his other bodyguard, who was bandaging the side. "We're in Benjamin the priest's house."

"I reached up and pulled you over the wall," said James. "Just as the Roman officer lunged at you, Levi pierced him below the shoulder."

"Is he alive?"

Levi shrugged. "The last I saw of him, he was staggering down the alley. Now we must hurry."

They helped Joseph through the back garden where a budding pomegranate tree stood. A body was propped against the trunk. As they passed Joseph saw Niger of Perea staring up at them grinning and dead.

Joseph felt his wound tear open as his aides dragged him away. They carried him down a cellar divided into large empty bins still powdery white. Wheat chaff lay strewn about and he could feel the grains under his boots. They circled a gray millstone embossed in a wood turnstile. "Here," said Levi. "It's through here. They helped Joseph into a round trough and James pushed the turnstile until the millstone moved, uncovering a gap. Both men had to lower Joseph through and into the arms of a third person waiting below.

"This leads to a cave. We'll be safe there."

"Arab bowmen are at the mouth of every cave waiting to kill anyone who tries to escape," said the third man. "They've captured a map indicating those caves which lead out of town.

"This one's not on any map," said James. "It's inaccessible."

"Inaccessible?"

"It's half way down a cliff facing Mount Atzmon."

Joseph was too exhausted to ask how they were to escape from a cliff below the south wall of Jotapata that fell one hundred feet into a defile. To keep conscious he counted the days of war. It was the forty-seventh day of the siege, the day of the new moon of *Panemus* according to Rome and the First of *Tammuz* by the count of the Jews.

CHAPTER XII — LIFE SO DEAR

i

Joseph lay half conscious in the cave under the town of Jotapata. The chamber swayed in the torchlight and he thought he was floating upon the sea. He focused on a wrinkle in the wall that dripped with rusted water. When he tried to sit up, a pain shot through his abdomen. Four women in black sat beside him, moaning as they rocked back and forth. Opposite them and alone sat the girl Shevah had taken as his bride the day Jotapata fell. She was sharpening a spear.

Rising and hugging the wall, Joseph made his way into another chamber where he found a half dozen men dividing stores of food and arms. A few others slept upon the floor. They were covered with lice. He worked his way slowly toward the mouth of the cave which was canopied by the star filled night. A hundred feet below lay the lights of the Roman camp. Drunken voices echoed up the canyon and carried with them the stench of roasting pig. The cave seemed too high for the odors to carry, and when he turned back to the chamber, he realized that it was the men who smelled and that they were not sleeping but dead. One man stared at him with glazed eyes. Each time he breathed a bubble the size of a cow's udder swelled blue out of his side. This time it was the face of Hanan ben Zevi, Mayor of Tarichea.

Joseph retreated into a third chamber where some armed men with their backs to him stood praying. Levi and James came sliding down a rope that hung through a hole in the ceiling. It must have been the way they had lowered him into the cave. The men stopped praying and gathered to hear Joseph's two bodyguards, both dressed now like Syrian auxiliaries, report on what they had scouted up above.

"It's the Xth Legion," said James, "and the butcher of Messina, the Legate Larcius Lepidus. Vespasian's given him the honor of upturning every stone and razing every structure higher than a foot off the ground."

"They're killing all males, six years and older, and women below sixty," added Levi. "The blood is streaming down the streets like snow melting off Hermon."

"Vespasian has refused to take prisoners or carry plunder back to Rome for the usual triumphal procession," said James. "The Commander of the East has decided that Jotapata was no victory when half the eighty thousand dead were Roman."

"*Ken yirbu.* May their numbers increase," they all declared in amen.

"We also heard," Levi hesitated, "that they would not leave the area until they found the Jewish commander. Dead or alive."

All eyes turned on Joseph. "Then we'll turn him out," declared a man still wrapped in his prayer shawl. "Then they'll stop searching the caves and we can escape and join John."

"I'm in command here," said Shevah, stepping forward. "John of Gishhalav preferred to retreat to Jerusalem and make his stand there rather than come to our aid at Jotapata."

"They want him, not you," said Levi nodding to Joseph without looking at him.

Shevah blinked nervously. "Joseph ben Matthias, no matter what we think of him, remains alive so long as we do." He then resumed his prayers. Joseph saw that he was stooped by the weight of the sword that he himself had captured from the Tribune Domitius. He was relieved to finally be free of command.

Back in the original chamber where he had awakened, Joseph noticed four low arches cut into the wall with a torch stuck in a crevice above each. He needed desperately to be alone. Reaching for a torch, he knelt and crawled through one of the openings and into a vault. The pain in his abdomen made him groan. Holding up the torch, he saw holy pledges tucked in the cracks of stones with the familiar raised borders that had been used in Herod's time to build the walls around the Temple in Jerusalem. Spears and poles were scattered on the floor, and a skeleton lay on a sarcophagus. Beside it stood a jug and a platter for the dead man's relatives to set out food for his nourishment while he sought his place in *Sheol*. A bronze armlet hung loosely from the skeleton's wrist and in his open hand lay a pair of bone dice, the mark of a man stoned for having trafficked in produce raised during the Sabbatical year.

Back in the larger chamber, Joseph saw Shevah with his arm around his bride. She was still honing her spear.

ii

For the next few days they could hear the barking and snarling of the bloodhounds above them and the grinding of plows that were levelling the town. From the mouth of the cave, Joseph saw Roman patrols dropping rope ladders down the cliffsides in order to search for Jews.

To occupy his time, Joseph read what he had recorded in his journal during the last days of battle. Whenever he looked up, his eyes met Shevah's wife. He read:

bannus used to say; concentrate on an idea, an image, a pin-

*point of light, and draw one question from it concerning life
and death. each day has one idea to teach us about our existence. we are incapable of absorbing more.*

He thought about the skeleton lying in the vault and wondered if
the reality of that man did not exist more in the pair of dice than in
the platter and wine jug left to sustain him in the Hereafter. He read
on:

*endurance and conciliation: can they be compatible? if they are,
then once again i have found that by enduring i have regained
my freedom of choice. if not, then the essenes are right in believing that endurance and conciliation can only exist through
death.*

Again he felt a stitch in his abdomen. And when he heard Shevah
pronounce the dread word, he remembered that his own pain was self
inflicted.

"Suicide," said Shevah. "We shall kill ourselves rather than have
the Romans profane our souls with their blemished swords."

"Not everyone is capable of taking his own life," said one of the
others.

"Those who are will act as the Angel of Death for those who cannot."

"There are those among us," said Joseph, "who believe in life's
possibility to the last moment."

"Then we shall help you arrive at that moment," said Shevah. "If
the decision is made, then it shall be made for all."

Shevah sent Levi and James out one last time to confirm the hope-
lessness of their situation. Glancing at Shevah's wife once more,
Joseph saw that she now had a krater filled with sheaves of wheat in
front of her and a jar of wine. She had scratched her face with her
nails and her black robe was spotted with blood.

Joseph returned to the last recording he had scribbled in his journal. He read:

*no. endurance and conciliation are, by definition, contrary. the
essenes are right. life and death are merely stages in the chain of
being.*

He raised his hand and slapped a fly that was crawling across his
ankle. He inserted:

*like that fly. an instant merging of time and space — serpent
and eagle — which makes one measure what has been created*

and what has been destroyed through the same creation. being one's own fulcrum, between the past and the present. the balance becomes clear only without the distorted rainbows of blood shaped by honor and land — jotapata — that have so cunningly deceived us all for so long. while roman generals think they are controlling history, it becomes obvious that conquering and being conquered are really the same thing.

The fly twitched its wings and rose. It buzzed around Joseph's nose, then flew out of the cave. Joseph smiled until he saw Shevah return with one of the scouts.

"Levi was caught and crucified," said James. "I escaped. No one's alive in Jotapata. Except for this side of the plateau, all the caves have been scorched. They'll reach us by tomorrow."

"It's time to prepare for death," said Shevah.

"The Law holds no such ritual," said Joseph. "In fact it denies burial until sunset to anyone who touches the blade to his own throat."

"Well might The Law groan aloud," retorted Shevah. "And God himself hide his face in grief — God who implanted in our souls scorn for death. Is life so dear to you, Joseph ben Matthias, that you can endure the pagan's hand of death more willingly than your own? We have fought for liberty. It would be a betrayal of our dead brothers, our children and our wives above and below the earth to allow the Roman to send us to everlasting unrest. By taking your own life, you die as the General of the Jews. By not, you die a traitor to Israel."

"Death," said Joseph, hearing himself contradict the last words of his journal, "gives liberty only to oneself. Not to those above who have died so that we might fight elsewhere. At least in bondage the light of hope still burns."

"The Roman kills," said James. "Walk out of here and you walk into a most shameful death."

"It's a chance worth taking for the eternity of Israel."

"The survival of Israel," said Shevah, "rests with those ready to die for her eternity."

"You should have gone to Masada with Eleazar ben Yair. Not even the beasts in the field commit suicide."

"Scorpions do," said Shevah's wife. "When they're trapped, they die with dignity."

"Nobody dies with dignity," said Joseph. "It's just nice to think so."

The others waited for Shevah to answer Joseph.

"Besides," continued Joseph, "such a choice calls for a private confrontation. A man must face himself alone. And God."

"At this stage," said Shevah, "God has already given us our choice. He's merely waiting for us to take it."

"Then twenty-four hours can change very little. There is a need for contemplation."

Shevah saw that the others agreed with Joseph and he relented. "Till sunset tomorrow evening," and wrapping himself in his shawl, he turned south, ignoring the others and began to pray.

Throughout the next day no one spoke. People were embarrassed to look at each other. Hunched against the wall, the girl continued to hone her spear. Shevah had not stopped praying.

Two locusts, left over from the *sharav*, lay at the mouth of the cave rubbing their antennae. They were larger than normal and Nile green. Joseph watched the smaller mount the other. They lay in the setting sun without movement. The female on top, stirred, then tightened her legs slowly around the wings of her mate, who shuddered, his antennae stiffening. The female's black, beady eyes looked up at Joseph. Then her wings whirred as she began to eat her mate. The male did not move, his eyes blinking as his head was slowly severed. The process of love making and dying now merged for Joseph, and he stepped on the two insects, crushing them under his boot. Endurance and conciliation, he thought. They *are* compatible. Looking around the cave, he wondered who would be his killer.

iii

The sun was almost beyond the horizon when Joseph began to panic. He saw no reason why he should not be allowed his own choice. He wanted to scream at them that he hated their revolt, opposed it from the start. If he could he would draw out a sword and declare them all dead in the name of Rome.

He breathed deeply. More and more he was convinced that he would be indispensible to the Flavians. Having fought against them, only he would be capable of turning their mediocre campaign into glorious history. So far as he was concerned the rebellion ended with the battle of Jotapata. Opportunity timed properly could twist fortune, his father and wisest teacher had once explained to him when he was too young to really understand. But opportunity implied patience — the freedom to act. He was tired of seeking the approval of others when all he needed was his own. Who was this Shevah to declare his destiny? Why was it that Eleazar ben Yair never apologized for his disaffections? And why did Bannus warn only him when he parted from the Essenes that "to walk humbly before God is merely an excuse to strut before one's own shadow'''?

The problem now was how to survive the other twelve still alive in this cave. To assure that the mass suicide would be joint and blameless, Joseph convinced the others that lots be cast, matching those who could not or refused to kill themselves with those who were ready to die. Joseph's lot fell with Shevah's wife.

Wishing to die privately, Joseph led his partner into the vault with the skeleton. The girl pulled out a Sicari dagger from the sheath strapped to her thigh.

"His?" asked Joseph.

The girl said nothing.

"Where did you get that bracelet?"

"This is my husband's ancestral vault," she said, pointing the dagger at the skeleton. In the torchlight her fingers glistened like Lucia's, and he remembered that for him the portents of disaster were always preceded by the act of love. He heard the groans coming from the other chambers and strangely they aroused him. Suddenly the vision he had had of Eleazar ben Yair dying against a stone wall in the synagogue of Masada, a dagger pressed through his heart, rose before him. He fell upon the girl, hearing the armlet crack beneath her, knowing that it was a lie her being married to Shevah because she had never before been penetrated.

When he got up he saw that she was bleeding between her legs and that the dagger had pierced her left breast. Her eyes were the color of ashes.

iv

Joseph dreamed he lay in the Temple of God. And in his dream he saw himself at the age of ten accompanying his father to the *Mikdash* on the eve of *Yom Kippur* as he had often done. There, in addition to the prescribed sundown to sundown fast in which all Jews partook, Matthias had spent the night prostrated on the stone floor, chanting psalms till dawn in order to purify himself. On the following day, as duty priest, he would attend the High Priest until he entered the *Dvir*, the holiest place in the Temple which he did once a year on this Day of Atonement. Joseph had fought to stay awake and follow his father's private ritual. The psalms floated in and out of his sleep until once he jumped up crying: "*Aba*, you called me?"

His father had smiled at him, his lips still mumbling prayers. Again Joseph tried to stay awake, and then for a second time, he leaped up and asked: "*Aba*, you called me?"

Matthias continued to chant, ignoring him. Huddled in the corner, the last thing Joseph remembered was seeing his own reflection in the laver, his hair completely gray.

"Joseph!" a voice called him. And he feared the wrath of the unanswered skeleton against which he lay. When he opened his eyes, he saw through the arched opening of the tomb that the outer chamber was filled with corpses.

"Joseph," a voice called louder. He knew he was no longer in his dream. He sat up and saw that he was holding the Sicari dagger of the girl whose name he had never known.

"Joseph. Out here," came the voice a third time.

Cautiously, he crawled out of the tomb and through the bodies toward the mouth of the cave. The shadows of the stalactites flickered closer and then retreated. Joseph groped along the wall feeling in his trembling fingertips a worn indentation. He wondered what balustrade or step it had once adorned. How many feet had trod its smooth surface? How much sweat of contrition had pounded itself into its polished stone? He saw a crude drawing where the girl had been sitting. With her spear she had scratched a gazelle. "*Tzvi Yisrael*," he said to himself.

"The splendor of Israel," said Titus who reached out to him from a straw nest of a wicker basket that had been lowered by a rope and dangled at the entrance to the cave and over the canyon. Lucia sat beside him.

"At the moment," said Joseph taking Titus' helping hand and stepping into the basket, "it reeks of catastrophe."

PART V
JERUSALEM

*Howbeit, neither its
antiquity, nor its ample
wealth, nor its people
spread over the whole
habitable world, nor yet
the great glory of its
religious rites, could
ought avail to avert its
ruin.*

Bellum Judaicum —
Josephus

CHAPTER XXIII — THE MATTER OF ROME

i

There is a legend that a man once slept for a hundred years and when he awoke, the world had not changed. The earth had become fallow and fertile in season; rain and sun shared the firmament; the oceans ebbed and rose, the rivers flowed down to the sea; trees bloomed and shed their leaves; beasts were born and slaughtered. Only man progressed. He made harsher wars against himself and hated his image because of his incapacity to attain its demands. God in his heaven remained steadfast, a reminder of what once was and what might yet be, thus holding the balance over time and space. Nothing was really new under the sun.

No doubt Joseph had his waking periods in the months he lay in his cell, but all he could remember were the cold stones and the constant crash of the sea. He must have been fed, have shit and pissed, but all he recalled was an abyss of shadows appearing and disappearing. If ever he had succeeded in reaching the Essene state of oblivion, it was during his imprisonment at Caesarea in the airless Tower of Drusion, named for Caesar's stepson. If, in fact, he felt anything of life, it was the fetters binding his ankles and the chains that made his wrists swell. Then, as must happen even in legend, he was given the choice between life and death. Naturally he rose to life when Titus cast a dagger of light into his cell. "What day is it?"

Surprisingly, Titus had changed. He looked haggard, and though his stomach still protruded awkwardly for a man under thirty, it sagged as did his face. He did not respond to Joseph's question, but led him out into a larger cell lighted by a candle in a brass holder. In it Joseph caught a distorted view of himself, his face dominated by eyes. He stooped as if he had been kicked in the groin.

"Let me give you some advice which is more than the day of the year," Titus finally said, beckoning Joseph to sit on a wood bench, the only object in the cell. "As you've discovered, Rome treats an ordinary soldier in the same manner as his commander. Defeat, like death, is a great equalizer. You have been imprisoned for nearly a year. Much has changed since then."

Joseph smiled. "Your last remark is relative. Nothing has changed here."

"Nevertheless, your prediction to Cestius Gallus whom, if you recall, you shared a cell with for the first few weeks of your imprisonment, was upheld. He's been reinstated as Legate of the XIIth Legion."

Joseph had always claimed a certain prophetic power. Often he thought of himself as a second Joseph of Egypt, and like his ancient countryman would become a new leader of his people beyond their narrow fold. The first Joseph, too, had interpreted the future and had been imprisoned before he was called to power. "The future of our nation," Joseph's father had told him, "was placed in that frail dreamer's hands. Its destiny is linked to your name as well."

Joseph's playmates, including his brother, would chide him whenever he insisted on leading them in their games, and ridiculed his passion for pronouncing their destinies. Once he had even dreamed how he was met by a conqueror who had just subdued a great city; how the man had knelt before him as he, Joseph ben Matthias, set a crown upon his head. Joseph had told his father of his dream who, unlike Jacob of old, acquiesced to his son's vanities. Joseph never told Matthias that in that same dream his hands were bound behind him to an endless chain of corpses. Bannus had deprecated dreams. Named them false prophets. True visions, said the wise Essene, come only from the angle of the sun on the trees and from the light that shadows cast.

To Titus Joseph said: "Perhaps I am the baker?"

Titus did not get the reference. "To begin with, Rome is again in turmoil. Vitellius is now Emperor and has become a new Nero, debaucheries and all. He's even reinstituted the Mulvian Bridge orgies."

Joseph's lips shaped the words Titus spoke, the effort distracting him from their meaning. "The cost of his extravagances are reducing the states and provinces of the empire to penury," continued Titus. "Soldiers have been declared a privileged caste and have become slovenly and habitual drunkards. Our western borders are again vulnerable to the wild-assed Celts, Franks and Teutons. Only the Army of the East, through the austerity of its commander, Flavius Vespasian, and his victories here, have kept the military establishment from disintegration."

Names and places lost their distances and Joseph found it hard to concentrate.

"After the defeat of Cestius Gallus, many of our colonies became restless, convinced that finally Rome was in decline. Your defeat at Jotapata, however, and the collapse of all resistance in the Galilee has made them hesitate in declaring a general revolt."

"Then nothing truly has changed."

"For the Jews, yes. Your defeat has made your countrymen living abroad, and I remind you that they already number as many as are here, to abandon their support of Judea. They've stopped sending their *shekel* tithe to the Temple and have included a special prayer to the health of the Emperor in their services."

"That kind acted so even before my defeat," said Joseph. "They like us to win all the time."

"We always do."

"Why am I being told all this?" Joseph's voice trailed off, having already lost interest in what he was asking.

"Because Nabatea and Parthia are still waiting to see what will happen in Jerusalem."

At the mention of his city, Joseph's face narrowed. "Jerusalem is still free?"

"Preparing for the final battle."

"And who is in command?"

"In ascendance would be more proper. Mostly the Sicaris."

"Simon bar Giora?"

"He hasn't made his move yet. He's quibbling with John of Gishhalav and your fellow nobles."

"And how is the Queen of Golan?"

"Queen Berenice is loyal only to us. She hopes through her brother-in-law, Tiberius Alexander, to win Egypt over to our side."

"Since when has Egypt taken on such importance?"

"Crops were disastrous this year in Gaul and elsewhere in Europe. Italy must rely on Egypt for all its grain. There are also two legions in Alexandria making a total of six in the east, nearly half the fighting force of Rome."

Joseph touched the bald spot that had expanded on his pate since his imprisonment, then pensively rubbed his wiry red beard. He was becoming aware of details, and the cell began to take the shape of a guard room. His tongue tasted of flour, and the itch on his nape that had long ago been displaced by the pain of his bound wrists and ankles returned. He smelled the garlic off Titus' breath.

"Eleazar?" he asked. "Where is Eleazar ben Yair?"

Titus shrugged. "Masada, I suppose. It's of no importance."

"To him it is. It might become so to you. To all of us."

"The crucial battles were fought here in the Galilee. All won by us. Even Justus ben Piscus has joined our forces. He now commands the Queen's Royals."

Joseph ran a finger along a line of sunlight coming through a window. "A real traitor. Without the shame of inconstancy."

Titus rose. "The Queen has asked for you to be brought before Vespasian. You will have to use your wits to convince him to spare your life. He doesn't trust you."

"Do you?"

"Twice before I've saved your life. I can promise you no more than that Vespasian is a fair man. He likes the jest of life. An oddity, not a plea; a prediction, not an apology. So think hard. Impress him not with your dignity but with that convoluted turn of your mind. Extemporize. The ruse — something which fascinates him, but which he is incapable of — may just save your life."

ii

Caesarea seemed more like an army camp than the bustling port Joseph remembered. Soldiers outnumbered civilians and the stench of horse piss and oil stifled the scent of the sea. The revolt had first broken out here, the seat of Roman administration in Judea. Once Jews were the majority of its residents. Now they had either been killed or fled. Joseph observed a woman kneading dough and a man nearby carving an idol from a piece of driftwood. Further along the quay, a man meticulously tarred the keel of a dhow as if it were a coffin. A smithy shoed a horse that nibbled grass off the roof of a seamen's hostel. Joseph scratched his wrists vigorously.

Titus led him into a small theater, not unlike the one in Jerusalem where he had once taken Hagla to see the *Medea* performed by a troupe from Crete. Hagla knew no Greek and had concentrated on the movement of the actors, while Joseph explained his own version of the play. He had always associated her with the heroine.

A statue of Caesar Augustus, in whose honor Herod had built the city, stood at the back of the sloping orchestra which fell away to a pillared stage. As he came down the center aisle, Joseph saw Justus and Queen Berenice chatting on the side. Behind them hundreds of vessels dipped and bowed in the harbor.

"My son keeps telling me nice things about you," a deep voice boomed from behind the pillars. "The Queen exaggerates still futher. The Jew, Justus, cautions me against you. All I know is you've managed to kill forty thousand of my men. Tell me, why should I spare your life?"

The shock of the sun and the sea made Joseph gasp. Vespasian and others of his staff loomed beyond the pillars like stallions about to charge at him in a race to his doom. Joseph fell to the ground and cried: "Hail Caesar!"

The echo of his voice resounded throughout the orchestra. Then there was only the breeze of the sibylline sea.

"That is no reason to spare your life," said Vespasian, amused. "In fact your words make you more a traitor than before."

"Not if they speak the truth," said Joseph.

"And how can they be true when Vitellius rules Rome?"

"Prophecies and omens," said Joseph looking up. "The God of Israel has made you spare me till now so that I might be an omen of life. By revealing his secrets to me, He has given me the key to my own life."

"I don't believe in omens. Get up."

Joseph rose slowly. Vespasian looked less forbidding now. He was bald and his teeth protruded like a skeleton's "Your majesty once spent three days with the prophets of the Baal, burning entrails that told false prophecies of your quick victory at Jotapata. Had he come to me, I would have shown him how it might have fallen like one of its overripe pomegranates."

"What omen allows you to address me as you do?"

Joseph's old instincts were alerted. He came alive to the excitement of the intrigue he was creating. Prophecy, he always believed, was a matter of convincing others. Fulfillment came later and was merely a matter of guessing right.

He stood erect. "Furthermore, your son by your side and the other in Rome shall be emperors in their own right."

Vespasian smiled. "Maybe, like Neptune, I should kill them before I do you. Before they kill me."

"I speak in terms of dynasty," said Joseph, glancing at Justus who wore a *clavi*, the striped toga of a Roman noble. "Not conspiracy. The first true Roman dynasty."

"You still withhold the omen."

"It came to me in a dream. Like the release of Cestius Gallus."

"You predicted that?" Vespasian turned to the legate who nodded.

"In a dream about the navel of the earth. God spoke to me and declared Rome the nexus of His new creation out of which shall come a new law of peace and order."

"Dreams are not omens," said Vespasian.

"As you see me in fetters and in this beggar's dress, so did I wake and find this chain around my neck, a chain and a medal engraved with the imperial Roman eagle. With trembling fingers, I turned it over and saw the face of Vespasian."

Those on the stage leaned closer as Joseph stepped up to show the general the medal. Vespasian fingered it, turning it over and over. "This could be Claudius, even Tiberius. Medals tend to put the same face on everyone."

Joseph shook his head. "Tiberius Alexander is on his way north coming to declare his allegiance to you and pronounce you Emperor of Rome. He will verify the prophecy."

Titus spoke to his father. Vespasian nodded and turned back to Joseph. "My son and myself find what you say possible. However, I fail to see what difference it makes to Judea."

Joseph bowed. "Your majesty knows of a plan your son fostered with myself and the Queen of Golan. Circumstances and the nature of my people delayed the plan. My destiny and my people's rest with the house of Flavius. There is still time to bring Jerusalem to Rome and through such communion bring glory to the Flavian dynasty. To this purpose I wish to devote my life."

"An exaggeration that again makes me fear your prediction."

Trumpets sounded followed by the entrance of a squadron of cavalry that rode up to the stage. "Sire," declared the leader. "The Legate Tiberius Alexander has arrived from Egypt. Because of fatigue he apologizes for not paying his respects. Urgent news, however, makes him beg your immediate attendance at his camp."

Vespasian frowned, his face flattening like a squashed plum. "The Emperor goes to be crowned," he said. "Take the prisoner back to his cell."

"Why not take him along," sugggested Titus. "Tiberius Alexander would enjoy seeing the execution of the Commander of the Jews. It was his old XIIth Legion that was decimated by the General Josephus."

"Maybe Cestius would like to witness it as well," laughed Vespasian.

Once again Joseph felt himself withdrawing among the stones and crevices beneath the sea.

"Order our chariots," said Vespasian. "The guard will follow with the Jew behind us."

Tiberius Alexander had pitched his camp a mile outside of Caesarea. Unknown to the others, he was accompanied by the New Governor of Greater Syria who together with Vespasian and Tiberius Alexander made up the triumverate of the Roman command from Greece to the edges of the Arabian Desert and half across Africa. The Legate Mucianus stood casually beside his roan smoothing its mane.

Titus, who rode alongside Joseph and his guards, whispered to him. "You're in luck. With those two legates present your ruse might just work."

"And in the process be forgotten," said Joseph sullenly.

Titus shook his head. "Once Vespasian is declared Emperor, I will be given command here. I still need you."

"He didn't sound too encouraging back there in the theater."

"That's because he and I have been quarreling."

Vespasian's chariot circled Mucianus, then stopped as both generals faced each other. For the first time since he had been captured, Joseph feared for his life.

"I see," said Mucianus, "that the Jews haven't worn you out yet."

Vespasian alighted just as Tiberius Alexander appeared from one of the nearby tents and came forward, embracing Vespasian in the Roman fashion.

"I brought Mucianus along just to feel safer," smiled Tiberius. "We generals of the east are always wary of you ambitious westerners."

"I suppose," said Mucianus, brushing his hands, "you realize why we're here."

"Regardless of the reason, welcome. I haven't seen you since Corinth."

"We've come to help you."

"Help?" Vespasian's face tightened. "I need no help from anyone. Judea is about to fall like a rotten," and turning back he winked at Joseph. "Like a rotten pomegranate."

"We've come to help you take up the sceptre of Rome," said Mucianus.

Vespasian looked at Titus, then over at Joseph who still sat chained in the chariot.

"Mind you," continued Mucianus, "Tiberius here had a lot of convincing to do. Personally I preferred young Titus. I've always thought of him as a son."

"One father is enough for any man," quipped Vespasian.

"I've watched him since he was a centurion, then as a tribune with my VIth Legion. He'll make a better emperor than you."

"So long as Flavius Vespasian is alive," said Titus, "I swear by the gods I will never accept the crown."

"Careful, son," said Mucianus. "We may then have to poison your father. Seriously, I've agreed to cast my fate with yours, Vespasian. Rome needs reordering, and quickly. It may not be so complimentary an offer to follow Vitellius. He is no divine Augustus or profound Tiberius. And though your own origins are lowly, and there may be superiors to you in intellect and talent, at this specific moment Rome needs a man of your stability and honesty. Needs us through you as your friends and advisers. The man who is afraid sees distinction enough in anyone he fears. I know that you fear no one. You are a hardened soldier, loved by your men. The rest will come to you by the fact of your position. To divide our forces now means victory for Vitellius, the collapse of our hard won order." Mucianus kneeled and handed his sword to Vespasian. "In the name of the Roman people," he declared, "from the cold shores of Atlanticus to the dark waters of the northern seas and down to our own blue waters, I, subject to the approval of the Senate, pronounce you on this Third day of Julius, Emperor of Rome."

Mucianus rose and embraced Vespasian. Titus kissed his father, without once glancing at Joseph standing beside him. As if by some magical power, the news carried across the city and a roar rose from the barracks and camps of the Roman troops stationed in Caesarea.

"Your brother, Flavius Sabinus, and your son, Domitian, have been alerted to our decision," said Tiberius Alexander, also embracing Vespasian. "The one doubt is the Praetorian Guard. Since Vitellius is a favorite of theirs, we suggest you dispatch Titus immediately to Rome and inform them of our ordinance."

"Impossible. He's essential right here for the final campaign," said Vespasian, showing no emotion over his new position.

"The matter of Rome is more urgent than the matter of Jerusalem," said Mucianus. "Reports are that the Jews are again fighting amongst themselves. Wait long enough and the city will collapse of its own."

Queen Berenice approached Vespasian and without bowing slipped her arms around him. "Come to Philippi," she said. "The Hermon air is clear and a fine place for contemplation. These may be the last days of your freedom."

Mucianus frowned. "You will return with me to Antioch. There's much planning to be done. Tiberius will take command here till Titus returns."

Vespasian hesitated. He loosened the Queen's arms from about his waist and turned to Titus. "See to it that Josephus is freed. Let him join our staff as an adviser." He then turned to the two legates. "If Jerusalem can wait, so can Rome. Until my son returns with the Senate's approval of my appointment, I shall be with the Queen of Golan."

iii

Joseph bathed then had his body oiled and his beard trimmed. He dismissed the orderly assigned to him and put on the uniform of a tribune that had been ordered earlier. He inspected himself in a mirror and after brushing his hair so that the bald spot was covered, he smiled at his own good looks. For the first time in a year, he felt that his body had been returned to him.

He was to dine with Titus and the other legates as their newly appointed adviser. His first request would be to ask for command of the Royals now under Justus.

He was surprised to find Lucia seated on the terrace at the head of the table beside Titus. By her flashing eyes and her trembling lips Joseph understood that she was attempting to reach beyond the zenith for which she had been trained, and for the first time in his life he felt compassion in his love.

On seeing Joseph, Titus raised his wine glass and, turning to the light, declared. "Truly a gift of the gods."

"Joseph or the wine," chided Justus fiddling with the amethyst he always wore.

"Who better than a priest in Israel knows the deific qualities of this clear, cool blood of the earth," said Titus, drinking from his sweating goblet.

"Only as a symbol of its fertility," said Joseph forcing a smile. "Merely one of God's attributes."

"Never for the pleasure of the thing itself," said Lucia, who rarely spoke in the presence of men.

Joseph nodded. "Only fools seek pleasure. Happiness is the house of idiots' fame."

"Your defeats have made you into a philosopher," said Titus.

"My battles," said Joseph, sitting beside Lucia, "have made me understand the haphazard order of the universe. I would no longer be surprised if the sun didn't rise tomorrow."

"Alchemiades suspected that the sun never rose," laughed Titus. "Why don't you come to Rome and begin your chronicles there? I suspect more action will be going on there than in Judea."

"Chronicles? What chronicles?"

"My father has instructed me to give you access to all our battle plans, past and future. You are to record the glory of the house of Flavius."

"Is that his definition of an adviser?"

"Oh, we'll use you in other capacities as well. In fact, you may partake in any campaign and with any legion you choose. So far as we're concerned, you're beyond the laws of war."

"As an experienced general officer," said Joseph, "I rather hoped you would appoint me commander over the Queen's Royals."

"What? and give you credit for conquering Jerusalem," Titus joked. "No, we've decided to put a halt to your separate Jewish army. They'll be integrated into our own legions. We can imagine how much you'll ask in return for a service we hardly need."

"And its present commander?"

"A man of many talents. We've invited him to join our staff as well."

Joseph turned to Justus. "You're accompanying the general to Rome?"

"No," said Titus. "But she is."

Joseph stared at his wine glass. His nebulous marriage to Lucia had ended as casually as it had begun. Cestius Gallus had said that girls of her class had a limited capacity for love, and that in the end it was what disqualified them from the higher seats of power. In five years she would be discarded by Titus or another legate, and manage through native frugality to save enough to set herself up in a villa in Ostia or Brindisium, where with a little luck she would still be able to charm some ancient senator or general who needed warming.

Nevertheless, she still provoked him. Not in her seductiveness, which he had recognized from the start as a feigned innocence that would always leave her somewhere between the ages of seventeen and twenty, but in how she managed through a desultory passivity to attract active men, men who barely had time to scent a woman. And that alone was enough to rejuvenate her for the next to enter her playground. Had he not expended his energies in a similar way? He turned to her, glimpsing her ugly toes deliberately rubbing against Titus' bare calf. A servant dropped a pink veined crayfish into his plate. He could barely swallow his wine.

The voices about him echoed like the sounds beneath the sea where he had spent the last year. He thought of the project the Flavians had set for him: a chronicler of war. Epaphroditus had claimed that more than anything, the everlasting word creates greatness; draws the spheres and the galaxies into one harmonious whole. For the Jew that word was GOD. Then he, Joseph, *was* ordained. Who, for example, would remember the events that had just passed if Joseph ben Matthias did not record them? Who would remember Lucia? Tiberius Alexander? For that matter even Titus or Mucianus crowning Vespasian, if he did not hurry now and set them down? Was not that why he had begun his journal in the first place? Chronicle. A more dignified word. He would recreate all these actors' deeds — mark them on the skies like the stars. *Was that why the sun never sets?*

He felt a new power surge in him. He would create history. By changing a place, a name, a time, he could invent eternity. Eleazar ben Shamia becoming Eleazar ben Yair. Masada replacing Jotapata. White ink upon black parchment, thus eradicating Vespasian or Titus or any emperor he wished. For as a Jew, he was coming to understand the continuity of time. Queen Berenice's ancestry, with its meager conquests and will to self-destruction, would long survive the alabaster record on pedestals in pagan forums which, being of stone, could be chiseled into other forms and other faces with new names, while Judah the Maccabee, with no recorded image, already had a date to his name, set upon a calendar of lights. And it came so that Joseph understood who really won the battle between the serpent and the eagle.

"I think," said Joseph half to himself, "that for the time being, I shall remain here. Set my day in order and learn the simple rule of existence. Living out of time gives one a desire to see the instant, literally to watch the movement of the grain of sand."

"Try shadows," said Titus. "They give more satisfaction."

Joseph smiled. "Tomorrow I shall spend the day watching the line of palms along the beach move across the sea."

The servants now carried out large platters of brown rice and squares of roast lamb mixed with pine seeds as large as pebbles and smothered in mint leaves. Titus paid no attention to Joseph and the others and busied himself showing Lucia how to eat the dish. Like a Bedouin, Titus used his hands to form little balls of the rice piled around the meat and tossed them into his mouth, together with a chunk of lamb. He washed it all down with the cold, pink wine, then chewed on a sprig of mint explaining that it cooled the palate. Lucia squirmed as some pine seeds slipped down her bosom.

"Understand," said Titus to Joseph, "that you're going to find other members of the staff suspicious of you. Especially the Tribune Silva and your compatriot Tiberius Alexander. Surprisingly enough, my father trusts you. So don't be afraid to ask for anything you need in your work. Whatever papers I have are at your disposal. My adjutant, Antonius Julianus, will see that you're comfortable. In any event you can always contact Vespasian in Phillipi." Titus rose and turned to Lucia. "Captain Markos informs me that the prevailing winds will last through the night. We must sail before the sun rises."

"Without dessert?" she asked coyly.

"I have much to do before we leave." He walked up to Joseph and placed his thick fingers on his shoulders. "Do nothing foolish. Just remember that from now on, it's I who make history."

iv

Later that evening, Joseph gazed out his window that overlooked the sea wall which was part of the harbor of Caesarea. He watched the waves turn like the bellies of dead fish. Only the stars counted the hours. At this moment the priests in the Temple would be preparing the sacrifice for the new moon of the month of *Ab* — the month the King of Babylon had destroyed Solomon's Temple six hundred and sixty years earlier. Nebuchadnezzer, too, had taken the Jews' destiny in his hands. Looking out across the lone and level sands, he asked: *Who was Nebuchadnezzer?*

The vibrations of human contact that evening had given Joseph the courage to face his journal. He had entrusted his papers to Titus at the time of his rescue from the cave and the legate had returned them this evening after dinner. Joseph's excitement increased as he unrolled a page and read the shaky handwriting in which he had made his first entry during his bout with the river fever in Lucia's own home. He read:

my father wakes me and i follow his legs to the temple...

He shuddered and forced himself to read on.

i begin to cry.
— i said don't be a coward.
— aba, why do the widows weep behind the sunrise? why in the evening do they gasp at the gloaming?

As he read on, he was embarrassed at his vanity. It would be different now. His recordings would no longer be purely his own but the voices and actions of others. To prove it to himself, he took up the quill. He wrote:

titus says that the sun never rises — that he alone conducts my destiny.

He stopped. As if waiting for something to happen that very moment, a flash blared through the night and made him wince. When he looked up, he saw a figure standing on the sea wall, framed by the bobbing lights of the Roman vessels. He rose and walked out across the beach which was ablaze with the fires celebrating the crowning of Vespasian. He climbed onto the sea wall that coiled like a dragon, its boulders teeth, frothing as they bit into the sea.

He came up to Lucia who stood barefoot on a patch of moss. Her hair breathed in the wind. "So now it's Titus," he said. "Perhaps you should have started with Vespasian."

Lucia faced the sea. "Like you, my destiny is in many hands."

"Mine rather seems more connected to yours."

"And the Queen?"

"If she's lucky, she'll survive long enough to live beyond hers."

"You give her more credit than she deserves."

"I had assumed she and Titus were lovers."

"The Emperor," said Lucia bitterly, "was intrigued to know what was so great about his son's Jewish mistress."

"And the son?"

She turned, her face covered with tears of sea spray. "He wanted to understand the pleasure of his father."

"You?"

She nodded. "In revenge against the Queen."

"And does he expect her to renounce his father?"

Lucia stooped to pick up a stone chip. She tossed it into the water and the sound broke the rhythm of the hissing tide. "She would have. Until he was declared Emperor."

"That's more of an excuse than you have."

"When the time comes, I shall need no excuses."

Above the lash of the sea they heard the drunken songs of men and women on the beach. From the harbor tower, a sailor called the eighth hour of darkness.

"How did the Queen get involved in your private life?"

"You," said Lucia. "She told Vespasian that you and I are husband and wife."

The sea spray burned in his eyes. He wondered if that was why Titus had tried to kill him in those last days at Jotapata. But he could just as well have let him rot in prison. No. Titus would not jeopardize his integrity over a woman. He wondered too if that was really why Vespasian had released him. "Well are you?" he asked.

"You've let your beard grow again," said Lucia without answering him. She slipped through an opening between the boulders and disappeared in a cavern. To abandon her now, he knew would be the coward's way out. Only by defying her could he finally exorcise her. He grasped the two boulders and lowered himself into the cavern. A small pool reflected the stars, and he saw Lucia lying naked on a wrinkle of sand against which the sea lapped. He stood over her and watched her shamelessly writhe, one hand forcing the other between her thighs, as she bit her lip. Her eyes now were the color of the sea. Then, like two claws, her legs shot out clasping Joseph around the waist, pulling him down upon her. He grabbed her knees, trying to free himself as he felt his breath explode in his stomach. He was being hauled, whether out to sea or to shore, he could not tell. As Lucia was doing now another woman had grasped him in the same manner the night before he had arrived in Rome, when their vessel had struck a reef. He had glimpsed into her tumid eyes and gasped, kicking himself free, refusing to test his endurance by trying to save both their lives. He had always feared the vacuum of waters.

Lucia contorted herself in such a way that their bodies became intertwined, her mouth covering his groin, his pressed between her thighs. And slowly he relinquished himself to her power as she took him once again in a way he had not known before. The sea crashed against the boulders spraying them both. Not till he lay panting beside her did he remember that long ago he had envisioned this scene. Only now the moon was faceless.

Then he felt the hardness at her side. He uncovered her gown and saw that she still carried the Sicari dagger Eleazar had given her.

"Judith," he breathed out hoarsely, calling her by her converted name for the first time.

She rose and walked along the wharf. "I must hurry. *Holofernes* is waiting."

Back in his villa, he wrote:

the idea, not the act, creates prophecy.

CHAPTER XXIV — A VOICE AGAINST JERUSALEM

i

Four Essenes sat by the gate at the entrance to the Ophel Quarter and gazed up at the *Mikdash* on the Temple Mount whose light they believed radiated holiness. The gold dome glared brighter than the early spring sun. Smoke rose from Jerusalem's forges that glowed day and night since the beginning of the revolt. The holy men wore tattered robes and their bare feet were spread before them. Nodding slowly and in rhythm to the same phrase, they chanted *ADONAI HU ELOHIM!*

One younger than the others repeated the words in an uncertain tempo as if embarrassed at his mumblings. His eyes would open often and glance away from the light, though he kept his head cocked to the sky. His side locks were tucked behind his ears and were as red as his beard. He was distracted by the strands of conversation he heard from the passersby "GOD IS GOD!" mumbled the younger Essene, as he listened to two Galilean soldiers discussing the situation in the city.

"Last night Simon bar Giora captured Hebron."

"And the Fortress of Herodion as well, I hear," said the other. "That's only six miles from here." They were setting up a punishment rack.

"He's got twenty thousand Idumeans with him and they're coming to attack us sure."

"John ben Levi doesn't frighten that easy. Some say he's negotiating with ben Yair."

"No one negotiates with Eleazar ben Yair."

"Together they can take over what remains of the nobles' militia in the Upper City and end this damn civil war. It's time we fought the Roman again instead of among ourselves."

They walked inside the city walls and returned carrying a heavy trough.

"John should never have provoked bar Giora by kidnapping his wife. They say that even more than liberty that wild man loves his woman."

"It's the desert in him. They're all that way. They think the bitches are more than for dropping kids."

"There's some who say that John did it intentionally. To decide the fate of Jerusalem between them."

"Maybe we'd be better off to let him have this bloody city. They don't like us Galileans down here. If they asked me, I'd rather raid those turds up in Zippori or even fight that traitor Justus of Tiberias than be cramped here up on those ramparts between sun and snow. In my life, I've never seen such climate. One day it's freezing, the next it's like a furnace.''

"That too's the desert. Everything around here is controlled by the desert.''

They set the trough down by the punishment rack and stretched their backs.

"One thing's sure, they treat us as if we're the enemy and not the Roman.''

"They treat bar Giora the same way. City folk trust no one. Least of all themselves.''

"Wait till they face those wild assed Idumeans. In my life, they're scary. I once was on a raid with them when Simon and John still worked together. They don't even hesitate to kill a fellow Jew.''

"*ADONAI HU ELOHIM. . .* GOD IS GOD!'' moaned one of the Essenes. The two Galileans turned as if first noticing the sun gazers.

The Legate Mucianus had been right, thought Joseph, brushing away a fly from his nose when the two Galileans weren't looking. The Jews were more concerned with their own squabbles than the fact that the Roman army was converging on the city from Jaffa in the west and from Jericho to the east.

Joseph had disguised himself as an Essene in order to enter the city and try to save it from destruction. Through Queen Berenice's intervention, Vespasian had consented to allow him to go to the capital and see if he could convince its leaders to surrender before the Roman attack. Nothing had changed since the legates of the east had declared Vespasian emperor, and in effect Rome now had two rulers. However with the rainy season ending, Vespasian realized that if he were to win the Senate's full support, he must end the Judean campaign in a burst of glory. Once again Jerusalem held the key to who would be supreme over the whole empire.

Inside the city the civil war persisted. John of Gishhalav and his Galileans, having been decisively defeated in the north, moved south and occupied the Temple compound. John had been less successful with the Ophel, the poorest of Jerusalem's quarters, and once the pride of the ancient City of David. Since the rebellion, the hovels of the Ophel had been jammed with two hundred thousand displaced peasants, who in times of crisis instinctively drifted toward the holy city. Neither the debates in the Gazit Chamber, the assembly hall of the *Sanhedrin,* nor the rivalries of the different war lords had any effect on these wretched masses. For them the stoic camps of the Christians or Essenes and the bands of the Sicaris were irrelevant. Even The Law became for them a denial of their crust of comfort, when instead of caring for their barest needs, it concerned itself with the dialectics of whether a bull was guilty or innocent when it gored a cow, or whether there was no king but God. The wily men of Ophel chose rather to wait for a practical leader to rise and declare God as hungry as they were: that the pain in the belly and the passion in the heart held the same faith. Only then would they prefer rebellion above their meanest joy. Which was exactly what Simon bar Giora was already doing around the towns and villages of the south and why they were waiting for him to march on Jerusalem.

A third force, made up of the Jewish nobles and their retainers, who had refused to abandon the capital, controlled the Upper City and the new Bezetha Quarter under the command of ben Gurion, Segen of the *Sanhedrin,* who still abided by the Supreme Council's orders. It was this last force that Joseph hoped would save Jerusalem from the fate of Jotapata.

A young woman approached and placed a crust of bread and some salt in a dish beside him. "GOD IS ELOHIM!" declared his neighbor, ignoring the offering. Looking down, Joseph caught sight of Raya, their family housemaid. He squeezed his eyes shut, contorting his face and turned his head back up to the sun.

Toward afternoon the air turned cold and the contrast between the heavy sun upon his face and the lightness of the rags he wore made Joseph shiver. People began to form in small knots by the gate and watch the Galileans testing the wooden locks of the punishment rack. Mostly they discussed the shortages of food and water, and how each evening raiding parties from the different factions burned the supplies of their opponents. Joseph wondered how long before the Jews would find themselves a minority in their own country.

After a while the square outside the gate became crowded, and soon a contingent of guards led a bald, red-faced man through the gate.

"What's he done?" demanded one of the crowd.

"That's Joshua, the slaughterhouse keeper," someone shouted. "Hey, what's he done now? Leave off the old fool. He's mad as a cootie in ram's wool."

The bald man's eyes rolled as he raised his bound hands. "A voice from the east. A voice from the west," he moaned. "A voice from the four winds. A voice against Jerusalem and the *Mikdash* of the Lord. A voice against the bridegroom and the bride. A voice against the people. Woe to Jerusalem!"

"Clear the way," cried one of the guards, who wore the fleeced boots of the north."

"But he's crazy," said a man in a smithy apron. "Always has been. So was his old lady."

"Move on, move on!" ordered the guards.

"Listen plow legs, what's he done? We want to know what crazy Joshua's done this time?"

"He's been sentenced to death for false prophecy."

"He's been howling the same shit for a quarter of a century. No one takes Joshua seriously."

"John of Gishhalav does. He's bad for the morale of the city," said one of the guards.

"A voice from the four winds," moaned the prisoner. "A voice against Jerusalem. A voice against the Sanctuary of the Lord!"

"Who knows what is and what isn't prophecy today," sighed a woman, shaking her head.

"The *Bet Din* military court has declared him guilty of seeing omens announcing the destruction of the city," declared a Levite, holding his staff of office.

As if suddenly the prisoner carried the plague, the crowd backed off, fearing even to ask what he had seen.

"A waste of time that way," said the man in the leather apron. "Stoning's faster."

False prophecy, as Joseph knew, called for death by *henek*, garroting. Squinting harder so as not to reveal that he was no longer in the state of trance, Joseph saw the guards lift the man off the ground and clamp the wood locks across his chest. They then raised his legs and placed them in the trough. The man's lips moved silently. In normal times only adults were permitted to witness such executions. Now children as well crowded around the rack. The trough was filled with excrement.

The Levite stepped forward and read the *Bet Din*'s verdict, then declared that it had been confirmed by John of Gishhalav. The guards unloosed the locks leaving the condemned man to dangle by the iron collar as his feet began to sink into the mire.

"Woe to the people! Woe to Jerusalem!" the man croaked, his lips falling open as if he were smiling. One of the Galileans forced a stiff waxed cord into the condemned man's mouth and pressed down on his tongue with a finger, making him gag and swallow at the same time. When the cord lost its slack, he lit it like a wick so that the flame burned down into the man's intestines. The round faced Joshua could neither gurgle nor groan, and died silently with his eyes still prophesying.

Only after the gate square had emptied did Joseph dare to look at the executed man, now covered with flies. Joseph gazed into the last sun, his eyes seething with tears. *ADONAI HU ELOHIM!*

He saw Raya still standing by the gate and staring at him. "My father," Joseph asked, hoarsely, the sun having dried his throat, "is he well?"

"The master's house is closed. I live alone in the wine cellar."

"And Mati, have you seen him?"

"The master's other son is among those in the desert."

One of the Essenes looked annoyingly at Joseph, who rose and followed the housemaid up through the Temple compound. The Temple guards were already lighting the oil lamps along the colonnades, and beyond the Great Altar, at the Nicanor Gate, Levites chanted hymns to the waning day. At this very gate Caligula had insisted on setting a statue of himself as god, and only through the intercession of Agrippa, Queen Berenice's father, was the mad emperor thwarted in affronting Jewish sensibilities. Joseph wondered again what it was in the nature of their faith that provoked others to compel Jews to their own destruction. He heard the widows wail as he and Raya came past the west wall of the Temple. The time post on the Antonia was fading across the *Mikdash.*

A guard from the nobles' militia nodded to Raya, giving Joseph a cursory glance as he let them both pass into the Upper City. A few moments later, Joseph stood before the charred remnant of the arbor where once he had made love to this same housemaid and where the family used to celebrate the Festival of *Sukkot.*

"Who burnt the arbor?" Joseph asked.

"They came, those others," Raya nodded in the direction of the Ophel Quarter. As always she spoke half turned away and eyes to the ground. In the fading light, he saw her dark skin was pocked and that her small nose had grown flat. Like most children of the desert, she had shed her beauty at puberty.

"My father must be in Jericho," Joseph thought aloud, relieved that Vespasian had taken that town without bloodshed. "Has the Palace been looted?" he asked Raya.

"Only palaces of the lords who have deserted the city," she answered, her eyes moving along the garden shrubbery already stiff with frost. "Ours has been spared because of the master's son's feats of war."

Joseph fidgeted. "I only did my duty."

"Not you, Sire. Your brother."

"My brother. What could he have done compared to what I went through?"

"At first they hailed you as a savior. They even prepared a hero's welcome. The news from the north was of victory."

"There are no longer any victories for us."

Raya waited after each sentence Joseph spoke to be sure he was finished. "They came," she nodded again toward the Ophel, "John of the north men. They told of your surrender. The people marched on the palace. It was then that I hid in the cellar."

"And then what happened?"

"The noble ben Gurion intervened reminding them of your brother's deeds in the south as a reason for not destroying our palace."

"Ben Gurion, what's he have to do with all this?"

Joseph waited patiently for the maid's answer. Her pause between each question, he knew, was the desert people's way of showing deference.

"Our Upper City has named him chief," said Raya.

"And this," Joseph nodded to the shell of the arbor, "Why did he allow them to destroy it?"

Raya stepped back. "The lord Ben Gurion allowed them to pour their fury upon it as a sign. They hung your effigy in it and burnt down the *sukkah*."

ii

Ben Gurion hurried into the palace to where Joseph had retired. Behind him stood Raban Johanan ben Zakkai. "Orders were specific about keeping this palace closed," said the commander of the Upper City.

"It's my home," said Joseph. "I can return to it when I please."

"As a traitor you've lost all rights. Even to the priesthood."

The ben Gurion family were Joseph's closest neighbors. Their family traced their ancestry back to the House of David. The fact that both eldest sons of the respective families bore the same name had led to confusion, and often, when they were young, each would answer to a call to the other. This in itself led to comparisons, which made Joseph retain till the present an envy of his more resolute compatriot. The two Josephs, as they were often referred to, had been appointed to the *Sanhedrin* at the same time where their different personalities often clashed. Joseph's arrogance had always been provoked by ben Gurion's diffidence. For Joseph ben Gurion had the ability to analyze and could be trusted. Though Joseph was shrewder, he was limited by his overpowering need to ingratiate.

"The priesthood is my inheritance from God. Nothing but death can deprive me of it."

"The people have burned your effigy here, then stoned another in the Valley of Gehenna."

"Then it takes twice to efface me. Once for each of my battles."

"A Jewish general never surrenders."

"The Romans say an ordinary soldier never does. Besides, I never surrendered. Ask Titus. He'll be here very shortly."

"Only you remained," said ben Gurion, whose slow speech had not changed nor did the haunted look in his sunken eyes.

"I fought as long as I had hope," said Joseph. "I think you've done the same."

"I haven't given up yet."

"That's what I've come to discuss with you." Joseph paced the long hall whose furnishings were covered. The palace still had the smell of summer, an odor Joseph associated with his childhood when the family would return from wintering in Tiberias. Since the palace was always cleaned before they left, it remained in a purified state called for by The Law for the Festival of Passover when they always returned to Jerusalem. It was the one time of the year that Joseph felt like a pilgrim in his own city.

"Four, perhaps, five Roman legions are converging on Jerusalem. Whether you hold out for a week, three months — as we did in Jotapata — or a year, in the end the city will be in ruins. There's only one way out."

"Surrender."

"Surrender with honor. I have the word of Vespasian who is now camping outside Jericho, at Quamran, that if the city open its gates, he will deal fairly with her. Mind you, we will be subject to some punishment for the rebellion."

"Like what he has done to the Essenes. Thrown more than a thousand into the Dead Sea, forcing them under the surface in order to see how quickly they can bob up again. His way of testing the legendary buoyancy of the waters."

Joseph received the news without reaction. "I'm authorized to offer Jerusalem in return for surrender and declaring allegiance to Rome —"

"Rome or Vespasian?" asked ben Zakkai.

"The same. Once he occupies Jerusalem his appointment as emperor will have been secured. It's our one bargaining point with him."

"What's his punishment?" asked ben Gurion.

"I'd rather begin with his offer. He has promised to reinstitute the *Religio Lecita* laws declaring us again an official religion; give every noble citizenship of Rome and allow the tithe to be collected again.

To show his respect for God, he would like to be blessed by the High Priest in the Temple, an honor he told me he deems second only to his coronation in Rome in the Temple of Jupiter."

"The comparison alone is degrading."

"He's a Roman. Not a Jew. If you wish to convert the Emperor, then join the Christians. For myself I have always had a distaste for all apostates."

"And for all this what price are we asked to pay?" asked ben Zakkai.

"A second tithe to cover the campaign costs up to the present, plus a levy for further campaigns in the east and the support of our forces against Nabatea and Parthia." He did not add that Vespasian had also demanded the heads of the leaders of the revolt.

Ben Zakkai shook his head slowly. "Does he realize that the country is penniless; that there is not enough produce for the next month; that a third of the population has been decimated by war and famine. Those with any wealth left are fleeing the land."

"There appears to be enough here for John and Simon to burn each others supplies," retorted Joseph.

"We have tried to keep out of their quarrel," said ben Zakkai, "Kalba Savua has been good enough to open his storehouses and feed the whole city, regardless of faction, free of charge."

"It's the first time I've ever heard of him being generous without a purpose."

"He loves the city as much as we all do."

"Love can destroy as well as shelter. Witness his daughter Rachel," Joseph was referring to the noted scandal of Rachel having run off and married an illiterate shepherd from their estates. Akiba then learned the *alef-bet,* and after attending a children's school for a year was accepted through Matthias' recommendation to the academy of ben Zakkai where he quickly became a master in The Law. None of this had softened the heart of his wealthy father-in-law.

"Nevertheless," said ben Zakkai, "he's kept us alive till now."

Joseph drew up a blind and looked out upon the silent city. He could almost hear the stars pop out, filling the void of darkness. The voice of the man executed that afternoon filled him with bitterness. *A voice against the bridegroom. A voice against the bride.*

"God pity us from our saviors," said Joseph turning back.

"There's another more serious factor," said ben Gurion. "Simon bar Giora has sent an ultimatum to John that if his wife is not released, he'll march on the city."

"Woe to Jerusalem if those Idumeans are allowed in," said ben Zakkai.

"Exactly why we must act at once. With your approval I'll signal the Romans to move immediately before the rains have ceased, and enter the city from this side."

"No army, not even under Pompey, has ever succeeded in conquering Jerusalem from the west," said ben Gurion.

"I mean for you to open the gates and let the Romans into the Upper City. The rest will collapse of itself."

"That's treason," declared ben Gurion.

"To whom? To John? To Simon? Certainly not to the holiness of Jerusalem."

"Nor to God," said ben Zakkai, who despite his age had eyes that flashed with a youthful surety.

Outside the thud of stones and the booming of a catapult sounded. A fire flared beyond the sheep market near the Tadi Gate. "Have any of you heard of my brother Mati?" Joseph asked. He almost asked about Hagla.

"He's with bar Giora," said ben Gurion. "So is Akiva."

"Then what I said earlier holds the more. We must act quickly. I shall go immediately and inform Titus that the western approaches to the city will be open to him. You, ben Gurion, must send messengers to Jericho informing Vespasian. You should also secure the passes into the city. We don't want bar Giora massacring another Roman legion."

Ben Gurion remained silent. Joseph saw that only ben Zakkai could convince him. "I shall inform the *Sanhedrin* immediately of your plan," said ben Zakkai, swinging his cane out before him as he left.

"For what it's worth," said ben Gurion.

"Help from any quarter is essential," said Joseph. "Nevertheless, be cautious, vague. Remember we're gambling with the future of the nation."

"You may be underestimating the Upper City," said ben Gurion.

"The average citizen of this or any city does what his leaders do. Jerusalem is no different. It's never really changed."

"Oh, it's changing. You refuse to see the changes. People speak less. They walk closer to the ground. Your defeat has had a tremendous effect on the price they put on their lives."

"Then I'm prepared to let them burn their own effigies."

"I mean it more honorably. After they heard of the Jotapata suicide pact, many took the oath to act in the same manner if the city falls."

"Merely the Jewish madness. The up again-down again syndrome that created the new state and will be its death. My defeat at Jotapata ended the revolt. Jerusalem's resistance is an anachronism."

"And isn't your *Religio Lecita*?" said ben Gurion.

"That remains to be seen."

"Then you have no real authority to speak for Vespasian."

"Let's say that Queen Berenice advised me to speak for him."

"The Josephean ruse again," said ben Gurion hurrying out.

Joseph watched Raya strip the covers from the furniture. "Tell me," he asked, "what were the terrible omens that poor devil saw to make them strangle him in so horrible a way?"

Raya stopped and backed out of the hall. "They say that Joshua saw — that last Sabbath, while preparing a cow for sacrifice, it gave birth to a lamb."

Joseph chuckled. "Do the desert people believe in omens?"

"They say further," said Raya, looking him in the eye for the first time, her voice quivering, "they say that for the past week he saw Nicanor Gate, that needs twenty men to move it, open by itself."

Joseph recognized these as the same myths handed down from generation to generation since the destruction of the first Temple and that were attributed to the prophet Jeremiah. "Peasant superstitions," he muttered and walked out upon the palace terrace. Snow had begun to fall, and small drifts piled in the corners. Though it snowed almost every year in Jerusalem, it was more like a cold rain and rarely stuck to the ground. Now a white blanket tucked itself into the edges of the sleeping city: around the Ophel, over the Bezetha villas and toward the white crenels in the finally completed wall begun by the late King Agrippa. Only the *Mikdash* dome stood stark and golden.

Suddenly he saw the comet, that for the past year had been streaking across the heavens, cut across the cinnamon skies. As it came over the city, it wheeled sharply and swooped down upon the terrace like a chariot of fire. Falling to his knees and covering his face, Joseph cried out, *"A voice against the City of Jerusalem!"*

CHAPTER XXV — THE ROAD TO PENANCE

On the Tenth of *Xanthicus*, being also the Tenth of *Nissan* according to the Jewish calendar, Titus Flavius led ninety thousand men consisting of the Vth, XIIth, XVth and XXIInd Legions, plus satrapies and vassel kingdom forces including troops from the Golan, Syrian auxiliaries, Dacian, Achaeans and thousands of labor battalion slaves through the passes of Shaar Hagai and up toward Jerusalem. A week earlier he had arrived from Alexandria with Queen Berenice to take command of all the Roman forces in Judea. His father had bequeathed her to his son, having been recalled to be ratified by the Senate as Emperor of Rome. Hardly having a chance to digest reports on the state of the Jewish revolt, Titus listened to Joseph's offer to open the Upper City and thus insure a peaceful surrender of Jerusalem. Since the outbreak of the revolt three years earlier, Joseph had not succeeded in fulfilling his obligations to Rome, and Titus had come to believe that Joseph had less influence among the Jews than he claimed. Nevertheless, because of the morale of his troops, who had been idle and debauching for six months, Titus considered it wise to rely on Joseph one more time. Four miles from Jerusalem, below King Saul's birthplace at the Valley of Thorns, he ordered a halt.

"Your torches are as numerous as the stars," protested Joseph, who insisted that speed was of the utmost importance at this stage of the war. "By now every child most know you are about to attack the city from the west."

"Maybe that will scare them enough into surrender," said Sextus Cerealius, Commander of the Vth Legion. "Just in case your plan fails."

"Doesn't make much difference," said Phrygius, new Legate of the XVth. "Their scouts have been following us since we left Jaffa."

They had all gathered in Titus' tent where he lay sipping wine on a mat spread with cushions. The general looked exhausted. Only a month earlier he had returned from Rome, where he had won support for his father by convincing the Senate that Judea was virtually conquered and that his return there was ostensibly to advance against Nabatea. The stiff walls of Jerusalem were the last obstacle in the way to extending the borders of the Roman Empire eastward. Just in case Joseph's ruse failed, he had asked Tiberius Alexander and Cestius Gallus, who knew the city well, to prepare contingency plans. To add to all his worries, the stomach pains he had developed in Corinth and which had persisted through the campaign in the north had become so acute that the army physicians had prescribed a diet of malva greens and fennel, banning all wine. Of course Titus knew better than they that what he was suffering from had nothing to do with his stomach and continued drinking to kill the pain. He had confided to Joseph that he was surprised that he had even managed to reach the age of thirty. This new disease was an omen for Joseph that not all Titus' moves were sanctioned by God.

"On the contrary," said Joseph to Phrygius. "We haven't been harrassed till now. As Cestius Gallus well knows, Jerusalem's first defense is always Bet Horon and Emmaus."

"Could just as well be a trap," said Cestius. "Well I know the treachery of the Jew."

"Not this time. It's all been prearranged with ben Gurion, head of the forces who hold the Upper City."

"I thought Simon bar Gioras ran these hills," said Titus, speaking with his eyes shut.

"Exactly why we should move into the city directly. In three days the Festival of Passover commences. He's temporarily thinned out his forces to give his people a chance to prepare for the holiday."

"He's not in the city?"

"They'd never let that cutthroat in," said Joseph. "He's camped at Hebron, twenty-five miles due south."

"There's only one way to attack Jerusalem," said Cestius Gallus. "To move north from here and cross over Mount Scopus. Set up normal logistical support and lines of communication with all legions and assault the city at its most vulnerable point."

"If the legate will allow me to remind him," said Joseph, "the city has improved its defenses since his attack two years ago. Agrippa's Wall has been completed. In many respects it's harder now to enter the city from the north side than from the steeper eastern or western escarpments. A half dozen squadrons of cavalry will be sufficient to verify my word about the Upper City."

Titus sipped his wine. "There's the Xth Legion that's on its way to meet us from Jericho."

"They were to swing around Anatot to the north of the city and meet us at the Ginnot Gate," said Joseph. "They're probably already waiting for us."

"For all we know, they might even be inside the city by now," said Tiberius Alexander.

"That's why we can spare a few days and let the troops get orientated," said Titus, sitting up as he saw Berenice standing at the entrance to the tent. "Gentlemen, the Queen of the Jews!" and Titus raised his goblet without, getting up. The generals toasted the Queen who entered the tent and sat beside the commander-in-chief.

"Now, if you will all excuse me, the Queen and I have our strategies to discuss. Keep lights to a minimum. A torch to a command post. Let the men sleep in the open and fully armed. Send out the usual patrols, and in the morning Josephus and I will take six hundred horse and see if he hangs or is made King of Jerusalem."

The jocular tone in Titus' voice made Joseph wince. Something had changed in the young commander since his father had been declared emperor. Or was it a new stage in his sickness?

Joseph bowed to the Queen who proffered her ring to him which he kissed.

"And your own?" she asked, noticing that his priestly ring was missing from his index finger.

"Not till Jerusalem is free again under your rule will I wear any sign of the priesthood. An oath I swore at the fall of Jotapata."

"Here's a present for you," said Titus, tossing a dispatch bag at Joseph. "Read it carefully. It might help you in your chronicles." Joseph caught it by the strap and then walked out to his own nearby tent.

The columns of soldiers were endless and a cloud of dust rose as far back as the coast. Joseph could see a few lights running all the way back to Lydda twenty miles westward. He passed a cavalry squadron lying beside their hobbled horses. Some of the men were grumbling about not being allowed to pitch tents and light cooking fires. There was a pre battle excitement in their voices, and many talked about what the Jews' holy city would be like. The Temple was mentioned occasionally and with fear. Not even their officers knew that there would be no fighting over Jerusalem.

In his tent Lucia was praying with the dedication of a convert.

"How was the Emperor's coronation?" Joseph asked.

Only after she completed her devotions did she look up at him benignly. "The coronation will take place only after the revolt here is totally surpressed."

"And the rest of the Roman season, was it exciting?"

"I never went to Rome. I became ill in Caesarea. The Queen came down from Phillipi and nursed me back to health through the winter."

"The swamps around there are as bad as those surrounding Rome."

"It wasn't the fever," said Lucia, her fingertips trembling along the pendant she wore.

Inside the dispatch bag, Joseph found a packet of oiled paper.

"What was wrong with you in Caesarea?" he asked as he leafed through the documents.

"I had a child."

"From Titus? Vespasian? or was it from Larcius Lepidus this time?"

"Yours. I told you."

"Mine?"

"It nearly killed me. In the end I won. I had it destroyed."

Joseph noticed the dark circles under her eyes and that her hair had lost its sheen. She looked like Hagla. He took her thin arm and felt the dampness of her hand. "There isn't much time, is there? Not for beautiful women."

"Some are luckier than others. Their beauty grows with wisdom. The Queen, for example. She'll never age."

"You're still young enough to mold your beauty into the same kind of wisdom."

"Because of my arrogance, I'm beyond wisdom. I've skipped a whole stage of living."

"At twenty-one there's yet a lot of living." He led her out of the tent. "Come, let's walk down the valley. The water still runs in the wadis and the stones sparkle like pearls."

Lucia took her hand from Joseph's and hugged herself in the cool night air. "Half of them will be dead in a few days," she said as they passed the sleeping troops.

"Not if I can help it."

Lucia stepped into a rivulet where the water ran swiftly. "Make love to me," she said looking down at her sandaled feet. "I haven't been touched by a man in three months."

Joseph took her in his arms, pressing a finger to her lips, then kissing it gently. "And I haven't slept with a woman since you at Caesarea. My road to penance. Both of us must pray so that Rome and Jerusalem might some day be bound together. Only then can we sort out our love."

"Jerusalem is my only penance," she said. "I intend to enter the city before the Romans."

The packet also enclosed a note from Titus, written, to Joseph's surprise, during the battle of Jotapata.

I thought it a good idea to put these and other documents of mine and my father's concerning our campaign against the Jews in your hand. I think you'll do better with them for us than if you tried to rewrite them in the light of your own deeds against us. Henceforth, I shall continue to place at your disposal what I deem essential, and wherever possible have you at my side even in the midst of battle.

Joseph glanced more carefully through the maps and charts which were interspersed with inventories of men and material of the Roman Army of the East; its dispositions, operations and movement of men in relation to time and terrain and how the weather would be. All contingencies were included, even in case Parthia and Nabatea invaded Judea or Golan joined the revolt. The last document was marked: APPROVED. It was the full battle plan for the destruction of Jerusalem.

He wrote:

the darling of rome wishes me to create him in his own image. the posterity of the flavians ironically is bound to that of israel. hence the conqueror of judea shall live only through the survival of those he has already ordered destroyed. my apologia, then, must be to jerusalem. again the superiority of the WORD over the ACT. to defeat your enemy is to record his victories.

CHAPTER XXVI — TREACHERY AT THE GATE

i

They climbed out of the Valley of Gihon at a slow pace, the horses sure-footed and trained not to snort. Joseph wore the uniform of a tribune of the XVth Legion and rode beside Titus. They approached the city from the side of the Serpent's Pool as planned and cantered up to the Ginnot Gate that led into the Upper City. If all went well, runners would carry back the news, and the rest of the legions would move up and surround the city. Jerusalem would fall without battle.

Like three abandoned chess pieces at a game's end, the towers of Herod's Castle stood out against the dawn. Joseph scanned the walls carefully to make sure that ben Gurion's militia were at their posts. No one was on the ramparts. They must all be busy with the holiday preparations, he thought. He saw smoke rising from the Temple courtyard, fires for the final cleansing of any *hametz* leavening in the compound. As peacemaker, he hoped he would be called upon to sacrifice the pascal lamb.

Galloping ahead, he shouted to the gatekeeper to get ben Gurion. His answer came in a hail of arrows that luckily struck his mount, who reared up like a shield.

Joseph fell down unharmed beside the corpse of his horse. The shadows of daylight revealed thousands of men rising from behind trenches and low stone walls of the gardens which sprawled across the western slopes and where Jews had hidden, waiting to trap the Romans who galloped past without noticing them. Their long robes and the scimitar-like mustaches identified them as Idumeans.

Titus, who believed in cavalry as the only true offensive weapon, charged forward, and bareheaded led his men over the trenches, cutting his way northward. But there too the Jews had outsmarted him. This time it was John's Galileans. Wearing fleeced boots, they poured out of the Psephinus Tower and forced the Romans toward the walls where bowmen began to cut them down.

"Our only chance," declared a centurion nearby, "is to dismount and use the haunches of our horses as a defense perimeter until relief arrives from our main force." As if the voice of this officer carried direct to his commander, Titus rode up and struck the man down, then shouted: "No one dismounts! Your horses are superior to swords and lances." And he pushed on to a narrow gap in the trench line of the Jews. In the midst of this confusion, the horse of the centurion just killed by Titus nibbled at some grass a foot from where

Joseph hugged the earth. Joseph leaped up and clumsily threw himself on the horse and galloped after Titus who was fighting his way down the path they had first ascended to the city. Anticipating this as well, the Jews now uncovered ditches, tripping the horses and then rolling stones down at the escaping riders. Titus wheeled back, charging past Joseph. He kept improvising, shouting orders and counter orders as the trap closed tighter around his men. Joseph saw that Titus was smiling.

Coming around the Psephinus Tower corner, fifteen squadron of the Xth Legion appeared. They quickly drove the Jews back into the city as they cut through to what was left of the embattled reconnoitering party, leading them down the valley and back to the camp. Two hundred and fifty-six Romans lay dead in the trenches that had become their graves.

ii

The fact that he wasn't immediately arrested upon his return to the camp gave Joseph hope that Titus did not blame him for the fiasco at the Ginnot Gate. He went directly to interrogate the few Idumean prisoners they had taken in order to find out what had gone wrong. The camp was feverish. Officers shouted at their men trying to keep them in formation as they awaited orders to move out. Roman retreats were never allowed to hang long. They were always followed by a harder thrust against the enemy.

At the edge of the camp, in a bend in the valley, a swarm of flies circled above Joseph, turning their turquoise bellies to the sun. Moving on, he saw twenty bodies nailed to crosses. Joseph studied the dead disinterestedly, noting how all their legs were crossed at the knee, the right one over the left drawn up in such a manner that brought the feet parallel and able to be fixed with one spike at the heels. This contorted the bodies into a half bowing position as if in gratitude to their tormentors. The prisoners faced west.

Joseph started back to the camp when he noticed one prisoner squirming on his cross in an effort to turn his head toward the holy city. "How'd you manage to get into the city?" Joseph asked bluntly. "From where did you come?"

The dying man struggled silently, trying to turn eastward. "You're not dressed like the others," Joseph persisted. "Who's your commander and I'll see that you're buried according to The Law."

Slowly the man moved his eyes and looked down at Joseph. His nostrils flared and his mouth twisted grotesquely spurting blood. "Eleazar ben Yair."

Joseph retreated to the center of the camp. Hesitating before Titus' tent, he was shoved aside by a tall man in a black burnoose.

"You're a lucky bastard we hung around for you," said Larcius Lepidus to Titus, throwing himself on the general's mat.

"What took you so long then?" asked Titus, grinning.

"Give me a drink or else I'll join the fucking Jews."

Titus poured wine. Before the man could drink it, Titus grabbed his ankle and rolled him over. Larcius was too quick and jumped forward tackling Titus and pinning him to the ground. "Now ask me again where I've been."

"All right, where've you been?"

"Fucking among the sheep," he said rising. "You can't imaging the tricks those little devils know."

Titus stood up and brushed himself off. "Hope it was female."

"Diana among the daisies. A tight twatted shepherdess, maybe twelve, thirteen years old."

"You always went for fresh watering holes."

"And you for those big splashy ones."

"It's faster. Faster to get in and longer to come out. Now where are the rest of your men?"

"Where we were supposed to be. On the eastern side of the city. You're lucky I sent out patrols. That's how we discovered you were in trouble."

"Eastern side?"

"That was the message we got. They got more dead Jews there than I've ever seen in my life."

"Mount of Olives," said Joseph entering. "Jerusalem's burial ground since its founding."

"Don't I know him?" the man in the black burnoose asked Titus.

"Josephus, once again, meet Larcius Lepidus, Legate of the Xth Legion, who thinks he's a better soldier than me. It's in this Jew's power," Titus pointed at Joseph, "to make you famous."

"When do we start?" Larcius scowled.

"We already have," said Joseph. "At Jotapata."

Larcius Lepidus lay back down on the mat, his legs bent at the knees so that his genitals hung exposed while he cleaned his fingernails with a Sicari dagger.

"As soon as this chronicler of our fortunes explains to me what went wrong this morning," said Titus.

Joseph, who had prepared his excuses even before the surprise attack against their reconnaissance party, was put off balance by Titus' lighthearted remarks. "I've been trying to question prisoners," he stammered. "They've all been killed."

"Here's one that isn't," said Titus, waving a hand at Justus of Tiberias, who now entered the tent. "He, too, can make you famous. You have your pick of Jews. They both lie beautifully."

"Sire," said Justus, his handkerchief already out of his sleeve as he dabbed his sweating chin. "I have just come from inside the city. Because of that man," he pointed at Joseph, "Jerusalem is about to be united as never before." He pulled out a scroll and handed it to Titus. Titus glanced at it and handed it to Joseph. "Translate it."

Joseph read it over twice, then handed it back to Titus. "It's a proclamation declaring a truce — not peace — between John of Gishhalav and Simon bar Giora."

"Much more," said Justus. "As you observed this morning, they've merged forces."

"You told me bar Gioras would never be allowed into the city," said Titus to Joseph.

"If the Legate will allow me, I think I can explain it all," said Justus.

"Doesn't really matter."

"You must realize that Simon bar Giora is a terrible man. If it's possible, worse than John ben Levi."

Joseph saw how Justus was slanting his story. "John's a tyrant and a cunning leader," said Joseph. "Simon is blunt and honest." The last words were said only to contradict Justus.

"Let him go on," said Titus, who poured wine for Larcius and himself.

"John's a very sick man and gladly agreed to merging forces. That is coordinating their fighting but not giving up their specific areas of control in the city."

"How did Simon get into the city?" demanded Joseph.

"The storm," said Justus, raising his eyes to the sky like a seer. "Didn't you feel it in Jaffa?"

"We were still at sea. We felt it coming up from Alexandria," said Titus.

"Worst I have ever witnessed. The storm strangled the winter, giving birth to summer without the pain of spring. The heavens opened and torrents washed down upon this sinful land for exactly one hour. Then God himself, instead of you, his messenger," said Justus bowing to Titus, "struck Jerusalem, which, I swear, heaved itself in a mass off the earth and settled back after a terrible crash of thunder and lightning. While all the time the ominous comet kept circling the sky, adding to the Lord's wrath against His once holy city."

Joseph was familiar with the rhetoric of half truths for which Justus was noted in his speeches before the *Sanhedrin,* and in his descriptions of his many voyages that made popular recitals on Saturday evenings in the salons of Jerusalem and Tiberias.

"Bullshit," said Larcius, belching loudly. "In Jericho it sounded like your god farted."

"Cut your imagery," Titus said to Justus. "Go on."

"Throughout the city, the sentinels sought shelter, sure that no attack would be forthcoming that night. For the wild Idumean desert dwellers, however, the fiery night held no fear and was ideal for a surprise attack. With twenty thousand troops, bar Giora assaulted the Gate of the Essenes, moving up the Tyropoeon Valley and firing the Archives, burning all the records of debts and indenture, thus winning the unanimous support of the Ophel Quarter."

"And the Upper City?" asked Joseph.

"They fought valiantly. The Idumeans under bar Giora took great pleasure in razing every palace and villa that was not already destroyed by the previous civil strife. They seemed to be avenging the blood of their pagan ancestors who suffered for so many centuries until John Hyrcanus compelled them to convert to our faith. They killed. They raped. They plundered the quarter for three days, but could not subdue it. Ben Gurion followed my defense plan of years before."

"What were you doing in the city?" asked Joseph.

Justus smiled. "The legate sent me."

Joseph snapped around and glowered at Titus. "I always cover my flanks," said Titus. "When I was told that my father gave you permission to secretly enter the city, I ordered Justus to go as well. For other purposes, you understand."

Joseph did not understand. What other reason but to check on him would Titus have to send this detestable man into the city? He decided not to protest but to question Justus further in order to trap him in a lie. "Ben Gurion, what happened to him?"

"Killed as well. He was not a good soldier."

Joseph tried to conjure up the face of the man whom he had never agreed with but always respected. So many of his contemporaries had died recently, both friend and foe, that his vision blurred and at that instant the face of ben Gurion became his own countenance. "Your words profane the passing of a brave man," said Joseph.

"Go on," said Titus to Justus.

"Finally bar Giora had to use a ruse which would have done you proud." He pointed his full hand at Joseph. "Since the Festival of Passover was approaching, the idea occurred to him to also free slaves, in this way winning them away from the forces of ben Gurion whose line soldiers they were. Within an hour after his proclamation of freedom the Upper City fell.

"Now the Idumeans began a systematic slaughter of the nobles. It was still going on when I escaped from the city."

Titus filled his glass, and when Larcius Lepidus tinkled his with a finger, he poured some wine into the legate's goblet as well. Both generals were getting bored with the Jews' internal squabbles. Justus sensed the mood and abruptly cut off his narrative. "Sire, I think the city is so weakened that all you need do is feign an attack and it will surrender."

"Unless you're lying to me as he did," said Titus.

"I told no lies," protested Joseph. "If this man's word is but half the truth, and I suspect it's less than that, I am already exonerated. Two weeks ago my plan was operative."

"If what he's been telling is true," said Larcius, "then let's get drunk, rope in some of those Nabateans and screw ourselves to death while the Jews kill each other off."

"Not if they fought as united as they did this morning," said Titus.

"How did you manage to get out of the city?" asked Joseph, trying desperately to trap Justus.

Justus sucked in his breath, controlling a titter. "The Christians. Bar Giora gave them permission to leave the city to go to Pella across the Jordan. He knew that they would never fight, and by getting rid of them, he could conserve food and water. I made a hasty conversion and joined them." He held up a cross that he pulled out of his toga. It was made of gold.

Just enough truth to cover his lies, and exaggerations, thought Joseph, who could not admit to himself that he had spoken similarly when he surrendered to the Romans in the cave below Jotapata.

"That, at least, is true," said Larcius. "I met this egg-sucking weasel with those sniveling beggars as they came down to Jericho."

Titus paced back and forth in the narrow tent. Once he even kicked Larcius' dirty feet that lay in his way. "Get back to the Mount of Olives and alert your troops," he ordered his friend. "We attack at dawn."

Larcius Lepidus jumped up. "Well, it's almost as good as fucking."

"You hit them at the Susa Gate, *here*," said Titus unrolling a map and spreading it on the floor. He pointed to the most easterly gate into the city.

"Impossible," cried Joseph. "It's the steepest point of entry. Furthermore, its sides are right up against the Temple."

"So?"

"If anything will unite the Jews, it will be an attack against the House of God."

"Fear for its holiness may work two ways," said Justus. "It can make them surrender more quickly in order to preserve it."

"Let's not worry about your Temple yet," said Titus tapping his finger on the map. Larcius is only going to feint an attack and draw off John's Galileans. They're tough bastards. I've fought them. The real attack will be even more impossible," grinned Titus. "Right here." He slapped the back of his hand against the western line of the Outer Wall.

"We've just reconnoitered it," exclaimed Joseph. "You saw what happened this morning."

"They'll never expect it again. The Vth, XIIth and XVth will break through here and move up to the old Camp of the Assyrians. There the XVth under Phrygius, moving northeast across the Bezetha Quarter, will open the Fish Gate to let Larcius into the city which he will approach by swinging north up the Kedron Valley. In this way they bypass your so-called Agrippa's Wall and immediately turn south against the Antonia Fortress.

"Meanwhile," continued Titus, "Cerealius and his Vth and Cestius and the XIIth break through the Iron Gate in the Second Wall, the former moving across the Tyropoeon Valley and hitting the Antonia from the west; the latter smashing his way through the First Wall and into the Upper City at the gate below Hanania's Palace."

"Insanity," declared Joseph, shocking Justus at his audacity in questioning Titus' strategy. Larcius Lepidus broke out laughing, and Titus, who unlike his father, was never averse to criticism, chuckled. "I'm making it up as I go along."

"Sounds pretty good to me," said Larcius. "Cause it's so fucking confusing."

"I won't even talk about the Xth moving up the Kedron," said Joseph, trying to regain his composure. "They face the toughest forces at the Outer Wall: the best Jewish slingers in the city. Your pivotal point at the Camp of the Assyrians is vulnerable to the highest hill inside Jerusalem. *Here!*" Joseph pointed to a promontory seven hundred and eighty feet high protruding above the city walls almost dead center in the Bezetha Quarter and up against the Second Wall. "The Arms Givah. The XVth will never get by it in time to open the gate for Larcius Lepidus, assuming he ever reaches it. Furthermore, Cestius Gallus, in attacking below the Hanania, will be up against the murderous enfilading fire from the inner walls of Herod's Castle."

"Sounds like more and more fun," said Larcius Lepidus.

"Finally," said Joseph, "may I question the Commander's initial breaching point into the city from the west on which everything else hinges? In that sector the Outer Wall is at its widest."

"Viktor," said Titus. "Your old friend the ram of Epaphroditus.

"We're going to smash through that wall before midnight."

Outside, Joseph saw the work battalions moving up the sinister looking machine. This time the ram's head at the end of the breaching post was painted vermillion.

CHAPTER XXVII — AMONG THE HARLOTS

That night Joseph came among the harlots. Three young maids, their faces scrawled with hieroglyphics, slithered around him, their thighs hissing as they taunted him with long fingernails the color of blood. At one tent a black girl jumped out in front of him, whacking a timbral of goat skin, her anklets clicking with elephant's teeth. Joseph was entranced by the contrast of her red gums and thick gray lips. She beat the drum faster and moved around him in long, dipping strides. Each time she came closer, running her hands down her naked sides and along the insides of her thighs. Her eyes were colorless and penetrated her oval skull like rays of light. Then she leaped in the air and landed in front of him blocking his path. She played with the tribune staff that hung from his left hip, rubbing her mahogany fingers up and down it, grunting as she moved them faster and faster. She pulled it along his belt together with his leather purse. Then she slipped the staff between her legs and began to swirl on it as her fingers jingled the coins in the purse. She moaned to the rhythm of her own movement until finally she jumped back letting the staff dangle wet and sparkling against his groin. Whirling about she stalked across the bonfire around which old whores sat muttering, their dugs exposed like rotting pears.

Joseph followed the girl into the tent in front of which a mangy dog slept. The tent had only a rug of intricate design in shades of brown and blue struck diagonally by lightning of green. A girl, hardly yet a woman, came and unwrapped the skirt of the black dancer. She handed it to Joseph for him to examine, and only when he saw her toying with the waistband of an underskirt did he understand the game she wished to play. He tossed her a silver coin for the skirt and sat down upon it. The girl brought a krater of wine and held it to his lips as he sipped it slowly. The familiar odor of Nabatean honey rose from a lighted punk the black dancer held between her teeth. She kicked off one of her anklets which landed beside Joseph. He tossed her another coin while the younger girl slipped off Joseph's tunic. The dancer handed Joseph the punk to sniff and then scratched one pointed nail down his chest to his exposed navel. Joseph thought he was tumbling.

The wine the girl tilted to his lips brought him back, and he shook his head clear. The black dancer rolled her eyes so that the irises disappeared, and for an instant she turned into a vision of stone. Lucia praying in Cana. She tossed him the other anklet, but he missed it and it burst, a mouthful of teeth, at his feet. The other girl unloosed the rest of his clothes and he saw that his purse had disappeared. The dancer straddled his body and forced him back slowly, squatting on his chest. She annointed his body with a white balm that had the acrid smell of a Sodom apple. The dancer covered her body as well, and Joseph felt he was sinking into the Salt Sea. The girl doused the torch and in the darkness he heard a voice command: "Faster! You can do it faster!"

It was Mati he was lying with, hidden behind a cactus bush from where they watched a cousin being purified before her marriage the next day. The rite was performed in the *mikva* bath in their garden, and Matthias himself was performing her initiation. Their father wore a crimson robe and a silver miter upon his head. He was intoning a blessing, and with the same casualness with which Joseph had seen him slaughter a yearling for sacrifice, he stuck his finger into their cousin's bare bottom, probing deep as she groaned. Unlike his and his brother's own initiation which they wiped on the leaves of the bush, Matthias wiped hers on a silk cloth, spotting it with the blood of her virginity.

Joseph felt his skin leak as welts burned across his thighs. The girl had pinned him down while he moaned in the pleasure of this new violation.

The Law obliges every Jew never to waste a *mitzvah* — to touch his fingertips to water in order to pronounce the commanded benediction over cleanliness even though his hands already sparkle. Was it not then also a duty to perform an evil before the Lord so as not to allow His punishment of the holy city to seem in vain? Joseph was pleased to become the scapegoat for Jerusalem's anguish.

His body trembled and he felt himself slide down the coasts of the earth. He heard screams as the tent was rent in two. The heavens were seething with the fires of battle that shattered the darkness into a dawn filled with ululations. His two playmates hovered stiff over him. He did not vomit when he saw that they were boys, and it was he who drew them down upon him, knowing that the attack on Jerusalem had begun.

"And the Children of Israel did evil in the eyes of the Lord," Joseph heard an unfamiliar voice prophesy out of his own. And it came so that he revelled in his abomination.

CHAPTER XXVIII — THE ARMS GIVAH

i

From the start the Roman attack went wrong. For ten hours the scorpion quick-firers hammered at the city from the central camp, moved north by now and on Mount Scopus. The booming echoed down the valleys as the missiles of stone and iron slammed against the ramparts and towers of Jerusalem. Catapults that heaved stones molded from clay and filled with iron smashed into the overcrowded Ophel Quarter, raising a crescendo of howls and screams only to be drowned out in the seventh hour of darkness when the order was given to attack.

Still dazed from his orgiastic absolution, Joseph moved between the grotesque machines that lined the hillside. He wished only to clamber up the streets of the doomed city shouting: *console ye! console ye!*

When he heard the artillery shift, which he knew was the signal for the Xth Legion's false feint to begin, he hurried to join the main thrust through the western sector of the Outer Wall. There he saw the men of the Vth, XIIth and XVth Legions and their Syrian auxiliaries waiting at their jumping off points to break into the city.

Joseph galloped by the Outer Wall, past the fluttering shadows of the work battalions, who were still heaving the ram against the thirty foot thick walls, sending sparks against the stars. But like the stubbornness of Jerusalem's defenders, the stones held. The slaves, all Jewish prisoners, labored faster, as if failure now would be their second defeat. Joseph wondered how many of them had fought under him at Jotapata.

The skies were already thinning when the wall was finally breached. A cry rose from the massed assault troops: "We are ready!" and the echo READY! READY! READY! rollback, bouncing off the oval crested Judean hills. First came the cavalry bearing the ensigns of the participating legions and Roman satrapies. Titus followed at the head of the Elite Guard in a square formation around him and holding standards topped with the imperial eagle. Behind them came the infanty in columns of six, the Macedonian mercenaries as usual bringing up the rear. Joseph entered the city with a unit of the Vth Legion and raced along the north road toward the Camp of the Assyrians.

He found Titus and Tiberius Alexander at the old ruined mill of the camp from where they watched the progress of the battle. By the light of two torches, he knelt before the same map that had been spread in the tent yesterday, only now four sentinels held down its edges. Titus' head was bleeding and he kept swatting the wound as if it were a mosquito bite. Messages began to come in from all fronts and interrupted their concentration on the map.

"Sire, the Legate Cerealius reports he's falling back," declared a centurion who looked like a death mask in the torchlight. "The Jews have set fire to the wood market lighting up the whole sector so that the Vth is a moving target from that jutting hillside ahead."

"The Arms Givah," muttered Joseph.

Another messenger arrived. "The XIIth is pinned down, Sire, below Hanania's palace. The walls were unmanned, but when we broke through the Second Wall, a horde of wild Jews stormed out of the storehouses just inside the gate and routed our advance guard, leaving a brigade cut off at the First Wall."

Titus pushed away his personal physician who was trying to apply a bandage to his forehead. "Any news from Larcius?" he asked. "That devil should have been at the Fish Gate an hour ago."

"The XVth under Phrygius has made no contact with him." said Tiberius Alexander. "His signal fires haven't been spotted."

"He's got to break through at once and attack Gioras's entrenchment on that fucking hill out there."

"He must be having trouble coming up the Kedron," said Joseph. "It's an impossible route."

"His best chance is to swing around north and approach us from Mount Scopus," said Tiberius Alexander.

Titus tottered for a second and had to lean on one of the sentinals. "All right, go tell him. Tell him to get into a position to attack the hill from the north. We'll swing the XVth back and have it hit them from the east. That should take enough pressure off Cerealius to allow him to move through the Second Wall beyond those markets and break into the Upper City over there by the Town Hall." He tapped his knuckles on the map and a drop of blood fell exactly on Joseph's palace. "From there we can cross the Tyropoeon Valley and still swing back up against the Antonia. We'll be there to join him."

Joseph shook his head. "The valley there is sheer cliff."

Titus ignored him. "Order Cerealius to mount those escarpments with grappling irons. I want that side of the Antonia neutralized before we move against that Arms Givah."

Joseph galloped back beyond the Hyrcanus Monument where Arab bowmen had managed to keep a lane open through the original breach in the Outer Wall. He turned north and followed the wall just below Mount Scopus, passing through the waiting reserve forces of the auxiliaries who were to attack in the second wave at dawn. As he climbed out of the valley, he saw the foothills of the Arms Givah piled with Roman corpses. The hill had been terraced into ledges and trenches from which the Jews had no choice but to fight till death.

ii

What Joseph found on the Mount of Olives was worse than on the west side of the city. But for a handful of guards, the camp of the Xth Legion was deserted. A Thracian officer explained to Joseph that the legion had marched across the valley at midnight hoping to surprise the Jews on the Temple walls. The Jews let them approach the Susa Gate and there, having barely ground to dig in until they could regroup to scale the walls, the Romans found themselves pinned down and were being decimated from above by the short bows of the Galileans.

Joseph looked out across the Kedron Valley where darkness still lingered, and by the few torches on the wall, saw thousands of legionnaires clinging to the little natural shelter below. The roar of Larcius Lepidus' voice resounded in the valley as he persisted in urging his men to scale the walls. The Legate of the Xth Legion, still in his burnoose, had disobeyed orders, and instead of a feint against the Susa Gate and then moving up toward the Fish Gate to meet the XVth Legion, he had countermanded Titus' orders and attacked the Temple compound head on.

The sun rose on myriad tombs which revealed a new army between the Romans at the wall and where Joseph stood. He saw the graveyard move, and from beneath the hoary stones, the dead rose and charged up to the Roman camp. Joseph barely managed to escape as the resurrected army of the Jews that had hidden all night under the tombstones now overran the Xth Legion's base. Once again Judah the Maccabee's ruse had saved the city of God, this time cutting down four thousand heathen at its walls.

Joseph retreated as he had come and reported to Titus what had happened. The commander-in-chief, his head bandaged, immediately ordered his Elite Guard out and led them along the foothills of the Arms Givah, then east out of the Fish Gate and down the Kedron Valley in order to rescue his old comrade. Drawing all the fire to his force, Titus allowed as many of the trapped men as he could to escape down the valley and toward Mount Scopus. Behind them, atop the Mount of Olives they saw their camp rise, like the sun, in a ball of fire.

iii

Joseph entered Titus' tent in the central camp on Mount Scopus and found the general lying on a sofa sipping some light wine. His head had been rebound and a deep gash in the calf of his left leg drained over a clay bowl. Titus dismissed his surgeon and motioned Joseph closer.

"Are you in much pain?" asked Joseph.

Titus shifted uncomfortably. "Soldiers and athletes are always in pain. Now read me what you wrote in that scroll about our opening attack."

Joseph unrolled a rough piece of parchment upon which the ink had smudged. He read:

today the words of john ben levi of gishhalav came true. the roman soldier showed that he was only a roman soldier. certainly jerusalem outfought rome, and the day was saved only by the daring of titus flavius. more than anything else this further roman defeat will encourage the extremists under simon. had titus listened to me originally, we might all be sitting in herod's castle instead of here on mount scopus, and tomorrow partaking of the passover sacrifice which most surely would have included the emperor vespasian's gift.

"Self-exoneration," said Titus. "You got it all wrong. My plan was flawless. What happened to the Xth was exactly as I planned it. A sham battle. The confidence the Jews gained today will be their destruction tomorrow."

"And did Larcius Lepidus know that the so-called sham would cost him four thousand dead?"

Titus smiled and sipped his wine. "No idea at all. Knowing him I was sure he would go for the Temple. Besides I never told him that most of his forces had been replaced by Syrian auxiliaries. His own men might just have broken into the Temple."

"But what of our losses in the west? The breakdown of our advance?"

"Sometimes a pause in battle is good for morale. The attack is about to commence at once."

"And this time will it be the XIIth Legion that you'll sacrifice?"

Titus shook his head. "Your defensive mind counts numbers instead of places. We are in the city after only twenty-four hours of fighting. We've got John guarding the wrong side of the Temple, since like you, he thinks he knows Roman tactics and is expecting us to attack again at the Susa Gate."

"You yourself once told me that the victories of the Roman army are based on repetition."

"That is correct. Only occasionally we mix up the order. I intend to repeat the tactic against the Antonia." He paused as they both heard the whizzing of the artillery start up again. This was followed by the whoops and shouts of the charging Romans that rolled across the city. "I suspect that both your and Justus' account will be wrong. Yours especially. You see things as you would like them to be and not as they are. You're more worried about how you'll be thought of than what you really think. It's your Jewish sense of history."

"It's the only one worth leaving. To record is what our whole purpose is."

"Most chronicles are wrong. Troy, Marathon, Actium — all myths. I, for example, shall go down as a great hero to the Roman and hated eternally by the Jews. Whose image do you think will last?"

"Right now the least we can afford is to create myths. Roman or Jewish. No one knows this city as I do. Every cave, every crevice has been explored by me at one time, and the intricacies of each attack in the past have been a special study of mine. Lest you forget it, your pivot point at the Camp of the Assyrians was named for the people who were once defeated in a similar attempt to capture Jerusalem."

"Myth again."

"History. This time history."

"The trouble with you is that you're comparing this battle with Jotapata. There you had a classic fort, and when a classic attack failed, my father, being a cautious man, used the classic last resort — siege. Here the situation is fluid. Neither John nor bar Gioras fight by the book. You did. They have the advantage of defending a city whose walls zig-zag at such angles that the attacking force is always outflanked. The road I'm choosing gives my men maximum protection."

"John's victory in the Kedron last night will whet Simon's appetite to outdo him. It's an eager bar Giora we face in the west at the moment."

Titus rose. He rubbed his back against the tent post, then drank more wine. "They're all busy sacrificing to that strange god of yours who inhales the fire of burnt offerings but has no frame to consume it. Maybe that's why he never supports you."

Joseph looked out and saw the smoke rising from where the Great Altar stood. The smell of sizzling lamb rose above the dust of war making him recall how as boys he and Mati would accompany their father the day before the holiday, and holding candles, search in all the corners of the slaughterhouses for any remnant of *hametz* leavening. The stalls and blocks had already been scrubbed clean and had a sickening odor of blood and lye. However in order not to waste a blessing, Matthias would place bits of bread around the long hall before the boys arrived, and together they would seek them out, brushing the crumbs with a feather into a papyrus folder. They would then burn it with a piece of unleavened bread, the only kind permitted to be eaten during the following seven days, and declare the Temple sanctified for the Passover. As the eldest Joseph had to fast the next day to commemorate God's saving the first born male child from being cast into the Nile by Pharaoh. Joseph remembered how jealous he had been that Mati could eat the rich egg matzah cakes which the cooks baked in the oven in their back garden for his breakfast, while he had to suffer for others' lives. To taunt his brother, he had once taken him back to the sheep pen after the slaughterhouse had been cleansed and the bread burnt. "Look," he had said. "A piece of bread!"

All the next day Mati feared for his father up on the altar, believing that he had sinned, and though unintentionally, that he would be struck down by the Lord. Joseph never told him that he had placed the crust of bread there without their father's knowledge.

Was Mati in the city now, perhaps performing the sacrifice? Or had God already made him pay for Joseph's sins?

Titus was about to offer Joseph a tankard of wine when a tribune entered and announced that the Jews had retaken the Hyrcanus Monument and that the headquarters of the XIIth and XVth Legions were cut off at the Camp of the Assyrians. Titus winced with pain as he strapped on his armor. "Round up Fronto, Tiberius and Cerealius," he ordered. Joseph hurried out feeling like a runner.

iv

In all his experience at Vespasian's headquarters in the north and at Titus' here outside of Jerusalem, Joseph had never witnessed Roman generals argue so vehemently with each other. Their formal Latin had disintegrated into their different native vernaculars.

"All right," declared Titus. "Now hear me and hear me once. Ten squadron of cavalry will again break through the breach in the Outer Wall, west. Archers will take up positions in a path and hold them like pillars of stone. Anyone who retreats will be shot from behind by his comrade. Cerealius, I give you one hour to make contact with the Camp of the Assyrians. Otherwise you might as well carry your head back to me. Fronto, I want every artillery piece of your reserve XXIInd aimed no further than ten yards ahead of our advance. If they bog down, pull back your fire. We'll break the Jew today or I'm dead."

That night Joseph listened to the clamor of battle until he could tell the difference between scorpion quick-firers and the catapult stone throwers. By their crash he could estimate their weight and the damage they were causing. The torching arrows gave frames to the heavens and made the mountains leap. He heard thunder that could only be the ram coming from the east and was sure that once again Larcius Lepidus was attempting to smash through the Susa Gate. If the Romans weren't careful, the Jews might yet capture the pride of Roman weaponry and turn it against their enemy's camp.

Joseph joined Titus at the head of the Elite Guard ready to charge through the breach with Cerealius. This time the Arab bowmen kept a steady barrage of arrows against Simon's men on Herod's Castle so that the Hyrcanus Monument was quickly overrun. Titus swung his force north beyond the Camp of the Assyrians, which was relieved by the Vth Legion, and charged right up to the Second Wall below the Arms Givah. Now Titus was indeed using the classic Roman strategy of repetition.

Cestius Gallus rode out of the Camp of the Assyrians and up to Joseph. "He's making the same mistake again." he shouted.

"He won't listen. At least he's given orders to move in the work battalions and they're to begin setting up earthworks immediately. Have you taken many losses?"

"From the artillery captured from us two years ago at Shaar Hagai," answered the Legate of the XIIth Legion, who was unaware of Titus' order for continuous artillery barrage regardless of the speed of the advancing troops.

"Look how they go when they see Titus," declared Joseph. "He's like their shield."

Cestius urged his horse on. "That's true on both sides. Your Jews fight as bravely when bar Gioras merely gazes down from those parapets."

Over to his right Joseph recognized the mustached, scimitar bearing leader of the Idumeans. He stood arrogantly between two torches so that his men could gain courage from his audacity. Men did not fight that way for Cestius Gallus, he thought, nor for himself at Jotapata.

They both stopped to watch a Roman trooper break the rhythm of battle as he charged past Titus and out between the advancing Roman cavalry and the Jews entrenched in the moats around the Second Wall. Titus kept shouting to his men not to bunch up. But like the Jews, the Romans too were watching the possessed trooper who had by now reached the Second Wall where he cut his way through a Jewish phalanx of archers. An Idumean challenged him to single combat, but the Roman pierced him through the neck with his lance.

Removing it quickly, he pinned another Idumean through the abdomen and against a tree that grew out of the whitewashed wall. Now a Jewish officer leaped out of the moat and fought hand to hand with the trooper who drew him off and back to the Roman lines where he was taken prisoner.

At the Iron Gate, Titus dismounted and walked up to the trooper whose hands were smeared with blood. "Your name?" asked the commander.

"Longinus, Sire," the ruddy face soldier beamed. Titus slapped him so hard that the trooper rolled over into the dirt. "For disobeying orders. I'd rather have us lose than break the disciplined ranks and tempo of battle. Let the Jew scorn death. Rome fights from the knowledge of its victory."

Once, in the bathhouse in Rome, Titus had told Joseph the story of a father killing his son for disobeying orders. Nevertheless, the soldiers in the trooper's brigade cheered him as they brushed him off after he rejoined them.

Titus signalled his aide to mark the man's name on the roll for a later award. He then ordered the prisoner nailed to a cross staked in the middle of no-man's-land, goading the Jews to come and redeem him. It made no difference to Titus that the prisoner was John the Essene, a Jewish general.

For two days the Jews attacked, desperately trying to save their commander. By the time the vultures began circling over the cross, fifty-two Sicaris had lost their lives. Simon bar Giora appeared on top of a storehouse. Despite the missiles flying about him, he drew an arrow and set it to a bow, then aiming carefully, let it go, piercing his companion-in-arms through the heart, ending his silent agony. Joseph had not dared to plead before Titus for the life of the wiseman Bannus' only son.

The Jews retreated to mourn their general, and Titus saw another chance to breach the Second Wall.

"Jews do not mourn their dead upon the battlefield as you Romans do," said Joseph. "Their retreat is a trick. They'll suck you in, then attack again from the Arms Givah."

Titus glanced at the rising hill still held by the Jews. The dead heaped upon it made it seem taller. Kicking his heels into the haunches of his mount he raised his hands in a V and spun about without holding the reins. A wild, continuous yell rose behind him as the combined cavalry of the XIIth, XVth and part of the Vth Legions charged back up the Arms Givah where twice before they had been repulsed.

"He's truly mad," cried Joseph, who found himself racing after

Titus. Half way up the seven hundred and eighty foot hill, they met Larcius Lepidus and his Xth whooping over the crest from the opposite side, overrunning the Jewish defenses as they dashed down to meet their own men. The haunches of the beasts glittered red in the sun.

v

In his tent that night, Joseph recorded:

roman strategy is never the same. it seems to repeat itself but each lesson learned in a previous encounter is added as a further stage to the plan. titus, who appears not to care about his men, controls his impetuosity and his own valor, merely giving the impression of devil-may-care, but in truth, every move he makes is calculated. larcius lepidus had not tried again to assault the susa gate, but instead moved a thousand yards north where the kedron valley is shallower and breached the wall opposite the janaeus monument with the ram. skirting agrippa's wall, he then raced up the arms givah in order to meet titus coming up the other side as planned. now he was ready to turn his forces against the temple of God.

CHAPTER XXIX — THE PAY PARADE

i

Two fortresses held the key to Jerusalem's defenses: Herod's Castle to the west, which controlled the Upper City where Simon bar Giora had his headquarters: and the Antonia Fortress to the east, which guarded the Temple and where John of Gishhalav was entrenched. Despite Joseph's prediction that Titus would now attack the Temple compound, the Roman commander decided to pursue Simon whom he still considered his chief antagonist. Furthermore, by conquering the Upper City, he would outflank John, causing the collapse of his defenses, thus avoiding a battle over the house of the Jewish God.

The fall of the Arms Givah, however, allowed Simon to consolidate his overspread forces, as well as absorb the Essenes who now flocked to join the revolt after Bannus' son had been killed. Simon had, therefore, a much more formidable force than Titus imagined.

On the First of *Sivan,* eight weeks after the initial attack on Jerusalem had begun, Titus ordered a twenty-four hour bombardment of the Upper City. The Vth and the XIIth legions were chosen by lot, as was customary, to lead the assault against Herod's Castle at a point where the Second and First Walls met. Having guessed the exact spot of Titus' assault, Simon bar Giora had tunnels dug, scooping out the earth below the approaches to the castle so that when the heavy equipped Romans and their cavalry moved up to the walls, the earth fell under them into a fifty foot hollow. From the Hippicus Tower, the Jews poured hot pitch on their enemy, raising a pyre over six thousand Romans.

ii

On top of Mount Scopus, the commander-in-chief of the Roman forces sat quietly and listened to his legates irritably accuse each other for their joint failure. His pock-marked face had turned the color of leather by the Judean sun.

"Alone," declared Larcius Lepidus, "with the half of my legion that's still left, I'll take the fucking city out there in a week, if you can give me the kind of artillery we really need and not that shit ratio of one a minute we've been getting."

"I can't even give you that anymore," said Fronto. "Our supplies are already below the ten day reserve point. Half the work battalions are busy carrying water up from the coast."

"The Jews can't have more than us," said Pyrygius.

"They don't require as much. They're veritable camels," muttered Cerealius.

"They shit like them too," snarled Larcius. "You can smell it all the way up here."

"That's because they don't waste water the way we do," said Fronto.

"Listen, Titus," said Larcius. "One last punch. The full impact of four legions smack against their goddamn temple."

"You tried that," said Cestius Gallus. "Besides there isn't much left of your legion."

"What's left of mine is still better than your whole barrel of piss."

Before the other could retort, Titus spoke in a tired voice. "You gentlemen fail to realize that if I commit all our strength and lose, my father loses the one power base he has. Those legates in the west are waiting for his head. And we hold it. One slip here and we'll have another new emperor in Rome."

"Victory brings renown," said Tiberius Alexander, "only when it's quick and decisive. Speed is what glory's all about."

"There's only one way to defeat Jerusalem," said Cestius Gallus.

"You ought to know," said Larcius.

Cestius Gallus ignored him. "One way," he continued, speaking slowly. "By starving them out. I've been discussing it with Justus. He claims he can construct an impassible wall circling the city within reasonable time so that no one can enter or leave. Reports received by arrow from spies inside the walls claim that famine and pestilence are beginning to take their toll. By mid summer Jerusalem will fold up its legs and die."

"Siege is a double edged weapon," said Tiberius Alexander. "Some of us believe that desperation — famine — will make the Jews more dangerous. Those men in the Temple compound have one desire: to fight until they have no choice but to fall upon their swords and die with the name of their god on their lips. It's the only suicide allowed Jews."

"Jerking off," said Larcius. "Sieges are like a man and a woman playing with themselves instead of with each other."

"There's another suggestion," said Titus, "which costs us little. Josephus, here, is a great believer in the ruse. Those of you who fought against him at Jotapata know well what I mean."

All eyes but Larcius Lepidus' turned to Joseph who was busily recording notes on the discussion.

"You must understand," said Joseph looking up and speaking with deliberation, "that we are not dealing only with the citizens of

Jerusalem who would long ago have acquiesed to Roman rule, but with a flotsom of embittered and fanatical Jews from all parts of the land who have little left to lose. They have gathered here, as Tiberius Alexander has said, to die. In this respect time is running out for us, not for them. By giving up his commitment to life, the suicide has all the time in the world. Let me remind you all that when pushed to the wall, we all have the instincts of a scorpion. Nevertheless, I believe that despite what Tiberius has said, the majority of those inside the walls would, as our Law states, choose life.

"That you will take Jerusalem, I have no doubt. Attack the Temple, however, and you attack Jewish survival. The cost, as Titus Flavius so aptly pointed out, would be no victory for Rome. I suspect that by now all classes in Jerusalem have had their bellyful of bar Giora's austere victories, of John's flamboyant promises that God shall never again allow His city to fall to the uncircumcised, as he likes to call Romans. I think all Jews appreciate that Titus chose to attack the Bezetha and Upper City rather than the Temple compound. Do not think that they are unaware that no artillery has as yet struck the Temple of God."

"Get to the point," said Titus.

"My own sources tell me that the leadership inside the city has reached a state of dilemma. The people are weary. Our last attack nearly caused the collapse of Herod's Castle. Had one more legion been at our disposal, we might today be sitting inside the First Wall.

"Fronto informs me," continued Joseph, "that tomorrow is pay day for the troops. From my days at Antioch, I remember it as always preceded by a full scale dress parade. Let us put on before these walls the most glorious spectacle ever seen by an adversary of Rome. Show them the pride of Rome not her wrath. Display the discipline that they themselves lack and fear. Then offer them reasonable terms, and I promise you that they shall see the futility of further resistance and accept Titus Flavius as the harbinger of peace, a messenger of God."

"It's worth a try," said Tiberius Alexander. "Costs nothing but a little time."

"And lots of back pay," chuckled Fronto.

"Might just be good at this point for the discipline of the men," said Phrygius.

"The men hate that shit parade," said Larcius angrily.

"What the men hate," said Titus, "makes them better soldiers. Tomorrow at noon each of you will have a complement of your best troops stand inspection in full gear. Meanwhile there's no reason why Fronto can't continue a logistical organization for another attack if

Josephus' ruse fails. So far as terms to the Jews, my father's offer still stands."

"Honorable terms," said Justus. "Jerusalem can live with them as Tiberias and Zippori already do."

Until Vespasian had appeared at the gates of Tiberias, this man was the ally of John, selling him out only a month later at the battle of Gishhalav, which had forced John to retreat to Jerusalem. Though Joseph could not help but agree with Justus' words, he turned away in disgust.

iii

The next day was the hottest Joseph remembered for the month of *Sivan*. He had asked and received permission to ride with a contingent of the XIIth Legion beside Cestius Gallus in the pay parade. Only the regular legions were massed in four enormous squares of men. Regiments of the line wore armor and leather cuirasses, all well oiled, their helmets pulled low and strapped around their chins. Swords swung on their left side, and on their right, shorter poignards. In their hands they held javelins, and baskets containing rations hung from their waists together with picks and axes and chains which clanged as they marched. Ahead of them came the legates surrounded by the Elite Guard, all mounted on gleaming, well-brushed horses. At the head of the parade rode Titus with Tiberius Alexander five horse lengths behind him.

At the order, twenty thousand men drew their swords and advanced in a thunderous tempo, the cavalry and the infantry keeping in perfect step to the booming kettle drums that lined the route they were to follow. The Jews crowded the city walls and the roofs of the buildings throughout the still unoccupied part of the city. Even they felt a holiday spirit and were awed by the perfection of the Roman spectacle. At the northeast corner of the city, four hundred yards from the wall upon which thousands of the city's defenders watched, command bounced off command as the parade came to a halt. Dust rose covering the golden dome of the *Mikdash* in a halo of red.

Just as the paymasters were about to receive permission from Titus to proceed, Joseph kicked his heels against the haunches of his mount and charged past the commander-in-chief, heading straight for the strongest of Jerusalem's defenses — the Antonia.

"*Shema Yisrael!*" he shouted as he dismounted and climbed the steps of the Tower of Hananel facing the fortress. "Hear O Israel! More than two hundred years ago our nation's path and Rome's crossed. For most of those years we lived allied and in trust. No one is to blame for the shifting sands of power. For have we not ourselves been the first anointed? the chosen of God, blessed be His name, to bear witness that the only permanence is His will?

"It is in the nature of our having been chosen, perhaps, to forget our purpose, — God's probation in declaring us His peculiar treasure — to resent others' tasks, and let our overzealousness lead us down the byways of blood into an abyss of despair that has always made us contentious and finally dangerously self-rightous. Rome tries to understand our peculiar complexity. How often have her leaders supported us once they understood our anxieties? Only when we confuse our mission with another kind of power — Rome's — have we blundered onto the road to annihilation. Let us not forget that for others Jerusalem is only part of the earthly empire that is Rome."

Like a chorus the wind hummed in echo to Joseph's oration, making him feel the weight of prophecy upon his lips. Instinctively his hands had been raised, his fingers spread in a V of the priestly benediction. He felt among the Jews again.

"I say to you, my brothers, war, rebellion have no place in our covenant with God. Let the arrogance of Gaul, the pride of Spain, the contumely of Germany make war upon the Roman century. Let the desert rats of Nabatea and the double tongued satrapies of Parthia whinny in defection. Let the Jew bow his head to the word of the Lord and declare as did once the prophet: *'Lo baherev velo bahayil, ki im beruhi, amar Adonai!* Not with the sword, not with armies, but with my spirit, saith the Lord!'"

"With blood and fire Judah fell! With blood and fire it shall rise!" came a voice resounding off the parapets of the Antonia and rolling over the heads of the Roamn army. Looking up Joseph saw John of Gishhalav and Simon bar Giora. Between them stood Eleazar ben Yair.

Joseph bowed his head. "One last call, O my people," his voice trembled. "You, you, all of you shall bear the burden of history if you continue in this suicidal folly against the will of God. Turn your gaze and look upon the miracle of the Shiloah spring which now flows freely for the Roman legions when but a week ago its bed was dry and sprinkled with dull stones. This miracle has occurred only once before: when the city was about to fall to Babylonia. Is this not sign enough for you, Simon, you John, you Eleazar, O hard-hearted men? Turn again and wonder upon this city and the splendor of its Temple. For it is you three who shall be accountable to history if these gifts, these holy treasures are devastated. You and you alone shall be liable to our brethren who because of our sins are already dispersed throughout the four corners of the earth. Make not our people weep once more in shame beside alien rivers. For I say to you that through Rome shall our destiny be named. To rebel against Rome is to defy the will of the Lord Elohim, King of the Universe."

His last words filled his ears with a new wind — the screaming imprecations of the Jews on the ramparts. And above it all, through his stifled cries, he heard a voice as old as the salted sands along the charcoal shores of the silent sea: *Israel alone is the instrument of God's will.*

Joseph did not budge when a stone struck his forehead and his blood mixed with the dung and excrement poured down upon him from the walls. His ears screamed at him: DEATH TO JOSEPH. TRAITOR IN ISRAEL!

With his head bowed, he let himself be covered in a new shroud of mourning for Jerusalem.

iv

For the next three days Jerusalem felt Rome's rage. After Joseph's failure at the pay parade, Titus decided that Larcius Lepidus was right, and ordered Fronto to concentrate all his remaining missiles on the eastern part of the city. On the Sixth of *Sivan*, while the Jews were gathered before the Great Altar for the Pentecostal sacrifice, the Roman artillery turned on the Temple compound.

That afternoon the ram, named *Viktor*, was brought up against Jerusalem's other key fortress, the Antonia.

Three hours later, Justus and the work battalions breached the First Wall. In desperation the Galileans sallied out in an attempt to capture the ram. But the same Arab bowmen, used so effectively by Vespasian at Jotapata, kept the Jews off.

Toward sunset the work battalions were ordered to wheel their machine away and the bowmen retired to allow the massed XIIth Legion to assault the Antonia. At that moment three Jews leaped through the hole in the wall, and carrying buckets like David's drawers of water, raced toward the ram and splashed it with pitch and oil. Then, while two kept the Romans off, the third man climbed on to the breaching rod and ignited it with a torch.

"Mati!" gasped Joseph, who sat on his mount beside Cestius Gallus at the head of the waiting troops.

Joseph's brother turned, a puzzled look in his eyes, as a brace of arrows struck him in the chest. He staggered back onto the flaming wood breaching post. The ram's head glowed red and withered like burning parchment, raising the scent of myrrh. There was no need for the Pentecostal sacrifice today, thought Joseph. This skirmish has substituted for the blood of the lamb.

CHAPTER XXX — THE WALL OF CIRCUMVALLATION

Despite the loss of two hundred and fifty men, the Jewish defenses at the Antonia held. The destruction of the ram had given them the courage to repel the Romans once again. Titus decided not to wait any longer and went to Jaffa to organize the replacement of the men and material for the final attack on Jerusalem. Meanwhile, he was forced to fall back on a strategy he detested. He ordered that a wall be built around those parts of the city still free, thus laying total siege to Jerusalem.

The Wall of Circumvallation, as it came to be called, was designed and constructed by Justus ben Piscus. Beginning at the Camp of the Assyrians, the wall ran oval shaped for five miles parallel to the Second and First Walls of the city. Thirteen towers divided it, and in many parts the wall was makeshift and built on the rubble of the destroyed Third Wall. No longer could Jewish women forage in the no-man's-land between the armies where pickets had now been posted to keep them off. As a countermeasure Simon bar Giora harassed the Roman construction crews unceasingly, forcing them, as the Jews had once done when the present walls of the city were first erected, to work with a trowl in one hand and a sword in the other.

In order to encourage the Romans in this tedious and dangerous labor, Justus suggested to Fronto that the legions compete against each other to see who could complete more of the wall. The prize would be first rights to plunder once the city fell. He did not tell Fronto that Titus had offered him a bonus if the wall was completed by the time he returned from the coast. It took Titus a month to refurbish his forces. Justus took only three days to strangle Jerusalem.

The summer equinox tightened its own noose around Jerusalem, searing what little vegetation grew inside and whatever water was still stored in its cisterns. The city starved in silence with only the flies buzzing louder.

In order to feed their troops, Simon and John ordered night raids against the Roman sentries who were required to carry three days' ration when on duty. To counter this, sentries were issued only one slice of bread and no water, causing many Jews to surrender rather than return empty bellied to the city. Roman prison stockades became so crowded that the captives soon dangerously outnumbered their guards. On the First of *Tammuz*, Titus proclaimed that only Christians on their way to other parts of the east would be allowed through their lines. Jews, regardless of age, would be crucified publicly. Despite this new horror, the nightly exodus from the city continued.

Finally, the Romans ran out of wood for crosses and began to nail new captives over the still squirming bodies of their compatriots.

One day Joseph wandered among some Syrian auxiliaries who were abusing a family. When he tried to intervene, the soldiers complained to their officer. "The more we taunt them, the less will they scurry out of their holes." The men laughed and began to shred the clothes off their captives with the tips of their swords, scratching their bare bodies and finally slitting open their stomachs.

"These are Christians," said Joseph, the screams of the slaughtered family still ringing in his ears. "They have permission to pass through our lines."

"If their cocks are clipped, they're Jews," said the officer.

"Many Christians are circumcised," said Joseph.

The officer grinned. "They carry gold in their guts. When they sneak past us, they shit it out."

"That's right," said one of the Syrians. "And as a unit of the XIIth, which won the wall building competition, we got rights to first loot."

"Where do you see any gold?" asked Joseph, waving a hand in the direction of the corpses whose intestines still steamed.

"The men of the Sixth Brigade found some. They say you just got to keep looking."

The officer had by now stripped a girl of her skirt. Her belly was already pregnant with hunger.

When Joseph later complained, Titus merely shrugged. "Most of those coming out are women and children and the old. That way bar Gioras empties the city of useless mouths to feed. It makes his resistance easier and more stubborn," said Titus, who seemed more distracted since his return from Jaffa.

"That still doesn't give us the right to allow those Syrians to play their bloody gold game."

"Right now I'm more concerned about our next attack. We've got one more left in us till the rains come."

"And if you should fail?"

"Then they'll look for gold in my stomach."

Joseph accepted the wine Titus offered him. After a few sips, he said. "Let me —" he leaned forward. "Give me one last chance to reason with them."

"I've given them every chance to surrender."

"John can be reached. He's the more reasonable of the two. I'm sure his own sickness has given him some compassion for others. Let me go into the city and talk to him."

"That's between you and the Jews."

"What can I offer him? What do you still offer John if he's willing to surrender?"

Titus tossed down his mug of wine, wincing at its sourness. "Nothing. Not even his life."

That evening, disguised once again as an Essene, Joseph entered the city through a secret tunnel leading from the Tomb of Absalom, in the same way Titus had once come to meet him under the Great Altar of the Temple.

CHAPTER XXXI — ONE LAST CHANCE

The pools beneath the Great Altar were dry. Rats, as big as jackals, gnawed at corpses stacked in the cavern through which Joseph made his way under the city. Above him the altar drains were clogged with blood that hung like bat shit. An Idumean guard looked up at Joseph as he came out of the cave near the Upper City *agora*, then nodded back to sleep. The sun was just rising and the Roman barrage had already begun. Joseph trudged across the city as in a dream. Buildings seemed translucent and merged in geometric chaos with the stone fences and gardens as if the entire landscape had been upturned and he was walking on his head. Much of this wealthy quarter, home of princes and priests, lay in ruins. Many of the destroyed palaces had been cleared and reshaped into redoubts with apertures on all sides. Titus was right. Simon and John intended to fight for every stone and crevice of the city which meant so little to them. Tears came to his eyes as he ran his hand along the warm marble facade of ben Gurion's ruined palace. Since Jotapata he found it easy to cry.

People roamed about listlessly, faces from Joseph's childhood. Bodies lay where they had fallen from hunger. The dead and the dying intermingled in piles under which occasionally a hand stirred, flexing in supplication. He saw a Galilean probe his spear into a body lying against a boulder. When it did not move, the soldier searched it, finding only a few blackened pine seeds which he stuffed in his mouth without bothering to crack the shells.

Two children sat and chewed the opposite ends of a leather strap dangling from the waist of a dead Sicari masked with flies. Further on he passed a man haggling with his master for a day's wages — a tuft of grass. A woman searched in a pile of rubble, tasting every shard. Dissatisfied she shuffled on picking up dried sheep dung which she ate greedily.

"Martha!" exclaimed Joseph. The former High Priest's daughter, who had once prided herself in never having need to walk, ignored him and continued to follow the trail of dung balls.

Though it was only the first hour of light, a queue had formed in front of the storehouses of Kalba Savua which Joseph joined, and with the others waited patiently as a guard let them in a few at a time. Inside two elders sat behind a wood crate and issued a fistful of grain and three dates per person. Even before they were outside, most had devoured the grains uncooked and gnawed upon the date stones which they had already stripped of meat. A boy held out his hand to Joseph, begging for a part of his ration.

"The good merchant Kalba Savua has opened his stock to all," said a noblewoman wearing a soiled silk robe. "Go stand in line like the others." The boy persisted, opening and closing his fist in Joseph's face, his eyes flashing with hate. Joseph gave the child his grain.

He was drawn toward the Temple. Below him the Tyropoeon Valley lay like a corpse. Wheys from the cheesemakers' vats that once flowed white, now cast green webs across the dried earth. The sun burnt his head and his neck itched. A barrage of ballista stones chased him to the bottom of the valley and he had to duck behind a stone ledge for shelter. He watched the missiles land, churning dust out of the earth, making the *Mikdash* seemingly rise in a cloud. Old corpses melded into the slopes, buried by the sun.

The valley also had life: gleaners among the dead seeking malva greens which flourished despite the lack of rain and which always sustained Jerusalem during sieges. Joseph plucked a plant, and after brushing away the blue flowers, he sucked on the palmlike leaves. They tasted of alum and he spat out the juice. The sun winked in the quartz embedded in the boulders that stuck out of the slopes. A monarch moth, red and yellow, floated across the valley and alighted upon a cactus thorn. Across the valley he saw two constables dragging away an old hag. As he climbed closer, he noticed that the woman was still young and that she was wrapped in a torn burnoose.

"Here now, let her be," said Joseph trying to free the woman.

Seeing an Essene approach, the two men backed off. "She's a murderess," said one constable who wore a blue band of office that had slipped to his wrist.

"They want my gold," the woman cried hoarsely. "Look, they want to steal my gold!" And flinging aside her garment, she exposed her groin which had been shaven clean and looked like a child's.

"She's mad," said the other constable. "Look what she's done." The man held the charred corpse of an infant.

"My gold," the woman shrieked. "Give me back my gold!" and she grabbed the corpse and bit into it. The men struggled with her as she chewed what remained of the infant. "It's mine," she snarled. "If you're nice, I'll share my gold with you." Her eyes flashed insanely at Joseph. "Want a leg? A breast? Not enough for you? It's good. Oh, so good. And sweet. Here!" and she held out a dried bone. "Take it for a mark of Jewish calamity."

It was not full morning yet and the air was dank with heat. Not till he reached the Ophel Quarter did Joseph stop running. He sat upon a step of a hovel beside a woman nursing two infants. Only by her ugly toes did he recognize Lucia.

"My God! What are you doing? You have no milk for sustenance." said Joseph.

She looked up at him defiantly. Her once lilac eyes were cracked with blood. "The sucking calms their dying."

"How did you get into the city? What in God's name are you doing here?"

"A vow. A vow I made at the stream of Shiloah where we last loved. If I do not fulfill it, I shall have sinned."

"There is no sin like forswearing life."

"I vowed life. To bear gifts to the Temple on the Pentecost."

"Come. You must come with me. As soon as I carry out my purpose, I shall get us out of this hell."

Lucia pressed the infants closer. "I cannot leave them." She spoke in the same tone as the mad woman he had seen earlier.

"They're dead. Come." He pulled her toward him gently. She resisted. "Wait here," he said. "I'll be back."

"No you won't," said Lucia. "You've left Jerusalem long ago."

Joseph rose and hurried toward the Upper City. He passed a mother who was calmly explaining to her daughter how to divide the water she carried in a jug. "You drank a mouthful, darling. Now we wash our bodies according to The Law. That water we reuse for the floors and the garden. In this way we make use of the water three times. Do you understand?"

"I'm thirsty," protested the child, who tugged at the jug.

"It's for your brother," the mother scolded. "To wash his wound."

Joseph hurried on. "Madness," Joseph lamented. "They all have the concentration of the possessed."

A one eyed leper crawled up to him and grasped the dates Joseph still held in his hand. He retreated up a street and across the heart of the quarter. Along the way he saw people sitting forlornly before shattered doorways, not daring to enter upon their own misery, yet incapable of abandoning it. Some leaned against the wall of their ruined shacks; others lay down to sleep knowing that they would never rise again. A waterbearer raced by, ignoring the half-hearted pleas of the dying, as his cart bounced across the uneven stones. Unlike the Upper City the streets here were narrow and the houses leaned toward each other so that the sun pierced through only in moted light. The stench of pus and blood mixed with the stink of excrement rising from the gutters. Animals had disappeared from the streets and the usual cackle of chickens had ceased. Only the clanging anvils in the smith shops persisted. It stuck Joseph that the buildings of the Ophel Quarter were no taller than himself.

A wail rose and a disheveled woman staggered out of her house. "*Ha-nega.* My child has the plague." Everyone scattered as she wrung her hands and pulled her hair. A few dashed inside to scrounge any leftover food. The mother fled with the others.

Nearby a gang of men were trying to pry open a shutter. "They're dividing food," said their long bearded leader. "Think they can fool us that they're still sleeping. Only the dead sleep in Jerusalem."

When they opened the window, Joseph saw an old man and woman pronouncing the blessing over a remnant of matzah. Before the woman could say amen, the gang leader burst in and grabbed the one stale wafer lying on a stool.

Above the Gate of the Essenes, Jewish soldiers, as exhausted as the civilians they defended, dozed against the parapets. Beside the gate six wise men, oblivious of the missiles falling around them, sat gazing up at the sun. Joseph joined them, and as always, he felt his substance among the Essenes.

He raised his eyes to the sun, and they burned, as tears streamed down his cheeks. Kneeling forward, he beat his head against the street. "*Ehkha? Ehkha?* How, O how has my city become a widow, her children abandoning her to the dying!"

A hand clawed, pulling him upright. The man's head was shaven and his faded blue eyes never looked away from the sun. "Why do the Sons of Light turn into the Children of Darkness?"

"You stare too long at the sun, old father," said Joseph trying to free himself from the skeletal fingers.

"The sun and the moon," persisted the old man, "are driven by the wind. Who drives the *merkava* of light? What name races the chariot of darkness?"

"There is no darkness," said Joseph. "There are always the stars."

"Human sin forces the spheres off their course. Like you, the stars are fallen angels."

Joseph let his hand fall into Bannus' lap and he began to sob. "Forgive me, Rabbi. I did not recognize you. "How are we ever to survive now?"

"Each of us chooses life once."

Still crying, Joseph felt a firmer grasp heave him to his feet. Two Galileans, their swords drawn, stood beside him. "Joseph ben Matthias," declared one, "I arrest you in the name of the Public Safety Committee of Jerusalem City."

Bannus remained seated, his childlike legs sprawled before him and his eyes still riveted to the sun.

The Galileans led Joseph through the Hulda Gate into the Temple compound which was relatively undamaged. In the Gazit Chamber, in the office of the President of the *Sanhedrin,* Joseph found John of Gishhalav, Kalba Savua, Johanan ben Zakkai and Eleazar ben Yair. Kalba Savua sat drumming his fingertips nervously upon the narrow table around which they were all seated. Ben Zakkai, his chin pressed against his clasped hands, leaned heavily on his cane. Though it was summer, John wore a long sheepskin coat. His eyes burned with fever and his lids were gray. He had lost much weight, and his once broad shoulders were hunched in a shrug. Joseph felt confident that his judgment would prevail.

"Action has run its course," he began. "It is now time for supplication."

Only John had looked up when Joseph was led in. "For you," he said. "You're under arrest."

"I've come to offer you a last chance," continued Joseph. "There's no longer room for bargaining."

"You stand before those who have already bargained away their posterity for the vanity of courage," said ben Zakkai, digging his cane into a crack in the stone floor.

"What is needed is a truce for burying the dead and an allowance of food to be delivered into the city for the non-combatants," said Kalba Savua. "We can then better face the consequences of the enemy's terms and test his compassion."

"Your usual practicality," said Joseph, "would make no sense to the Romans. It's you they are testing. They mean to conquer the city through pestilence and starvation. There are a few, however, who wish to spare the splendor of Jerusalem. Tiberius Alexander and Cestius Gallus are among them."

"And the price?" asked Kalba Savua.

"Some of you will have to be sacrificed."

John's chuckle turned into a hacking cough. "Like at Jotapata."

"I was there," snapped Joseph. "You refused to come to our aid."

"Everyone was sacrificed there. Everyone but you."

"Neither vanity nor valor can save Jerusalem," said Kalba Savua.

"Never again must Jerusalem be destroyed," said Joseph.

"And I'm here to see that it will never again surrender," said Simon bar Giora, who strode in wearing the same crossed straps with daggers across his chest and a scimitar still at his side. Two Idumeans stood beside him. "I understand that this man has been arrested as a traitor," he said addressing John. "Who are these others with still a voice in Israel?"

John breathed heavily, then coughed, this time spotting his handkerchief with blood. His once thick fingers were wrinkled with ridges.

"We still represent what is left of the civil government of Jerusalem," said Kalba Savua.

"This man entered to spy on us," said Simon. "One of the young spotters we have throughout the city saw through his disguise when he accepted a ration for the poor. Being an Essene himself, the boy knew that none of theirs eats when others go hungry."

"Judge not others, all of you," said ben Zakkai sadly, "until you reach their dilemma."

"I judge only myself. It's you who worry about the judgments of others."

"The judgment of Jerusalem," said ben Zakkai, "is the judgment of God."

"The sword. The sword and fire are what's left for Jerusalem. In that order."

Kalba Savua jumped to his feet. "I'm not here to be lectured to by a brigand, a desert war lord, about a city my ancestors have resided in since the days of Ezra. My fortune, my family, my life, in that order, have been squandered upon a rebellion I adhered to only to preserve Jerusalem."

"With less food and added restriction, the people might become a little more desperate. Only then they'll really defend your city," said John.

"Without The Law," said ben Zakkai, "there is no Jerusalem."

"The time has come to die for The Law," said Simon bar Giora. "*Al kiddush Hashem.* To die in the holiness of the Name."

"Burning Jewish supplies, starving our people, confiscating gold from the Temple treasuries without authorization is not fighting in God's name, but for death itself," said ben Zakkai, a froth of spit hinging the corners of his mouth.

"Since when has the Raban concerned himself with the place of sacrifice and Temple rites? For your information that gold has been converted into weapons: swords, lances, bucklers." Simon grabbed a shield from one of his guards and held it up flashing it into the old Pharisee's narrow eyes. Ben Zakkai looked back without blinking.

"The Temple is still under my control," said John "I allowed Simon the use of the treasuries provided that they were for the defense of the compound. So long as we stay on the defensive, we stand a chance. Unlike his father, Titus hasn't the patience for sieges. It's been three years that he's been at war with the puny land of the Jews."

"Defense is logical only so long as it give us a fulcrum for bargaining," said Kalba Savua.

Even as the city's defenses were crumbling, the old quibbling had not ceased. "The Romans," said Joseph, "are beyond the point of bargaining. As John says, Titus is no Vespasian, and will attack as soon as he's ready." He spoke with deliberation, one hand tucked in his robe and one foot forward. "Is it possible to explain to you who have been sealed in here that Jerusalem no longer matters? Rome and only Rome holds the fate of us all. We count for nothing. A tumbleweed in the Roman way. Our pride has cheated us, cajoled us into choosing a suicidal course. If we accept our fate, we can recuperate sooner than you imagine. If we persist in our stubbornness, it will be a millenium — more — before the new mark of Cain is erased from our national consciousness. For the moment God has chosen Rome over Jerusalem. The mystery of His ways is beyond our comprehension. Let us never forget, however, that it is He who ordained that our signature shall finally set the seal to history.

With a combination of disgust and resignation in his voice, John asked: "What have you got for us, priest?"

"Johanan ben Zakkai. He must go before Titus. You, Raban, must come with me immediately and plead, beg, not for Jerusalem alone, but for the posterity of our people."

"The time is now," said Simon. "As soon as you stop wasting mine, the battle commences. Whether your Roman friends like it or not, when the time post on the Antonia crosses the valley, we attack the enemy in his camp."

After a few seconds of silence, Johanan ben Zakkai spoke. "Your kings and your states, what are they but substitutes for *Torah*, which is the continuum of history. A state, as the Greeks and the Romans perceive it, is an abomination to the Jewish ethic. It is man's kingdom, hence finite. *Darkai hagoyim* — the way of the gentile — not Judaism. The day we preferred Saul to Samuel, the Maccabees to Simon ben Shetah, we compromised His Covenant."

"You mean to sit there, you in your wisdom, in your love for *Torah*," declared Simon, "and say that by fighting for a place, our land, we are doomed? that by denying ourselves, we earn the Kingdom of God on earth?"

Ben Zakkai nodded quickly. "Say henceforth that this is our *segula*, our peculiar treasure. Never should we have allowed the Roman to enter our process of survival."

"Law, glory, choices," sighed Kalba Savua, "these are words. They won't feed the city for another week. Nakdimon and ben Zizit inform me that the wells in the Temple, our last water, will be dry before the week's out. Our granaries are empty. Even the supplies I managed to salvage while you two," he pointed to John and Simon, "were still burning each other's stores. To die is not my kind of survival."

"To die is to bring down as many of the Roman as you can with you," said Eleazar ben Yair slowly, almost haltingly. "And leave a record of how a handful of Jews destroyed the greatest army of heathen ever assembled. That's survival." He had not spoken until then because Joseph knew he was meditating.

"There are twenty more legions where those came from," said Joseph. "There will also be greater battles against the heathen."

"And until they come," said Simon, "ten years' time for us to raise another generation ready to survive."

"Even that might not be necessary," said John. "Rome is already fearfully looking north. Four emperors in less than three years proves the rot of Rome."

"Wrong. All wrong," said Joseph. "Rome is entering into new greatness. A new era of dynastic rule. The Flavians will never again allow the Senate to elect an emperor. Vespasian shall pass the mantle to Titus and Titus to a child by a Jewish queen."

"Titus' child, maybe," said Kalba Savua. "Never by a Jewish queen."

"The Empress Poppea was a Jewess. Prophecy says that soon a Jew shall rule the world."

"That is what the Christians claim," said ben Zakkai.

"I'm speaking about Berenice, daughter of King Agrippa, scion of the house of the Maccabees."

"To be a Jew is to live like a Jew," said Simon.

"The Queen's more Jewish than you. A *gair,* an alien. At this moment she is in Rome pleading before Vespasian for the life of our city."

"Berenice is Jewish," said ben Zakkai. "Her mother was Jewish. Her mother's mother was as well. So too was Simon's."

"The absurdity of your arguments is astounding," said Kalba Savua. "Jerusalem burns and you're worried about who is or isn't a Jew; about posterity, about history, when every day our future dies with those children lying out there, food for rats. Simon is a patriot. No one denies it. Berenice, though I have no personal loyalty to her, acts in what she sees as our best interests which could also be her own. But right now the only Jew is the one who survives, and that means getting food, water, medicaments. If necessary, even from the Romans."

"Parthia," said John, "is about to move. We can hold out."

"Parthia moves only when Rome retreats," said Joseph. "Even their Jews have abandoned us."

"Then Nabatea. Right now Simon's emissaries are negotiating with their chiefs."

"Who still hire out their best bowmen to Rome in order to shoot us down."

"Joseph ben Matthias has reason," said ben Zakkai. "To place ourselves at this moment again on the pinpoint of history will allow us to wiggle a little longer before our blood is once more drenched with the victory of others."

"And you recommend, Raban?" asked Kalba Savua.

"The survival which exists only through *Torah*. Eternity is in the *Word*, given to us because no other people accepted it unquestioningly. The *Word* goes beyond power and pride and honor and victory and defeat. Only through its flexible abstractions can we conquer the limits of action. Say then, what Jerusalem needs is to retire onto itself among more modest stones in the vineyard of the Lord."

"The road to God is in sacrificing yourself to him," said Eleazar rising. "Not others."

Ben Zakkai shook his thick head of amazingly dark hair for a man his years, and tapped his cane against the floor. "Once the Lord God demanded human sacrifice: 'Take now thy son, thine only child, whom thou lovest and get thee into the land of Moriah and offer him there as a burnt offering.' That was an ordeal commanded by the *Almighty* out there where the Great Altar now stands," ben Zakkai pointed his cane. "And was redeemed by a lamb in the brush. One other time *man's* vanity demanded victory in promise for the sacrifice of an only daughter. You are the progeny of Jephtha and I of our father Abraham."

Simon bar Giora blocked Joseph when he tried to walk up to Eleazar. "You may think you hold Jerusalem's fate in your tongue. I know I hold yours. According to the powers vested in me as commander of this city and under its emergency laws, I sentence you to be stoned no later than when three stars appear above the *Mikdash*."

Johanan ben Zakkai shook his head. "As president of the highest court of the land, I absolve Joseph ben Matthias of any treasonable act until such time as his whole career, beginning with his mission to Rome for the *Sanhedrin,* is thoroughly investigated."

"We've already done that last year," said John. "When his wife accused him of sodomy."

"I was never found guilty," protested Joseph.

"The court postponed its verdict because of a more recent matrimonial involvement," said ben Zakkai.

Joseph lowered his head. "We have all paid more than enough for our transgressions." He felt the tears like gnats tickle in his beard, and the sensation encouraged his crying. "My lords, each of us has already witnessed his own personal tragedy that parallels the greater one of our nation. I have lost my only brother, who, as I once did, fought at your side; my cousin Niger lies decomposing amidst the ruins of Jotapata. And my bride walks the pavements of Jerusalem nursing the dead progeny of others."

Joseph paused and wiped his tears on his sleeve. John looked at him with the indifference of the dying. Simon toyed with one of his daggers and Kalba Savua wept. Raban Johanan ben Zakkai's lips trembled and he dared not raise his eyes to meet Joseph's. Only Eleazar ben Yair glowered at him with contempt. "Your wife," he said, "has the strength of many bodies." He rose and walked out of the chamber.

The guards at the door did not stop Joseph as he rushed out into the gallery. He found Eleazar sitting on the base of a pillar as he watched smoke rise from the Great Alter. "Bannus is in the city," was all Joseph found to say, ashamed now of his outburst in the Gazit Chamber. Eleazar's eyes searched for the sun.

"I intend to return to Titus and convince him that Jerusalem is bent on self destruction."

"Bannus is not so sure that Jerusalem has earned that right."

His impatience with Essene solipsism wiped away Joseph's self-pity of a moment ago. "To save this city is my only concern."

"Ben Zakkai is concerned with the idea of the nation."

"Right now Jerusalem is the nation of Israel."

Eleazar's eyes were blank like a blind man's. "Bannus says this is all merely the beginning."

"In times such as these beginnings and endings become confused," Joseph sighed. "How much God demands of us."

"How little we demand of ourselves," said Eleazar.

"I think, in the end, ben Zakkai and his academicians will be our survival."

"Bannus says there are many definitions to survival."

"And you?"

Eleazar turned his head up to the sun. "When do wonders cease?"

Joseph climbed the slopes leading back to the Upper City. The smell of the sun lingered in the stones. Helmeted men crouched behind the battlements, the shadows of their weapons wiggling against the gleaming white *Mikdash*. He felt the crushing missiles in his bare toes as the city quivered like a dying beast.

CHAPTER XXXII — THE TOMBSTONE OF JERUSALEM

i

Convinced that the final assault would not be mounted until he reported back to Titus, Joseph decided to tarry a little longer in order to record the last days of Jerusalem. He recalled Tiberius Alexander's words that only over the Holy Name was a Jew permitted to take his life. Looking down upon the Temple compound, Joseph envisioned it as a huge altar, its buildings and defenders the final offering. *Or maybe it was God who was committing suicide.*

Stumbling among the ruined palaces and the secret gardens of his youth, he saw that the only hope now was to try to salvage the Temple. And for that a new voice was needed to plead the cause of his people. The missiles that fell around him hammered one name in his ears: BEN ZAKKAI. BEN ZAKKAI. Once again the necessity to action welled up in him, but as usual it was quickly dissipated by the compulsion to the ruse.

He turned back and walked through the dyers quarters where ben Zakkai lived and which still reeked of ink like the scriptoria of the Essenes in Ein Gedi. The Raban's house was a pile of rubble. Moving past his uncle Caiaphas' palace, he saw that only two walls still stood, and the once beautiful fountain, where a man named — it came to him slowly — Petrus had denounced some Christians, had been smashed, its marble spotted with blood.

He followed the Outer Wall up to Herod's Castle and saw the place where he and Mati had once hidden behind the Serpent's pool, and where he had lain for the first time with a Bedouin harlot whose face he never saw, but whose body had already been moistened by his father. In the distance stood the Psephinus Tower from where he had once descended in an attempt to convince Cestius Gallus to save the city. Now the same XIIth Legion manned its turrets as an artillery observation post, guiding the destruction of Jerusalem.

In the Upper City *agora* death squads were selecting corpses and neatly stacking them into carts.

"Why are all the dead brought here?" Joseph asked the one-armed man who was in charge.

"It's to get them away from the Temple so that they don't corrupt the few sacrifices still being offered. Keeps the plague under control as well."

"And who are those in the carts?"

"Priests. We take them out and bury them at night."

Because of its holiness no one was allowed to be buried within the precincts of Jerusalem. Not even during its worst days did Jotapata have so many dead. Bodies were stacked ten feet high, waiting to be carted away while half crazed cats and dogs attacked them. Rats that normally came out only at night, stalked the gutters of the city. One bloated rat stood in Joseph's way, and when he stamped his foot, it merely sucked its red whiskers and continued to tear at the cheek of a child's corpse. Joseph forced all these scenes upon his memory, already seeing himself the engraver of Jerusalem's epitaph.

And the Jews fought on. Guards still manned their posts, and reserve troops gathered at strategic points ready for the next Roman attack. The little food and water left was distributed first to these guardians of the city. Women and children worked diligently, gathering the Roman ballista stones and other missiles in order to resupply the patiently waiting Jewish artillerymen. The few remaining Christians in the city stood by the Ginnot Gate waiting to leave, totally indifferent to the plight of their former brothers. Justus had escaped by joining them, something Joseph could not get himself to do. He was surprised to see among these pacifists men with daggers flashing beneath the folds of their garments. Using the familiar Jewish tactic of attacking the enemy from the rear, Simon bar Giora had disguised some of his men as Christians, in this way allowing them to infiltrate the Roman lines.

He walked down Yedidya Street and intentionally let the cactus thorns hanging over the garden walls prick his fingers. Mati used to hide his childish treasures here among the loose stones, and once they had sworn a blood oath, touching their pierced fingertips to a piece of parchment in signature, that they would never allow strangers to occupy their city. That was after the riots under Cummanus and when Joseph had fallen in love with the young Princess Berenice who had defied the Roman procurator. The Upper City smelled of camels.

The gates of Joseph's palace had been dismantled and he could see the wilted garden from the street. His favorite lemon tree had been uprooted, and the burnt arbor showed the broken lattice where old grapes had left their stains. He entered the palace through a hole in the wall and gasped when he saw his father.

"*Aba*," he cried, falling to his knees and kissing the hem of the old man's robe. "I've come to save Jerusalem."

But like the city, Matthias was already dead by his own hand.

ii

Joseph sat crosslegged mourning his father. He nodded back and forth intoning psalms, his clothes rent and his forehead smeared with ashes. He had anointed Matthias with holy oil, then dressed him in his priestly robes and folded his fingers in a *V* across the *ephod* that he himself had once worn upon the Great Altar. In his hand, Joseph held a scroll that he had found rolled beside his father's body. It was a *Ketuba* signed by Matthias, the official document of Joseph's marriage to Lucia.

Toward dawn, Johanan ben Zakkai appeared. He stood before the bier and mumbled a prayer.

"His death, not your plea saved your life," said the old Pharisee scholar leaning heavily on his cane.

"You knew?"

"We all did."

Joseph took his father's hand. "You, Raban, can still save Jerusalem."

"Jerusalem has lost its purpose. Matthias," said ben Zakkai, nodding to the coffin. "He can free us from the bondage of Jerusalem."

Joseph understood. He gazed at the yellowed cheeks of his father and at his soft, peppered beard. The faded rust colored bristles linked him with the dead.

iii

Because of his rank, Matthias was permitted a small funeral procession, which Joseph led through the Dung Gate. They passed widows in black, mourning old death, ignoring those about to be buried. The women pounded their heads against the west wall in the way of the gentile. Again the scent of camel dung tingled in Joseph's nostrils. Under a steady barrage, a shallow grave was dug beside the Serpent's Pool and Joseph handed the gravediggers the honey he carried so that later they might use it to preserve his father's body. Only when the Conductor of Lamentations handed him filled *Y*-shaped cups did Joseph realize that the wailing he had heard came from the professional mourners who were to be paid according to the amount of tears they shed. This, too, he thought, was the way of the *goyim.* And he felt only disgust for the pain of his people.

While Joseph recited the *kaddish,* the gravediggers tilted the bier, sliding the corpse into the soil from which God had first molded it. To everyone's amazement the body rose. Holding the bone of an animal which had simulated the smell of death, Raban Johanan ben Zakkai emerged from the coffin and blessed the pallbearers.

iv

Still wrapped in the ephod of Matthias whom he had replaced in the coffin in order to escape from the city, Johanan ben Zakkai bowed to Titus outside his tent. "*Shalma alakh, Malkha,*" he declared. "Peace upon thee, King."

At these words Titus keeled over, grasping his thigh. "You mistake me for my father," he moaned, rubbing his swelling leg.

Ben Zakkai shook his head, his beard parted by the breeze. "You too shall rule Rome."

"Right now my problem is your black magic. What's to be done about my leg?"

"I know nothing of your pain. Only of my own."

"Spare Jerusalem," begged Joseph, who had escaped with ben Zakkai. "What's left of her."

"It's too late," said Titus, waving at his massed troops sloping down the hillside. "The Antonia will be ours by noon."

"And the Temple?" asked Joseph..

"You're the one who once said that when the house of your god is squared, it will lose the protection of the holy spirit. The fall of the Antonia will make your temple walls a card box."

"Give me," ben Zakkai's voice trembled. "Give me Yavneh and her wise men."

"And my bloated leg? What can you give me for that?"

"I am a teacher of The Law, not a physician. Only God can see to your infirmity."

Titus turned to Joseph. "You're a magician. At least by the way you've managed to stay alive."

"A priest, Sire."

"Cure me or you both die."

Titus had indeed changed since the campaign against Jerusalem. He had become short tempered and his robustness had turned to sagging flesh. "Where is Queen Berenice?" asked Joseph, trying to distract the general.

"In the Golan where she belongs. Now which one of you is going to cure me?" he demanded, drawing out his sword.

"Cross your hands over a man who hates you," said Joseph, remembering what Eleazar ben Yair's wife, Shlomit, had advised him when they were still children and when she had them walk through the hot pepper bush at Ein Gedi.

Titus sheathed his sword. "No one hates Titus Flavius," he said with the old sarcastic lilt in his voice. "Didn't you know? I'm the darling of the world." Turning to ben Zakkai, he said. "Until Jerusalem falls, you'll remain my guest at Gofna. You'll find comfortable quarters there where already a community of priests is established. So far as your request, it will depend on how long Jerusalem holds out." To

Joseph he said: "The only people who hate me are Jerusalemites," and he passed his hands over Joseph's head.

Joseph backed away. "Let me join you in the attack on the Antonia and find you a man who really hates you."

v

"Watch and record," were Titus' last words to Joseph. "We're going to repeat and repeat and repeat."

Joseph scanned the battlefield from the top of Mount Scopus, behind the line of artillery, now replenished with larger weapons that had been brought up from the coast. Beyond the Wall of Circumvallation stood a new array of catapults, scorpion quick-firers and ballista stone throwers which now bombarded the city unceasingly for twenty-four hours. Towering pagodas ninety feet high on wheels and equipped with their own fire fighting gear as well as thick armor plates stood ready to push against the last of Jerusalem's walls. Behind these came endless columns of attack legions, backed by reserves — also refurbished with arms and troops from Jaffa. When the artillery raised its sights and commenced firing over the Antonia Fortress and into the Temple courts, three companies of sappers from the XIIth Legion dashed to the wall where they quickly dismantled the obstacles and traps set there by the Jews during the night.

The Wall of Circumvallation burst open and from behind it, like carnival giants, the pagodas rolled down by themselves followed by twenty battering rams toward the last city wall, smashing through the Tadi Gate. The dust lifted slowly, the sun tottering on its own rays. Jerusalem tilted on its axis. In all his military experience Joseph had never seen breaching weapons lead an attack. Titus' audacity would save Jerusalem from further agony. For surely now the Jews would surrender and in this way hope at least to spare the House of God.

Then he saw the spear points, the head bands and armorless chests of the Idumeans rise from the Tyropoeon Valley in their thousands. Led by Simon bar Giora, they climbed like mountain goats and came racing along the sloping walls of the Antonia, outflanking the Romans and cutting off the undefended rams and pagodas. Ben Zakkai had been right: Jerusalem had indeed lost its purpose.

Suddenly, Titus appeared from beyond the Janaeus Monument. Behind him came the full Vth Legion charging down upon the Jews. This time the Romans repeated not their own strategy but their enemy's as well. With the precision they were famous for, the Roman assault teams cut down the hordes of undisciplined Idumeans, forcing them back down the valley. In desperation, Simon climbed atop one of the pagodas and roared at the Galileans: "Tell that bastard, son of a bastard, John, that as soon as we finish with the Roman, we'll see that he dies before he chokes on his own diseased bile." Simon then pulled out a flag and waved it toward Herod's Castle to the west where a sentry relayed the message south.

Titus' gamble had worked. Figuring that John was too weak to take the bait of the undefended breaching machines, he hoped that Simon would rush into the trap. Once the Vth Legion was released, no pleading by Simon could bring the Galileans out from the temporary security of the Antonia. Simon bar Giora had no choice but to call up his reserves in the Ophel Quarter. Ben Batia, the nephew of Johanan ben Zakkai, and Akiva, the disinherited son-in-law of Kalba Savua, rushed up Tyropoeon Valley in order to relieve Simon. What the Jews did not know was that Larcius Lepidus with his Xth Legion lay waiting behind the Mount of Offence ready to swoop down upon them, closing both sides of the valley. Titus had finally lured the major Jewish force outside the walls of Jerusalem.

The time post on top of the Antonia was just slipping past the sheep market, when suddenly a torrent of water exploded against the Tadi Gate in the city's First Wall. Joseph's horse reared up, almost tossing him, as the line of pagodas and rams toppled over and were washed away in a tidal wave below the Antonia and down the steep escarpment of the Tyropoeon Valley. John had opened the locks of Jerusalem's last water reserves in the Pool of Israel, sweeping away thirteen thousand first line Roman legionnaires. Once again ruse and the energy of despair had defeated order.

iv

By the second week of *Tammuz*, Justus convinced Titus that the waters of the pool had so weakened the foundations of the Antonia that the manually operated ramming rods that he had hastily constructed would be sufficient to bring down Jerusalem's most crucial fort.

In his journal, Joseph wrote:

craftiness and procrastination have saved jerusalem for a few more weeks. now, in mid summer, after three years of war and four months of siege, the city is about to be destroyed due to the stubbornness of its sons.

He refused to inscribe the name of Justus ben Piscus for posterity.

The deluge had also softened the earth along the wall and a wood foundation had to be laid to sustain the weight of men and ramming machines. Luckily, since hardly a tree still stood in the whole land, Tiberius Alexander had arranged for planking to be transported from Cyprus and Rhodes and as far as the Nile. Nevertheless, the heat and the low morale of the Romans hampered the work. The artillery had meanwhile continued to hammer away so that the only signs of life inside the walls were the cries of the watchmen on the ramparts sounding the alarm as missiles hurtled across the city. *"HAEBEN! STONE!"* they shouted, which to Joseph's ears sounded like "haben," the son. And he remembered the unburied corpse of his father.

And Titus brooded. Except for an occasional whore, he saw no one and revelled in the increasing pain in his thigh as recompense for his failures.

"On the Sixteenth day of *Tammuz,* Joseph observed Larcius Lepidus enter Titus' tent on Mount Scopus. He was accompanied by a veiled woman. "Titus Flavius," he bellowed in drunken hoarseness, "I've brought you a true whore. Now get your cock up and let's move our ass into that city!"

An hour later Titus addressed his troops. He told them that new omens had predicted full Roman victory by the morrow, and that the temple of the Jewish god would be theirs to plunder. Then raising his gown, he showed the men his right leg. The swelling was gone. Titus had passed his hands over the woman Larcius Lepidus had brought him — Judith — Lucia Paulina.

CHAPTER XXXIII — SLAUGHTER AT THE WEST WALL

i

As Justus had predicted, the foundations of the Antonia had been so weakened that in less than a day the XIIth Legion breached its walls and broke inside. John of Gishhalav and his Galileans, in disarray, retreated into the inner Temple courts. Titus ordered these and the *Mikdash* to be surrounded but not entered until the rest of the city was conquered. He now turned to the other fortress, Herod's Castle, dispatching Larcius Lepidus to break into the Upper City, while he himself prepared to circle south with the XVth Legion and take the Ophel Quarter, in this way assuring that none of Simon's men escaped into the Judean Wilderness. The Tribunes Bassus and Silva were to move south immediately against the remaining pockets of resistance at Herodion, Machaerus and Masada.

The last of the three named forts indirectly caused Titus' strategy to fail once again. Larcius Lepidus had long ago sworn to avenge the two hundred dead of his own legion, pushed off the cliffs of Masada three years earlier by Eleazar ben Yair. That vow he decided could only be satisfied by attacking the *Mikdash*. Since his advance took him up the Tyropoeon Valley, flanked in one side by the Upper City and on the other by the Temple, he needed only a good excuse to disobey Titus. He found it through Sabinus, his arms bearer, a tall, black boy of sixteen from Tyre where his father had been a merchant and his mother one of his wares. The boy informed his commander that because this side of the Temple Mount was steep, only a handful of untrained Levites manned these ramparts; that it was also at this same spot that Antiochus Epiphanes, the Seleucidian king against whom the Maccabees had revolted two centuries earlier, had used an old Syrian trick to goad the Jews to attack. Throughout the campaign Sabinus' one obsession was to be the first legionnaire into the temple of the Jewish god.

On the seventeenth day of *Tammuz*, Titus waited patiently for news of Larcius's conquest of the Upper City so that he might finally enter the Temple triumphantly and declare it a prize of war. The legate of the Xth Legion, taking his arms bearer's suggestion, had meanwhile stampeded a thousand swine through the Temple's West Gate. With no other thought in mind, the Jews chased the unclean beasts back down the valley in what could have been taken as a sally against the Romans. Larcius Lepidus wheeled his cavalry to the right and charged up towards the Temple's west wall.

Zakharia ben Hakotsev, chief steward of the Temple slaughter-houses, and a thousand of his own fearless butchers happened to be on the adjacent section of the wall. Seeing the Romans moving up the slope, Zakharia signalled Simon across the valley on the Upper City walls.

The flames that rose from the west warned Titus that something had gone wrong. He held up his own advance until stragglers appeared and reported the complete rout of the Xth Legion's cavalry. Ignoring the pain in his thigh which had begun to bother him again, Titus jumped on his roan and rallied the XVth Legion behind him. By the time they got down the Tyropoeon Valley, they found only the corpses of Romans and swine. Three days later Joseph recorded what later became known as the Battle of The West Wall. He wrote:

we came riding hard along the first wall, and though it was getting toward evening, the sun rose miraculously, blinding us and making any advance impossible. simon bar giora had cleverly melted the gold vessels he had filched from the temple treasuries, forging them into shields that now deflected the gloaming in our eyes, blinding us so that we were compelled to slow our charge to a canter. suddenly, out of the blare of gold, a horde of two hundred camels mounted with jews loped down upon us at a speed that the elite corps of roman cavalry guard could not believe. they broke up our formation, biting man and horse, their barks rising up to the darkening heavens. only GOD's cover granted me life and i and a handful of cavalry managed to escape. now the groaning, scorched men of the Xth legion melded with the syncopated groans of the mauled twenty-seventh cavalry.

only after dusk, after the rising of a full moon, did we see how the jews had routed one of the bravest legions of the roman army. the once green valley was as black as the makhtesh crater. charred bodies lay curled like dried worms. even the birds that usually nested in the wall had disintegrated from the heat. the valley, too, was lined with the corpses of the cavalry, the dead foaming at the mouth.

as we approached the west wall, we saw that it was shadowed with stains of bitumen. below the bodies were so burnt that they fell apart when we tried to remove them. those still alive looked like demons: no hair, their faces all eyes. for the first time titus lost control of himself and ran crazed among the steaming carcasses as he searched for his comrade larcius. only when he spotted the dolphin and galley insignia of the Xth legion, that he he himself had once awarded his friend, did he kneel and gently unhook his armor. it was filled with ashes.

eleazar ben yair had brought up herds of wild camels from the arabian desert at the same time as zakharia ben kotsev had poured kettles of boiling holy oil, used on the altars, upon the assaulting troops of larcius lepidus. no one, not even GOD, could now save jerusalem from the wrath of the roman.

CHAPTER XXXIV — THE SERPENT'S TOWER

Despite his grieving, Titus blamed Larcius Lepidus for the new defeat. A man who disobeys orders, he told Joseph, deserves to die. Nevertheless, the Romans went about razing the part of the city already in their possession with a passion that foretold the havoc they intended to wreak upon the Temple.

In the vaulted chamber below the Antonia ruins, a staff meeting had been hastily convened. The cellar smelled of piss and armor grease.

"For all purposes," Tiberius Alexander opened, "Jerusalem is done. The corpse thrashes only because its heart is still beating. The maw is empty. The skeleton hollow. We've had ample proof by now that the temple of the Jewish god must go if total victory is to be ours." Only the dripping water over the trough at the far end of the chamber cushioned the shock of the chief of staff's words.

"What's the difference between victory and total victory?" asked Titus mockingly.

"When it comes to the Jews," answered Tiberius, "it's got to be total, else in a decade, a generation, at most fifty years, we'll be back here with another revolt on our hands. The only way to truly defeat them is to wipe out any connection they have with this blood drenched land."

"And you other Jews," asked Titus looking at Joseph and Justus. "Does your historic sense confirm Tiberius' proposal?"

Justus pulled out a handkerchief from his sleeve and wiped his sweating lips. "No doubt about it. The Temple has become a fortress."

"Then by your own law, as I understand it, it's no longer holy," said Tiberius Alexander.

All his life Joseph had admired the Legate of Egypt, nephew of the great Philo who had been a friend of Johanan ben Zakkai, and though he had chosen Rome over Jerusalem, never had he doubted the sanctity of the Temple. "Holiness in the Hebrew sense," said Joseph, "is a word that does not exist in Latin. *Shekhina* — the Holy Spirit which dwelleth therein — can only be explained in the Roman term *Gloria.* Surely the time will come when Rome too shall merely be a mark on the facade of history, a time when men will have assimilated as their own your genius for order and law; when even the names of battles and places of victory shall be absorbed into the tactics of a new breed of conquerors whose swords in turn shall be as ephemeral as our own. Only in the monuments you leave shall Rome's greatness rest eternal: in the footfalls clicking through the

Palatine halls, the roars echoing in your circuses and arenas; in the swish and sparkle of a thousand oars shipped at once across the confluence of Lake Cinnus and the River Liris; the preservation of Neptune's Temple at Sunian; yes, in the myrrh and frankincense rising through the golden heaven of the Temple here in Jerusalem, preserved and rededicated by the house of Flavius, shall your posterity lie. Not in the sands of destruction."

"Write all that down in your chronicle," said Titus. "And you, Justus, see if you can outdo him. Right now I'm concerned with the numbers and the lives of my men."

"The city must be broken," declared Justus, pointing a finger at Joseph. "As in the time of Jeraboam, the power of Jerusalem over the Jews has got to be erased and another capital raised."

"Tiberius, no doubt," retorted Joseph, who could never reconcile this fop, whose hands were soft and well manicured like a courtesan's, with the architectural genius he was reputed to be.

"I've been informed that Titus had that in mind."

"And the changing of the name of our land as well?"

"Palestina always sounded more majestic than Judea," said Tiberius Alexander.

"The Hellenism of Egypt," said Joseph angrily, "has caused you to forget that the Philistines in whose name you wish to call this country are today as Jewish as the Idumeans and the Galileans."

"Once they were your utmost enemy," said Titus. "Antecedents of the Greek-Syrians you all detest."

"No one has ever succeeded in erasing the Jewish presence in this land."

"That, my friend, depends on what the Jewish presence becomes."

"Our rabbis ask," said Justus, "the tower that harbors the serpent, what's to be done with it?"

"Ben Zakkai says you kill the serpent," Joseph answered.

"I should think," said Titus, wincing as he shifted his weight from one leg to the other, "you'd destroy the tower. That kills the serpent as well."

Titus strapped on his sabre. "Gentlemen, in twenty minutes we attack again. You have your instructions. Before this Ninth day of *Ab* is over, I shall be the new Jewish god."

After the others left, Joseph waited for Titus while he doused his face with water from the trough. "Once, because it was the law of yours," said Joseph, "you saved a synagogue in Rome. That Temple out there represents every synagogue in the world."

"Do you really think that John, trapped in there like a wounded she bear in its lair, will surrender before every stone in that compound is upturned?"

"For a Galilean the Temple is merely an expiation for his ancestors' idol worship."

"And for a true Judean? For you?"

"It holds the heart of God."

"He must have a proud heart to need so grand a dwelling."

"Only the *Dvir*. The place where He commanded."

"In that glittering marble, gold domed sanctuary. Is that where your *Shehin* is?"

"*Shekhina*," corrected Joseph. "*Shehin* means boils. One of the Ten Plagues cast upon Egypt."

"And now upon me. Ever since that old Pharisee named me king, my groin has been fired with boils. The swelling has moved from my thigh to my balls. What other treasures do you keep in your Holy of Holies?"

"Once the *Dvir* held the Tablets of Moses."

"The ones from Mount Sinai?"

Joseph nodded. "Nebuchadnezzar looted them on this very day from the Temple built by Solomon."

"Sinai," Titus mused. "I think after this is all over, I'd like to rest there. Right on top of that mountain where he received the Commandments."

"No one knows which mountain it is. Our chronicles left it vague so that there would be no worshipping of place."

"What a trophy that would have been," Titus clicked his tongue and shook his head once. "To bring those Tablets back to Rome."

"The Temple is a greater trophy."

Titus moved toward the arched doorway. "I have a feeling it's already been decided. Maybe your *Shekhina* really resides up on that desert mountain?"

"The XIIth has again won the lottery and will be first to move into the Temple compound. Do I have your permission to join them? John will surrender to me."

"And bar Gioras? He's the real serpent in the tower," said Titus wincing again as he buckled on his armor.

"You're still in pain?"

"I think I need a real whore. One of our own."

Alone in the vaulted chamber, Joseph ran his fingers along the rim of the trough. Beside it he could still make out the squares and circles of games scratched upon the floor by Roman soldiers once garrisoned here to protect the Temple from heathen profanation. Joseph prostrated himself upon the bulging stones like upon the belly of a woman, feeling the ground tremble from the breaching rams that now pounded the Temple walls. And he remembered Lucia and how they had always made love by waters.

When he rose he saw that his tunic was wet. Searching for something to dry himself, he found a leather bound packet beneath the table the staff had sat around. He pulled the thong free and unfolded a binding. Inside he read:

Beware the traitor Josephus!

It was a journal like his own, and by the fastidiousness of the handwriting, he knew that it could only be Justus ben Piscus' own history of the Jewish revolt.

CHAPTER XXXV — WE ARE DEPARTING

Joseph climbed the still standing south parapet of the Antonia where he found Cestius Gallus looking down upon the Temple courtyards. "You're three years late," said Joseph approaching the legate.

They both looked across the Hel rampart of the Inner Temple. An occasional missile whizzed overhead. "It's incredible," said Cestius. "It took sixty years to complete."

They watched the Levites keel over into the blazing fire upon the Great Altar as Roman bowmen easily picked them off. "Mad," Cestius exclaimed. "Really mad."

"The sacrifice has ceased. It's their way of relinquishing their vows to God."

"If they'd only surrender, I'm convinced Titus would stop the attack."

"And the legions?" asked Joseph. "Do you think revenge can be checked by discipline alone? Even Roman discipline?"

A trumpet sounded to the west. "Titus is advancing," said Cestius hitching up his sword. "What building is that to our left?"

Joseph leaned over the parapet. "The Chamber of the Hearth. Where holy oil for the Eternal Lamp in the *Mikdash* is stored."

"John's headquarters. It's been confirmed. Let's move out and see if we can cut off his escape."

Joseph scanned the compound one last time, taking in the order of the courts, the chambers, the gates and what remained of the porticoes. He saw a procession of wounded dragging themselves up the fifteen oval shaped steps of the Nicanor Gate whose bronze door had long since been melted into arms. Many of the stragglers fell dead before they reached the Court of the Priests, their glazed eyes seeking the holy sanctuary of the *Mikdash*. The snow white edifice loomed over the whole compound as its variegated marble base crouched like a lion between the two columns placed in memory of Jakhin and Boaz, the popular names for the pillars that fronted the Temple built by Solomon. Above it the cupola glowed complementing the imperfect sun. Upon the altar, the last smoke curled in the rising breeze, no longer sure of the path to heaven.

First John:

With a company of lancers, Joseph came out of the Antonia and fought his way through the Outer Temple Court. He would take John of Gishhalav prisoner, causing his few remaining Galileans to surrender. He could then block the south gates to the compound, the only access Simon bar Giora still had to the Temple. Titus might then be willing to spare the *Mikdash*. He led his men under the north porticoes just as they collapsed in flames. The Romans fell back leaving Joseph alone less than one hundred yards from the Chamber of the Hearth.

Undaunted, Joseph ran through the flames. At the entrance to the Chamber, he met ben Cathla, Simon's second in command. Simon's Idumeans were already in the Temple compound fighting for every inch of the hallowed ground.

Ben Cathla retreated inside the Chamber of the Hearth. Two torches hung diagonally from holders forged into the thick stone walls. The hearths were charred and cold, and the few vessels still whole glistened with oil. A table with a torn map spread on it stood near a large smouldering urn into which John of Gishhalav was tossing torn documents. Ben Cathla drew out two daggers and circled the urn, coming between Joseph and the entrance. John unsheathed his sword and lunged at Joseph. Joseph was too quick for the sickly Galilean commander and leaped over one of the hearths, coming under the wall with the torches, in this way covering his rear from ben Cathla.

"In the name of God," cried Joseph. "Stop this suicidal slaughter and I will guarantee your safety. If you must fight, at least continue outside the city. For the sake of the Temple."

John sneered. "There is no God," and he thrust his sword with all the strength left in him, slashing the thongs of Joseph's armor. Joseph raised his sword as ben Cathla moved in on him, ready to sacrifice himself in order to let John strike the final blow. *So now you will finally discover,* thought Joseph, *if you really are capable of killing a Jew.*

Two Romans burst into the Chamber. Ben Cathla whirled about stabbing a dagger into the abdomen of one, drawing it upward. The other Roman turned on John who was gripped by a coughing spell causing blood to trickle through his lips. Joseph stepped between them and fended off the Roman, giving John and ben Cathla a chance to flee.

"Traitor!" cried Sabinus, the black Syrian, pointing his sword at Joseph's throat.

"Just see that you obey orders," declared Joseph backing off.

"You're a Jew. A Jew won't ever kill another Jew." He lunged at Joseph, who grabbed one of the torches overhead and threw it at Sabinus, forstalling him long enough to regain his footing. Joseph could feel Sabinus' strength in the whip of his blade as his own forearm muscles began to ache. If he could only switch sword hands the way Eleazar ben Yair did in mid fight. Sabinus forced Joseph deeper into the Chamber of the Hearth, his hand clenched on the hilt of his sword and pressing against Joseph's. Using the wall for leverage, Joseph made one last effort and heaved the Syrian back, dodging around so that now he had access to the exit. Sabinus jumped on to the table, then leaped forward, piercing Joseph's heart. Surprised that Joseph had not fallen dead, Sabinus dropped his guard long enough for Joseph to thrust him through. The Syrian tumbled back into an oil trough, his legs dangling over the rim as if he were shitting. From inside his own armor, Joseph withdrew the pierced packet of Justus ben Piscus' journal which had saved his life.

And Simon:

In the Court of Priests, Joseph saw the Idumean leader with the last of his men desperately trying to stop the Xth Legion, now under Titus, who were scaling the west wall of the Temple and fighting their way to the *Mikdash*. These last defenders of the House of God raised their voices in psalms as they threw themselves, many without weapons, against the relentless drive of the Romans. Not Simon. In silence, his scimitar never leaving his hand, he gained strength with each heathen he killed. His face glowed from the blood gushing down his cheek.

A ram's horn blared from the trumpeting tower, and the familiar cry rose up:

TO THE TEMPLE!

Turning back, Joseph gasped as he saw the miracle he had tried to conjure up in the many dreams and prophecies that had possessed him in his thirty-three years of life. Thousands swarmed through the Beautiful Gate to the east: the young, the old, the maimed, the dying — their eyes like magnets drawing them to the steps of the *Mikdash*. Joseph was swept up in their procession, and tearing off his armor, he led them in praise of the Lord, his high priestly chant rising above the pandemonium.

> The Lord is the strength of my life;
> whom shall I fear?
> Though a host shall encamp against me,
> in this I will be confident:
> That I shall dwell in the House of the Lord
> all the days of my life,
> to behold His beauty,
> and to enquire in His Temple.
> Hide not Thy face from me;

when my father and my mother forsake me.
Deliver me not over to mine enemies:
for false witnesses are risen up against me.

An apparition in red staggered out of the multitude. With his remaining strength, Sabinus flourished a torch in the breeze, then let it fly. It bounced off the gates of the west wall, splashing against the pillar of Boaz making its color bleed. Like a serpent's tongue the flames leaped up into the golden dome of the *Mikdash*, bursting in an amber whirlwind that finally eclipsed the sun. The Levites, standing in their *azarot*, plucked harps and lyres.

And we shall bring upon them their iniquity
And shall cut them off —

The Jews, many of them wrapped in *Torah* scrolls, leaped into the flaming *Mikdash*, finally victorious over the living.

Seeing that the temple of the Jewish god was merely another temple, the Romans charged up the twelve steps leading into the *Mikdash*, slaughtering the Levites at their choir desks in the midst of their singing.

"The Lord God shall cut them off," cried Joseph, completing the psalm as he dashed ahead of the Romans into the sanctuary. In a distance a horn blasted. "The Sabbath," he gasped.

Then he was running through the galleries until he found himself standing before a gate. There, like a stone arbor, stood the indestructible *Dvir*. Joseph backed away. He drew out his sword, vowing that no one, neither Jew nor gentile, would cross this threshold which only the High Priest entered on *Yom Kippur* in order to atone for the sins of all Israel. It was the closest he himself had ever come to the Holy of Holies.

Something struck him from behind and he fell back, mumbling. *Adam had prophesied the end of the world twice: once by water, once by fire.*

— But it is forbidden, cried Joseph, as hands threw an *ephod* over him, urging him into the *Dvir*.
— I am Theopolis, High Priest in Israel. The watch of Jehoyariv is on duty. Enter!
— Theopolis is dead. There is no High Priest.
— The *ketoret* of incense. Take it and rededicate the *Dvir*. Here are the keys.
— Even so, only on the Day of Atonement is it permitted to enter.

— Henceforth, every hour is the day of atonement.

Darkness.

No light even in the corners of his eyes.

No battle.

He saw the Table of Shewbread, the loaves corrupted and gnawed. Behind it stood the *Menorah*, its cups turned away from the central light. The Tree of Life, he thought, only it shed petals like the almond tree hanging over the terrace of his room at the palace. When he reached out to touch it, the *Menorah* curled into itself like a Sodom apple and disintegrated.

Two tapestries hung from the ceiling; one portrayed the panorama of the heavens overlaid with the Zodiac; the other, embroidered in scarlet and made of fine blue and purple linen, represented fire, earth, air and water. Incense rose out of the shattered dome. In the far corners of the *Dvir*, against a wall of gold, stood the *Ehven Hashtiya* where once perched the Tablets of Moses. The sun shaded the heaven.

"*Yaveh!*" he screamed, prostrating himself and touching his lips to the marble floor as the flames hissed:

WE ARE DEPARTING

The words extinguished the lights. He let his breath out, and like a drowning man, this time he gave himself to waters.

Mati holding the slaughtering implement over the Great Altar, ready to slit the throat of the sacrificed — himself.

The soaring waves below Masada heaving up the jackal — himself.

The pokers goading the race of scorpions — himself.

The grinning Christian, his mouth choked with genitals — himself.

The Nabatean witch, blood oozing from her circumcised loins, and Eleazar stooping to the tipah — himself.

The barren face of Hagla — himself.

Lucia in the middle of the pool, curled around the serpent's pillar — himself.

Night fell suddenly. The half moon cast a cage over the *Dvir*, and Joseph saw that his eyes were open. Scales of ashes were sprinkled over his bare chest, and he was sweating. A mosquito whirred in his ear.

The Eternal Lamp was cold, the stones above charred by half a millenium of holy light. Voices whispered upon the *Ehven.*

"Not yet. God, it's taking so long."

"Hurry. It must be now."

"Upon the King's altar and his Foundation Stone."

"In a land that devours its people."

Joseph saw Lucia unsheath the Sicari dagger Eleazar ben Yair had given her at Masada. As she lay upon Titus, she raised it, ready to plunge it into his passion. She had entered the *Dvir* as she always desired and she was about to make sacrifice in the Holy of Holies.

"No," cried Joseph rising. "Thou shalt not raise a sword against the anointed of the Lord!"

Titus rolled over Lucia, his stained tunic uncovering his naked thighs. Her dagger slit the hanging tapestries and blood flowed from the Zodiac. Across the *Dvir* shadows lamented the death of God.

Joseph staggered to his feet and grabbed on to the stem of the *Menorah.* His beard was filled with blood. The Holy of Holies was empty and on the Foundation *Ehven*, where the two had lain, a parchment of *Torah* flapped in the open breeze. A cluster of keys, which in his delirium Joseph imagined Theopolis, the last High Priest had handed him, lay like a talon on the marble tiles.

"The serpent," he whispered. "Not the eagle."

CHAPTER XXXVI — THE MATTER OF JERUSALEM

i

On the Eighth of *Elul*, Jerusalem fell for the fifth time in its two thousand one hundred and seventy-seven years of existence. During the three years of revolt, nine hundred thousand Jews and two hundred thousand Romans and their allies perished, while ninety-seven thousand Jews were taken prisoner. John ben Levi of Gishhalav, Simon bar Giora and Eleazar ben Yair had disappeared.

On the day before the Honors Parade, Titus summoned Joseph to his new headquarters up at Castel, outside of Jerusalem. Joseph had not seen the general since the night in the *Dvir*.

Joseph wore a simple gray robe whose edge was cut in sign of mourning.

"Why do you mourn?" asked Titus. "You made your choice long ago. Rome is now your Jerusalem."

"I mourn the death of my father," said Joseph.

Titus continued to eat the newly ripened figs, squeezing their red flesh out of the green skin into his mouth. "The awarding of battle honors begins this afternoon. Tiberius Alexander has had twelve young she lions sent up from Abyssinia to fight some hot-blooded Idumeans for the occasion. I've offered them pardon if they live."

"Offer me the same," said Joseph.

"Don't be an ass. I offer you the glory and comforts of a Roman prince. You shall sit by my side at the festivities."

The sounds of wrecking machines came from over the hills. "You can still save part of the city," said Joseph. "Justus is going at the destruction with a vengeance."

"This land is always crying out for vengeance against itself. Besides he's only following my orders. Nothing but the three towers of Herod's Castle are to remain standing."

"A monument to Rome's prowess."

"To the death of Jews."

"Death has always been part of our history. We learn to live with it."

"I almost died with it."

Joseph said nothing.

"You saved my life. What can I offer you?"

"Lucia. As she once was."

"She's disappeared. I never thought a Roman could take life so seriously."

"She took everything seriously."

"But you."

"I am more Roman than she."

"Once she took the Mulvian Bridge seriously."

"Another kind of death," said Joseph.

"You might think of death as a new kind of freedom. With the problems of statehood in our hands, Jews can devote themselves to their real purpose on earth: to pray to that nebulous god of yours to forgive us all our sins. We shall not disturb you in that."

"You confuse the Jew with the Christian. Without that city out there, there is no God."

"Ben Zakkai says your god is the god of laws. He thinks the rabbis will do a better job preserving Jewry than you priests did."

"You gave him the town of Yavneh. I ask nothing for my loyalty."

"I award you your father's estates for posterity. Those in and around Jerusalem will be replaced by land in the Valley of Jezreel, including Jotapata. As for yourself, you're to return to Rome under our patronage."

"I need time to sort out my priorities. I would like permission to go alone into the Wilderness."

Sextus Cerealius has been given command of the Xth Legion. They've been assigned mopping up duties. First on their list is your Judean Wilderness. You'll have no peace there."

"I wish to go among the Essenes at Ein Gedi. There lies the true loneliness of the hour."

"There are no Essenes. Those along the Jordan and the Salt Sea have either been wiped out or escaped to Masada."

"I'll go to Masada."

"The Xth Legion has been ordered to take Masada."

"They haven't surrendered?"

Titus shook his head. "Your friend Eleazar ben Yair."

Joseph waited to be dismissed, but Titus was in a talkative mood. "We need you in Rome. To tell how it really was. You'll be given all the help and leisure you need to finish your chronicles."

"And Justus?"

"It appears that his journals were lost during the fighting. Yours is the only record." He rubbed his nose vigorously. It was swollen to the size of one of the figs he had been eating.

"Your malady, it's spreading," said Joseph looking out across the hills where an obelisk marked the tomb of Samuel.

"A damn mosquito."

"It looks more serious."

"The Baal priests say it won't heal until John and Simon are captured.''

"You think they're still alive under that destruction?'' Joseph waved his hand toward the city over which a pale yellow nimbus hung.

"We're still searching.''

"The last time I saw John, he was just about dead from the sickness of the lungs.''

"Simon's alive. I'm sure of it. He'd make a fine gladiator.''

There was a long silence while Titus rubbed some ointment on his swollen nose. "You're disappointed in us aren't you?''

"More in myself.''

"You did your duty. Out there was just a battle of Jewish vanity. It could have been avoided.''

"You burnt the Temple out of vanity.''

"Your god's will.''

"Your men are acting like beasts, crucifying women and children. It takes long to die that way.''

"It's the only compensation I can offer them for this long plunderless and bloody campaign.''

"You claimed you were bringing civilization to us barbarians. Roman discipline.''

"Free anyone among your family and friends,'' said Titus.

An aide came hurrying in. "Sire, John ben Levi has been found in a ruined synagogue down in the Ophel Quarter.''

The Freedman's Synagogue, thought Joseph. "Is he alive?''

The aide hesitated. "After a fashion. He seems to be dying of his own body.''

"And bar Gioras?'' asked Titus.

"We're still searching.''

That evening, in the midst of their drunken celebrations, a group of Syrian auxiliaries staggered along the remnant of the west wall of the Temple which Titus had left standing in commemoration of his dead comrade Larcius Lepidus and the bloody battle that had been fought there. Suddenly an apparition dressed in white and caped in a purple mantle rose from the bowels of the earth. The superstitious men cast their cups at it and fled down the Tyropoeon Valley. It made its way slowly toward the ruined Temple, passing Joseph who happened to be wandering among the rubble. At that moment a patrol passed and grabbed the apparition which they discovered to be a Jew. Before Joseph could intervene, the Romans castrated Simon bar Giora upon a mound where once had stood the Great Altar.

Back in his quarters at Castel, Joseph made the first recording in his journal since the battle of the west wall. He wrote:

and it came so that on the ninth day of ab, six hundred and fifty-seven years and forty-five days since its construction, the TEMPLE OF THE LIVING GOD was burnt down through the instrument of HIS will. from the castel i see the outskirts of jerusalem TABUR HAOLAM. i can see the sea where the valley of timnat opens, the place where samson fell in love with his lucia. king david once hid in the cave of adulam below. to the east lies the dead sea, its sparkle muted by the hulk of masada. the jordan already virile at this season, makes me drowsy and i imagine walls wiggling like caterpillars up and down the hills dominated by the blue and gold snow field of marble that was the temple.

the bark of dogs desecrating the rubble and the grinding of machines reminds me that justus ben piscus of tiberias is plowing under my only estate. titus is right. in rome i shall repossess my soul, freed from the demons of this land. space is merely extension, and only in pain is there texture to time. woe to jerusalem! woe to my people! woe to the four winds!

He set the scroll aside and stared at a cork into which he had earlier stuck a silver pin. His eyes began to turn inward, and like mirrors against the sun, deflected all the sight off the panel of his brain. What Bannus had not succeeded in teaching him in three years at Ein Gedi, he had learned through the blood and fire of the Temple's destruction. He could meditate now for almost an hour.

The leather pouch beneath his bed broke the spell, and his eyes became unglazed as he regained his normal solicitude. He opened the pouch and read in Justus' journal.

if ben zakkai can abandon jerusalem for yavneh, certainly i might return to tiberias without shame. berenice says she no longer cares what happens to the city or for that matter judea. is it because she has lost her lover? or the crown of rome? intuitively she knows that titus cannot marry a woman that has slept with his father. also, that the lords of rome would never accept the possibility of a jewish empress. lately she speaks of retiring to that indestructible part of her patrimony, the red desert of idumea.

Joseph skimmed the next few pages and found nothing that he did not already know. Only when he reached the last notation did he start to read more carefully.

how little we know of the gentile and even less of ourselves. as boys we believed that the girls of the syrian neighbors were more exciting than our own, and we gave unto them without restraint of sin. until one day sabinus, our black stable boy, laughed when i found him lying with my cousin leah. later he told me that there was no lust like the lust of a galilean maiden. in like manner the romans think that they have conquered our pride instead of merely subduing our generosity, having thus succeeded in setting a new law to our alienation and we a fresher contumacy.

Joseph let the scroll roll shut. He hated to admit that Justus' words had more compassion than his own.

Replacing the journal it its pouch, he walked outside. His servant was just removing a kettle filled with a supper of lentils and parsley. Since the destruction of Jerusalem, Joseph had eaten only what the earth and the sun provided. He stood over the fire and watched its hypnotic tenticles draw from his fingers the journals of Justus ben Piscus. "Let there be but one truth," he muttered as the flames enveloped the pouch. He knew that he would use Justus' last line in his own next recording.

ii

The awarding of prizes for gallantry opened the Honors Parade. Those who had shown personal bravery were promoted one rank and had gold crowns set upon their heads by Titus. Eight hundred of the bravest were also given land to settle at Castel. All the troops, including those of the satrapies and the Syrian auxiliaries, were presented with new ensigns made of silver commemorating the victory over Jerusalem. In honor of Larcius Lepidus, Titus set standards of the Xth Legion where once the Susa Gate stood. Throughout the ceremonies Joseph wondered under what upturned stone Lucia was buried.

The games came next, held along the slopes of Mount Scopus. The towers of Phasael, Hippicus and Miriamme stuck up from the ruins like sentinels over the dead. Once again blood flowed down the Tyropoeon Valley as Jewish gladiators were torn by young lions. Beyond the levelled city lay the lavender hills of Judea, shocking in their serenity. Somewhere out there, Eleazar ben Yair waited.

iii

Dawn rose on *Yom Kippur*. Joseph, who was to depart for Rome that evening, spent his last moment among the upturned stones of the *Dvir*. He prayed aloud, even naming the unnamable Name, no longer fearing recrimination.

> Yaveh who Elohim!
> Jehovah is God!

he repeated seven times, trying to convince himself. Finally he added:

> *Yaveh is mine enemy.*

Behind him the hacked porticoes stood in mute amen.

Hurrying by the west wall, he passed a group of widows, beating their breasts and marking their brows with sweat against the huge stones. As the sun rose, he saw that instead of doves and sparrows, vultures flushed out of the hairy crevices of the wall. They dived and screamed, then circled above the razed city into the panic of daylight. *And god descended into the valley below and did not ask why.*

PART VI
ROME

*Life, not death is man's
misfortune.
(Eleazar ben Yair's
parting speech at Masada.)*

**Bellum Judaicum —
Josephus**

CHAPTER XXXVII — ARCH OF TRIUMPH

i

The Emperor Vespasian had Josephus installed in a small palace on the Palatine Hill. With access to the former library of Epaphroditus and all the documents and battle plans of the Judean campaign, Josephus worked daily and into the night to complete his history of the Jewish wars. Only on the Sabbath would he cease his labors and retire to the synagogue by the river. There were times when he felt that by reliving the experience of the past five years, he was really escaping them. Often he would wake from the sweat of a nightmare in which he saw himself tossing the first torch that had set flame to the Temple of God. Though he received regular reports from Palestina, he could not gather the courage to return to the ravaged land.

On the Eight of *Gorpiaeus,* two years to the day on which Jerusalem had fallen, the Temple of Peace was completed and Vespasian declared a week of festivities. Titus invited Josephus to sit beside him during the parade through the streets. Since returning to Rome, Josephus had rarely seen the general. Nevertheless, the pinpoint of his meditations had become the scene he had witnessed in the *Dvir.*

He was shocked at the state of Titus' health. Most of his hair had fallen out and his once large head had shrunk to the size of an asp's. He had lost much weight and only the festive vermillion dye smeared on his face and worn at victory celebrations covered the corruption of his nose.

"The poison of your god has entered my blood, gnawing like an iron claw at my brain and firing my intestines with dragons," said Titus, looking out beyond the Forum and the legions already lined up for the review.

Josephus turned pale. Only the night before he had dreamed that Titus died and that his ashes were spread over the sea. But a wind had risen from the east and gathered them back into the urn in which they were fired. Once again they were burned and shaken over the water. Before Josephus could force himself awake, Titus had been burned alive five times.

"The Rose of Jericho," said Josephus. "It's a venomous hornet known in the Wilderness of Judea."

"Nonsense. Already at Jotapata you and I knew what it is that's devouring me."

"The prophecy says that you shall reign next as emperor."

Titus struggled to rise, one hand pressed against his stomach, as he saw the royal retinue coming out upon the tribune. "In the next life it will be whores first, then war. It's much faster that way. By the way have you finished your chronicles of the war?"

Josephus exaggerated the slight stoop he had lately acquired from all his reading and writing. Despite the three scribes he had at his disposal, he trusted no one with the final words. His eyes had narrowed to a squint from too much work by candlelight. "It's all recorded. The problem is organization. The manuscript reads more like an apologia for my sins than laurels to your and the Emperor's great deeds."

"The Romans have given me laurels enough for burial. Just keep to the truth."

"The truth lies only in heroes," declared Josephus. "It's hard to find the hero in those wars."

"Still defensive," said Titus. "Make Jerusalem your hero."

Vespasian came across the bridge leading from the palace to the Forum. He was followed by his personal guard all in silver armor. The Emperor wore the purple and gold robes of the god Mars and held a sceptre topped with an eagle. His face too was marked with dye. He led the way down from the tribune and into a chariot drawn by four wreathed horses. As the legions came to attention, Titus and Josephus entered a second chariot where the poet Valerius Flaccus already sat. He handed Titus an ecstatic hexameter he had written over the burning of the Temple. At the blast of the long horns, the chariot lurched forward behind the Emperor's.

They moved through the rose-petal-strewn Forum which since dawn had been lined with thousands of citizens. A mist thickened the morning sun, magnifying the eminence of the great square. Glancing at Titus' disintegrating face, Josephus thought how equivocal was the power of survival when stamped on its opposite side was the will to self destruction. Maybe the next time a new force will be created great enough to annihilate others with ourselves, finally extending history beyond God's judgment or even the magnitude of his destruction.

They passed the circus where years before Josephus had watched Titus win the races. There they were met by cartloads of booty from Judea and huge floats framed in ivory and gold illustrating the glorious battles of the Jewish War. There were scenes of the devastated countryside, the scaling of city walls, the naval victory on Lake Gennesaret and the burning of the Temple. One float, three stories high, had a replica of the ravines and pomegrante groves of Jotapata.

The procession turned up the Via Sacra and instead of stopping at the Temple of Jupiter as was customary, it continued to the top of the hill. Josephus was about to ask why, when he saw Simon bar Giora in a halter, with Syrian auxiliaries scourging him, followed by seven hundred of his handsomest and bravest Sicaris, all in chains.

"And John?" asked Josephus. "Where is John of Gishhalav?"

"Choking to death in the Marmeline Prison," answered Titus. "He too has been stricken by your god."

"What will you do with Simon?"

"As the acknowledged leader of the Jewish revolt, he'll be crucified upside down at the climax of the ceremony."

The Xth Roman Legion followed the prisoners. They were massed in a rectangle headed by the new commander Flavius Silva.

"But they're supposed to still be in Judea," Josephus whispered to Titus. "I saw your order only this morning."

"Palestina. They're back for the celebration," said Titus tartly.

Silva approached the first chariot and saluted. "Hail Caesar! Judea is captive!" He then dismounted and handed Vespasian a *Torah* scroll captured from the Fortress of Masada, the last pocket of resistance in Judea.

The Emperor's chariot led the way into a small square where a new statue of Mars stood, paid for, Josephus knew, by the *Fiscus Judaicus* as a war indemnity. Immediately in front of the statue, a gleaming marble arch was now unveiled, releasing a flock of ibises. Josephus jumped up from his seat, and as on other occasions he felt his body rising out of itself. He was about to hail Titus as Imperator of Rome, when he saw that the frieze above the arch depicted chained captives, their ankles shackled, carrying what he recognized as two silver trumpets from the Temple, the Table of Shewbread and the seven branched *Menorah*, all of which had stood in the *Dvir*. He slumped back breathless beside Titus.

"Dedicated to my son," said the Emperor, pointing out the inscription to Silva.

Before the chariot moved through the arch, Josephus slipped off and hurried back to the Palatine. He vowed to record in his chronicles an admonition to the Jews never to walk under the Arch of Titus.

ii

Throughout the night, Josephus heard the celebration. Like Jerusalem during a pilgrimage holiday, the palaces and arches and temples of Rome were lighted with torches. Only instead of voices in praise of God, the heathen capital heaved with orgy.

In his study Josephus pondered the last entry in his journal, trying with its words to drown out the Roman holiday. He knew that tonight every city and settlement along the shores of the Great Sea were celebrating the defeat of the Jews. His eyes shot open when the scroll snapped closed. Looking up he saw Judah Hakohen standing in the doorway with a frail woman beside him.

"I leave tomorrow for the Rhineland," said the leader of the Jews of Rome, "where our brethren are migrating away from their shame in Rome. There will be need for much instruction there."

Josephus sighed. "There are times when I think that the further we disperse from our land, the more bitter shall our lot be."

"Perhaps that is our new burden," said Judah, still wearing the outmoded flounced robe Jewish priests had worn twenty years earlier.

"Perhaps. Perhaps whatever befalls us shall mirror like prophecy what will eventually happen to others. It's all written here." Josephus tapped his journals. "I would like you to store them in the synagogue Geniza Room."

"That is only for the holy writ," said Judah.

"This is the story of our holiness. As a record of the Jewish War, it might be of some instruction for the future survival of our people."

"I am informed that it was proscribed by the Emperor and his son."

"I have told the truth as I saw it. As I participated in it."

Judah turned to the woman beside him. "Your story cannot be completed without hearing hers." Judah left without having entered the study.

Josephus stared at the woman who stood in the doorway. "You've come from Judea, I assume," he said, rising.

The woman kept her eyes to the floor.

"Has your freedom been purchased?"

She remained silent.

"Come, have a *davla* and let me hear your story." Josephus held up a plate of flat cakes. "The figs are not so good as those of our Negev. Nor is the dough baked in the proper clay oven."

The woman retreated. Without raising her head, her eyes flashed up at Josephus as she pulled off her shawl. "I've come from Masada to finally offer myself to you."

The plate of cakes crashed to the floor. "Shlomit!" gasped Josephus. Her hair was clipped almost to the roots.

Josephus fell back into his chair. For a long while he dared not speak. Finally he rose again and led the woman to a seat beside his writing table. "Tell me the story of Masada. Tell me all."

"Suicide. That is all the story of Masada."

Josephus' heart pounded. Even with her clipped hair, she remained beautiful and defiant, the perfect end to his chronicle. "Suicide is a sin against the Lord," he said.

308

"Theirs was done in the name of the Lord."

Josephus nodded slowly. "At least you're alive. I shall tell their story in your words."

Again the blazing eyes glanced up at him. "My words are no different from yours. Like you, I cheated death at the expense of Eleazar."

"The judgments the living make over the dead are the only patrimony left them by the dead."

"A curse. Ten were chosen to kill us all. Nine hundred and sixty men, women and children. Eleazar spoke his few words and convinced everyone but me."

"He was not a man to be defied," said Josephus.

"He, Yoav his aide, myself and another were the last. It was near dawn. The winds prayed. The Roman was at the Snake Path Gate. He cut off my braids, then loved me on the hot floor of the cistern below Herod's Palace."

She stopped as if the story were over. In his mind Josephus saw Jotapata, the place of his own equivocation. "Then he spared you," he said. "Freed you from his burden of death?"

"I stabbed him to death with his own dagger."

Josephus breathed deeply. He reached out and touched the clipped edges of her hair. Her tawny skin was already losing the sun and her cheeks were cold. He could no longer lie. "Once before I came to Rome. I cut off my beard so that I would not be recognized as a Jew. Now I force myself to wear it, rejuvenated by its mark of shame."

"I hate braids. I hate beards. I hate the blood they make me bear."

Josephus kissed her gently on the brow. She grabbed him and kissed him fiercely on his lips. "No," he said, pushing her away. "To have loved the truly brave allows no shame. Go with Judah, with the new dignity of our people. They will have need for your pride."

"That other," she said. "That other at my side when I killed him. I killed her too. Her name was Judith and she was his mistress."

Alone, he understood now the way of Eleazar was also the way of the *goyim*.

He wrote:

three cycles exist in our national memory: to die with the philistines, masada, yavneh. not samson, not eleazar ben yair, but through raban johanan ben zakkai shall we survive. for only if a nation enters history when it is truly defeated does history become its weapon against annihilation. the LAW was given to us unto eternity. for a jew, then, punishment cannot be related to sin but is merely a part of the ordeal of his faith: THE

PROMISE. for is it not written, "hath HE said and shall HE not do? hath He not spoken and shall HE not make good?" in HIM, therefore, the act is infinite, the word timeless — both agents of his will. say henceforth: JERUSALEM NEVER FELL.